Always *a* River

TODD ALLEN HENDERSON

Always a River

To Chris ~
God Bless, Br.
Ra VaMil!

TATE PUBLISHING
AND ENTERPRISES, LLC

Published by Tate Publishing & Enterprises, LLC
127 E. Trade Center Terrace | Mustang, Oklahoma 73064 USA
1.888.361.9473 | www.tatepublishing.com

Tate Publishing is committed to excellence in the publishing industry. The company reflects the philosophy established by the founders, based on Psalm 68:11,
"The Lord gave the word and great was the company of those who published it."

Book design copyright © 2013 by Tate Publishing, LLC. All rights reserved.
Cover design by Errol Villamante
Interior design by Mary Jean Archival

Published in the United States of America
ISBN: 978-1-62510-816-6
1. Fiction / Christian / General
2. Fiction / War & Military
13.07.18

To Joyce, who believes in my dreams.

There is always a river to cross;
Always an effort to make
If there's anything good to win,
Any rich prize to take.
Yonder's the fruit we crave,
Yonder the charming scene;
But deep and wide, with a troubled tide,
Is the river that lies between.

—Josephine Pollard

THE RIVER

Jack,

I've heard it said there is a reason for everything. Although the circumstances and situations in which we find ourselves seem so unrelated, there is a thread running through them that connects them all, sewing together our individual lives and all of history in a weaving too complex for us to understand. But it is there all the same.

Some say it is chance, and others fate. But I have seen it firsthand. It is too convenient for chance, and too wonderful for fate. Instead, it is the very hand of God that threads the loom, carefully weaving the turns of our will and imperfection, until even our very flaws are woven into something perfect and beautiful.

You will see it soon,
Ted

Jack finished reading the letter, slowly folded it, and buried it deep in the pocket of his Sherpa jacket. From the edge of the Yukon River, he could see the red-orange glow along the horizon hinting that the sun would be up within the hour.

It was a brisk morning, numbing cold, almost too cold to be early fall, and it had Jack shivering in short, uncontrollable bursts. He was glad his hands were comfortable, his fingers not numb at least, pressed down in the soft woolen lining.

And then he felt it.

Anna, Anna, Anna.

She pounded against his heart to the rhythm of the river, twisting everything inside him. She always came to him in moments of solitude, in waves, furious and devastating. Still, there was the picture of her perfect beauty, a sense of something good. But it faded quickly, leaving him with a dark emptiness he could not begin to fill.

It's cold. Got to be below freezing. Why are you running, Ted?

Earlier the weather was much nicer, almost sixty in Anchorage, but Alaskan winters descend quickly. They come howling down the sides of mountains with the dusty edge of snowline, and find their way to the banks of rivers in September.

I'm back to the water. Just like back home. Only difference is this one's faster, deeper – twice, maybe three times the James. Still, being on the river – it's just like the old days.

The old days. Paddling up and downstream on the James River in southern Virginia in his dad's leaky old aluminum johnboat, he would fish under the sprawling arms of the sycamores and white oaks, and among the river birches and weeping willows that reached down and trailed their fingers in the water.

"What are you thinking about?"

The question ripped through the silence, echoing against the river banks and startling Jack. He had not heard Mr. McClain walk up behind him over the burble of the river's current lapping its rocky edge.

"Uh, just thinkin' about back home, about the James," he answered.

"This is a bit bigger," McClain said. "What's on your mind about the James?"

"Chasing Ted. It reminds me of tracking and trapping on the James as a kid. Dad never would let me use his rifle to hunt with, probably afraid I'd shoot him, so the fellas at the Co-op showed me how to make a snare," Jack said.

"Did it work?" McClain asked.

Jack could sense the nervousness and shame in McClain's voice, and the questions seemed to be awkward attempts to reconcile.

"Caught a rabbit once. Took it to Dad to see if he would show me how to skin it. He had a real sharp hunting knife, but he was so drunk he ended up layin' his hand wide open. Then he took it out on me. Busted my mouth and nose pretty good with a back hand I never saw coming," replied Jack.

"How old were you then?" McClain asked.

"I think about eight," Jack answered.

McClain thought for a moment. "I'm sorry to hear that. What did you do?"

"I just ran," Jack replied, "like I did most of the time. Hid a mile down river. Stayed there for three days."

"At eight?"

"Yeah, but it wasn't that bad. The river was more like home to me back then."

"Hmmph," McClain said as he looked back out over the water.

Jack busied himself searching for a flat stone.

"Dad killed everything that was important to me. Guess it's just what he was good at," Jack said, still picking through the rocks along the shore. "One time I found this baby raccoon hangin' on a skinny limb of an old elm that overhung the shore about a half-mile downstream from the farm. I paddled out in the johnboat and rescued it right before it fell into the river. Coon hunters must've got its momma. You ever raised a coon, Mr. Mack?"

"Can't say that I have," McClain replied.

"Smartest animal I've ever seen. We took to each other immediately. I raised it for a year and a half before it bit Dad one night. He took a bat to it right there in front of me on the back porch,"

"Geez son, did he kill it?"

"Yeah. I cried but he kicked me and told me to get that—well, he used a lot of language—animal off his property. I brought it down to the river and buried it under a pile of rocks. It was the first time I ever prayed."

"For your raccoon?"

"No," Jack replied, "for God to kill my dad. At that point, I'd have given anything to see him suffer a horrible death." Jack threw the rock out and watched it skip several times. "Maybe God does give us what we ask for," Jack said.

"Yes, maybe so," McClain said. "Jack, there's something I've got to tell you."

"You don't have to say nothin' Mr. Mack. I know how hard it's been on you and Mrs. McClain, and now this. No, you don't have to say nothin'," Jack said.

"I know, but it's something I have got to tell you."

A brisk gust swept across the river, whistling through the scrub spruce on the far bank. Jack shivered in a burst, again. He waited for the wind to die down.

"I'll make you a deal, Mr. Mack," replied Jack.

McClain paused for a moment and cleared his throat. "Well, I'm really sorry about everything. I mean, really sorry. I've been foolish for so many years, and now it's catching up with me, but go ahead. What's the deal?"

"The deal is this: let's focus on the mission—on finding Ted. Then, I'll listen to anything you want to tell me."

"Sounds fair enough."

Jack watched Mr. McClain looking out over the river. He seemed relieved, and it made Jack feel good about turning back his confession, whatever it would be.

"Let's get this gear bundled up and on the boat. Got a lot of river to cover," Mr. McClain said. "We'll finish this before the day's over. Right now, I suppose we need to get rolling. I just don't want Ted to die alone up here—and he will soon, if we don't get to him."

"I know, and we'll find him. I promise you that, but I've got a question," said Jack.

"What is it?"

"Why do you think Ted's here? I mean, why's he running? What's it all about?"

"I don't know for sure, Jack, but I'm assuming it has something to do with the tumor. It's gotten worse."

"Why did you need me? Not that I mind, or anything. It just seems…"

"I wanted you to be here for him. You know Ted pretty well and you think like him. An investigator isn't going to do this, and you know Annabelle is a wreck over everything we've been through."

Jack sensed something missing from McClain's explanation. It was a whisper of insight that McClain was holding back.

"I'm headin' up to pack the gear. We'll be on the river in about thirty minutes," McClain said.

He turned and walked back up the steep bank toward their campsite. Jack stayed, tossing a few more stones in the water, occasionally skipping a flat one. He did not suspect McClain had anything new to tell him until that moment as he stood with a flat sandstone, cold and gritty between his fingers.

What is he going to tell me? Why me, here, helping him look for his own son? Ted's still out here, somewhere. We'll find him, bring him home.

Jack dropped the stone, stooped down and scooped some sand between his fingers, rubbing them together to get the feel of the loamy soil along the bank. Holding it close to his nose he breathed in deeply and took in the smell of the water.

Trout muck. Glacier silt. Yeah that's the difference in the smell of it. Be my guess, anyway.

He loved that smell—fish waste in mid-decay mixed with stagnant water and mud. Swirling around in his consciousness were the sensations of his childhood—the euphoria of snake hunts and boiled crawfish, and the feeling of willow webs broken across his face, wet with summer sweat, all tangled in the smell of river. It was a familiar melancholy to which Jack often retreated when things weren't going well.

I need some coffee.

He picked up another stone and flung it with an effortless whip of the wrist into the current. The stone skipped once and then splashed. He watched for a moment as the ripples radiated out, and then just as rapidly, dissipated as they were consumed by the powerful current. He wasn't in Virginia, and these weren't the docile waters of the James.

Jack turned and headed up the rocky bank and made his way along the ridge he had followed down to the river. It was about thirty yards to a clearing along the wood line where Mr. McClain tended to their meager campsite of a two-man dome tent and a Coleman stove.

"There any coffee here?" asked Jack.

"Coffee in the thermos," Mr. McClain said.

"Thanks," said Jack as he picked up the thermos and poured some in the cup that Mr. McClain had set out for him. "Hope the river moves this fast the rest of the way. We need to make up some time."

Mr. McClain handed Jack a bowl of something that looked like dog food. "Eat up. Looks like it might not warm up today. Almost froze last night. You'll need all you can get."

"Looks like something that might make a sled dog pretty happy," Jack said, taking the bowl with a shaky hand.

Stop it hand. Sit still. Stop this shaking. The cold. Hope Ted ain't dead, yet.

"What in the heck is this?" asked Jack.

"Camp food. Corn beef hash, a little grease—good for ya stuff! Cooks fast, too," Mr. McClain shoveled in a mouthful.

"I suppose," Jack said.

He took a few hardy bites, then slung the rest out on the ground.

They had flown along the Yukon in a guide's Piper Cub the day before, but saw no sign of Ted. It was just too much to try to see from the air. The guide landed them on the river near an outfitter, and with a healthy outlay of Mr. McClain's cash, they were stocked with a boat large enough to carry a fifty gallon fuel drum, and enough gear to cover several hundred miles of river and sustain them for more than a week.

They covered about twenty-five miles, but had gotten on the river late. The early fall evening would not allow them any late navigation, and when it decided to get dark, it did so quickly. Mr. McClain didn't want to fight keeping a twenty foot long johnboat out of the mud in the dark.

They camped near the inside of a hairpin bend in the river, both getting fairly wet securing the boat, and learning a quick lesson about Alaskan nights, as the temperature plummeted. They were nearly hypothermic before they got a fire going well enough to dry out. Each took turns keeping the fire going, but Jack struggled to sleep. He worried about wolves, and kept the rifle, a Remington .308 Mr. McClain had purchased at the outfitter, near his side. That's how they found themselves on the bank of the Yukon River, early in the morning, miles from anywhere.

Mr. McClain had already stuffed their sleeping bags and other assorted personal gear in the duffle bag they had quickly thrown together back in Anchorage. Jack began to break down the dome tent and get the gear ready for them to carry down to the boat.

Jack and Mr. McClain grabbed all of the gear and toted it to the riverbank. Once they had everything loaded, Jack sat at the edge of the river while Mr. McClain busied himself with the rigging.

Good, time to think. Doubt. He might've made it this far. Maybe. Why here? After all this. Can't figure it. Doubt he's over Anna and all, even if he knows the truth.

Something new was brewing inside of him and he couldn't put a finger on it. His gut burned, he teetered on the edge of grief, and his hands seemed to tremble in waves. Jack couldn't nail down exactly what it was he was feeling.

So he sat there, at the edge of that swift, silent river, somewhere deep in the arctic wilderness, thinking and waiting.

"You ready to roll?"

"Sure, let's do this," Jack replied.

Jack pushed the bow into the river, and carefully hopped over the edge into the front.

Mr. McClain lowered the thirty horse outboard into the water and pumped the primer a few times. When he cranked it, the motor fired up without even a sputter, which struck Jack as a sign of good luck. He had messed around with enough outboard motors and knew how temperamental they could be in the morning.

Mr. McClain cranked the throttle and immediately they were outpacing the current as the bow spun around and they headed down river. Jack sat stoically with his eyes pinned forward.

They had gotten to a point where it began to spread out and show its immensity. He unfolded one of the maps that Mr. McClain had bought from the outfitter before they put in. They were topographical, which made it a bit easier to find their location using the terrain and landmarks on the map.

Jack traced the river from the outpost to the big bend where they had camped. He was impressed by the size of the geography. Mountain ranges shot up into the sky just to the west, and river valleys as wide as some states extended beyond the horizon. This was big country, and he felt dwarfed and insignificant in it.

The outboard motor hummed as they moved steadily down river. Jack found himself almost hypnotized by its constant buzzing noise, but would break out of his trance enough to keep up with the river bank and make sure he or Mr. McClain had at least a distant visual of every foot of it.

He could see that Mr. McClain knew what he was doing, maneuvering the boat through a chicane of shallows and debris jams in this wider part of the river. They began circling back upstream to get around some of the islands where the river had spread out and divided. It was going to take quite a bit of time.

Impossible. Gonna take all day to cover twenty miles. There must be hundreds of cabins on the river. Time. Running out of it quick.

"What's on your mind, Jack?" McClain asked.

"I dunno. It just seems like this is a tough way to find somebody out here. I know it's worse for you, bein' he's your son and all," Jack answered, still looking along the river.

He worked his way back to the seat in front of Mr. McClain so he wouldn't have to yell across the length of the boat, and over the whine of the outboard. Even though Mr. McClain had made amends with Jack, Jack still felt uncomfortable, his words stiff and formulated.

"Oh, we'll find him, Jack," McClain said. "I have a certain peace right now. There are a lot of people praying."

They paused for a moment as they concentrated on the passing riverbanks.

"You know, Mr. McClain, I used to love to take that old johnboat out on the James when it was up in the spring. I'd think of myself as Huck Finn on the Mississippi. It helped me conquer some fears and it toughened me up a bit. That and the back of my dad's hand, I suppose."

Mr. McClain smiled and took in what Jack had just said. "Was there ever a good time with your dad?" he asked Jack.

"I guess there was. Sometimes I think hard to try to remember any time that was good, and I can remember a couple good things. That fear I was conquering on the river was my fear of him. Well, and I suppose that constant sickness in my gut."

"Have you been able to forgive him?" McClain took his eyes off the river to face Jack.

Forgive him? He's dead. No reason for that. Mr. Mac knows he's dead. Why bother?

"I don't always know what forgiveness is. I mean, we say we forgive somebody, but whatever it is that they did still happened, and it never really goes away. Bloody noses and black eyes, they go away, I guess. He broke some ribs in my back. I still feel it when I breathe in deep. There were nights without food, heck, weeks without anybody home."

McClain shook his head and looked down.

"When he *was* home, he was usually drunk and mad. I guess I've come to terms with him, I mean, I don't hate him. I actually miss him. Guess I miss him kicking me around."

Jack looked away, thinking.

"No, not that, not really. I probably shouldn't say that. In a way, though, I wish he was still around to see me now. Maybe he'd be better. Maybe even proud of me. I dunno, maybe that's what forgiveness is."

"That just might be it, son," Mr. McClain replied, still looking forward, still watching the river.

Jack kept his eyes peeled. As he looked at the river banks on both sides with their thick brush and scrub trees that appeared to have been ravaged by the years of bitter cold and wind, he began to think about the bond that brought him to this river to find a lost friend.

God knows they all die. Or worse. Everyone I touch. Why does it have to be like that?

There was a bond with Ted unlike any other that Jack had experienced. He had been a loner when he first met Ted and his family. He had been suspicious of all people, trusting no one. The *beast* had taught him that.

It was the monster that had grown up inside of him with all of the agonies of his childhood. Like a heavy shadow that rested on him and kept the best of him hiding in some dark internal cavern, it had crushed his spirit long ago and turned him into something stoic and reclusive.

As he talked to Mr. McClain, he would feel the internal waves of grief beating against a place in his heart. He had learned to fight the waves back, but they were softening him, and he prayed that God would somehow stop them before he was overcome.

No. Not gonna answer these questions. Not ready. Don't have the right things to say. Enough for now.

He knew, at the same time that God was up to something, but he was not sure if he should be eager for whatever it would be.

His thoughts warred inside him, ripping him apart.

Hang on, my brother. We'll find you.

PART 1

BROTHER RAT

CHAPTER ONE

FEAR

LEXINGTON, VIRGINIA
THREE YEARS EARLIER

"Just the two bags, son?" asked the taxi driver.

He was a short, stocky, middle aged man with gray hair buzzed in a 50s style flat top and a freshly shaven face. His off-white short-sleeve button down Cuban shirt with an open collar left no doubt that this guy was from an earlier time. Jack could smell the Old Spice as the driver walked around to the trunk to give a hand with his seventy-some-odd pound duffel bags.

Wish I could've slept last night. I'm tired—too tired for all of this. I'm not ready. Not ready. Why am I doing this? Quit shaking, it looks stupid. Stupid.

Jack stared at the man for a moment.

They stood in the parking lot of the motel in a fog that had settled in the thick, early morning Lexington air. A familiar late summer event, it rolled in and blanketed the small towns and farms that dotted the southernmost tip of the Shenandoah Valley. It dripped with wetness, fed by the dew of thick green fields and the slumbering rivers that wove their way through the patch quilt countryside.

"Yeah," Jack replied. "I mean, yes sir."

Voice is shaky. Don't do that. Sounds like a kid. Scared kid.

"Bags in the back seat, trunk in the trunk," the driver replied as if he didn't hear Jack.

"Uh, no trunk, sir," Jack said.

"Oh, you really meant just the two bags," the driver said. "Sorry, son, just used to everyone havin' a trunk. Guess you travel light."

"Didn't really have a need for one, sir," Jack replied. "Everything fit in the duffel bags."

"We can put 'em in the trunk then, son," the driver said. "You ain't bringin' civies? How in the heck you gonna run the block?" the driver asked.

"I don't reckon I know what you're talkin' about."

"First year, huh?" the driver asked.

"Yes sir. Do I look scared or something?"

"Not so much that. But our conversation aside, y'ain't got a haircut yet. No one shows up without one, except the newbies"

Jack rubbed his hand over his hair, messing it up a little.

Wow, I am an idiot.

"Oh yeah, I guess so," Jack said.

The driver held out his hand to shake and Jack obliged with a decent grip.

"I'm Jim King, good to meet ya."

"Jack Hartman, good to meet you, too. Oh, okay," Jack said pointing to the door logo, "King Kab. That makes sense. Family company, huh?"

"Yeah, it's my stock and trade these days. Bought the company about eight years ago when I moved back here to Lexington. Retired military, had to have something to do. Run six cabs here in town, and just started running four more down in Lynchburg. It pays the bills," he said as they loaded Jack's duffel bags in the trunk.

"Alright, Mr. King," Jack said, "let me just turn in the room key I'll be ready to go."

"You're a polite young man. I can tell someone must've raised you right. Don't call me Mr. King, though. You make me feel old," he said chuckling. "Matter of fact, most folks call me Jimbo."

"Alright, Jimbo."

Yeah, if you only knew how somebody raised me right. Beat down. I'm feeling sick. I feel like I'm gonna puke.

Jack walked over to his motel room door and closed it. It was a small motel just on the outskirts of Lexington, Virginia, snuggled neatly in the country just past the edge of Washington and Lee University along US 60. Jack stayed there because he didn't want to be picked up at the Boys' Home, and it was one of the only places he could afford.

Jack walked to the office and turned in the key, and then returned to the cab. He sat up front with Jimbo.

I hope he doesn't talk much more. I don't wanna talk this morning.

He was queasy for the first time since he even considered going to school. It sounded fun, then. It sounded like a stupid idea, now.

Jimbo pointed out a couple spots as they drove through Lexington's main drag—hot spots for cadets. He took every opportunity to break the long stretches of awkward silence. Jack obliged with a brief reply each time, still staring out the window in a pensive daze, studying the town as it passed.

Jack knew Lexington. He'd lived near Rockbridge County all his life and was used to the town with all of its historic architecture. The colonial red brick buildings with their thick white-railed porches passed by his window while the manila fortresses of the Virginia Military Institute lined with their battlements looming over the town in the distance grew closer.

Traffic thickened with the family cars of other matriculates from every other part of Virginia, and a variety of other states. They drove slowly past the rows of formidable brick academic buildings with their plantation style columns that made up the façade of Washington and Lee University.

Though he'd seen it all before, today it seemed new and fresh and remarkable. Jack sat there perspiring, hands shaking slightly, quietly looking out the passenger window. There was a comfort in the scent of pine and honeysuckle in the cool August air leaking its way in the cab through the slightly opened back window. Still, he could feel the tempo of his heart rising slightly in his neck and chest.

"Is this your first time?" Jimbo asked.

"Pardon me?"

"Your first time here, at the ol' Virginia Military Institute?"

"Oh, no. I live over in Botetourt County, on the river. I've been up here a time or two. Well, a bunch of times to Lexington, a couple to VMI." Jack answered glancing over to Jimbo, then back out the window.

He had seen it, but only from the outside, and though it was quite impressive to a young boy, it was far from being within reach. He never thought he'd find a way to attend. But a couple months after he applied, a crazy scholarship came through.

Money. He'd never experienced much of it, and it remained a mystery to him. But there were generous people in the world, and though Jack had never met any, he was able to benefit from at least one of them.

He had been excited about the adventure, the chance to escape his life. But at seventeen it was only an idea. Now, it was like a monster that loomed somewhere directly in front of him. He could sense its stomach growling for him, and knew that it would eventually consume him, along with all of his past.

He thought about his dad.

"My dad spent some time in the state prison. I wonder if this is what he felt like on his first day there," Jack said.

It was the truth, but almost immediately, Jack regretted saying it. It was too much to offer a perfect stranger.

"Where's your dad now?" Jimbo asked.

"Died when I was fifteen," Jack said almost monotone.

"Sorry to hear that, son. What about your mom?" He asked.

"She left my dad and me when I was a baby. I never knew her," Jack answered, still looking away.

The conversation stopped for a moment. Jack was thinking about what he'd already gone through to get there—the foster homes and Boys' Home, fighting to get his grades up in school, long work hours in the summer, and sleepless nights worrying about how to do something with his life.

"So how did you manage? I mean, getting into a school like this is tough, isn't it?" Jimbo asked gently.

"I dunno. I guess a lot of people helped me. The folks at the Boys' Home and my sponsors. Oh, and I had a case worker. He was a big help. Helped me with some scholarships and grants and such. Did you know there's even a pretty big scholarship for bein' an orphan in Virginia?"

Jimbo shook his head.

"It's a decent one," Jack continued. "Covered most everything. I guess you just do what ya gotta do and hope for some help along the way. It's worked out so far."

Jack stopped abruptly. They sat at a stop sign waiting for traffic to clear enough to squeeze in.

Jack knew no one could understand the demons he had battled. He thought about how his past chased him with all of its darkness like a menacing shadow. He knew if he slowed down it would catch up to him and engulf him in its blackness. It was both grief and addiction, and he had been struggling to shake it for years.

It so often would surface inside of him and torment him, like a beast intent on his destruction. A beast. Jack believed somehow that this move in his life might help him shed this "beast" once and for all.

"So, you still got a caseworker?"

"Yeah, though I don't know how much I'll see of him. I think unofficially he'll check up on me from time to time. I'm eighteen. I'm pretty much on my own," replied Jack.

"I like a fella that can pull himself up by the bootstraps."

His heart started racing as they pulled onto Letcher Avenue and began the ascent to the front gates of VMI. He could hear the blood pound in his ears as they crested the hill and the panoramic view of the barracks, white washed and bathed in the morning sun, spread across the horizon in front of them. Jack's hands began to shake. He never imagined he would be so anxious.

He had been alone for all practical purposes, never really attaching to anyone after his dad was killed. But he knew that there would be conflict and darkness and change. For the first time in many years, Jack was afraid.

A slow procession of cars moved through the gate, directed by a cadet with white gloves and a white short-sleeved shirt with epaulettes. He wore a dark blue service dress hat with a brightly shined VMI emblem on the front. Jimbo followed the cars moving slowly along the road bordering the parade ground.

"Well, there it is," Jimbo said, gesturing toward the VMI barracks spread out in front of them.

A cadet waved at Jimbo from the sidewalk.

"You must come here a lot," Jack said.

"You might say that. There are a couple cadets I check up on from time to time, and I provide taxi service for the Institute when they need me."

"Well," Jack said, "I sure do appreciate you gettin' me over here."

"Now look, son, here's my card. If you need anything, you call me. I'll come by and check on ya too," he said handing Jack his card.

"Yes sir, and thanks. Be nice to know someone from around here," Jack answered as he took the card. "I really don't know a lot of people that would visit me."

They were pulling up to the front of the massive fortress. The large archway stood gaping like a man-thirsty mouth, consuming the small crowd of parents and new cadets. Jimbo pulled the cab up to the curb just beyond the arch and threw it into park. He popped the handle on his door and turned to Jack.

"This is it. Jackson Arch. Named after Stonewall."

Jimbo turned and looked at Jack.

"You ready?" Jimbo asked.

"Yes sir. I'm good."

Certain calm had come over his voice as the fear flushed away. He was finally here.

"How much do I owe ya for the ride?" asked Jack.

"Nothin'," Jimbo replied, "first ride for a new cadet is free. And no tip, either. That's why I make a point of driving one of these on matriculation day. Besides, and trust me on this, one day this year you're gonna be broke and you're gonna find a five in one of your pockets for an 'X-check' that gets ya through. You'll know what I mean by that soon enough."

Jimbo popped the trunk and got out. Jack followed. They met at the back of the cab and Jimbo pulled the duffel bags from the trunk, one at a time.

"Good luck, son." He handed him the bags.

Jack slid one strap over his right arm and then slung the bag around to his back. He picked up the other by its canvas handle in his left hand and looked over his shoulder at the archway.

"Remember; call me if you need anything. Don't think you're imposing if you do. I don't mind helpin' a Rat out!" Jimbo said.

It was the first time Jack had been called a Rat. He knew it was about to be his station in life for the next seven or eight months. Jimbo reached out and Jack reached back. They shook hands heartily.

"Do good in there, and be tough," Jimbo said like a concerned father.

"Will do, thanks again," Jack replied.

He turned and headed into the arch.

"Whoa, Rat! Is that bag properly marked?" The question came from his front left.

He looked quickly in that direction and there was a rather impending looking cadet with wide shoulders and rock-hard forearms twice the size of Jack's rapidly walking toward him. There was a definite purpose in his steps, and Jack stopped immediately to pull the bag off of his shoulder and answer.

"I think so," He replied.

"Ya think so?" the cadet mocked. He laughed briefly, then leaned in close to Jack, his face stern. "Look, ya 'think so' isn't gonna cut it here. You either know or you don't. Just answer 'yes,' 'no,' or 'I don't know.' Now the bags gotta have two-inch block letters of your last name, then first and middle initials," he said as he looked at the side of Jack's duffel, "which you got, so you can follow me." He spoke with a strong New Jersey accent and walked so fast Jack had trouble keeping up.

As they walked through the two-story archway Jack's attention was drawn to the engraving on the second floor bridge that cut across the middle of the arch about twenty feet from the opening. In letters a foot tall were the words "'You may be whatever you resolve to be.' – Stonewall Jackson."

I suppose, Stonewall. I can handle this. Guess I don't have any other choices at this point. Guess I'm gonna be whatever they resolve for me to be.

It wasn't the architecture or the ritualistic traditions rooted deep in the nineteenth century that drew Jack. He loved the very nature of southern culture that he saw here when he visited as a boy. Cadets were models of respect in public, and it was a place where the boys still tipped their hats to ladies.

Being raised in the south was something that Jack always felt was the one blessing in his tragic life. A deep genteel spirit and the almost Victorian naiveté were woven into the southern way of life. Inside his gut, he had a natural distaste for things urban and northern. He found it comical in this bastion of southern tradition, the first cadet he would meet was from someplace like Jersey.

"Putcha bag down over there. Make sure you can still read the name," the Jersey cadet said pointing to a large pile of duffel bags in the middle of the courtyard, stacked like cord wood.

Jack obliged. He turned to go back and was startled to have another cadet face to face with him.

This one seethed of something mean. The brim of his hat was pulled down low enough to cover his eyes. His face was firm and thin, and he appeared to be angry, but with great control. His jaw was clenched and he was breathing strongly through his nose like a vicious animal defending its territory.

"Where you from, Rat?" he asked in a low voice through his clenched teeth. He had a strong southern accent. His voice sounded familiar to Jack.

"Buchanan, Virginia, sir," Jack replied, still unsure of his military courtesies.

"You live on the James River down there in Buchanan, Rat?" There was a distinctive pause before "Rat."

"Yes, sir."

I know this guy.

"Let me guess." He moved even closer to Jack's face making Jack a little uncomfortable, "You probably think you have an advantage over your Brother Rats because you come from around here, don't you, Rat?" This time his head cocked back a bit and Jack could see him raise his right eyebrow slightly when he said "Rat." He was clearly mocking. Jack did not answer.

John Phelps.

Jack felt his heart begin to pound and his face flush. Sweat quickly beaded on his cheeks and nose. His hands were visibly shaking.

"Look here!" The corporal kept his voice low and continued to speak through his teeth. "You ain't nothin' more than a worthless piece of sewage. You think you're smart and you know everything about this place because you come from around here, but you need to get in your head right now, you are an idiot. Your days here will be few."

John Phelps…I didn't know he made it in here.

"It is going to be my personal mission to see you standing in front of Jackson Arch with your raggedy duffel bags, waitin' for the cab that dropped you off to come and remove your sorry butt from this place, hopefully never to return. In case you haven't figured it out yet, Rat, I hate townies," the corporal said.

Great. Can it get any worse? I'd be better off leaving now.

"And don't look an upperclassman in the eye," he said. "You keep your eyes straight ahead."

With that, he turned and walked away.

This is starting well. Save yourself the grief, Jack. Just do what he said. You can go to college somewhere else.

Sudden anger welled up inside Jack. His teeth clenched and his hands shook even more.

I hate him.

A string of foul words ran through his mind. It was a like a floodgate opening every time someone or something made him angry. Two years ago he'd sworn never to cuss again. He'd been successful on the surface, but the battle in his head seemed to be one he was losing more often than not.

The words were always there—words he had picked up from his dad, from a couple of the boys at the home, from high school classmates. They would give him temporary relief and he found himself allowing them more and more leeway. He hoped he could keep them out of his mouth, because they were a part of his dad he despised.

"I see you've met Corporal Phelps," yelled the Jersey cadet from the same place along the stoop he had dropped him off. "Don't worry about him. Someone peed in his grits this morning. I actually think he liked it!"

The humor brought Jack back from his internal fury.

"Now follow me. You gotta matriculate before Corporal Phelps can have his way with ya!"

The Jersey cadet led Jack and two other Rats to a building connected to the barracks. He called it Lejeune Hall, one of the newest buildings on post, named after the famous Marine Corps Commandant and former VMI superintendant. When they entered, Jack immediately noticed the aura of the place was a little more serene and civil than the barracks' courtyards from which they had just come.

They followed the corporal to a lower level where they began academic and military in-processing.

Then he heard it.

Down a long hallway leaving the room where he was moved from station to station along with dozens of other new cadets, he could hear screaming. Not the kind you hear when someone is trying to get another's attention, but men screaming and yelling with anger and intensity Jack had never heard before. He began to get a sick feeling in his stomach, again. He knew when it was his turn to walk down that long hallway and through those doors it would be like walking into hell. Jack wanted to go home.

He just wasn't sure where that was.

Jack made his way through the matriculation line and arrived at the last station.

"Rat Hartman, J. M., this is your Rat Bible." A rather blunt and serious cadet was standing in front of him, holding a pink pocket-size booklet with a cartoon caricature of a sweating rat-like animal in a cadet uniform. He held the booklet about four inches from Jack's face.

"You will," he continued, "from this moment forward, be responsible for knowing the entire contents of this book. I recommend at every moment of idle time you have, you pull this out and memorize the contents. You will also be responsible for the security of this book. You must have it on your person at all times. You will never give this book to any other person, cadet or otherwise, for any reason unless an upperclassman or military officer requires your book for instructional purposes only. Now take it from my hands like a man."

Jack yanked the book from his hands.

"That wasn't good enough, Rat Hartman. Give it back and let's try it again!"

Jack handed the book back.

"I thought I told you not to give this book to anyone unless told it is for *instructional purposes only*! You're already starting out on the wrong foot, Rat Hartman! Did you understand me when I said not to give this book up?"

"Yes, Sir."

"I'm trying to help you out here, 'cause when you cross through those double doors down that hallway there'll be at least twenty requests for your Rat Bible before you can…" he paused, pointing down the hallway. "Well, you'll find out soon enough. Now go straight down that hallway and knock on those doors. Make sure they can hear it!"

He stuck the book out and Jack snatched it firmly and quickly. He began the long walk down the hallway. Jack could hear the yelling intensify as he approached. He stood, intimidated for a moment, then raised his clenched fist and hammered on the door three times. It swung wildly open to the inside as if he had knocked it open with that third strike.

"Get in here, Rat!" a cadet screamed with force and rage.

It was the loudest scream Jack had ever heard from any man, even his dad.

Jack complied, looking straight ahead. He could see through the commotion of new cadets lining the walls and cadet trainers, or cadre, surrounding them screaming, they were in a long corridor. He was pushed against the wall to his left. Several members of the cadre converged on him simultaneously.

"Quit cuttin' your eyes, maggot!"

"Get your stupid face against that wall!"

"Why you lookin' around, Rat. You lookin' for a date to the Hop?"

Even the humor was delivered viciously, mocking.

"Rats, get your Rat Bibles out and start reading and memorizing," another commanded above the din.

Jack held his Rat Bible up in front of his face, but with his face so close to the wall, he couldn't read the words.

At least look like your reading it.

He was surrounded by at least a dozen men yelling and screaming commands, questions, and insults so loudly and rapidly Jack could not begin to process what was being said, or asked, or commanded. He was spun around several times until he came to rest with his face pressed firmly against the wall. Sometimes he was told to put the book in his pocket, sometimes in front of his face.

"Why are you here, Rat?"

"I...uh..." Jack had attempted to actually answer a question, but was amazed to find he couldn't coherently mumble anything that made sense.

"You...uh? You...uh? You...uh what, maggot?"

"Get on your face!"

"Knock out twenty push-ups, idiot!"

Jack quickly got down in the push-up position and commenced to doing push-ups as rapidly as possible.

"Why aren't you counting the reps, Rat?"

"Get on your feet!"

Jack jumped back to his feet, facing away from the wall. He was breathing hard and was disoriented. A very vicious sounding cadre corporal had his face almost touching Jack's ear. He didn't scream, but his voice was every bit as virulent.

"How many times do I have to tell you to get your stupid, ugly, idiotic maggot face against the wall?"

It's him. Him again.

It was Corporal Phelps. He screamed a few expletives in Jack's ear, and then moved along to the next Rat.

Jack spun around and faced the wall, squeezing as close as he could until his chin, lips, and nose were all firmly pressed against it. There was another tumult brewing a few new cadets from Jack.

"I've got his Rat Bible!" A cadre member was dancing gleefully.

"Rat! Why did you give up your Rat Bible? Did the corporal ask you for your Rat Bible for instructional purposes?"

"No, Sir!" the bewildered Rat yelled.

"Then why did you give him your Rat Bible?" He emphasized each of the last four words, screaming them at point blank.

"Everyone drop and give me twenty!"

Jack dropped down in the push-up position, Rat Bible under the palm of his hand, as did most of the new cadets at his end of the hall. One new cadet did not drop down, which immediately drew the attention of almost every nearby cadre member, temporarily easing the tension off Jack and a few others. They began to do push-ups, but still not counting repetitions out loud.

The cluster of cadre was like an angry mob, flowing in unison to every opportunity to wreak havoc. As Jack cranked out one push-up after another, sweat began to roll down his nose and drip on the floor.

Hot in here. Too soon to be sweating like this. Guess I'm a little too nervous. What number am I on? Twenty? Twenty-five?

"On your feet!" The command came from somewhere down the hall.

Everyone jumped up. Suddenly, all the commotion ceased.

"Rats, look at me!" It was a tall, lanky handsome cadre cadet who apparently outranked the corporals who had been chewing on this group for the last few minutes. Jack could see about twenty Rats along the walls of the hallway.

"At this time you will be heading back up to the courtyard from whence you came," he said in a stout voice. "You will follow your cadre corporal whom I will assign to you right now. You will be under his supervision until otherwise told. Do you understand me?"

"Yes sir!" they, to Jack's surprise, shouted in unison.

CHAPTER TWO

C ORPORALS

"I'm Corporal Johnson. You seven nasty maggots have been assigned to the Third Squad of Echo Company. I am your corporal. You are such low scumbags on the food chain you are not even worthy of being called Rats. Therefore, I will refer to you as maggots."

Immediately, he dropped them on their faces for push-ups and a muscle-burning exercise he called "mountain climbers." It seemed to Jack that screaming and push-ups were the way things were communicated by these guys. It had been less than twenty minutes since he had knocked on the double doors. He was already thinking he had gotten into something way over his head.

"Rats McClain, Kolwinski, Hartman, and Burkes: fall out and fall into room four thirty-two," Corporal Johnson said as he took the others further down the stoop.

All four of them, each carrying two duffel bags, peeled off and went into the room. They plopped their gear down and stood in silence for a moment, not sure what to do next.

Jack looked around the room. It was Spartan, almost like an old prison cell. The walls and ceiling were an off-white plaster with cracks showing points of stress. An old radiator style heater sat along the back wall beneath a high double window. Four bed racks leaned lengthwise against the back wall, and a white wooden rifle rack was bolted against the back wall a couple feet to the left of the window.

One of the Rats decided to break the silence. He stuck out his hand to Jack first.

"Darryl Burkes."

Short, fat, never make it.

"Yeah, of course, Jack Hartman." He shook his hand.

"Guess I'm next," said another. "Mike Kolwinski."

He was the tallest in the room and Jack could tell by his handshake that he was quite strong.

Strong enough. Sounds kinda dumb, though.

"Cool, a Russian," Darryl said as he shook Mike's hand.

"It's Polish, and I'm from Tenafly, New Jersey," Mike replied shaking his head and laughing at Darryl's naiveté.

That's why—Yankee.

"I'm Ted McClain," said the last of the four, the best dressed in his Izod button-down, khakis and docksiders.

Prep. Silver spoon. He's here on the family tradition plan, be my guess.

"At the risk of stating the obvious," Darryl said, "it looks like we'll be rooming together in this shoebox."

"Looks like we're in luck," added Ted, "If we work it just right, there might be enough room for us to sleep without even touching each other."

"I'm for no touching," said Mike.

They all laughed.

"Don't count on it, being lucky. There'll probably be three more guys in here before they get finished." Jack said with a wide grin as two cadre members walked in behind him.

"When an upperclassman walks into your room, the first to see him will call the room to attention. You will say in a command voice, 'ROOM ah ten SHUN'! Am I clear, Rats?" one of the cadre asked.

"Yes, sir!" they shouted together.

"Okay then, let's try that again."

The cadre left the room and the four roommates stood watching the door. After a minute they relaxed, assuming the cadre would return later.

Darryl began to talk casually. "So where were we? I think you were saying…ROOM ah ten SHUN!"

Ted and Jack snapped to attention, but Mike Kolwinski was looking out the window and simply laughed.

"Instead of all that attention stuff, let's just jump 'em and kick their…"

As he turned around, he saw the two cadet officers. He shut up and snapped to attention, but was too late.

"Rat Kolwinski. You're a tough guy, huh?" one of the cadre asked.

"No, sir! Not really, sir," Mike answered nervously.

"Looks like today is your lucky day. Matter of fact it looks like this is room four thirty-two's lucky day!" the other cadre replied.

"This is going to be the luckiest room on the fourth stoop. You will all get to prove that Rat Kolwinski is tough rather than stupid," the first bellowed. "Front leaning rest position, MOVE!"

The four quickly jumped down into the push-up position. Before it was over Jack had lost count of how many push-ups and mountain climbers they had done. It was hot in the room, and a puddle of sweat accumulated on the floor below each boy. Jack was mesmerized by the sweat dripping off of his nose. Renegade droplets rolled out of the hairline on his temples and snuck into the corners of his eyes. The four Rats were soaked. Jack could see his watch. They had been working out for fifteen minutes.

Jack tasted the salt. His body trembled. His eyes stung.

"It's been one heck of an introduction," one of the cadre said loudly. "My name is Mr. Henson, your Echo company commander. And this is Mr. Bogart, your first sergeant," he said pointing to the other cadre member.

"If Rat Kolwinski has anything else to say, I will assume from this point on he will keep it to himself. Do I make myself perfectly clear Rat?" Mr. Bogart screamed, bending down to get close to Mike's face.

"Yes, sir!" Mike yelled.

"Good. On your feet!"

They all jumped up to attention.

"Your corporal will be in here momentarily," said Cadet First Sergeant Bogart.

"Nice to get a chance to meet you, four thirty-two. We'll be keeping a close eye on this band of misfits. At ease!" Mr. Henson said.

The two cadre walked out of the room quickly.

They were quiet for a moment. They could hear Henson and Bogart lighting up the next room. Jack laughed nervously, still keeping a wary eye on the door, and that was enough to loosen things back up and get them talking again.

"I'm from Richmond," Ted said. "My dad's an alum. Even at that, I still wanted to go to VMI. Strange, huh?"

"I suppose if he told you about all this," Jack answered with a teasing smile.

"I loved the Institute since I was a kid. Dad's stories about it, about how tough it was, just made me want it so much more."

"A son after Dad's heart, how cute," Darryl said.

"I know, but in a healthy way. I think boys should try to emulate their fathers, and seek their approval. There's nothing wrong with that, I suppose," Ted said.

"You never met my old man," Jack answered.

Ted was lean, muscular, and tan. He seemed to Jack to be a straight-shooter, not pushy, with a strong spirit.

"I'm a legacy, too," said Darryl.

"What's a legacy?" asked Mike.

"Someone whose dad is a graduate," answered Ted. "It's a guaranteed slot into this fine exercise program."

"Yeah, but unlike Ted, here, I wasn't too keen on the idea of attending," Darryl continued. "Dad talked me into it. Hey, Ted, maybe I'm searching for my father's approval, too."

"Yeah, maybe," Ted answered.

"More so after his money. This is the only college he would fund. A full ride from Dad sort of thing. He thinks it'll get me in shape. Says I'm fat, but hey, I'm just horizontally tall," Darryl said.

They all laughed.

Nice guy, and all. Never make it, though.

Jack was about to tell a little about himself when a corporal and the company master sergeant walked in the room. This time Ted called the room to attention and everybody snapped to.

The master sergeant and Corporal Johnson led them downstairs, lined up along the wall again, and one by one led them in to have their heads shaved. The screaming cadre in the hallway directed their assault on those new cadets just entering the fray.

Jack noticed those coming out of the barber's room did not have a normal military buzz cut, instead their heads were almost completely bald. Once Jack's and his roommates' heads had been quickly shaved, they moved along through various rooms to be measured for uniforms and issued uniforms and equipment.

Jack's military issued duffel bag was filled with the new items. It was a blur of activity. He knew he would never remember what instructions were being given, when he would be expected to pick up items, what he was signing for, or what his account was being charged.

With freshly shaved heads and bags full of gear, they hustled behind Corporal Johnson up to the room, where they were put at ease. He told them how to set their bed racks down on the floor and showed them the arrangement in which they would be required to place the racks.

He showed them how to roll out their bed rolls or "hays." He had them dump their duffel bags on their own beds, and went through a checklist with them to ensure they had all of the required items. He took them through the Blue Book section concerning room arrangement; there was a place for everything.

Socks were to be rolled up, and the top folded over the roll forming a smile and placed in a row on the second shelf of the locker, the smile facing out. Then there were gloves; stretched and pressed flat with the fingers extended, each pair neatly stacked on the others.

Then underwear. Then shaving kits. And then, and then, and then.

Their new uniform items were marked with permanent ink, last name, first and second initial. It was tedious, but working steadily they had everything knocked out in about an hour and a half.

They filled the rest of the morning with training sessions in everything from basic military courtesy to shining shoes and "taking down" and shining every brass plate and button.

Corporal Johnson showed them what they would be required to wear. He called it "Rat Dyke" and instructed them to change into it. The term struck Jack as strange. Darryl laughed out loud when Corporal Johnson said it. Corporal Johnson gave little more than a pointed look at Darryl and left them to get dressed.

They changed quickly in their room into a uniform which consisted of black low-quarter shoes, olive drab fatigue pants, white short-sleeve shirt, and a black tie tucked in between second and third shirt buttons. The uniform looked intentionally dorky topped off with an olive drab fatigue cap.

"At VMI, one of the meanings of the word 'dyke' is uniform," Corporal Johnson explained. "That may seem a bit weird, but it's something that has evolved in the VMI lingo. Your basic uniform will be 'Rat Dyke' or, informally, 'Idiot Dyke' because it looks idiotic. The term originated from the phrase 'dyke out,' which is an old fashioned way to describe getting dressed for a parade. Full parade uniform also known as 'parade dyke.' Confused yet? Good, 'cause you'll figure it out in time," he said with a rather cavalier smirk.

He continued, "Some say the phrase actually is an evolved version of the term 'decked out.' It often takes the help of another cadet to wrap the sash around a cadet officer, or put on other parade gear. You will be assigned a first classman to mentor you while you are a Rat. He will be known as your 'Dyke,' because one of your duties will be to help him get dyked out for parades. Additionally, you will take care of a myriad of daily chores for him. This is why you will be called his dyke and he will be your dyke. Does everyone understand?"

"Yes, Sir!" they lied in unison.

"Good. The next thing I need to show you is the actual Ratline. The Ratline is defined as the longest distance between any origin and destination inside the walls of these barracks. You will be walking the Ratline for the next many months. You will begin as soon as we complete this training. You will never deviate from it and will never be excused from it, unless you are granted the right by a first classman. Follow me."

They followed him single file. He walked them through the Ratline around the different parts of barracks. There was no physical line, only a darkened trail from years of Rats walking the specified route. Corporal Johnson demonstrated each turn and direction AD nauseam until the group of Rats had memorized it.

Finally, he walked them out of the barracks, where he told them to salute the statue of Stonewall Jackson every time they exited Jackson Arch. Finally, he showed them where they would form on "the bricks" in front of the barracks for every formation.

"Alright, Rats, listen up. We've got a great deal of work to get accomplished," Corporal Johnson said. "As soon as I give the command to fall out, you will immediately return through Jackson Arch and follow the Ratline directly to your room via the Sally Port stairwell. You will finish getting your room in military inspection order. You will have fifteen minutes to complete this task at which time I will inspect your rooms. Any questions?" There was a short pause. "Then fall out!"

And they did.

—⟅⟆—

"Whoa, Rat Hartman."

Jack had just entered Jackson Arch and stopped suddenly in the Ratline. He could feel several Rats pile up behind him like a traffic jam.

"One step to your left, idiot."

"Yes, sir," Jack said as he obliged.

"I just want you to know that you will not make it through the end of the week."

It's him. He won't stop till I'm gone. I won't give him the satisfaction.

"No, sir, I will make it through this week," Jack replied, still staring forward at attention.

"We'll see. We'll see how much you can take, maggot. Get out of here."

Immediately following his inspection, Corporal Johnson led the entire squad down to the armory where a number of cadets and an Army officer issued their M-14 rifles and bayonets. The cadre at the armory gave instructions on the use, maintenance and security of their issued weapons.

By one, Jack and his roommates were standing with the group of Echo Company Rats against the fourth stoop railing, holding chairs straight out over the edge by the back legs, waiting for a few stragglers to join them, a torment significantly worse than push-ups.

"This is insane," Darryl whispered to Jack.

"Shhh," Jack replied, "or they'll be dropping us all for push-ups, again."

"Which would be an improvement," whispered Darryl.

If this goes on any longer, there'll be a pile of broken chairs down in the courtyard.

"Rats! Get out of the Ratline! Bring your chairs over here and take a seat in a semi-circle around me!" It was a first class officer of some sort. Jack didn't care who he was, he was just relieved to put down the chair.

"My name is Mr. Tranjik. I am one of the two prosecutors on the Honor Court. The next thirty minutes will be the most important training you will receive at VMI. If you get everything else wrong, get this one thing right."

Truth. Honor. Never taken lightly, never gray. Every cadet was to speak truthfully and live honorably at all times, even when away from the Institute. Mr. Tranjik even covered "quibbling," which included intentional omissions of the truth in an effort to deceive. It was complete and comprehensive to the nth degree: don't lie, cheat, steal, or tolerate those that do. Even tolerating another's lie was a violation of honor.

Tranjik looked over the group of Rats sitting around him as if he intended to make eye contact with every one of them.

Honor was serious here. Any breech of it would be prosecuted. If found guilty, it would mean permanent expulsion from the Institute, and if you were expelled, cadets would be forbidden to mention your name inside the barracks ever again. Jack imagined it would be a difficult shame to bear.

Mr. Tranjik finished with one statement.

"When I leave the Institute, and I am wearing this ring, other men will recognize it and there will be an implicit trust, because they will know I am a VMI man, a man of honor."

"When you are given the command to fall out, you will begin double timing and moving through the entrance to the mess hall behind your corporal," the company master sergeant said to the formation of Rats that he had just marched down the hill to Crozet Hall, the corps dining facility.

"Do not pass your corporal! Do you understand, Rats?"

"Yes, sir!" they shouted in unison.

"Fall out!" he commanded.

They began double timing, mostly in place as they followed their corporals into the building. Other cadre would walk by them holding a hand out slightly higher than waist high, telling them to get their knees up. Once inside, still double timing, the cadre led each of their squads to a table.

First meal as a Rat. Starving.

"Rats, stop double timing and look at me," Corporal Johnson instructed them. "When I give the command to take seats, you will sit on the front three inches of your chair. You will eat one bite at a time with arms and hands down to your sides when you aren't taking a bite. Heads straight forward, eyes looking down at the plate, in a modified position of attention."

Jack found it difficult to get much to eat. Corporal Johnson remained incessantly lively and angry at every move one of them made, especially if it was not consistent with one rule or another.

It was like that for everything: physical exercise and mental stress.

Their two fists of force. They'll beat us into shape with them.

They were drilled in the hot August sun on a freshly cut parade deck for what seemed hours. They ran everywhere and the punishment for each mistake was, of course, push-ups and mountain climbers. Jack figured he had done several hundred of each by then, and though his arms were like rubber, he grew numb to the pain and struggled through set after set.

"Hey, idiot."

"Yes, sir," answered Jack.

Jack could not see him, but recognized the voice immediately.

The courtyard, the barracks basement, Jackson Arch, now here, on the parade ground. Doesn't anyone see what this guy is doing?

Suddenly he was right behind Jack, breathing on his neck.

"Don't go to sleep tonight. I wouldn't recommend it, anyway."

Jack could feel him move away, his presence always heavy like a thick cloud of something evil. His attacks were inconspicuous and under his breath. Jack realized he was operating under the radar, not drawing attention to his subtle abuse.

It will be hard for him to get to me. Too public. Still…

"Right face, I said, Hartman, you moron!"

Jack executed the right face, startled he had slipped so deeply in his thoughts.

Jack caught on quickly, and was seldom dropped for his own mistakes. But when one Rat in the squad messed up, they would all feel the pain together. So they pushed against the freshly cut grass, and they pushed against the concrete on the stoops, and they pushed against the asphalt in front of the barracks in the area known as *the bricks*.

As the sun was setting, they formed in companies as units in the Rat Battalion formation for retreat – the ceremonial lowering of the flag for the evening. They marched down to Crozet in their companies and double-timed to tables. They ate what they could, but not enough. At that table, that first evening meal, Jack was deep in thought. He wondered if he had the stamina to stay this course for the long run. He wasn't the only one. He would find out in time all of his roommates were questioning themselves about their decision to attend VMI and whether they would be able to make it.

All of them.

CHAPTER THREE

CADRE

"I can't lift my arms up," Darryl said in a low voice.

Everyone in the room groaned, and then laughed as if they were amused by their newly discovered paralysis.

"That ain't nothin'," Mike whispered as he rolled onto his side in his creaky bed rack, "compared to how my head feels like sandpaper every time I lay it against this pillow. Nice classy buzz-job."

Jack lay on his back, trying to make out the features on the ceiling. The room was dark, but there was a slight bluish glow from a security light in Jackson Arch which held the pitch black at bay. He couldn't help but think of it as a prison cell.

The plaster walls and ceiling were thick with layer upon layer of flat latex paint a shade darker than white, one florescent light fixture in the middle of the ceiling, and a single sink in the front corner. The paint wasn't peeling, but had some distinctive and ornate cracks along the top of the wall over the uniform hanging racks.

"Hey Ted," Jack whispered. "Did you say you were from Richmond?"

"Yeah, still am when I'm not gettin' my head shaved and doin' push-ups all day," Ted replied. "What about you?"

"Not too far from here, down around Buchanan in Botetourt County."

"Hey, you're close enough to be considered a townie," Darryl interjected, "home right around the corner and all."

"I don't know if I call it home. Things'd have to get pretty bad to make me wanna go hang out there," Jack said.

"They're not bad enough for you yet?" Mike joked.

"Where about in Richmond?" Darryl asked Ted.

"Forest Hills, across the river from the city. We live right on the James, there."

"That's cool. I grew up on the James River," said Jack.

"All I want to hear are sleeping noises!" a corporal outside their door shouted.

No one said a word. In the silence, Jack heard his heart pounding and it made it difficult to even think about falling asleep. The warning from Corporal Phelps kept ringing in his ears. A few minutes passed and Jack could hear a mild snore coming from Mike, making the whole effort to sleep even more futile.

He won't try anything here. There's no way he would get away with it. That is, unless everyone is in on it. Unless they protect each other.

Jack felt muscular pain and weakness in almost every part of his body. As he turned on his side, his shaven head bristled against the pillow. No position seemed comfortable enough to allow him to think he might possibly get any sleep. His mind raced across the day's events: the insanity, Phelps, his new roommates, the Honor Court.

Don't try so hard to sleep. What the heck, I'm resting anyway. Resting is good enough. Long day. Hit the hay at twenty-two hundred hours—I think. Wake-up at five-thirty, be my guess.

As he shifted and stared, and shifted and stared, Jack could hear his roommates snoring lightly or breathing drawn-out inhalations and exhalations typical of sleep.

Sleeping noises.

Jack reached down and fished his watch out of his shoe. He pressed the button for the background light and checked the time. It was twelve-thirty, but he could still hear strange noises from the courtyard. Shuffling and whispers.

Then he heard the distinctive *clink* of the button being pressed on the barracks public address system microphone. Jack had been hearing it all day.

"Welcome to hell, Rats!" A voice boomed over the courtyard speakers.

Wham!

The door of their room seemed to explode as someone kicked it open. The light flipped on and six cadre flooded their room screaming like men on fire. The company master sergeant flipped Darryl's rack and sent him sprawling on the floor before he could even wake up. One short, psychotic looking corporal Jack had not met yet was standing on the tables in the middle of the room, beating on them with a metal dustpan and screaming at the top of his lungs. The veins were standing out on his head and he was nearly frothing as saliva foam was building up in the corners of his mouth.

"Get up! Get up! Get the heck up you stupid maggots!"

The scene was surreal.

Ted and Mike jumped up, obviously still asleep, and ran straight into each other, colliding head-to-head. Ted crashed back down on his rack, but Mike landed flat on the hard floor and was scooting around on his side in a circle trying to get his balance back and stand up. It was the image of a fish flopping helplessly on the dry ground that immediately popped into Jack's head.

Jack bent over and helped him up. He saw Ted pull on his red PT shorts and grab for his running shoes. Jack quickly began donning his PT shorts and shirt, though he couldn't remember hearing anyone tell them to do so, as everything being shouted was so garbled with six men screaming all at once.

"Get out on the stoop, your Brother Rats are out there waiting on you!" One of the cadre yelled.

How in the world?

They were dressed and on the way out the door with Mike right behind them pulling on his yellow PT shirt. Darryl was half-way under his bed trying to get to his shoes while the Master

Sergeant and two corporals were bent down screaming at him. Mike stopped to help Darryl, but another corporal grabbed him by the shirt and pointed him out the door.

The three of them ran out onto the stoop and were directed by other cadre to stand against the rail facing the courtyard. Jack was surprised to see most of the other Rats out on the stoop already in the darkness, illumined by a sliver of moon.

These guys must've been sleeping in their PT uniform.

Darryl finally barreled out the door with his two new friends in tow. He squeezed in between Ted and Mike and the two cadre released and went along the stoop to a room several doors down.

"Combs, Anderson! There's an idiot still in five!" the Master Sergeant yelled to the two pit bulls that had finished chewing on Darryl.

"Oh, this is gonna be fun," one of them said as they headed quickly down the stoop.

Various corporals were walking back and forth commanding each Rat to stand at attention, giving direction laced with an occasional expletive, and talking among each other. Jack heard a familiar voice between Ted and Darryl.

"Why are you improperly dressed on my stoop, Rat?"

It was Phelps.

"I, uh, don't know, sir." Darryl answered.

"Where is your stupid shoe, idiot?"

Four or five cadre corporals and sergeants immediately latched on to Darryl. He was well into his twentieth push-up when they decided to drop the entire company. As everyone did push-ups on the stoop, Darryl was sent back to the room to look for his shoe. He was back out in about thirty seconds.

The Echo Company Rats were directed to get back on their feet, face right, and squeeze tightly together and move along the Ratline somewhere downstairs.

"Butt to belly, butt to belly! Make your Brother Rat smile!" one cadre member yelled.

Down the outside of the stairs to the pillar, right turn to the wall, right turn along the wall, right turn along the wall again, right turn down the outside of the stairs to the pillar, right turn to the wall, right turn along the wall, right turn along the wall again, right turn down the outside of the stairs along the courtyard rail to the center of the arch, right turn through the center of the archway, salute Stonewall and follow the leader...

"Run Rats!" a cadre member yelled.

They ran, guided in the darkness by a gauntlet of cadre, across the front of the barracks in single file into an old gym. It was pitch black inside. The only thing Jack could see was the very dim light from red lens flashlights the cadre used to direct them. When the last Rat was in and guided into position the doors slammed shut, and all of the flashlights went out.

Jack heard only an occasional cough, and a few scattered footsteps of hard sole shoes against the wood floor. Suddenly, a spotlight shot across their heads to the gym's second level. Standing at the railing was a very stout looking cadet in the grey VMI blouse and white sharply creased pants.

"Rats, look up here!" he shouted.

Jack already was. He could see a row of cadets behind the speaker, wearing the same uniform, and standing at parade rest: feet shoulder width apart and hands clasped together at the small of the back. Jack was both impressed and intimidated. The speaker placed both his hands on the railing and began to speak.

"My name is Mr. Warner, president of the First Class. Many of you are already wondering why you even came to the Institute."

He paused for several uncomfortable seconds.

"Some of you are here because you wanted to come. Some of you are here only because your parents made you come. It really doesn't matter because here's a news flash, hero: Your mother is gone, your father is gone, and they aren't the ones going through this torment for the next year. You are officially alone—some of you for the first time in your lives. You need to understand this clearly: You have a new mother. He is your corporal. Your new brothers are to your left and right. Your new dad is the First Classman assigned to mentor you. You also need to get this straight: the First Class runs the barracks. We own you!"

He paused for several seconds.

Someone whispered close to Jack's right side, "Go ahead Rats, keep cuttin' your eyes."

Mr. Warner continued.

"Make no mistake about this. You have just matriculated into the toughest military school in the country! When I looked at all of you walking around the barracks, I saw a gaggle of nearly four-hundred individuals whose only care was for themselves! For you to make it through the Ratline you will have to function as a single unit. You will have to become a class. Until then, you are just a lowly mass of Rats! You will learn to take care of yourselves. Some of you don't even know how to do that. Then you will learn to take care of your Brother Rats. You must rely on each other and work together. Until you do this as part of your daily life, you will not be a class."

"Half of you will quit tonight," one cadre member whispered somewhere behind Jack.

"If you think you're going to get out of this any time soon, you might be better served quitting right now, because it ain't gonna happen," Warner continued. "I do not care how long it takes. The leaves will fall from the trees, and you will still be Rats. The air will turn cold and snow will fall and you will still be Rats. The snow will melt away, the birds will start singing, the trees will bud and the leaves will come out again and you? You will *still be Rats*!" He hammered those last three words out, paused for several seconds, and yelled, "Rats, meet the first class!"

The room filled with light and an explosion of voices screaming. They were surrounded by first classmen in grey blouse. One very marine-looking cadet with a mass of chevrons on his sleeves singled out Jack, Ted, and another Rat who wasn't from Echo Company.

"Get your knees up!" he yelled, as he held his hand almost chest-high, making them touch their knees to his hand every step of running in place.

"Get used to it, Rats. You'll be doing this everywhere you go. Front leaning rest, move!"

They dropped.

"Twenty push-ups in unison. Ready, begin!" he yelled.

They counted out twenty push-ups, all grunting on the last few. The din of hundreds of grey blouse clad First Classmen yelling and screaming commands at the whole gym full of Rats was overpowering. Jack could barely hear the commands from the Marine-looking First.

"On your feet and get your knees up!"

They jumped back up and began running in place.

"On your backs!"

The three of them quickly dropped down on their backs.

"Twenty sit-ups! Ready, begin!"

They began doing sit-ups, this time well out of synch on the last several. They were beginning to tire.

"On your feet!" the first classman barked.

They jumped up and began running in place again. They knew what needed to be done, that there would be no breaks in the workout.

"Good Rats. Now get those knees up. We don't need any fall-outs in this sweat party. We're no different than any other college, are we? We like to party till two in the morning here, too!"

He held his hand waist-high as he paced back and forth in front of the three Rats.

They ended up with a few more rounds of push-ups and mountain climbers. They were spent, soaked in sweat, and unable to do any more exercises correctly.

Before they reassembled in a mass formation, the first classman taught them to strain.

"The strain is a modified position of attention. Look straight up, Rat Hartman."

Jack looked straight up till his chin was pointed at the ceiling. The cadet officer placed his hand an inch from Jack's Adam's apple, and then had him bring his head back down without touching his hand. It was almost impossible and very painful.

"How old are you, Rat Hartman?"

"Eighteen, sir!" Jack answered.

"Then I better see eighteen wrinkles under that chin! You other two do the same."

"Now, squeeze your arms in tight against your sides so there are no gaps between your arms and your sides."

All three complied. He grabbed Jack's right arm and pulled it away from Jack's body. Jack yanked it back down.

"You trying to fly away Hartman?"

"No, sir!"

"I shouldn't be able to pull your arm away that easily. Next, squeeze your shoulder blades together. You should be able to pinch my finger if I put it between them," he said testing Ted's back.

"Good job, Rat McClain. That's how you strain Rats! You will strain at all times in the Ratline, in formation, and any time you are being addressed by an upperclassman! Do you understand, Rats!"

"Yes, sir!" they shouted in unison.

Jack immediately understood why they called it "the strain." It was very painful, requiring most of the body to be very tense. He felt a Charlie Horse clenching up under his chin.

The first classman got very close to Jack's face.

"Do you know who your dyke is, Rat?"

"No sir," Jack answered, "we haven't been told that, yet, sir."

"Well, congratulations, Rat Hartman, you seem like you might just be tough enough to be my Rat! I'll see you in a couple days!"

The cadre ran the Rats back to the barracks in single file, the same way they had gone to the gym. Then it was up the Ratline and back to the fourth stoop where the cadre corporals and sergeants were waiting for them. As they arrived in the room, corporals were yelling at them.

"Get your soap and towel and get back in the Ratline and head down to the sally port showers! Y'all smell like a bunch of nasty, stinkin' rats and we're gonna make sure you have a chance to get clean and fresh! Tighten up this line, butt to belly!"

We're going to take showers as a group?

Jack was beginning to feel panicky. He realized someone would see his scars.

The lines stacked up from each direction of the barracks converging on Sally Port, the connecting corner of New and Old Barracks. As they stood packed together, sweating on each other and waiting to make it into the showers, they endured constant harassment, and spent much of the time doing push-ups or mountain climbers when singled out for not straining hard enough.

There were a few moments of quiet. Jack was relieved, hoping maybe they had tired of it all and were willing to just let them shower and go to bed. Jack wanted to be invisible. His body was in deep muscular pain and he was completely exhausted. He pressed close to the sweat-soaked Rat in front of him.

The Ratline became a two-lane path moving quickly as Rats were entering and leaving the showers, but the whole shower experience was every bit as miserable as the work out. Rats were given just enough time to get their PT gear off, walk through the showers, and rinse some of the sweat off their bodies. One of the corporals saw it immediately when Jack took his shirt off.

"What happened to your back, Rat?"

Jack wanted so badly to lie, to tell them it was from a farming accident, but he knew he couldn't. He knew they would see through such a violation of his honor.

"My dad did it," he said in a whisper.

"Speak up, Rat."

"My dad did it…when I was younger, sir," he said loudly.

"Well, get your gear on and get out of here."

It was obvious the corporal was considerably shocked and at a loss for words. Jack was glad the shock squelched the questions.

There was no time to dry off and, of course, no change of clothes. They put on their sweaty PT shorts and shirts, and walked the Ratline back to the room, wet, cold and rank.

Ted stood beside his rack, shivering slightly, looking stunned, while Mike and Jack helped Darryl get his rack back up and his bedding back together.

"What just happened?" asked Ted.

"Well, with the help of our illustrious cadre, we just met the first class, and what a joyful bunch of fellows they are!" Mike said.

"Does this happen every night?" Ted asked.

"Probably, except, tomorrow night they'll come in with bullwhips and cattle prods!" Jack answered.

They laughed, cautiously.

"They'll need 'em if they keep wakin' us up every hour!" Mike added.

A corporal walked by the door.

"All I want to hear are sleeping noises!" he yelled.

"I'm really starting to hate that guy," whispered Ted.

Each got his gear cleaned up and stowed, and got into his cot.

"Jack, I saw your back. You said your dad did it. On purpose?" asked Ted.

"Yeah, drunk. But he's gone now. He died a few years ago."

They lay there, quiet for quite some time, listening to the cadre harassing the last straggling Rats. Jack heard Darryl sniff twice in his bunk. At first he didn't think anything of it, but only seconds later he could hear Darryl's whimpers, muffled in his pillow.

"Hey, Darryl, you okay, man?" asked Jack.

It took Darryl a moment to answer.

"I'm fine, just trying to clear my throat," answered Darryl.

Jack knew better. He had cried quietly in his bed too many nights growing up not to recognize it.

"Yeah," said Ted, "this has gotta be good for our health."

"I heard the corporals talking. They said the 'fat one' wouldn't make it the first week. I know they were talking about me," Darryl said.

Jack could tell by the way Darryl's voice was shaking, and how he gasped for a breath when he finished talking, he was still fighting back an emotional flood.

These rotten…

Jack's mind filled with darkness.

They're gonna try to run this guy out of here.

"Listen here, Darryl. Nothin' is gonna happen to you. They'll have to come through me first," Jack said.

"And me, too," said Ted.

"Oh, you know I'm in," added Mike.

"Then it's settled. What they do to one of us, they do to all of us," Jack said.

"That's it. If any one of us gets singled out for push-ups or whatever else they can come up with, the rest of us join in," said Ted.

"Sound good, Darryl?" asked Jack.

"Yeah. Thanks, guys."

"And by the way, you're not fat, you're thick, and thick is good," said Jack. "Thick is stronger. Thick means you can carry more weight on your back, and the military likes guys that can carry more weight. You got it?"

"Yeah, Jack, I got it."

Bristly hair, dried sweat and nerves could not keep Jack from sleeping, and within minutes, he was.

⟞〜〜⟝

The 0530 wake-up, complete with corporals and sergeants and all the yelling, made for a short night's sleep. By 0600, the Rats were formed in their respective companies on the bricks in the cold, wet air.

More fog. Just like yesterday. Like home on the river.

After a battalion stretching and warm-up, they began to peel off in company units and run around the parade field. The road circling around the parade field was just under a mile loop. By the beginning of the third pass, many of the Rats who were not in the kind of shape they needed to be in were getting quite desperate. Jack could see the fear in their eyes.

Each squad was led by its assigned corporal. Another corporal carried the guidon front and center. The company first sergeant and a line sergeant traded calling "jodies" from the left of the formation, while the Rat company commander, a lieutenant, ran on the right side. The master sergeant and another line sergeant ran behind the formation looking for stragglers and fall-outs.

Jack loved it. The jodies called out and sung by each company echoed off the facades of the buildings surrounding the parade field, and became a cacophony of men's voices, garbled with brief hints of rhythm.

> C-one thirty rollin' down the strip,
> Airborne Ranger on a one-way trip,
> Stand up, hook up shuffle to the door,
> Jump right out and count to four.
> If my main don't open wide,
> I've got another one by my side,
> If that one should fail me too,
> Look out ground, I'm a comin' through!

A couple of the Rats fell out. One peeled out of the squad to Jack's right, but as he came alongside, Jack grabbed him to push him along and the Rat on the other side did the same. It was enough of a push to help the Rat finish with the company.

Another Rat was not quite as fortunate. He peeled off to the outside of the formation and gasped for air, grabbing his chest and throat.

Crybaby! We're all tired. What's your problem?

Two line sergeants went on a feeding frenzy and gave him some personal attention all the way back. He joined up with the company after they had already finished the run and started cool down exercises.

By the afternoon, Jack noticed the Rat that had fallen completely out of the run was gone.

Corporal Johnson said, "He quit and went home to Mama."

Why quit? Run out, I suppose. Don't want too much attention.

In the day and a half he had been there he was already exhausted and sore and anxious. But he couldn't quit. Something inside him wanted to be where the action was, where it was tough, where it was tough enough to overpower his nightmarish childhood. By then he was convinced he was certainly at the right place for that.

"Maybe Warner is right," an exhausted Ted had said that morning. "Maybe this is the toughest school in the country."

Darryl laughed as he massaged his arms and said, "That is, unless hell is admitting students."

CHAPTER FOUR

A Crowd of Honorable Youths

"I'll gut you, you fat, worthless pig."

Jack stood, petrified, a few feet from the door to the room. Darryl had been stopped By Corporal Phelps in the Ratline just outside the door. Jack knew coming to Darryl's rescue would be a complete disaster. He froze in place, afraid.

"You, and that scumbag Hartman. So make it easy on yourself. Go in that room and pack your stuff. Why suffer for a few weeks when we're gonna run you out eventually, anyway?"

Corporal Phelps walked off. Darryl stood in place, straining and shaking.

Jack pulled the door open.

"Get in here."

Darryl stepped into the room. "Did you hear all of that?" Darryl asked Jack.

"Yeah, I heard it."

"Why does he have it out for us?"

"Not us," Jack replied, "me."

"You?"

"Yeah, looks like you're collateral damage," said Jack.

"What, you had a run-in with this guy already?"

"Yeah, a bunch of run-ins. That's just since I've been here," Jack said.

"Since you've been here? You knew him before this?"

"High school a couple years back. John Phelps was a bully and a punk. Tried to torment me his senior year. He was a rich kid, at least fairly well off. Preferred to act like a redneck, though. I don't know why, but he hated me something fierce."

"Wow," said Darryl, "this all stems from some high school feud? Nice. Some guys just don't grow up."

"I guess. I still wonder why he picked me to hate. I think it had something to do with my dad."

"Why would you think that?" asked Darryl.

"He was always hung up on telling me that I had something to do with my old man's death."

"Oh, sorry to hear that. How did it happen?"

"Tractor accident when I was fifteen."

Darryl didn't answer for a minute or two.

"Jack?"

"Yeah."

"I'm afraid of this guy, Phelps. He's not like the rest. I think he's crazy."

"Best I can tell, he was crazy long before he came here."

"Every day will be the same in your miserable, stinking Rat lives. Doors kicked in every morning at zero five hundred hours. Physical Training, or PT, at zero six hundred, Breakfast Roll Call or BRC, followed by drill, inspections, Dinner Roll Call, training classes on everything VMI, and more PT," shouted Corporal Johnson.

I'll punch him if he gets in my face again. Why am I here? I can't wait to be the guy doing all the screaming. I want some stripes.

"Get used to it. You see the pattern, Rats? Everything has an abbreviation. Know what they mean."

The evening started officially with Supper Roll Call, at which the Battalion presented arms, the bugler sounded retreat and the evening cannon fired prior to the lowering of the flag. More assemblies and drills and classes followed SRC, and even more PT to end the long days.

Jack was amazed how well they began to move and learn and react as a unit in that first week. They were soaking up information at a feverish pace. The memorization of drill movements, military courtesies, the Honor System, and all of the history and "pertinent information" in the Rat Bible was more intense that anything he had ever done.

"Guys, I can't win," Darryl said when he made it back to the room Thursday afternoon. "It's like the snowball effect. You mess up on one thing, they want to destroy you. Then they put more pressure on you, and it just gets worse and worse. I might be beyond help, and I'm pretty sure Corporal Johnson hates my guts."

The other three were sitting at their desks, shining brass and shoes.

"The guy's just doin' his job and we're Rats. Can't expect more from him than that," replied Ted.

"Johnson is an idiot," Mike said. "Just for taking his side, the room will nickname you 'Teddy' for bein' soft and mushy like a little girl's teddy bear."

"That's fine, it's what my family calls me. While we're on the subject, though, maybe we need to call you 'Ski' for bein' such a lame Pollock," Ted replied.

"Room attention!" Ski shouted.

They snapped up to attention, their chairs screeching as they scooted out suddenly and one fell over backward, the back bouncing quickly a couple times as it hit the floor. Jack didn't even know who had come into the room. His heart sunk a little when he recognized the breathing pattern of Corporal Phelps. It took Phelps fifteen seconds or so to position himself to the right of Jack, face close to his ear.

"Holy..." he rattled off an expletive. "You ain't left yet? Well, we'll just see what needs to be done about that. Rat Kolwinski!" he shouted turning his head to read the block letters on Ski's PT shirt.

"Yes, sir?" Ski inflected as a question.

"What is your assessment of Rat Hartman?"

"He's a good man, sir."

"Rat," he paused as he read Ted's shirt, "McClain, what do you think of ol' Hartman?"

"Same, sir. Good man."

"Burkes, you worthless piece of…" releasing the same expletive, "I'm not even going to ask your opinion. You're too stupid!"

Phelps leaned over till he was only a few inches from Jack's ear.

"Looks like you've snowed your roommates. Glad to see they all like you so much. It just means I won't feel as bad if they all wash out."

He walked around the table, stopping beside Darryl.

"Get on your face!"

Darryl jumped down into the push-up position. Jack, Ted, and Ski followed suit.

"I didn't say for everyone to get on their faces, just this Rat! Get on your feet!"

All four jumped up to their feet.

"I meant the other three, not you, stupid!" he snarled at Darryl.

Check. Check.

He walked quickly over to Jack, who had just snickered.

"You think this is funny, Hartman, you maggot?"

"No, sir! I mean, yes, sir."

"If we weren't on post, I'd take you right now." Phelps was speaking almost at a whisper.

Jack broke all military bearing, and turned and looked at Phelps in the eyes.

"Whenever you're ready, just go for it," Jack said.

Jack continued to stare right into Phelps's eyes. Phelps let out a one-syllable laugh, and then turned to walk away.

Checkmate.

"Your day is coming, Hartman." he said as he left the room.

They all relaxed. Darryl picked his chair up from the floor and sat at his desk.

"Maybe he'll get the message," Jack said.

"Oh yeah? What message would that be?" asked Ski.

"I'm not going to take it, anymore. Not like this, anyway. He's out of control."

"I hate to tell ya, Jack," said Ted, "but I don't think our psychotic friend gets any messages."

"So what am I supposed to do, just lay down?"

"I don't think you get it, so let me put it in southern for you— it ain't never gonna stop," said Ski.

"Well, I'm sure not going to let him take it over the top with me, and I'm not going crying to anyone else," said Jack.

"You really think you got the upper hand today with Phelps, don't you?" asked Darryl.

"He backed down. That's enough."

"He played you like a deck of cards."

"What do you mean by that?" asked Jack.

"He was just trying to find out what your biggest weakness was."

"And?"

"And he did," answered Darryl. "He's countin' on that short temper you have to take you down."

"On your feet!" echoed the command from the back of the J.M. Hall, the Post Chapel.

The entire group jumped to their feet in one succinct movement. Along the center isle a group of cadre marched forward in two columns as their heels, drumming in unison on the wood floor, counted their cadence. Jack dared not cut his eyes.

Once they had reached the front, the two columns of men split and walked up the stairs on both sides of the stage. Twelve of them took seats in a row of twelve chairs arranged in a slight semicircle well behind the podium. They were all dressed in their grey blouses, which Jack knew by now meant something serious was about to happen. The thirteenth man needed no chair, but took his place behind the podium.

"Rat's, look up here!"

The command seemed ridiculous to Jack. It was the only place his eyes could look in the sanctuary. The lights had been turned off. They had been herded in and seated shoulder to shoulder in the pews facing the dimly lit stage. Behind it, on the wall, there was the stunning, life-size antiquated mural depicting the VMI Cadets' charge during the Civil War against the Union cannons at New Market, Virginia, a small town about seventy-five miles up the Shenandoah Valley. The dimmed lights above the stage gave an eerie feel to the assembly.

"Take seats!" the cadet at the podium yelled in a two count military command.

It took less than a second to execute the command. He began speaking in the very military manner—shouting out clear and staccato sentences.

"My name is Mr. Maxwell, president of the Rat Disciplinary Committee. I am also the Rat battalion commander. Many of you have already had the unfortunate experience meeting me personally. All of you will have the same experience before the Ratline is over. You will learn in short order I am not your friend and I am not your big brother and I am not your dad. You made the choice to enter the toughest military college in the country, and it is my job to ensure you are not let down."

He went on to introduce the RDC. Each member stood when Mr. Maxwell introduced them. They maintained faces of stone and each one wore a scowl. It was more than just military bearing; it looked more like contempt or even anger.

It intimidated even Jack, who was familiar with the cruelty of men. When Maxwell finished, he explained the responsibilities of the RDC, and talked about what Rats could expect from them. He paused for a moment and looked around the room. Suddenly, he pointed to someone near the front on the pews, opposite the isle from Jack.

"Mr. Martin, wake that Rat up!"

Martin and two others jumped off the stage and began screaming frantically as soon as they reached the Rat in the second row. They continued for about two minutes while the Rat did push-ups and ran in place.

Those around him didn't know what to do. A couple got down beside him and started doing push-ups until Mr. Martin told them to sit down and shut up.

The whole affair had Jack giggling inside, though he was careful not to exhibit anything which could be construed as laughter. He bit the inside of one cheek to take his mind off of it. Finally, the three released the Rat and he sat back down, gasping for each breath.

"Don't *ever* fall asleep when I'm talking," Martin said. "Tomorrow, you will face one of your first real challenges here. Tomorrow, you will be climbing House Mountain as squads with two-hundred pounds of sand. My hope is half of you will quit. If I was a Rat, and I was thinking about quitting, I'd quit tonight. It will certainly make my job easier. Those of you who make it will be better for it, but keep in mind you will still be Rats."

He paused again and looked around the sanctuary of the chapel appearing satisfied with all of the fear.

"One more thing, Rats. Many of you have received cards already for failure to properly execute one of your Rat requirements. You will eventually get a summons on your door, inviting you to a meeting of the RDC. Every Rat will eventually attend an RDC meeting." He paused. "Be scared, maggots. RDC, fallout," He said.

Be scared.

The RDC stood and quickly walked back out.

———

"We can't go up without you, Scotty!" Darryl barked in a Scottish accent.

Scott Holman was not from Scotland, but earned the nickname "Scotty" because he resembled the television character.

His roommates tagged him with it the first day, and always said it with the appropriate accent.

The cadre corporals had caught on quickly, and used it too. Scotty was a member of the third squad, and had a reputation for not being in good shape. He often struggled to keep up during Rat PT.

"My legs are cramping," he complained. "I don't think I can make it."

"C'mon, Brother Rat, you can make it," Jack said.

"Hey, if Kirk was here, he wouldn't let you get away with that. C'mon, let's go!" Darryl said as he slung Holman's sandbag on his shoulder, giving him two to carry.

Jack and Bobby Mitchell, one of Scott's roommates, grabbed him by the armpits and dragged him stumbling back to the group about twenty feet up the hill. By this point, they were all exhausted.

It had rained steadily all Friday night, and though the rain let up for a few hours in the morning, it started pouring by the time the buses arrived at the jumping off point on the farm at the foot of House Mountain.

The mission was simple enough: the squad was to climb House Mountain while carrying six thirty-plus pound sandbags. With ten Rats in the squad, they could take turns carrying the sandbags, allowing each of them to get a break at different times.

The climb started out miserably. The rain was so dense they could barely see or hear each other. The first five hundred meters were extremely steep up the side of a ridgeline. It was difficult to climb without any extra weight, but next to impossible dragging or shouldering a sandbag in the deluge and resultant sloppy mud.

In the time it took them to climb the first ridge, they were covered in mud, soaking wet, and several were pretty banged up. Jack had taken a swat from a sapling limb across his right eye and it was burning and watering so much he had to keep it closed most of the time.

"Where's Darryl?" asked Ted.

Jack spun around to look back down the ridge. The rain hammered down in thick drops, so dense Jack could not see clearly more than fifty yards. He didn't see Darryl anywhere.

"Burkes!" Jack yelled.

His call was lost in the roar of the rain.

"Corporal Johnson!" Ted yelled uphill.

Jack began backtracking. He ran back down the ridge about fifty feet, then turned and slid down the muddy trail they'd left on their ascent. He had covered about fifty yards when he heard Corporal Johnson's voice up the ridge behind him.

"Rat Hartman, stop!" he yelled.

Jack stopped and turned around. Johnson was sliding down the trail, trying to stay on his feet.

"If you've decided to make your bolt for freedom, this is about the worst place to do so, idiot," Johnson said as he approached.

"No sir, just looking for Brother Rat Burkes."

"He's not up with the rest of your squad?"

"No sir, just came from there. I thought maybe he'd gotten hurt and was still back here on the trail."

"Well, I don't see Rat Burkes from here. Let's get back up with the squad before we lose someone else. I'll get some cadre on the radio and see if we can locate him on the trail."

They fought their way back up to the top of the ridge and found the rest of the squad.

"I guess this means you didn't find him," said Ski.

"No, Corporal Johnson's going to call some other cadre and try to find him on the trail."

Corporal Johnson was already talking to another cadre member on his PRC-77 about fifteen feet behind them on the ridge. It was another corporal monitoring the trailing squad. Several cadre reported they had not seen Rat Burkes.

Corporal Johnson looked up at the squad.

"We can turn back and look for him, sir," Jack said.

"Hang tight Rat Hartman," Johnson said, "no one's died on House Mountain since the Civil War, I'm sure Rat Burkes is just draggin' butt."

The radio interrupted.

"Delta Two Three, this is Bravo One Four, over."

Jack immediately recognized the voice from the transmission. *Phelps.*

"Two Three, over."

"You missing a Rat, Two Three? Over."

"Affirmative, One Four. You seen him? Over."

"Got him right here, Two Three. Seems he had a little accident. I've called the medic up. Gonna need to take him back, over."

"Roger, One Four, over."

"Let his BRs know he's in good hands, over."

He meant for us to hear that. Darryl's in trouble.

"Roger, out."

Johnson hooked his plastic wrapped handset back onto his shoulder strap and headed up to the squad.

"Corporal Johnson, was that Corporal Phelps from Bravo Company?" asked Jack.

"What's it to ya, Hartman. Let's get moving."

"I was just going to say…"

"Rat, I don't care what you were going to say. You don't have the privilege of speaking freely with me. Now fall in and let's get up this mountain before it washes away," Johnson yelled.

Jack got in line on the trail as the squad began a hasty ascent. There was no way he could know where Darryl was, and no way to get there if he did.

When they arrived at the top, Corporal Johnson led them to a large rock outcropping overlooking the valley. For miles, the valley floor and its surrounding mountains were only partially obscured by the cloud cover beginning to thin out.

"The Shenandoah Valley," He said gesturing to the valley laying before them.

A handful of cadre stood at the top. Jack could hear radios cycling on and off with short bursts of communications from other cadre along the route. Corporal Johnson talked about the blood of southern and northern men which stained the valley, and how, right or wrong, each paid dearly for what he believed to be honorable.

"You need to understand, Rats, honor is not just telling the truth and not being a thief," Corporal Johnson said, "but it's about the way you live your whole life. Rat McClain, you got anything you believe strongly in?"

"Yes, sir," Ted answered.

"Good. If someone started stepping on those beliefs, would you stand up for them?" Corporal Johnson asked.

"Of course I would, sir."

"That is honorable, Rat McClain, and people will recognize the honor in it, even if they don't share the same beliefs. From Lexington to Gettysburg thousands and thousands of men from both sides fought honorably for beliefs they held dear," Corporal Johnson said, gesturing to the valley again.

"We'll visit New Market just up the road in a couple of weeks where the VMI corps was committed to battle against the Union forces in a farmer's field in order to fill a gap in the Confederate lines. Ten cadets were killed in the battle and over forty wounded. It was their time to be honorable, and it was their field of honor."

Phelps is out there, waiting. No honor, just hate, and he has Darryl. I will stand alright.

As the wind kicked up, they sat contemplating everything Corporal Johnson had said, and how it blended in with all they had been through together.

"Ted," Jack whispered when Johnson had moved far enough away, talking to some other cadre, "we've got to tell somebody about Corporal Phelps."

"Johnson won't listen. You heard him," said Ted.

"I know. What about our dykes? Have you talked to yours yet?"

"Not yet."

"I'll find mine tonight. I think he's in Room 128."

"Isn't he on the Regimental Staff?" asked Ted.

"Yeah, Jim Donahue, the S3."

"What if he shuts you down like Johnson?"

"I don't know. I'll burn that bridge when I come to it," said Jack.

Muddy and weary they got the command to move out, but before moving, they dumped their sand on the top of House Mountain, and tucked the empty bags in Corporal Johnson's rucksack.

They returned to barracks as the rain tapered off, and Jack got permission for his room to go to the infirmary and check on Darryl. When they arrived they found him sitting up getting dressed to return to barracks. He had a neck brace he wore loosely, more to support an icepack on the back of his neck than to support anything else.

"So Mr. Agility, did you have a nice trip?" asked Jack.

"Yeah," Darryl replied, "but I think I would've preferred to use my stunt double for that one."

Ted grabbed Darryl's loose things as Darryl signed out, and the four of them headed up to barracks together. When they got to the arch, Ted and Ski got into the Ratline and began making their way up to the Fourth Stoop. Darryl grabbed Jack's arm, stopping him from following them.

"I've got to tell you something, Jack."

He motioned for Jack to follow and led him over to the parapet, where he stopped on the steps behind a wall.

"What's up, Darryl? We can't be over here. We're supposed to be in the barracks."

"Phelps was there."

"I know. I heard him on the radio talking to Johnson."

"Jack, when I grabbed Holman's sandbag, I was at the back of the squad. I had to stop to take a leak. Next thing I know, I'm waking up, my head is pounding, my neck was numb, I was too dizzy to stand."

"They said you fell quite a way down the ridge."

"Yeah, even I thought something like that must have happened. Then I saw Phelps."

"He indicated to Johnson he was the one who found you."

"Of course he did, and I even thought I'd fallen at first."

"What do you mean?"

"Well, Phelps was being nice to me. He didn't make any usual threats. I thought maybe the guy actually had a heart, but then he said it. It's like he couldn't help himself."

"Said what?"

"When they were loading me in the van to take me back to town, he leaned over me and whispered *Be careful, Burkes, the falls just get harder from here on out.*"

"I'd say that's pretty obvious."

"It's worse. They checked me out at the hospital and I didn't have a concussion or broken neck, thank God, and they sent me to the post infirmary. While I lay there, everything started coming back to me."

Jack peered over the wall to ensure no one was listening, and no cadre were close by.

"Okay, go on," said Jack.

"I didn't remember anything until back at the infirmary. Jack, I didn't get hurt when I slipped down that ridge. Matter-of-fact, it wasn't very exciting, but when I stood up, the world exploded. Then I'm waking up. You know the rest."

"How can you be sure it was Phelps and not, um, the result of a lick you took on the way down?"

"Well, I didn't put it together till the infirmary—what he said and what I saw."

"What?"

"When I came to, Phelps was standing a few feet from me with a big stick—thick—like two or three inches thick, and maybe four feet long. He didn't see me coming to, and he ditched it when he got off the radio. He never picked it up after that."

"You're pretty sure he hit you with it?"

"All I know for sure is someone hit me with something. It just adds up."

"Think we should tell our dykes?" asked Jack.

"I'm not sure who we can trust. Everyone knows everyone. They're all connected," answered Darryl.

"I can't imagine one of the firsts letting this go on."

"Me neither. But what if Phelps is allowed to stay? If they don't kick him out, he'll keep coming back at us."

"We can get back at him next year," Jack said, grinning widely.

"Yup, long as we survive this one."

—◦◦◦—

"Permission to enter, sir," Jack asked, standing in Jim Donahue's doorway.

Jim Donahue was a no-nonsense marine-type with broad shoulders and thick, muscular arms. He stood an even six feet tall, and all of his upper body muscle tapered down to a thin waist. Jim maintained a high and tight marine haircut—buzzed off to the skin on the sides, and a narrow patch of very short hair on the top.

"Rat Hartman, what are you doing visiting your dyke during cadre?" Donahue shouted.

"Well, sir, I wasn't sure if I could, but something came up that made it important to try to talk with you."

"Rat Hartman, if I misjudged you, if you're a whiner and I'm stuck with you as my Rat dyke for the rest of the year, I'm gonna puke in your face right now."

"No sir, I'm not whining. I'm just kind of worried about the way a cadre corporal from Bravo Company has picked me and Brother Rat Burkes to try to run out of here."

"Run out of here?" Donahue asked with a puzzled look. "I assure you no one is trying to run any Rats out of here."

"Sir, Corporal Phelps has made a number of threats to both me and Brother Rat Burkes, and today at House Mountain, I believe he struck Burkes from behind and knocked him out."

"Somebody would have seen him. That climb is well monitored."

"Somehow he got away with it. I can have Darryl come down here and…"

"Look Rat Hartman," Donahue interrupted, "if Rat Burkes thought it was important enough to tell someone, he'd be over telling his dyke, and his dyke would get it taken care of. In the meantime, I'll keep an eye on Phelps. You're dismissed."

Jack turned around to leave, but then stopped and turned around to face Jim again.

"Actually sir, I'd rather you didn't. I'd rather you just go on like this never happened."

"Why's that, Hartman?"

Because he'll come at us with a vengeance. You couldn't watch him all the time, even if you intended to.

"I don't know, sir. Maybe I am just overreacting."

Jack began to turn.

"Jack?"

"Yes sir," Jack answered.

"I want you to call me Jim from now on. Understood?"

"Yes sir, I mean, Jim…sir."

The last day of Cadre Week, the cadre had the Rats load onto buses after PT and BRC, and drove down winding roads to God knows where. Jack could have known, he knew the area well enough, but he could not keep his eyes open long enough to keep track.

All he knew for sure was after they arrived and were briefed, they got off the bus and he could smell the James. He loved that smell. It was the musty smell of river life all rivers, and maybe all waters, shared. Fish waste.

They ate hot dogs and played horse shoes, touch football and a tug-of-war between companies. At the baseball diamond, a cadre member poured a duffle bag of gear and began to rally support for a game of softball. It was as if everything was suddenly normal, like they were normal guys at a normal picnic, other than the fact there was not a female within miles.

It was also a time the Rats met their first class mentors, or Dykes.

Rats were allowed some badly needed rest time, and Jack took full advantage. He found a spot away from the game playing and food just outside of the right field fence. Looking across the old dirt road and to the banks of the James, he felt at home among the lofty elms leaning slightly over her silky waters with scattered tufts of fescue grass tipping in the afternoon breeze.

"Jack Hartman?"

It was not a cadet's voice breaking the solitude. Jack looked up to see an air force colonel in his camouflage fatigues squatting down beside him.

"Don't get up. It's a good day to relax and take in a little sun," he said.

The colonel kicked his feet out one at a time, and leaned back against the fence like Jack. Jack looked at him and smiled, noticing the gentleness in the lines of his face.

His camouflage fatigues were crisp, with sharp creases and his sleeves rolled up to just above his elbows, with the exterior cuff rolled back over so the lighter inside did not show. His camouflage fatigue cap bore the flat black rank of a Lieutenant Colonel and his collar the branch insignia of a Christian cross.

"My favorite part of Cadre is finally getting to meet each Rat individually," he said looking directly at Jack and offering his hand. "I'm Chaplain Campbell."

"Rat Hartman," Jack replied shaking the chaplain's hand.

Jack looked back out toward the James.

"Alright, Rat Hartman, but if you don't mind, I'll call you either Jack or Cadet Hartman, depending on the situation, of course."

"Yes, sir."

"I know a little about your background, Jack," he said, staring now along with Jack at the river. "You had one heck of a run getting here."

Does he know everything? Does he know about my dad?

"Oh, just did what I needed to do," Jack answered safely.

"I suppose you did, son," he said. "Look, I got this letter. I mean, they didn't mail it. They brought it by my office. They said they wanted me to hand deliver it."

He pulled an envelope from his cargo pocket, and looked at the front.

"It's from Jerry and Linda Martin, your sponsors," he said, handing it to Jack. "Are you very close to them?"

"They're nice folks, alright. I've really only known 'em for a little more than a year. They helped a lot with getting into school here and all."

"Well, you read the letter, and if you need to talk, we'll talk," he said pushing himself back up off the ground. "You're gonna do just fine here, Jack. There are people very interested in your success. Keep your head up!"

What people? Why would they be interested in me?

"Yes, sir!"

Jack opened the letter and was elated to see two twenty dollar bills inside. It was an encouraging letter, but the Martins had written it to tell Jack they had finally gotten finished with all of their preparations to leave for missionary work in Southeast Asia. It wasn't unexpected, and Jack was happy for them.

Before the whole day was wrapped up, Rats began grabbing their respective corporals, carrying them overhead as a squad to the end of a small fishing dock sticking out into the river, and throwing them in. It was a tradition to "baptize" corporals during the Rat picnic, Jack overheard.

A wet Corporal Johnson came up to Jack afterward. "Rat Hartman, you doin' alright?"

"Just fine, sir," he replied, not sure whether to pop to attention or not.

"At ease, Rat. Lighten up. This'll be your last chance to do so for quite a while."

"Uh, okay."

"You can still call me sir or Corporal Johnson, though."

"Okay, sir."

"I saw you sittin' over here by yourself. Everything okay with your room and your squad?"

"Oh, yes sir," Jack answered, "everything with the other guys is great. I just needed a little alone time. Thought this'd be a good time for it."

"Alright, I just thought I'd check. You're a pretty good Rat, Hartman," he said, and then he paused as if he had just been hit by a piece of wisdom he couldn't leave without sharing. "You're gonna need these guys from here on. When we get back to the 'I,' things are gonna change. Obviously, I'll be mean again, but more than that. And it ain't gonna stop for a long time. You hear me?"

"I hear you, sir," Jack said with a smile.

"I don't think you do," Johnson said. "There are people gunning for you. You make sure you keep your head in the game, you got me, Rat Hartman?"

"Loud and clear, sir."

—ᔑᓍᔑ—

There was heaviness hanging over the Rats on Jack's bus as they wound their way along country highways eventually leading back to the main drag through the middle of Lexington. They were all headed back to it, back to the pressure cooker. As the caravan of buses rolled up Letcher Avenue, Corporal Johnson stood up in the front of the bus, and seemed to be back in his cadre mode.

"Welcome back, Rats! Things are about to get ugly like you've never experienced ugly. While you were out having your little picnic, it seems the corps returned."

No more Mr. Nice guy, I suppose.

"Typically, when this many men are reporting back to a place that might as well be prison, they tend to be a bit fired up. When you get off this bus, you're going to get to meet twelve-hundred of the meanest muthas you've ever seen. I recommend you strain real hard."

As they filed off the buses in front of the barracks, Jack, Ted, and the rest of the room formed up with the cluster of Rats massing at the entrance to Jackson Arch. They listened to the roar build to a deafening howl, like the rising of a hurricane.

The noise and bedlam they heard at the mouth of the arch extended deep into the bowels of the barracks as the stream of Rats moving along the Ratline were being screamed at and interrogated by the enraged mob of upperclassmen. They all knew it was going to be a long, tough trip up to the fourth stoop.

Jack looked at Ted.

"Another fine day in the infantry," Jack said.

They popped into a strain and entered the arch.

CHAPTER FIVE

ANNA

To Jack, the military duties and academics rolled into a plodding routine, and though their lives were turned upside down, even VMI Rat life became monotonous.

"You know what I think is great about right now?" Jack asked Darryl as all four roommates sat at their desks in the room shining shoes.

"Enlighten me, Jack," Darryl answered.

"Nothin'."

"Nothing?" Ted asked.

"I think this is the first several days in a row we haven't heard corporals screaming in our ears, sweat parties, or any of the insanity," Jack said. "I actually got all my class work done today."

"I suppose nothing can be a good thing," said Darryl. "Come to think of it, I've been so wrapped up in routine I forgot when I got the 'Gross Body Award' last. Must've been a couple weeks ago."

"Definitely good, guys," Ski piped in, "because the only alternative is trouble."

"Yeah," said Ted. "College life is great. Every other eighteen year old is out there havin' the time of their lives. All we can hope for is nothing."

The days were piling up into weeks. Summer faded, but the heat of it still lingered. There were moments of excitement and dread, but even being a Rat had its dull, predictable pace.

"It will all change soon enough," said Ted. "Everything will ramp up again like cadre week."

Our own prophet of doom.

"How do you know?" asked Ski.

"Dad told me on the phone last weekend. He said that's how they usually do things around here."

"When will it happen?" asked Jack.

"Don't know, but I wouldn't get to comfortable. It's gonna happen."

After SRC the Thursday before Parents' Weekend, the Rats were held in formation while the company first sergeant covered some important details and requirements pertaining to the weekend. Sweating, bald heads donned in blue-gray covers, canted forward in their awkward strain. Heat radiated from the asphalt beneath them. Jack's mind wandered.

Maybe it will rain. Cool this off. Cancel the parade.

Before being given the command to fall out, Mr. Martin addressed the entire Rat Battalion.

"Look at me, Rats!" he shouted. "This will be the first of many tests you will undergo as a Rat mass! Your appearance and your discipline as well as your execution on the parade field tomorrow, will be carefully scrutinized by me and the rest of the RDC. If you meet our expectations, *and* I'm in a good mood we might give you the weekend out of the Ratline."

He panned across the battalion with his trademark stare and clenched jaw that teetered on the edge of something psychotic with all of its anger and authority.

"I won't give this away! Don't let me down!" He paused for moment. "Fall out!"

Ted, Jack, Darryl, and Ski headed as a group toward the arch.

"My folks will be in Saturday morning just in time to attend the parade," said Ski. "Jack, you have plans for lunch?"

"Yeah, Ted invited me a while back to hang out with his folks and his sister," Jack answered, "but thanks anyway."

"Yeah, but don't mind my sister. She's gotten a bit snobby since she started at Hollins last year." Ted said.

"Is your girlfriend gonna make it, Darryl?" Jack asked.

"Oh, yeah. She won't be in till Saturday morning, though. But my parents will be in Friday night. We're going to have dinner."

"Well, sure hope we can get out of the Ratline. Make for a nice weekend," Ski said.

"Yeah, real nice," Jack said.

As they returned to their room, they continued on in the same fashion as when they were walking toward barracks. The Ratline had been relegated already to not more than an inconvenience—a pause in a conversation. Darryl came in a little after the others, and though he had been stopped along the way and written up to go to the RDC, he didn't seem to mind.

"What the heck! I think I've got about five of these things from the same third. When they do call me up there, it should be a good time," Darryl said. "Just BRC, two classes, parade, and I'll be with my girl!"

"You do know this is supposed to be Parents' Weekend, not Girlfriends' Weekend," said Jack.

He envied everyone who had parents visiting. Joking around about the upcoming weekend was his way of masking the emptiness in him when parents were talked about. They remained quiet for a few moments, as each busied himself with his military tasks of folding socks and shining brass. Jack's awkwardness about parents had a hushing effect on his roommates.

"You'll like my folks, Jack. You'll be one of theirs in no time," Ted said.

Jack smiled, still looking at his laundry as he folded it. He knew Ted was being genuine.

"Getting out of the Ratline would be cool enough. It's been awhile since I've experienced walking through the barracks without being hassled. Matter of fact, I never have," Jack said.

"Oh, yeah. You got on Phelps' hit list before you even matriculated," Ted said.

They all laughed. It was a good laugh—one of the best they had experienced since the first day of Cadre. Still, the sore subject of Phelps tormented Jack. He knew it would come to some kind of confrontation, and it made Jack sick to think about it. It was as if the beast was gnawing at him, again, waiting to leap out. So, Jack laughed with his roommates to press it back down.

———

Saturday morning was fairly normal with BRC and classes. Upper classmen laid off the Rats for the most part as family and girlfriends showed up in the arch waiting for their cadet to make his way down after receiving their message slip from the guard room. Pretty girls in summer dresses stood two or three at a time with wind tossing their perfectly primped hair from shoulder to shoulder.

A potpourri of everything female carried on the breeze and permeated the barracks. Young men longingly stared through open doorways and from behind door windows, sometimes even loitering on the stoop with others, while leaning against the stoop rail handsomely, and chatting in their white VMI blouses. A hush of civility had fallen over the barracks.

Real life around here is a secret.

Somewhere lying twisted inside him, Jack harbored a thought that it would be fun to see a third go nuts on a Rat with his mother or girlfriend standing in the arch, witnessing the abuse of their loved one.

Hilarious. That would bring some tears. If they only knew.

Still, it was nice to see the rest of the corps so engaged in other things that the Rats could slip up to their rooms without ever being stopped. Jack was only asked one question on his way up to his room.

"Whoa, Rat. What's for lunch?" It was a second just coming out of the sally port showers, wearing only a towel on his shoulders, PT shorts, and flip-flops.

Before Jack could even answer the sentinel in the old barracks courtyard called him down.

"Second stoop, improperly dressed, sir!"

He hustled along, back toward his room.

"Don't worry about it, Rat. It all tastes like slop anyway!" he yelled.

Back at the room, Ski was putting the finishing touches on his shoes, while Darryl was kicked back on his rack reading the Richmond Times-Dispatch sports section, grinning.

"How's your girl? It's obvious you've already seen her today," Jack said.

"Man, you should've been there," Darryl replied, slapping his paper down. "I was heading back from class, I walked into the Arch in the Ratline, straining, and out of the corner of my eye I caught a glimpse of her smiling at me. I didn't know what to do so I just stopped."

"Stopped? Like, just standing in the middle of the Ratline?" asked Jack.

"Yeah," Darryl continued. "So this first classman walks right up to me and asks me what I'm doing. I told him that I thought I just saw my girlfriend. He says, 'Was it some kind of a vision, or for real?' Then he says, 'Are you just going to stand there?' I didn't say anything. I just froze up. He told me to get out of the Ratline, take my girlfriend to the 'X,' and get back here to get ready for parade. When I turned and looked at her, she laughed out loud at me. Aaaagh!"

Darryl flopped back on his rack, fists clenched as he let out the guttural scream.

"Please tell me you didn't start bawling, because if you did it would make generations of VMI men look like total sissies!"

"No, but she did. She's over at Lejeune Hall with my parents waiting for the parade. Sure hope we get out of the Ratline. I don't need her seeing me like that again," Darryl said.

"It would be nice. See if you can remember to shoulder your M14 on your right shoulder during rifle manual. That would probably help," Jack said with a sneer.

"It must be a bummer *not* having a girlfriend. Huh, Jack?" Darryl said.

"Only when I'm reminded a flabby, mediocre-in-just-about-every-sense-of-the-word, ugly frump such as you, actually has one!"

They both laughed.

Ted made it to the room a few minutes later, and they all began to get ready for the parade. They each donned their white belt, ammo pouch, cross dyke, and breastplate. The Rats wore the grey wool blouse while the rest of the corps wore coatee—the formal blue-gray coat with brass buttons and tails. When they were finished they each went down to their dykes' rooms and helped them get ready. Eventually, they assembled in formation inside the old barracks, ready to march through Jackson Arch.

Following the parade, the four boys headed quickly from the courtyard to their room, negotiating the Ratline without being stopped by an upperclassman. They changed out of their parade uniform and into the white blouse with shoulder epaulets.

"Ted!" Mr. McClain shouted as Ted and Jack walked through Jackson Arch.

"Hey, Dad," Ted said as he quickly approached him. They embraced for a moment. Ted peeled out of the embrace and with his right arm still around his dad's back, he introduced Jack. Jack and Mr. McClain shook hands and then they all turned to walk along the sidewalk around the parade ground.

"We could see you when you passed in review. Your mom got some pictures. You boys looked sharp today."

Jack could smell the fresh cut grass hanging thick in the air. *The smell of parades.*

"I think the Rats looked better than the old corps. Your mom wanted pictures by the cannons, pictures in front of the arch. She's a nut with her camera. I talked her out of it for now—too many people. We'll meet the ladies over at Moody Hall." He paused for a moment. "Jack, so you're from Buchanan?"

"Just up river. We had a small farm up there. Went to James River High," Jack answered.

"So, and stop me if I'm prying, but I understand you were at the boys' home there. Is that right?"

"Yes, sir. Dad passed when I was fifteen. It was tough, but they were good to us at the home. I have nothin' to complain about."

"Who's keeping up with you now?"

"I had some sponsors, but they've left the country on some kind of missionary thing. They were good folks. When I decided to come here, they did what they could to help."

"Well, I'm impressed, son," said Ted's dad.

He meant well, Jack felt certain; but something inside him churned. It was a sense that others always looked down on him, like he wasn't from a decent class of people.

Such an accomplishment to come from scum of the earth, trailer park trash to a school filled with Virginia gentlemen.

He let it go, hoping for a better shake from Ted's family.

"There's Mom and Anna," Ted said as the trio approached Moody Hall.

The two stood at the stone and concrete half-wall on the balcony overlooking the parade ground. Annabelle gazed out at the sprawling beauty of VMI. She was, of course, taking pictures.

Ted ran over to his mother. They embraced.

"Jack, this is my wife, Annabelle," said Mr. McClain.

Jack tipped his hat to her.

"Nice to meet you, Ma'am."

She obliged with a warm smile and reply. Jack thought about her elegance and beauty—what a real mother might look like. Her light brown hair piled in a perfectly arranged bun behind her head, with just the right amount escaping in strands and ringlets to frame and accent her thin face, pretty and lightly made-up.

"And this is our daughter, Anna Marie. Anna, Jack."

ALWAYS A RIVER

Anna was strikingly attractive, with long sandy-blonde hair given to a slight wave, thrown fetchingly over the front of her shoulders. Her eyes, a dark brown complement to her tan skin, gave Jack the impression of something deep, mysterious. She wore some make-up, but clearly didn't need it.

She did not dress as casual as most college students, but appeared polished in her skirt and short, tailored suit jacket emphasizing her slender feminine frame. With her heals on, she was almost exactly the same height as Jack.

A breeze tossed her hair around her shoulder, some even across her face. She tamed it with a slight toss of her head to the side a casual brush from the back of her hand. The breeze carried her perfume, light but distinct.

Roses. Her perfume is some kind of rose.

Jack was taken aback for a moment. He touched the rim of his hat, but with much less precision than when he greeted Annabelle. He said nothing. Every time he felt the slightest attraction to a girl, he flushed with shyness. He never felt comfortable around women in general, but uncertain and clumsy.

And then Anna's beauty. Jack had known plenty of pretty girls, but Anna was immediately in a higher category in Jack's mind. She had yet to even utter a single syllable, but in the few seconds of awkward silence, Jack saw something truthful and pure.

He cleared his throat to cover for his delay.

"Anna Marie, nice to finally meet you," Jack said.

Anna did not present a gushing smile like girls usually did in the south, and especially Virginia. It was more of a smirk that dripped of disdain. She held out her hand to Jack as if to say she wasn't impressed by his display of southern charm—the hat tip just didn't do it for her. Jack obliged by shaking her hand with a moderate grip.

"Charmed," she said.

Jack figured her coolness was a façade. He had been warned by Ted. It presented a challenge.

83

"Well, let's get going. I'd like to get a real dinner in before the game." Mr. McClain said, giving Anna a stern look.

"May I?" Ted asked his mother, holding out his right arm in genteel escort fashion.

The gesture struck Jack deep in the heart, as he had always wondered what it would be like to have such a relationship with a mother. He had never had the opportunity to do so, and it remained a mystery to him that he longed to experience.

They all headed down the stairs to a spot along Letcher Avenue where their Cadillac was parked. The McClain's gave Jack the impression of means. It did not rattle him, but was more of a novelty, having a friend with money.

Jack did not completely miss Anna's coolness. He had seen something deeper than her demeanor which had really gotten to him. He could not comprehend the stirring happening inside of him. It had never happened before.

She's so good-looking. Why does she have to be Ted's sister? With my shaved head, I'm sure I look like an idiot.

They sat at a table on the patio at the College Inn, a quaint little bar and grill on Washington Street, just off Main. It was a rod-iron fenced outdoor dining area just off the sidewalk. A beautiful warm day in early fall, the breeze kept the air fresh with an occasional hint of French fries and apple fritters. It was the aroma of a carnival to Jack.

From their umbrella sheltered wooden table, they agreed on sandwiches all around to the waitress, a pretty and petite college-age girl who, best Jack could see, caught Ted's eye. As they ate Ted told the whole gamut of war stories from Cadre to classes to ROTC. Jack loosened up and even piped in from time to time, but his mind was racing and his heart pounding.

Three times he caught Anna looking at him. Their eyes met and she looked away, trying to seem uninterested in him, as well as the whole conversation taking place around them. Jack knew better. He stared at her until she looked at him, and then he smiled dramatically and cocked an eyebrow as if to say, "Gotcha!" A little embarrassed, she finally broke her silence.

"So tell me, Jack, what exactly are you planning on doing with this wonderful military education?" She asked.

"Oh, I don't know. The military option is always available. I think I'd be good at killin' folks," Jack answered, finishing with a grin.

"Okay, you got me. But really, why are you here? What are you majoring in?"

There it is. I'm not good enough. I'm not from their side of the tracks.

"To answer the first, because I've wanted to attend VMI since I saw a parade here when I was eight. The second, English."

"A VMI guy that's not an engineer? How quaint."

"I'm just surprised you are so cliché."

"Cliché? What is cliché about me Mr. Hartman?"

"A blonde Hollins girl in a suit concerned about my major."

"Jack!" She laughed genuinely for the first time since they had met over at Moody Hall, "Touché. Maybe I am cliché."

Jack enjoyed the verbal dance. As shy as he was, he was usually a disaster around girls. He felt somewhat at ease with Anna, though.

The conversation between Ted and his dad went on as Annabelle engaged lightly. Anna, sitting across from Jack, decided to break with etiquette and carry on with him.

"So, what do you like to read? What are you reading now?"

"If you're talking about anything that could be mistaken for literature, nothing. It seems my reading time has been consumed as of late with this little gem, here." He pulled his Rat Bible out of his hat. Anna laughed again. Jack felt as if he was on a roll.

"Do you like poetry, or fiction? American or English Lit?"

Jack thought about the things Ted had said in passing about Anna being a poet.

"Hmmm, I noticed you said poetry first," Jack said, leaning toward her and speaking quietly. "I'll assume that if I say poetry, then I will have checked the cultured drivel box, and I am automatically in the Anna club. However, if I say science fiction, you will think of me as boyish instead of manly, and write me off as a complete nerd. Okay, you got me—romance. But not just any romance, something along the line of a cheap, drug-store novel."

"Typical guy. I'm not shocked."

"No, you don't know the half of it. I love to pour into a nice quality paperback romance novel. The kind with the masterpiece artwork on the cover depicting the guy with long flowing hair, big pecks and absolutely no, God forbid, chest hair."

"Jack!"

"Don't stop me now, I'm on a roll. His massive arm supports a swooning woman with a wickedly plunging neckline, which is obviously styled so to tempt men like me to buy the book on the remote chance it might have pictures. That's what I love to read. And you?"

"You are truly ridiculous, Jack Hartman."

She smiled warmly this time.

"Good one, Jack," Ted said. "I didn't even know you could read."

"I try to keep it a secret so I don't embarrass my Neanderthal roommates."

Jack couldn't help it. He wanted to intrigue and entertain Anna in case there was even a remote chance she might see something in him. He wanted to be attractive to her, but felt sure by the way she greeted him she wasn't impressed by his looks the way he was with hers.

To Jack she was one of those girls he would deem as an impossible catch and would not even entertain the notion that there might be a chance. In Jack's mind, as impossible as Anna was, he felt he had an opening, being Ted's roommate and friend, and Jack was feeling his flirtations with Anna were actually going somewhere.

"When do you fellas need to be back for the game?" Ted's dad asked.

"Thirteen hundred for formation," said Ted.

"Well, we better get going. You guys will be sitting with the rest of the Rats, and your mother and I have seats with all the other old fogies. We have a seat up there for Anna, unless she wants to try to sit next to you, Ted."

"Actually, I think I will. I haven't seen Teddy since he joined up with this charade. His shaved head is so fuzzy," she said as she rubbed her hand across the top of his head.

—ɷɷɷ—

The corps marched into the stadium to the cadence of the snares, and unit by unit, took their respective places in the reserved areas of the bleachers. It was only the second home game of the season, but the rules were clear. The Rats sat as a mass in one section of the stadium and were not allowed to intermingle with visitors, save those lucky few that sat on the end of a row, or along the top row of the Rat section.

Jack was able to finagle seats along the coveted outside edge. Anna finally found them just after kickoff, and made her way up. Ted sat to the inside and Jack sat next to Anna. Ski and Darryl sat behind them.

"Wow, you think they'd let us sit down after trying to work us to death last week," said Darryl.

"Sit? What does that even mean?" asked Ski.

"It's a position that those lazy civilians take from time to time. I think it's a position of rest. We Rats have the front leaning rest if we're tired," said Ted.

The Rats stood for most of the game, sitting only during field changes between quarters and the halftime break. Rats were required to scream almost constantly, but especially when the opposition's offense was on the field.

A couple times Anna leaned over to talk to Ted, and when she did, she supported herself by holding on to Jack's outside shoulder and leaning across his chest. Jack could feel her body press against his, and it sent a tingle that felt almost like an electrical charge through him he was sure she could feel. He felt goose bumps up and down his arms and legs.

Oh gosh, I hope she doesn't notice. She's smart. She's gonna figure me out. Worse yet, she'll know soon enough I'm just a poor farm kid from Nowhere, Virginia. Can't let her in too much. She likes me, I think. I hate not having anything except an old beat up truck. She's way out of my league.

"Think we might actually win one, Jack?" asked Ted.

"Don't know. We've got that guy Andrews that put up some yards last week. Maybe he breaks out this week. Maybe not. Close game—we don't finish well, though."

"Losing is not an option," said Darryl. "If we don't get out of the Ratline, It might be a bad day."

"Why's that?" asked Jack.

"Phelps is on guard tonight."

They didn't lose. With a fourth quarter touchdown and an ensuing interception, The Keydets pulled off the win, much to Jack's surprise. The boys sang the Fight Song and the Doxology with enthusiasm rather than fear. There was a euphoric spirit of victory and celebration other schools experience when they win a conference championship.

We won a game. Amazing.

Anna stood beside Jack, smiling and staring at him. It seemed a little odd, and he turned and faced her. For an extended moment they looked into each other's eyes. It was flirtatious, and even a little beyond flirtatious.

As cadets around them began to work their way out of the bleachers, Anna and Jack stood there transfixed. She reached her hand up and ran her fingertips down the side of his face as if she was memorizing its every curve and angle.

"I have to go. Daddy will be waiting at the gate for me."

"See you again?" asked Jack quietly, his rapid heartbeat evident in his voice.

"Again it is, then. We'll make it a date, Jack Hartman. Until then, I need to know a little bit more about you, Mr. Mysterious."

"I'm not very good at writing letters…"

She put her finger to his lips.

"Then just write an essay, English Major."

"That's brilliant. Sounds a lot better than writing letters."

"Oh, I'll bet you're a great writer, Jack Hartman," Anna replied. "And I'll write you, too."

"Pen pals, how nice," he joked.

"Yes." She laughed and then reached over and tugged on Ted's sleeve to get his attention. "Teddy, I'm going over to meet Daddy at the main gate. I'll see you." She hugged him and kissed him on the cheek.

"We'll walk with you," Ted said.

"No don't, it's just over there. I'll be going back to Hollins right away. I have a paper to do, so I'll see you next weekend."

She looked with a raised eyebrow at Jack, then waved and turned to head down into the throng of cadets and girlfriends and mothers and fathers flowing toward the bridge and the main entrance.

"So what was that touchy, feely thing going on with you two?" asked Ted as they watched her drift away into the flow of humanity.

"Oh, you saw that. You were talking with the other guys, but it, uh, I don't really know." Jack paused, a bit flustered, then perked up. "We're gonna be pen pals."

"Wow, that's romantic. Guess I don't need to worry about you taking advantage of my sister."

"I suppose," Jack said, still on a bit of an endorphin high. "Teddy."

They walked across the bridge and up the hill where Darryl and Ski met them half way between Crozet Hall and Old Barracks, gleefully announcing they had been let out of the Ratline. Even though Jack heard them, it didn't sink in. As he walked into Jackson Arch he popped into a strain.

They all laughed and Ski reminded him of their temporary privilege. Jack was somewhere else, distant. He had lost track of the game, his roommates, and VMI for that matter. All he could think about was Anna.

Anna, Anna, Anna.

CHAPTER SIX

THE CRUCIBLE

In the seven weeks he had been there, Jack had received only three letters. The first from his sponsors, then one from Jimbo, the owner of King Cab. It was a nice note he wrote just to encourage Jack. He even included twenty dollars, which Jack really needed at the time. Jack sent him a thank you note a few days later.

The other was from Anna. He had received it the Thursday after Parent's Weekend. It was exciting to Jack to think she had written him a letter as soon as she got back to school. It was a friendly letter that carried the scent of her perfume. Jack was not sure if had intentionally scented it, or if it had inadvertently rubbed off her wrist as she wrote.

Rose. Wish I knew what it was. Makes me think of her. Her hand on my face.

He replied the same day. It had been ten days since he sent it.

There was a struggle going on in his mind when he passed by the mail room that Monday morning. He wanted to check his box, but he was afraid to be let down. Curiosity overcame him, though, and he braced for the empty box let-down when he checked.

When he opened the door he thought he saw a glimpse of something white, but even then was careful not to become overly excited. Almost immediately though, he smelled the perfume and his heart began to race. It was certainly Anna.

Yes, Anna, Anna. Second letter.

He quickly stowed the letter in his literature book and bolted for the barracks. It had been raining off and on for two days, and as he entered the stairwell heading up to the first stoop from the basement concourse, he was immediately drenched. Jack plowed on though, up to the first stoop, and was quickly out of the rain, hoping he would have time to change and put on his rain gear.

He had made it most of the way without being stopped, but as he crested the top of the sally port stairwell onto the third stoop, he heard someone standing at the railing near the base of the stairs that led to the fourth.

"Whoa, Rat!"

He stopped still facing away as he hadn't made the entire outside square of the stairwell.

"Idiot Hartman," he said as he approached, "why are you still here?"

"Still where, sir?"

Jack was straining hard and facing the wall. He wasn't sure what he meant by the question, but he recognized it was Phelps doing the questioning.

Phelps breath.

"You are one stupid Rat. Here, at the Institute, idiot!"

"I like it here, sir."

"Then, apparently I haven't done my job. You will quit, Hartman. I'll see to it. Oh, you might make it till Christmas, but you won't come back. What's for lunch?"

Jack knew he was asking a pertinent question to cover his harassment, because third classmen could not stop Rats in the Ratline for any other reason unless they were in their direct chain of command.

"Spaghetti with meatballs, green beans, garlic toast, and milk, juice, or coffee, sir."

His voice got very quiet. "And just in case you do make it back from Christmas break, I'm gonna do everything I can to get you drummed out. I've got ways. I can trip you up. You can't be perfect all the time."

"I will not break the honor code, sir," Jack said.

"Your old man was a worthless drunk. You were an idiot and the laughing stock of James River High. You're trailer trash of the worst kind. I may have had to put up with you then, but this is my world, the Institute. You see, it's been in the family for years—four generations—and you're not going to mess this up too."

"Is that all, sir?"

"One more question Rat Hartman—and remember the honor code—did you kill your old man? I mean, I know what you told the cops and all, but what's the real truth? Did you run him down with that old tractor? You can tell me. I won't hold it against you. You did the world a service, killin' that loser."

It had finally crossed a line in Jack's head. A surge from inside of his brain felt like sparks shooting from his head down his spine. The beast exploded from the doors Jack kept it locked behind. He couldn't hold it in. He didn't care, either.

In a sudden movement, Jack grabbed Phelps by the face and smacked his head against the wall. Phelps was completely startled and failed to offer any defense until he was against the wall with Jack's hand now slipped down over his throat. Phelps began grappling with Jack until they were entangled on the floor of the stoop against the wall.

"If I kill anyone, I'll kill you," Jack heard himself repeating over and over.

From every different direction, third classmen ran into sally port and pulled Jack off of Phelps. Unseen hands felt as if they would tear Jack apart. Phelps leapt up and began swinging. His fists pummeled Jack's ribs and twice connected with his face. Jack flushed with a new wave of adrenaline, this time a flash of fear of death struck his mind like lightning.

But quickly, the fists and tugging stopped, and the yelling began, more vicious than he had yet seen. There were about fifteen of them surrounding Jack, all of them screaming at him simultaneously. None of them knew the truth.

It was obvious to Jack they assumed he was just a Rat out of control, insane or something. Jack began straining as a form of defense. He was shaken up pretty bad, and had taken a few cheap shots when he was being pulled off of Phelps, causing him to gasp to get air back in his lungs.

"That's it, Hartman! You're out of here! You just struck an upperclassman. No one gets away with that—especially a Rat. I knew you couldn't make it, here you..." Phelps hissed the expletive through a swollen, bleeding lip.

Someone yelled above the din and almost as quickly as the event had erupted, it ended. Everyone fell silent except for one command voice. Jack was fighting back sobs, but would suck in air in short gasps through his mouth and nose, blood beginning to trickle from each.

"Rat Hartman, get out of the Ratline, grab your books, and go to your dyke's room."

It was Mr. Tranchik, First Battalion S-3 and honor court prosecutor.

"Yes, sir."

As Jack ran down the stairs he could hear Tranchik questioning the thirds very aggressively. Jack figured his stay at VMI was about to end.

Maybe Phelps is right. Maybe I don't belong here.

When he got down to the first stoop, he went straight to his dyke's room and knocked on the door. Jim was actually in, lying back in his rack doing some reading. Jack hardly ever saw him that way. Usually, he was up and working on something either at his table or on his feet.

One glance at the mirror to his right told Jack just how bad he'd been beaten. Jim looked at him and a look of terror washed across his face. Jack's uniform pants were torn and muddied, and he was soaking wet.

"What the heck happened?" Jim said, standing up quickly and walking toward Jack.

"Just got in a fight with that third. Y'know, Phelps…" He let go of a sob which sent blood and mucus spattering across his lips and chin.

Jim had him clean up, and get control of himself. Jack proceeded to tell Jim the whole story of the fight and the way Phelps had been bent on seeing him leave the Institute.

Jim questioned Jack, who did his best to recall every event in which Phelps had harassed him and his roommates. Jack told him about the past and his father and about how Phelps had come after him in high school, bullying him until he left for college.

"Jim," Jack said, "this is the best my life has ever been. I don't want to leave it. But if this is what VMI's all about, I don't want to be a part of it."

Jim turned to Jack, his face firm and showing intense anger.

"Your problem with Phelps has nothing to do with VMI! It's some garbage you brought in from the outside world. VMI is about honor, and discipline, and developing the whole man. Does any of that sound like your issue with Phelps?"

"No, sir."

"Then don't blame VMI. Look, Rat, all I ask is you keep your head about you. When things go critical, you need to be able to think clearly. Keep your temper in check. It's time to be a man."

"I'm sorry, Jim." Jack paused for a moment. "So what happens now?"

"Phelps is gonna get it handed to him. He'll at least get a Ten, Six, and Thirty, maybe even a Number One. Whatever it is it'll be bad and he'll be busted back down to private."

"And me?"

"I'm gonna go talk to Steve Tranchik. I'm sure he's done with those thirds by now. I don't think you're gonna get in too much trouble over all this. There'll probably be a little issue with the RDC and maybe some of your corporals."

"I guess it won't be boring around here."

"Anything but. A Rat can't just punch a third and get away with it, even if he was justified, but you'll be okay. You're a tough nut. Now, get out of the Ratline and go to your room. Do not stop for any reason. I'll talk to you after SRC."

"Yes, sir."

Jack turned to head back out onto the stoop and into the Ratline.

"Jack, one more thing," Jim said.

Jack turned back around.

"If this is the best your life has been, then that's pretty messed up," Jim said. "There ain't nothin' good about being a Rat."

"Yes, sir," Jack replied, turning to leave.

Jack bolted up the stairwell on the back corner of old barracks and bee-lined to his room. Ted and Darryl, just back from classes, were waiting for him. Word of Jack's fight had made it to the fourth stoop.

"Dude, you can't beat down a third and not tell us in advance. I'd have paid ten bucks to see it. More if you'd let me jump in," Darryl said.

"What happened? I know it was Phelps, but what did he do this time? Did you whip him?" Ted asked, sounding happy someone had finally lost it with Phelps.

"Well, I wouldn't exactly characterize it as a whipping. More like a draw. I think I ended up on the bad side of it before it was over."

"Did ya get a couple licks in for me?" asked Darryl.

"It was *all* for you. He was just standing there mindin' his own business, when all of the sudden I got the hankerin' to waylay him a couple times just for you Darryl," Jack said, his voice still a little shaky.

"Really?" asked Darryl.

"No, not really," Jack said, shaking his head.

They laughed.

Jack smiled, and then told them what had happened.

When the Rats fell in for SRC that evening there was still a steady rainfall, and uniform included rain gear. Jack was worried about the repercussions and knew there would be a barrage as soon as the formation was called and corporals were released to check their squads. He hoped he could hide in the noise of the falling rain and the camouflage of the extra uniform.

Corporal Beard from first squad called back to Corporal Johnson.

"Hey, did you know you have a Rat in your squad who likes to fight thirds?"

"No, what's up?" Johnson asked and they stepped aside and began whispering.

Here it comes.

Within a few moments, several corporals gathered around them, and then broke their huddle heading straight to Jack. There was an explosion of screaming, again so furious Jack couldn't answer one question. He was up and down between straining and the front leaning rest, knocking out push-ups and running in place.

It was a personal sweat party. As if that wasn't bad enough, the rain water began filling his shoes and had soaked his hat, which had fallen on the ground open to the rain.

"Do you somehow think it's okay for you to hit an upperclassman when he ticks you off, idiot?"

"What is the name of every member of the Honor Court?"

"You're gonna wish you were never born, Rat!"

"Drop and give me twenty!"

"Do you think this is funny now?"

"Do you hate thirds, Rat? 'Cause thirds hate you!"

"Get up! Get back down!"

Jack began to just tune it all out. He was pulled out of the formation, because the rest of the Rat Battalion was waiting on Echo to move to the mess hall. Eventually, the Echo Company first sergeant called them down and told Jack to run down and fall in to his formation. By the time he made it to Crozet Hall they were already in. He began double timing with the Rats from Band Company, but as soon as he entered, he was told to follow a first classman he recognized as a member of the RDC.

"Do you know who I am, idiot?" the first screamed.

Little drops of spit sprayed out of his mouth, hitting Jack in the side of the face. Jack did not care. His face was still dripping with rain water.

"Yes, sir!"

"Well, who am I?"

"Mr. Hall, Sir, RDC!"

"You're the first Rat in two weeks who actually knew that," he said.

The sudden switch to low key didn't surprise Jack. The RDC guys seemed a bit psychotic at times going from one emotional extreme to the other.

At the RDC table, Jack could see out of the corner of his eye, as he double-timed in place, the table had already been served their meals. He didn't expect to eat much.

"Gentlemen, I'd like to introduce you to Rat Hartman. He likes to be known as Hart-*nan* the Barbarian because of the ruthless way he beats the crud out of thirds. Have a seat Rat Hart-*nan*," he commanded.

Jack sat down quickly in the usual manner on the front three inches of his chair, arms straight down to his sides, head straight but eyes looking down at the plate. It was a position that would often give him headaches from staring straight down the sides of his nose. Mr. Hall slid a fresh plate of food in front of him.

The RDC let him take a few bites before the harassment started. It was more of the same, only these guys were scarier. They finally made him stand on his chair and yell.

"Alright Rat Hartman," Mr. Hall said, "stand on this chair facing the rest of the mess hall and shout as loud as you can, 'Thirds eat...'" He used a profanity.

"I'd rather not, sir!"

"It's not your choice you..." he finished with another word even more profane.

"I don't want to cuss, sir," Jack answered.

"You can't make a Rat swear, Steve," said another RDC member, "but you can make him do push-ups for beating down a third."

"Well, then say it in another way. I don't care how you say it."

He could see he wasn't going to get out of this. He was going to have to do it, and it was going to bring a tremendous amount of heat on him. These guys didn't care. It seemed to Jack they were almost happy he'd done what he did. He turned to face the rest of the mess hall still standing on his chair.

"Thirds eat..." he yelled with the slur.

I said it. My old man's favorite word for me. I broke my promise.

"Louder!" several of the RDC yelled.

"Thirds eat..." he yelled, using the expletive again in hopes he would appease the RDC.

The first one had gotten most of the mess hall fairly quiet. The second one had every third's undivided attention.

Things are going to get ugly when I get back to barracks.

And they did. When the Rats double-timed out of the mess hall and marched back up, Jack marched up by himself with two RDC members. Ted was held in formation when all other Rats had fallen out, and was being run through the wringer with several corporals.

Ten minutes after all the Rats had been released, Ted and Jack were still on the bricks being disciplined. The Echo Company first sergeant once again told them to cut it short as it was almost CQ.

Ted and Jack moved quickly and as inconspicuously as possible along the Ratline to their room. When they arrived, there were several Brother Rats from different companies in the room.

"I know Phelps and I know what was said to you and I'd have done the same. Phelps is my corporal. There's something wrong with him. He ain't right," Chip Willis from Bravo Company said.

"I appreciate it, guys, but I don't want anybody getting' in trouble over something I did."

By now, Jack was wishing the whole thing would not have caused such a stir, and it would all go away. He didn't want the parts of his life that embarrassed him to become common knowledge.

When everyone but Jack's roommates had left the room, he asked Ted why he was singled out after SRC. Darryl jumped in to answer.

"When you were yelling at the thirds, Corporal Johnson had us look at him, and wait, let me do my Corporal Johnson impression," Darryl said, then cleared his throat.

"Rats," he said in the raspy voice similar to Corporal Johnson's, "look up here! Looks like Rat Hartman is really stepping on it today. It's only gonna get worse for him. When you lose your military discipline, you end up in a deep pile of kimchi. His is getting deeper. That's all. Eat!"

"I was pretty ticked," added Ted. "I mean, I knew why you had lost it; why you cut loose on Phelps."

"Yeah, so Ted asks Johnson if he ever considered Brother Rat Hartman may have been justified," said Ski. "You could hear a pin drop. Johnson went berserk on Ted. Said he was going to get a few things straight with Ted's point of view. It was crazy."

"Thanks, Ted," said Jack, smiling.

"Just another fine day in the Infantry, BR."

Jack expected he would be answering to the commandant for his actions, and the result might be something really severe. Striking another cadet could be punished by dismissal or a Number One, the highest penalty just short of dismissal which carried a sentence of four months barracks confinement, thirty demerits, and sixty penalty tours.

On the other hand, it could be handled within the corps if nobody placed him on report for it. Jack hoped for this. He could ride it out. He anticipated this would drag on for awhile.

Should be over by Christmas.

He lay on his bed staring up at the ceiling, listening to the rain, thinking how lucky he was to be able to hear it, to be on the top floor where the sound of it still penetrated the ceiling. Thoughts of curling up in a homemade tent by the river on a rainy night played in his mind. As the anger cooled, he felt a sense of loss, a grief for the death of his idealization of VMI and the military. The perfect plan to dig him out of the mire of his life had been stolen by the hatred of a young man bent on his destruction.

Finally, Jack sat up, gathered his books, and joined other Brother Rats in the Ratline on their way to evening study.

The following morning, Jim let Jack know he had met with the RDC president, the first class president, and Steve Tranchik. They had decided the incident didn't warrant any action outside of the corps, and would be handling Phelps through both the executive committee and general committee. Any residual disciplining of Jack would be handled through both the RDC and corps chain-of-command.

As the rain tapered throughout the week, so did the pressure on Jack. At each meal he would sit at one of the staff tables, and undergo a barrage of harassment.

Thursday SRC, Jack had been sent to the regimental staff table for another night of fine dining. Jim was at the table. It was the usual harassment and physical workout Jack had seen for the last several meals since he tangled with Phelps.

After a few minutes, the table fell silent. Jack was happy to be able to get more than two bites in a row without running in place beside his chair, or answering a barrage of questions.

"Rat Hartman," Jim broke the silence, "I want you to tell the regimental staff why you came to VMI. Take your time, and be upfront."

Jack finished chewing and swallowed. He thought for a few seconds.

"I came here because I always dreamt about being a VMI cadet and then being an officer in the army. I guess I really just wanted to do something with my life, sir."

"And what about your folks? Tell us about your dad."

"My dad? Well he died when I was fifteen, sir."

"Yeah but what was he like, your dad, before that?"

"Um…" Jack was reluctant to talk about it to the whole regimental staff.

"Jack, I need you to talk to us here. These guys are on your side, and they need to know about where you came from. Just describe your dad to them."

"Alcoholic. He was hard to live with. Y'know he'd get mad and all."

"And that means?" asked Jim.

"When he was drinkin' he would, um, rough me up."

"And your mom? What about her?"

"Left us when I was one. They say she may be in California. I've never talked to her. I don't know her at all, sir."

"So in a nutshell, you had a pretty rough time with your parents growing up, and when you were basically orphaned, you still got yourself accepted here, and somehow put some funding together to pay for it. Is that accurate, Rat Hartman?"

"Someone gave a big donation that helped out with the bulk of it, but you could say all that is true, sir."

"When Phelps confronted you the other day, what did he say that caused you to retaliate?"

"He said something about my dad being a drunk and I had some part in the way he died. I didn't do what Phelps said I did. I didn't kill my dad. It was an accident. I wasn't in the barn when it happened. And I'm just not gonna lay down when someone says those things about my dad and about me." Jack's voice broke and he had tears welling up in his eyes.

"He said that to you?" asked Mr. Morgan, the regimental commander.

"Yeah, Joe," Jim said, "and in my opinion, if someone attacks a guys family like Phelps did and makes those kinds of accusations about an issue as hurtful as losing a father, and he doesn't punch him out, he ain't a man. We need to yank a knot in this Phelps's rear end, demote him and send him to the EC for conduct unbecoming."

"I agree," Morgan said. "Look, Rat Hartman, your dyke has talked to me about you. He seems to think you have more character than the whole third class combined. After listening to you here tonight, I'm inclined to agree you've got a lot in the character department. I'm gonna keep an eye on you. You strike me as a good Rat! Now, your company's falling out of the mess hall. Double-time over there and join them. Keep your head up, and your chin in! Go!"

With that Jack was double-timing as he blended in with the Echo Company Rats. For the first time since the whole incident, Jack felt good. Satisfaction and peace.

After they had marched back up to barracks and had fallen out, Ted and Darryl asked Jack if he was okay after the Regimental Staff table, and he gave them a quick rundown. He dropped by Jim's room to say thanks. It was almost time for the CQ stick, so Jack headed up to the fourth stoop as the stick was running. On the third stoop, he was stopped.

"Whoa, Rat!" A third was approaching him from the front. "Give me the Honor Court."

Jack began to rattle off the names. "President, Mr. Stuart; Prosecutors, Mr. Tranchik, Mr. McClelland; First Class Representatives, Mr. Young, Mr. Allen, Mr...."

"Time is now nineteen-zero-four hours. You're up to the RDC for failure to know pertinent information, i.e., the Honor Court." He was writing up the three by five card.

"Sir, I was in the middle of..."

"Did you give me the whole Honor Court, Rat?"

"No, sir because you stopped m..."

"Take it up with the RDC. Now, give me the Regimental Staff."

"Regimental Commander, Mr. Morgan; XO, Mr. W…"

"The time is now nineteen-zero-five hours. You're up to the RDC for failure to know pertinent information, i.e., Regimental Staff."

Jack knew there was not a good way out of this. He thought as quickly as he could. He remembered during CQ no seconds or thirds were allowed to stop Rats in the Ratline, and it was always forbidden for a Rat to be dropped for push-ups by a third, except by his direct chain-of-command in formation or inspection. So he did the only thing he thought might put an end to it.

Jack jumped into the front leaning rest position and yelled, "Yes, sir!" loud enough to echo throughout the barracks. He then began cranking out push-ups and counting the repetitions loudly.

"I didn't tell you to do push-ups, Rat, get on your feet."

"Yes, sir!" Jack said as he jumped up to his feet and began double-timing in place with his arms over his head.

His voice boomed around the barracks courtyard.

"Why are you running in place, Rat? I didn't tell you to do that. I'm sending you up to the GC for taking a third class privilege and working yourself out!"

Jack jumped back down into the front leaning rest, and began knocking out more push-ups, counting the repetitions loudly.

As Jack was doing push-ups, he could see Ted, Darryl and Ski jump out of the door of the room across the courtyard, run along the Ratline and then double-time down the stairs to the third stoop. By the time they arrived Jack was on his thirtieth push-up and they jumped down and joined in.

With all four of them doing push-ups and counting repetitions the noise was loud. The Rat sentry in Old Barracks could see what was happening. Instead of calling them down for the noise on the third stoop, he got down, laying his rifle across the back of his hands and joined in. The third who had been harassing Jack was standing there, frozen in place, not sure what to do.

Suddenly Rats started streaming in from all over the barracks up or down to the third stoop and joining in on the push-ups and cadence. It was a tremendous stir at a time when barracks were supposed to be quiet.

First classmen came running out of their rooms and seeing most of the Rats doing push-ups on the third stoop, automatically assumed they had been dropped by thirds. The firsts began running up to the third stoop telling the Rats to get out of the Ratline and to go study, then began lighting up third classmen all over the third stoop.

The four ran back to the room, and busted through the door before they broke out in laughter.

"Jack," Ted said, "that was really smart, really good."

"Yeah, it was. Really good," added Darryl.

Ski was still laughing.

"Did you see the look on that moron's face?"

"Yeah," Jack said.

Jack grabbed a couple books and headed out of barracks to study in Scott-Shipp Hall. For the first time in a week, the sky was crystal clear and the stars seemed to light the sky from horizon to horizon. The air was crisp and cool, and the light sweat Jack had worked up in the all the activity felt invigorating.

In Scott-Shipp Hall there was a small classroom on the second floor authorized to be used for late study. Jack would often camp out there to do his required reading and assignments because it was seldom used by anyone else. He grabbed a cup of coffee in the Timmons Music Room, and headed upstairs.

It was always an incredibly good feeling to walk up to the room and see the light was off. As he walked in, he flipped on the light, set down his coffee and spread his books out on the table.

Something was sticking out of the bottom of his American Literature book. He immediately recognized the letter he had received just days earlier from Anna, and he was flushed with anger at himself for forgetting about it.

At last, he excitedly opened it. His hand trembled as he read her words.

Dear Jack,

I don't really know where to begin. I cannot stop thinking about you. Then, I ask myself if it is possible to become so infatuated with a guy I hardly know. Regardless, I must tell you I dreamt about you last night and it was so vivid I have been praying for you since.

It was weird, as dreams tend to be. You were fighting someone and I was looking on from a distance, helpless. Then, somehow, I was right beside you and we were fighting a blackness I can't really explain. I felt I had to save you (the Joan-of-Arc in my subconscious, I suppose).

Once you were free, you began pushing and shouting and fighting. And they were gone. Just like that. It was weird enough to wake me. My heart was racing.

I don't know if you really were going through any struggles, or if it was just my overactive imagination, but I hope it comforts you to know I am praying for you, and will continue to do so.

I miss you. I want to see you again, soon. I want to reach out to you and touch your face.

Love, Anna

Jack sat with the handwritten, sweet-smelling note in his shaking hands. He read it again and again. Brick by brick, she dismantled a wall somewhere inside him. Anna had known somehow prophetically, and in a way far too mysterious and wonderful for Jack to comprehend. She had protected him with her prayers, and though he couldn't understand yet completely, he knew something spiritual was happening.

He knew his heart was twisting like a towel being wrung out. For the first time in his life, he knew he could at least hope to understand love and there was a kindness beginning to seep out from somewhere deep inside of him.

He found himself there in a chair in an empty room, exhausted from battle but resting in this new hope. Though the knot of grief kept trying to well up inside of him, he was too euphoric for melancholy. Finally, he quit studying the words on the piece of paper, folded it back neatly and slid it into the envelope. He laid his head on the table and dreamt of Anna touching his face.

CHAPTER SEVEN

THREE STEPS

The first Thursday evening in November, Jack sat at a pay phone in the concourse, fidgeting and sweating, waiting for Anna to answer. It was hot in the underground hallway, almost eighty. Summer had not fully given up it seemed, and had fooled the old steam-generated heating system which continued to run even though it was in the seventies.

Jack sat in the dampness of his sweat, in an effort to answer a message slip he had received from the guard room two hours earlier. Anna finally picked up.

"Hello?"

"Hey Anna, it's Jack. I got your message. Everything okay?"

"Fine," she answered, "I just thought I'd see what you were doing this weekend."

Jack laughed.

"What am I doing? Let's see. The only difference between me and anybody serving a four-year sentence in the state pen is that I'm paying five-thousand dollars a year. I'm being a Rat this weekend, which probably means I'll be hauling large blocks of limestone up House Mountain to work on the superintendant's pyramid."

"Ha, ha," Anna replied. "First of all, you aren't building any pyramids. Second, I am fully aware that even Rats get time off on the weekends. So tell me now, what are you guys doing on Saturday?"

"You guys? Wait," Jack said, "this isn't just about me?"

"I meant 'you guys' as a generic term for you, or you and your roommates, or you and the rest of the little Rats," Anna answered.

"Well," Jack said, "I was thinking about making an X-check at about twenty-one hundred Saturday night."

"The PX on campus?"

"The PX on post, yes," Jack answered.

Anna laughed.

"You're so ridiculously military," she said.

"Yes," Jack replied, "I suppose it has something to do with the fact that I'm attending a *military* college. Now, why the sudden interest in my lame social life?"

"Well, I don't drink, and I'm neither a shut-in nor a nerd, and though there may be a plethora of wonderful cultural events on campus this weekend, none of them really grab my attention. Hollins is boring on Saturday, at least this Saturday, and you're the closest friend I have to visit. I'm sure not driving all the way to Richmond. Not to mention, I actually have a brother going to school there," she answered.

"Oh yeah, *him*."

"Is Ted going to the PX, too?" she asked.

"No, he's going to the movies."

"That sounds much more exciting than the PX. By himself?"

"Naw, I think he's going with Darryl and Ski."

"We should all go," Anna said, excitedly.

"So you were really calling to see if you might be able to see Ted this weekend," Jack said.

"I want to see Ted, yes," she admitted, "but I want to see you even more."

"Y'know, no one could ever accuse us of moving too fast in this relationship."

"I don't know what too fast is anymore. I'm a romantic, I guess."

"Yeah," Jack said, then chuckled, "but you haven't even seen me with any hair on my head. What if it grows out and I look like a putz?"

"I wouldn't be the first girl to like a putz, I suppose," Anna answered.

"Hmmm, it's getting hot in this booth," Jack said, "and I'm already wallowing around in my sweat-soaked class dyke."

"That's gross."

"How 'bout your folks? Are they okay with this?"

"With what?"

"Y'know, us."

Anna was painfully silent for several seconds.

"I've been trying to figure all this out, and I suppose just ignoring the issue won't fix anything," she said.

"What issue? What's going on?" Jack asked.

He was taken completely by surprise. He fully expected her to affirm her parents liked him. His mind raced back to Parents' Weekend, and he was certain the McClain's gave no indication they had a problem with him.

"I suppose…" she said, and then paused briefly. "Okay, look, I happened to mention to Dad that I've written you more than once. Suddenly I was in the middle of an argument. He said it wasn't about your friendship with Ted, but he had plans for me, plans that would be best served if I did not get serious about a guy right now."

"We're not exactly serious, Anna. Are we?"

"Not exactly. Not yet anyway. I think it's more than just that, though."

"Like what?" asked Jack.

Here it comes.

"I don't know. No, I do. They have their ideas about who they want me to marry, or at least the kind of guy. I don't like saying these things, Jack. You know I don't think that way."

Jack could hear her voice break.

"So they don't approve of me because of my background, because I'm an orphan from the wrong side of the tracks, from the wrong kind of family."

"He didn't say that, exactly."

"Yeah, but we both know what he meant."

"I suppose, still…"

"So why are you calling me and asking about Saturday?"

"Dad didn't forbid me seeing you. He just said he was against it, and I would understand someday."

"Great, just what I need," Jack said, "another fight with someone."

He stopped short of saying anything else. He was afraid he'd just hurt her feelings.

It's just a roadblock. I can work around it. Is Ted gonna start running interference for his dad? I am serious about her.

"Anna, did you mean it?"

"Mean what?" she asked.

"When you said 'not yet,' we weren't serious yet."

"Maybe, but really I think I lied a little."

"Oh," Jack replied, sighing.

"Yeah, I am serious about you," Anna replied, then giggled. "See you Saturday?"

"Saturday."

———⧓———

It was less than a week before Opening Hop, and shortly before taps Jack busted through the door of their room, laughing, digging in the inside of his hat.

"This is going to be one monumental visit to the RDC!" He belted out as he produced a healthy stack of three by five cards.

"You didn't get all those tonight, did you?" Darryl laughed as he grabbed them and started reading them.

"Naw, that's the whole collection since the Phelps deal."

"Hey don't we still owe your boyfriend Phelps a little visit in barracks during OCMNI?" Ski said, from under his comforter.

"I'm more concerned about being on the RDC's ten most wanted."

Jack chuckled as he sat on his bed and began pulling off his shoes.

Taps began to play and the stick started.

"Ah, the primal rhythm of clicks from bundled hangers tapping doors," Darryl said as he looked out of the doorway.

The guard members ran around each stoop and tapped each door. When the stick tapped a door, all of the members of that room just had their status checked. If they were each doing what was authorized at that given time they were okay, but if any wasn't he was considered "un-alright" and honor-bound to place himself on report.

"The evil sentinels gleefully run along each stoop, swatting the doors as they pass," added Ted.

"A visit from the Angel of Confinement for those wayward souls who have wandered into the land of un-alrightness," Darryl said followed by a long, dramatic sigh.

"Engineers," said Jack.

"At least we'll have jobs when we graduate," answered Darryl.

"Hey, Darryl could you hit that light before we get busted for unauthorized late study in barracks?" Jack said.

Darryl shut off the light and felt his way to his rack. Jack lay down. Ski was already asleep across the room and well into his deep rhythmic breathing that bordered on snoring.

Jack was amazed that Ski could fall asleep so quickly. It seemed to take Jack hours. He was used to about five or six hours of sleep a night. It had been that way since he was fifteen, when his father died.

"So," Ted broke the silence, "that letter that you got from Anna, it was more than just friendly, huh?"

He's fishing. No way would he know.

"Yeah, I mean, it was friendly, a lot of friendliness." Jack could not help himself.

"Whooooaaaah, hittin' on your roomie's sister so soon—shameless," Darryl said.

"Well, what's the skinny? You guys were flirting around a little on Parents Weekend, then holding hands at the movies Saturday. I'm just surprised Anna would have any interest in a VMI guy," Ted said.

"I like your sister, Ted. But I don't know where it's all going."

"The truth comes out. That's gross, dude. She even looks like Ted. Not to mention that you look like Ted. You might as well be dating *him*. It's all confusion. I think I'm gonna puke," Darryl said.

"She doesn't look anything like Ted. I look more like Ted than she does," Jack said, but with a grin while shaking his head.

Ted lay quietly for a moment.

"First of all, I'm okay with you and my sister. Keep in mind, though that she's a good girl. She needs to be treated right, Jack. She needs to be treated like a lady in every respect, if you know what I mean."

"Yeah, I know."

"The other thing is," Ted continued, "I ain't the one you need to impress. Dad's pretty old fashioned. He won't let just anybody date Anna. You've gotta be approved. You've gotta get his blessing."

Mr. McClain told him. He's worried about me and Anna.

"Blessing?" Jack asked.

"Yeah, blessing," Ted replied with a sigh of exasperation. "I'm beginning to suspect that you're not even *from* the south. I'm thinking you're a spy from somewhere far north of the Mason-Dixon Line; some place where the people don't know about anything southern. Here in the south, one gets a blessing, kinda like permission, before he starts dating a girl. I know, it's so old fashioned, but…" He left the sentence hanging.

"That's more than old fashioned," Darryl said, "that's just plain stupid."

"You may be able to go further south than Botetourt County, but ya can't get more southern. We're just not society folks like y'all," Jack said, smiling. "I suppose I'll get your dad's blessing. You just gotta put in a good word for me."

"I'll see what I can do," said Ted. "Y'know, Anna's really a good person, Jack."

"The best," Jack replied.

———◦✻◦———

The next morning just before classes, Jack and Ted were the last two in the room.

"I really want to ask your sister to the hop, but man, it's been awhile. And look at us," he said as he was looking in the mirror rubbing his buzzed scalp, "we look like we're POWs or something!"

"Look, I've got one of Anna's old friends coming down from Richmond to go with me. Give Anna a call. You know she won't say no. Dad, on the other hand, if he finds out, probably will. Then again, who knows? If you don't make it out to be anything serious, he probably won't deny her going to a VMI hop. He might see it as a way to get her to like VMI as much as he does," Ted said.

"Alright, I'll call her," Jack played it off as if he was being talked into the whole thing, but inside he was churning with excitement.

"Oh, by the way, you're right, you do look like a freak!" Ted laughed.

Jack left the room early for class. On his way his mind could not stop racing, thinking about a conversation that he would have with Anna that evening. Telephones in the concourse were off limits to Rats during CQ, so he would have to wait until 2200 to call her because he knew there would be little chance of catching her during the day.

Timing and consideration made his anxiety grow even stronger because he was afraid that she would not be in, or would already be asleep. He found himself being overwhelmed by his rampant anxiety.

He exited the barracks, saluting Stonewall in the usual manner, and walked over to the top of the parapet to wait for class formation. Sitting on the wall near one of the old French cannons he spent some time thinking about how even in the midst of all this turmoil, this was clearly the best his life had ever been.

Now, with the inclusion of Anna, he had no desire to ever go back to the farm. It represented his father. He could not look at the old house without seeing him standing there, waiting to unleash his dreaded anger. The thought of the tiny broken-down farmhouse was enough to turn his stomach. But the river – the river was Jack's.

He sat and thought deeply, as an autumn breeze with a hint of summer magnolia rustled the reddish brown leaves in the half-naked sycamores that lined Keydet Drive. Some let go, parasailing along with the wind to careful landings along the sidewalk and safely in piles at the base of the parapet.

Jack could let the farm go. It was his part of the great river that had been a symbol of his mangled, tumultuous existence. But now everything pointed forward. The dark soil and the flint rock, as well as the waters that passed over it had become the only thing that anchored him to his past. It was by law his, held by the state till he turned twenty-one. Then it would be his right to let it go.

"I'll do it."

Right there among the ghosts of French cannoneers, he made up his mind. He would find a way to sell it as quickly as possible.

"You're very witty, Jack," Colonel Gavin said as he smiled, still studying the paper that Jack had turned in that morning.

"Thank you, sir. I think," Jack replied.

"Now," Colonel Gavin said, looking over his glasses, "are you certain that you want to be an *English major*, Jack?"

The question took Jack by surprise. Colonel Gavin was Jack's professor in Early American Literature and had been assigned as Jack's academic advisor.

This was the second time since classes had started that Jack had found himself in Colonel Gavin's office, reviewing something he had turned in and discussing his academic direction. The first meeting had been an effort on Gavin's part to encourage Jack to live up to his potential. Not great, but still Jack left it with the confidence that he was doing the right thing, something he loved.

Now he seemed to be questioning Jack's very dream—to write.

Colonel Gavin was a tall, thin man that appeared to be in his mid-sixties. Jack particularly liked his deep baritone voice, which seemed to complement anything he read aloud, especially poetry. He was respected in academic circles for the body of his life work centering on Milton. His books were published and well-known. He spoke eloquently, but not in a pompous way as he was a humble man whose passion was focused on his writing and his students.

Jack sat motionless for a moment, not sure what his answer was supposed to be.

"It's a simple question, unless you would feel more comfortable if I appeal to your current station in life, and end the question with *Rat.*" Colonel Gavin laughed.

"Jack is fine, sir, and yes, I really do like English. I like to write. I want to be a writer, or a journalist, or something like that."

Colonel Gavin looked out the window for a long moment, and then took a deep breath.

"The beauty of the Institute is that I am able to spend more time with the students I teach and advise here than I would at many other colleges. It is my job to find out what each of them desires to accomplish while he is here and when he graduates. You're going to get a heck of a hard time from me, Jack."

"I'm used to it, as you know," Jack replied, gesturing over his shoulder toward the barracks.

"Yes, of course," Gavin continued. "Now, since you've started classes, I have received three papers from you. Your writing, Jack, is promising for a college freshman. It started out horribly, but has improved since our last meeting. Still, there are some strange moments, but it has promise. If writing is really what you are passionate about, then neither of us can be happy with the status quo. You might end up decent at it. A fellow can make a living doing something he loves."

He had leaned forward in his chair, and was speaking with excitement.

"Thank you, sir. So what does that mean?" asked Jack.

"Nothing except you need to read more and write more and generally work harder. I'll be running you through the wringer. You know, sort of pushing you."

He stood up and walked behind his chair, grabbing two very old looking burgundy clad books off of one of his bookshelves.

"You'll need to take a look at these," he said to Jack. "A couple of old volumes on writing. Don't believe everything you find in them, though." He said. "Some rules are meant to be broken. Right now, you need to focus on the basics—chemistry, math," He looked down at Jack's class schedule trying to remember his math course. "Probability and Statistics, nice. World history. Those will give you the fits, I suppose. Of course, your American Lit and composition. Then you can take a little more liberty with your schedule. This year will be tough enough for you. Lord knows it was for me. Is this too much?"

"No, sir. I'm ready. You know, be all you can be and such. I want to write well," Jack said.

"Good, then we're done here. I'll want to meet with you in two weeks."

"Thank you, sir," Jack said as he stood up.

"And, Jack, there is a good writer in there," he said pointing to Jack's chest and then finished with a wide grin. "You need to commit to digging him out. Read, Jack, read."

He handed the two books to Jack.

CHAPTER EIGHT

FALLING

Walking back to the barracks, Jack was feeling satisfied. He had finally voiced his interest in writing, and was glad to be taken seriously. He walked slowly past the parapet, remembering his commitment to sell the farm and wash away his past with it.

He knew, however, that he needed not loiter anywhere to baste in his thoughts and feelings, no matter how unlikely it was that he would be bothered during the class day. He was still a Rat, and certainly still a target.

Jack had learned when to be noticed and when not to be. The latter was most of the time. He tried not to move faster than upperclassmen, but moved at an unassuming pace, never drawing attention, blending like leaves piled along the parapet.

He had to enter barracks through Jackson Arch, but he could skirt around the first stoop and take any of the stairwells other than Sally Port. Sally Port tended to be where everyone converged going to or from their rooms. Naturally, he figured his chances of running into a rather unsavory Third as he passed through the third stoop would be greatly reduced using one of the other Old Barracks stairwells. It had been working great for him over the previous few days.

Jack headed into Jackson Arch and turned left on the first stoop, and then walked the Ratline around Sally Port all the way to the far left stairwell known as "Ghetto Corner." But before he could double-time up the stairs, he heard the dreaded "Whoa, Rat!" from one of the doors just before Ghetto Corner. Jack stopped on the first step, and then backed off of it.

"Well, whadya know, it's Rat Hart-*nan*, the scourge of the third class, come to visit the fellas in the Ghetto. Third time I've seen ya using *this* stairwell this week. Let me guess, you're steerin' clear of Sally Port since you took on the whole third class up there."

It was, of course, Mr. Hall from the RDC.

"Yes, sir!" Jack replied without hesitation.

"Well, y'know Hart-*nan*, you oughta use the stairwell closest to your room, but I like your ingenuity and your sense of survival, so I guess I don't really care. But when I see you over on this side of barracks, you will have to pay the fine."

Jack felt a sense of dread as he asked the obvious question.

"What's the fine, sir?"

Mr. Hall moved from his doorway and leaned on the rail at the edge of the courtyard. It sounded to Jack like he was lighting a cigarette.

"I'm a big fan of the Parapet. Never was much into poetry, that's for chicks and English majors. But the Parapet, that's something else."

He took a couple drags on his cigarette and blew the smoke in Jack's direction. He was referring to the quote from Colonel J. T. L. Preston that was engraved on the parapet wall outside Washington Arch that overlooked William H. Cocke Hall, where Jack had been sitting earlier. It was considered "pertinent information" that all Rats had to memorize. Being early enough in the year, most were still having trouble with it.

"That's it? You want me to recite the Parapet?"

"Well, I don't want your lunch money, cowboy, and my Rat shines my shoes already, so I guess for you, it's the Parapet. C'mon let's hear it."

Hall had changed suddenly from Dr. Jekyll to Mr. Hyde.

"The healthful and pleasant abode of a crowd of honorable youths, pressing up the hill of science with noble emulation. A gratifying spectacle, an honor to our country and our state, objects of honest pride to their instructors and fair specimens of citizen soldiers, attached to their native state, proud of her fame, and ready in every time of deepest peril to vindicate her honor and defend her rights. Colonel J. T. L. Preston, sir."

Fast and flawless.

"Well, well, well, Hart-*nan*, you're okay for a smelly ol' Rat. It is truly going to be a pleasure to have you as our featured guest at the RDC meeting tonight. The invitation is posted on your door. Carry on." He crushed out his cigarette with his shoe, and headed back into his room.

Jack double-timed up the stairs and quickly made his way along the Ratline to his room. When he arrived, just as Mr. Hall had said, the invitation was on his door. It read:

> Name: Hartman, J. M.
> Room: 432
> You will report to the RDC
> Date: Thursday October 12, 1980
> Time: 2200 hrs
> Uniform: Grey Blouse

He realized as he read it that his chance to call Anna was quickly evaporating. General Quarters was not until 2200 hours and taps was 2300. It fell over the period of time Rats were allowed to use the pay phones in the concourse. Being the first official meeting of the RDC, Jack was certain they would be disciplining Rats until taps.

Jack sat down, exasperated. He plopped his books down on his desk and tucked the invitation under the top edge of his blotter. He leaned into the back of his chair and stared at the top corner of the wall across the room.

It's the way of the Institute – constant torment. Don't dare plan anything. Don't try to have a life. What am I doing? I'm acting like a big baby. This is ridiculous. Still, though...

Jack felt selfish and even immature as he evaluated his own emotions. He thought quietly there for several minutes, and then opened his drawer and pulled out his letter tin. He opened the lid just to smell the perfume, but once he smelled it, he could not stop there. So he pulled out Anna's letter and read it again.

And again.

Later in the room, Darryl stared across the table at Jack.

"Hey Jack, Ted's sister blow you off already?" Darryl asked.

"No."

"What's wrong, man?" Ted asked.

Jack sat down at the desk and slid the RDC slip out from under his blotter.

"This."

"So that's what one of those looks like," Ski said, looking over Jack's shoulder.

"RDC, very cool. Not for you, though," Ted said.

"That makes two of us. I got my invite this morning. I'm *so* looking forward to a wonderful evening with the death squad."

Darryl was his usual chipper self. Nothing seemed to bother him.

"It's not so much the RDC, as it is the fact that I can't call your sister, Ted. I really had my mind set on talking to her tonight. Besides, I don't want her to make other plans."

"Let me clue you in, she's gonna be here. A little bird told me today that if you don't ask her, I'm supposed to ask you to go with her."

"Would the little bird be Anna?" Jack asked.

"Most likely," Ted replied with a grin.

It was a huge weight Ted had lifted off Jack with those few words.

"Excellent," Jack sighed, leaning back in his chair.

"Look you focus on push-ups, mountain climbers, flutter kicks, running in place with knees high, and up-downs, breathing hard, and puking 'cause I have a feeling your gonna be quite involved in those activities tonight. You can call Anna tomorrow. I'll let her know tonight that you said yes."

"Hey," Darryl piped in, "it's like you're in junior high again."

"Yeah, make sure you put the 'yes or no' blocks on the note you pass to your sister," Ski added, and then laughed.

"Not funny, Yankee. You're probably bringing a W and L frat boy for your date," Ted replied.

"Yeah, and after he hears how you were making jokes about him, he'll come over here and beat the snot out of you with his hair," Ski replied.

"That actually would have been funny, if I wasn't scheduled for the RDC tonight," Jack said.

———⟨∘∕∘∕∘⟩———

Sweat.

The odor of sweat filled Jack's nose as he stood in a single file pressed tightly against the Brother Rat in front of him and behind him. At the rail above, someone was shouting into the courtyard below.

"Brother Rats! The RDC is killing me! Brother Rats! The RDC is killing me! Brother Rats! The RDC is killing me!"

Jack dared not cut his eyes to see who was doing all of the screaming. He had been on the stoop either straining with his face against the wall, or at the rail straining, sandwiched in the ridiculously tight line waiting to see the RDC.

They were taken from the line one at a time and made to face the wall several times to endure POW-like questioning and be given instructions. In between the rail and the wall were, of course, an endless series of push-ups for not moving fast enough, or for answering a question unsatisfactorily.

The RDC meetings were held in a two-room block on the fifth stoop above Jackson Arch. The fifth stoop was an additional level that only cropped up behind the peaks of the three arches, the others used for overflow rooms if a Rat class was a few too large for the fourth stoop alone. A narrow interior stairway ran up to an indoor landing that split the rooms.

Finally, Jack stood at the front of the line, feeling as if he was about to jump out of an airplane. Two RDC members were screaming in his ears, and he found himself running up a very narrow, dark stairway where he met the next RDC member at the landing. A very dim light hung a few feet above them, swinging back and forth, giving an eerie feel to the hallway between the two rooms. He pointed to a poster on the wall directly in front of Jack. It had three bullet statements printed in two-inch block letters.

The RDC member explained them to Jack at a very high volume.

"When you are read the infractions on the card for which you have been sent here, you will be asked to answer. You will answer either *correct, incorrect* or *correct, but wish to explain.* Do you understand, Rat!" he yelled.

"Yes, sir!"

"Now go and knock on that door, maggot, and you better knock it off the hinges."

Jack ran over to the door, still straining. The hanging light in the landing did very little to illuminate the door. It was dark, almost black. He banged on the door with the side of his fist three times as hard as he could. Sharp pain shot through his arm to his elbow. A very large RDC member yanked the door open, and another yanked Jack into the room.

A bright light was positioned behind a row of five men sitting at a table so that Jack could only see their silhouettes. To Jack, it was all a blur, and it blended together in his brain until he could not process it cleanly.

Someone was screaming, another was reading out the write-ups on RDC cards that sounded vaguely familiar.

Huh? Yes, correct! Yes, yes!

Almost as quickly as it started, he was whisked across the hallway to the other room, where he joined a packed room full of Brother Rats being worked out with all of the screaming and intensity that six or seven RDC men could muster. The lights in the room were flashing on and off, and a boom-box was blaring music ranging from Nugent to Wagner. The psychological tension was worse for Jack than the physical stress of the sweat party.

And like that, it was over. Sweating, weak, and disoriented, Jack walked the Ratline quickly back to his room. Ted was there. Ski was out studying late. Jack hung his sweat soaked grey wool blouse back up, kicked off his shoes, and lay on his bed.

"Bad, wasn't it?" Ted asked.

"It was crazy, weird. My head's still spinning. I mean, the work out was about the same as they always are. But there were lights and crazy music and so much screaming, it was confusing. I'm not sure I can tell you what exactly happened. I think I got like fifteen penalty tours, as well."

"Man, I wish I'd gone tonight with you guys," Ted replied.

"I don't think you want to go there," Jack replied.

"Everyone gets at least one visit."

"Oh," Jack said, "I forgot about that."

"Yeah, and now that you've told me this, well, I'd rather just be ignorant."

"It's more 'weird' than anything else. They try to be all psycho. I guess it works a little. I wouldn't sweat it. By the time they get you, they'll be bored with the whole thing. You'll get off easy."

"Liar," Ted joked.

"I know, but I'm trying to be encouraging. They'll eat your lunch."

"Thanks, BR!"

"No prob. Darryl made it back yet?"

"No, didn't you hear him earlier? He's been up there screaming all night that that RDC is killing him."

Anna's perfume.

To Jack it was unique and perfect. It graced the letters Anna had written him, and though there may have been no medical explanation for it, he could always count on his heart noticeably racing the second it hit his nose.

His heart was racing again. It was Saturday, Opening Hop night.

Jack could hardly look at Anna. His hands were shaking when she met him at Lejuene Hall. But it was that perfume, her signature scent, which had him gutting out wave after wave of butterflies. Jack could sense that he was feeling stronger about her, that they were somehow becoming emotionally intertwined.

He held Anna's arm draped over his in courtly fashion as they entered William H. Cocke Hall. The scene of their first Rat mass sweat party had been transformed into a ballroom with a tremendous layer of decorations that covered its marred antique walls and ceiling. But there was still a hint of that musty scent of sweat and old gym socks. A large mirrored ball hung in the center, and the stage lighting beamed reds and blues that spilled across the middle of the room.

"Oh, I love this band, this music," said Anna, looking to the stage. "I've heard them. They're really good."

"I guess they sound okay, but the fella that's singing could use a haircut," replied Jack.

"I heard them last June in Virginia Beach. They really got everyone dancing when they played old Tams or Drifters songs. You know, beach music."

Jack thought about beach music. It was the rage among those who called the East Coast home; whose fondest memories were always of weekends spent in Virginia Beach, or Myrtle Beach or anywhere along the Eastern Shore of Virginia and the Carolina coastline. It was a music symbolizing a status that had been unreachable for Jack, till now.

"Jack! Anna!" Ted yelled from a few feet away, just on the dance floor.

He made his way over to them, his date in tow.

"Ted," Jack replied.

"Let me introduce Miss Jenny Lipscomb. Jenny this is Jack," Ted said.

Jack nodded once nervously. "Nice to meet ya, Jenny."

Anna had set them up. Jenny was pretty, with dark brown hair and large blue eyes, sparkling with life. She smiled at Jack and held out her right hand. Jack shook it.

Ted rolled his eyes a little, then let out a one syllable laugh.

"When we get done here tonight remind me to show you how to dazzle the ladies when introduced," Ted said, intentionally loud enough for the girls to hear.

"Jenny's a sophomore at Richmond, and a very close friend of mine," Anna said to Jack. "Please don't mess that up, Ted."

"Don't worry about me, Anna. I can handle your little brother," Jenny said, slugging Ted's shoulder.

"Alright, enough of this nonsense. You guys come on out and dance," Ted said, already pulling Jenny toward the dance floor.

"Of course, but maybe in a few minutes," Jack answered.

"I'll see you in a minute, Anna," Jenny said over the din of music and conversation, "and Jack, it was nice meeting you."

She gave Anna a raised eyebrow look as if to say she approved. Ted and Jenny slipped through the crowd toward the center of the room.

Jack didn't like to dance. He had always been awkward with it, not too rhythmic, not good with his feet. He wasn't really into music. He didn't expect a bunch of military guys would care so much about it that the dance floor would be packed. He thought most guys would be like him, so it never crossed his mind to worry about his lack of skill where dancing was concerned.

For Jack it was neither music nor dancing that had him standing at the edge of the room, nervous and perspiring, listening to the band and trying to figure out what to say next. It was simply Anna. He just wanted to do anything that would give them time together.

Jack could tell that Anna sensed his nervousness.

"Hmmm," she pondered out loud, "I'm sure you were much more confident last time I saw you. Let me guess, you don't dance."

"I've danced a couple of times, two dances in high school without a date. I know, that's a little weird. I was kinda dumb then. 'Bout all I could think about was fishing," he replied.

"Would you mind learning how? I love to dance, and I refuse to whittle the night away with a pair of left feet," she said with a silly grin, fluttering her eyelashes.

"Sounds like I've run out of options."

"You have, Jack Hartman, but I'll make you a deal."

"Okay, I do deals."

"Fine, you find us a corner somewhere, where we can be as inconspicuous as possible. I will teach you a little dancing, and we won't have to do so in the middle of this whole assembly."

"You're on, Miss Anna," Jack replied.

He grabbed her hand and led her through the throng of cadets and dates that filled the perimeter of the dance floor. Jack could not find a corner that was not already crowded, but he remembered the stairwell that led up to the running track. Anna began to get tickled at Jack's determination to find privacy, and Jack began to feel the same amusement when he heard her giggling.

"What?" Jack said laughing. "I'm doin' the best I can!"

They barged through the double-doors, laughing childishly. Finally, they came to a stop, and Jack turned toward Anna. Anna held her hands out, palms up, and Jack obliged by placing his hands in hers.

"Okay, I'm going to teach you a dance called *The Swing*," she said.

"Oh, that one half of them are doing in there?" He motioned toward the gym.

"You know it?"

"Yeah," said Jack, "but in the same way I know physics. I know it exists, and that people do it."

"Well, I can't help you solve the mystery of physics," replied Anna, "but maybe I can help you be a little less shy around the ladies when it comes to dancing."

Jack sensed a need for confirmation in her statement.

"As far as I'm concerned, I don't need to impress any other ladies, just this one."

Her face flushed and she smiled. Jack knew he had guessed right.

The music from the band hammered against the door. It managed to press through, still loud, but muffled and echoing up and down the stairwell. *Myrtle Beach Days*.

"Okay, watch my feet…"

And they were off. For the next thirty minutes or so Anna worked feverishly to make a dancer out of Jack. He was normally agile, but did quite poorly with this. Jack struggled with anything when a girl was involved. He was awkward and shy, and his being head over heels for Anna just made it worse. Not a lost cause, but Anna quickly realized he would be years in the making.

They wound up sitting in the box window sill in the stairwell, looking out over the lights of the neighborhoods just beyond the football field. It was just big enough for her to sit with her knees together and bent tightly, but canted just slightly to her left and sitting on the side of her left thigh, knees toward the window. She leaned against the old metal casing, and the tug of it pulled at her dress, revealing her left shoulder. Moonlight highlighted the features of her face. Jack was mesmerized.

She held the hem of her dress over her knees, so that she would be proper, and not reveal too much. In her innocence she could never have known how badly Jack burned for her. He sat with his left leg hanging over the ledge, and his right leg pulled up close to his chest with his arms loosely wrapped around it. He leaned his head back, looking out the window quietly, fighting the battle raging inside of him.

He did well.

Somehow in this moment, he squelched his desire enough to stop him from making a foolish move. Something inside of him was saying over and over that he should not, that she was too good for that, as if there might have been a girl who was not too good for that. It was frustrating, even for his better nature.

She looked at him with the strangest expression, squinting like she was looking into him.

"Sitting here like this has made me realize that you are not like most other guys, Jack Hartman."

"How's that?" He sighed.

"I don't know. It's hard to say. You're good, I guess, but not in a nerdy or weak way. When I think about it, I guess I feel safe and, y'know, happy with you. It's a good feeling, hard to explain, really. The goodness in you, I don't know that anyone else can see what you've let me see. It's like I've found the secret, and no one else knows it."

"What's the secret?"

She paused and looked down, twisting a fold in the hem of her dress. She seemed a little nervous to Jack.

"I think we're supposed to be together, Jack, and I don't think I know why. Maybe it's a God thing, I don't know. Maybe he wants us to be together, to fall in love. Is this too weird?"

"No, not at all. Maybe that's a sign that things are changing between me and him," Jack said.

"You and God?"

"Yeah, I mean you know my past. My life with my dad, then him gettin' killed and all. Then havin' really nobody for so long. I mean, there were always people who cared, but I still felt alone, disjointed. I don't know, but it just seems that things have been better here. And now, you. I don't know too much about God, but maybe things are changing."

"You know, it's funny," Anna said, "but Dad would never want me to be seeing a boy that was not already a strong Christian.

He also only likes certain boys, a good upbringing, and the like. I suppose it's what our argument was all about."

"I never got his blessing to take you to the hop," Jack said, looking out the window.

He didn't want to confront her eyes.

"I suppose it's for the best."

"I'm from the wrong part of town, no money, no pedigree."

"Dad's not like that. He just has his mind set on certain things."

She reached out with her hand and grabbed his hand, squeezing it once.

"If you only knew what I was thinking right now, you wouldn't think I was any different from other guys, like you said I was," Jack said.

"That's just the point, Jack. I can't know exactly what you're thinking or how it is affecting you. But it isn't exactly what you're thinking right now that is the important thing. It's what you are doing with those thoughts."

"How is it any different?"

"I used to like this boy back home. Last summer, I went out with him. He was supposedly this strong Christian boy that really seemed to believe and have his spiritual life in order, but he wouldn't stop pressuring me. It was awkward, and I certainly wasn't Miss Perfect in all of it. I'm not always the strongest one when it comes to affection. But it worked out okay. Nothing happened and we stopped seeing each other."

Jack looked into her eyes for the truth. He wanted all of her if he was going to restrain himself for however long it would take. Anna continued.

"Tonight you had the same opportunity, but you've reacted totally different. Whatever crazy male hormones are running through you, whatever effect your male eyes are having on your body, you've fought it back because you think more of me than to waste it. At least, that's how I perceive it."

"I've fought it back, 'cause I'm not good enough for you," he replied, looking down.

It was a selfish thing to say, and Jack knew it. He searched for something to lower her inhibitions.

If she feels sorry for me.

"Don't you go there, Jack Hartman. We are no different."

Jack looked out the window silently for a moment, shocked that she had somehow read his mind, and dismantled his self-pity so easily.

"So, that's the secret?"

"Yes, that's the secret."

Jack wanted to tell her that she was wrong. A part of him wanted to go exactly where that other guy had gone, to satisfy his desire, to "waste it," as she had put it. There was, however, another part of him that saw her as something different than any other girl he had ever known. It was a part of him that wanted everything to be perfect, to see something in his life work out right for once.

They stayed there in the box window for awhile, both being quiet, occasionally looking at each other to smile and sharing some of their thoughts, almost in a whisper. In Jack's mind he wrestled with a decision: to flush away his past and rise up to be everything that Anna needed, or to go on and be the same he'd always been–not taking the chance and not risking pain.

He studied her face, glowing in the fullness of the light blue moon as they sat quietly listening to beach music swirl through the stairwell. Jack felt closer to Anna than he had ever felt to any other person. He wondered if she felt the same for him. He wondered.

Does she? Does she love me?

And so, he reached slowly out to her, and she conceded, interlocking her fingers with his. They held hands as they sat there, still perspiring lightly, even in the coolness of the Shenandoah autumn night.

PART 2

A CODE OF HONOR

CHAPTER NINE

THE ECHO OF DRUMS

It had been a full night of study and Jack was tired, but he was moving around continuously in and out of sleep. It just seemed impossible that night to get comfortable.

Click, click, click, bang! The old steam radiant heater knocked. It heated the room well enough. The rest of Jack's roommates never seemed bothered by the incessant noises it made.

He propped himself up and looked at his desk clock. It was already two in the morning.

Gotta get some sleep.

He slid his comforter down to his feet, and then slipped out from under it. The room was warmer than normal. Old faithful clanged away in the corner.

Jack sat on the side of his rack and rubbed his eyes. He thought about wrapping up in his comforter and stepping out onto the stoop for a few minutes. The cold air would do him some good, he figured. But as he grabbed his comforter he heard a strange sound emanating from somewhere in the courtyard.

It took him a few moments to figure out what the sound was. It began as an almost undetectable hiss, but as it began to slowly crescendo, it became obvious that it was the sound of a snare drum roll.

There must have been two of them because it continued to build until it was very loud. Then it stopped suddenly. There was a pause, then a single boom from a bass drum. The snare roll and bass drum strike took twenty or thirty seconds, and then was repeated over and over.

As the drums were rolling Jack looked through the door window and could see and hear several upperclassmen on each stoop going from door to door. They would flip on the light in the room and say in a very stern voice, "Get out on the stoop, your Honor Court has met!"

Every room was being awakened, and cadets on every stoop slowly moved like zombie figures wrapped in blankets to line the rails surrounding the Old Barracks courtyard.

Jack woke his roommates, and a minute afterward, their door was flung open and they were told the same. It was a first class Honor Court member in coatee and white gloves. He flipped on the light long enough for him to recite the same command, then flipped it off again, moving on to the next room.

There was an ominous rhythm to it all, between the commands and the rolling drums and the boom of the bass drum echoing through the barracks.

"So this is it, a drum out," Darryl whispered.

"Shhh," said Jack.

"Weird," Mike whispered.

"Yeah, weird," said Ted.

They quietly stepped out onto the stoop.

At two in the morning, there was an eerie feel to the old courtyard. A cold, starry night, without even a hint of moon created a dungeon like blackness. The ghostly figures surrounding every level were dead silent. It was difficult to make out the shadow formation assembling in Jackson Arch.

An occasional cigarette fell from the second or third stoop, trailing its embers like a meteorite burning out. Finally, the drums stopped rolling.

It was quiet.

"Honor Court, ah-ten-shun. For-ward march."

The shadowy formation marched out of the arch toward the center of the courtyard on the wide concrete walkway that led from the arch to the circular patio around the sentinel box. They were dressed in formal coatee and white gloves. No cadence was necessary. It was a short march.

"Court, halt!" The heels of the Honor Court members clicked together in unison. As soon as they halted, the Honor Court President began walking briskly around the perimeter of the circular patio.

"Tonight, your Honor Court has met! And has found Cadet Second Classman Williams, E. J. guilty of making false official statements to a member of the guard! He has placed personal gain above honor and has left the Institute never to return! His name shall never be mentioned within the walls of these barracks again!"

There was a mumbling among those looking into the courtyard and they all turned and headed back into their rooms. Jack watched as the court executed an about face, and marched back into the arch. Jack, Ted, Darryl, and Mike stood mesmerized by the whole event, and finally headed back into their room.

As he lay back down, Jack felt nauseous. It was that kind of feeling in which he sensed that something terrible had happened. Not because it was wrong, or there was anything wrong with the justice of it, but because it was so serious.

Now the honor system was real and verified. There was an impending gravity of the meaning and significance of honor weighing on him.

Devastating. Maybe not to someone else—someone on the outside. But here. You pour your sweat and blood out to be here—to make it through. To be a part of the corps.

No one said a word as they lay there. Jack didn't even know who he was. His name was Williams and he was a Second. He may have been a great guy.

Someone's friend. Never bothered me that I know of. He lied. That's all I know about him.

In the silence and darkness, with his restlessness gone, Jack fell asleep.

—⟋⟍⟋⟍⟋—

December rushed in with some of the coldest winds the Shenandoah Valley had experienced in ten years. There were a couple of light snows the first week of the month, but it quickly turned colder and the idea of snow seemed driven away by the biting, chapping wind.

It felt to Jack as if a thousand parades, rifle runs, and Rat training sessions had come and gone. He also agonized over the eternal monotony of his academic classes, and had begun to long for the fresh air and freedom of his life on the James. It wasn't only him feeling the stagnation of the early winter.

Ted was eager to get home for Christmas. He included Jack in all of his plans. Darryl and Ski were no different, everyone counting the days until they would get to experience home and family and most importantly, freedom.

Jack did long to see Anna away from Lexington and VMI. The opportunity of a week at the McClain home with Anna filled Jack's thoughts. They had been out with Ted a couple of times since that first hop, but mostly their time together was on the phone twice a week and, of course, about as many letters. Jack had told Anna everything he could about himself and had listened as she did likewise. He could not help feeling disconnected though, and longed to sit with her as they did at Opening Hop, quiet and connected.

"Get your chins in, Rats!"

Jack snapped out of his daydream about Anna when Sergeant Thompson yelled near his ear.

"This is my favorite Jodie tonight," Sergeant Thompson said. "How many days left till we get to vacate this prison for a couple weeks?"

"One day, sir!" several Rats yelled, not in unison.

"I'm in a good mood tonight, third herd," Corporal Johnson said as he walked along the front of his squad. "I will not look at your nasty shoes or your foul brass!" He stopped in front of Ski.

Corporal Johnson scraped the sole of his shoe across the top of Ski's shoes. Ski had spent an hour spit shining them to a high gloss.

"Rat Kolwinski," Corporal Johnson said, almost apologetically, "I thought I had busted you wearing corfams. You spit shined those?"

"Yes, sir!" Ski yelled in a marine bark.

"Well, Rat Kolwinski, I only have one thing to say," Corporal Johnson said with a sneer. "Don't ever wear scuffed up shoes to formation again."

The squad laughed in staccato hisses trying to maintain bearing.

"Company, attention!" Sergeant Thompson yelled.

Corporal Johnson took his position at the left end of the squad.

"Left face," Sergeant Thompson commanded. "Forward march!"

They began marching along the front of the barracks and down the hill toward Crozet Hall.

"Alright, Rats, it's time for my favorite song!" Sergeant Thompson yelled over the cadence of the drums. "Hit it!"

One of the corporals in the front of the formation began to sing in rhythm to their marching and all the rats in the company joined in singing a familiar Christmas song with a new lyric.

It was a song they sang every evening on the way down to the mess hall since the beginning of December. They counted down the days till Christmas furlough with it. This time it was more important, because it was the last time they would ever sing it as Rats.

> "Hark, the corps of Keydets shout,
> One more day till we get out,
> One more day till we are free,
> From this place of misery.
> No more ball and no more chain,
> Let's all run for the nearest train
> Hark, the corps of Keydets shout,
> One more day till we get out."

One more day. The thought of it caused Jack to drift off mentally, to go through the motions of marching and dining and marching again, but give them little conscious thought. He felt intimidated and jittery and ecstatic every time he thought about spending Christmas break at the McClain's, about spending time in the home of the girl with whom he was in love.

—⟋⟋⟋—

Ted and Jack didn't get on the road till late the next evening. They signed out on furlough at the guard room, walked the two miles to the secret hiding place for Ted's car, a friend's garage, and drove the three hour drive to Richmond. They got in around eight, and spent several hours talking with Ted's parents before going to bed. Anna was not home yet. She was to be in the following afternoon.

Jack woke up around six and slipped outside for a run. He needed the fresh air and time alone to think.

Ted's neighborhood was a Christmas postcard. Richmond had been covered in a thick blanket of snow for almost a week. More was on the way, only a couple days out. Even with snow still thick on the trees, Jack could smell the cedar and pine that grew readily in almost every yard. The brisk, cold air burned his face, but Jack didn't mind.

Black lamps lined the neighborhood streets, and almost every yard was groomed and decorated for the Christmas holiday. Red brick or keystone homes with oversized lots lined both sides of the road. Black iron fences and brick walls seemed fairly standard in this old established neighborhood.

Rich folks. Must be nice. Oh, one of those old fashioned English style homes. He didn't get the memo. Probably a northerner.

He ran listening to the rhythm of his breathing, feeling good in the cold. He liked running. It gave him time to think. He would spend time in his memories or dreaming about his future and concocting plans for his life after school.

This run was no different. Jack felt a smidgen of envy for the life that Ted had, but quickly found himself back in his own memories. The cold air that morning reminded him of how difficult it was just keeping a threadbare pair of tennis shoes on his feet for school when he was in eighth grade.

He remembered once when two girls snickered in the classroom, pointing at his feet. His right shoe was falling apart with the tongue missing and laces tied in two different places because the lace had broken in half. He remembered sliding his left foot, whose shoe was only in slightly better shape, over the top of his right, then tucking them both back under the chair so his feet wouldn't be so obvious. He was thirteen.

Jack never really had noticed how poor he was until then. He never had any friends that were any better off. Ted was the first wealthy kid with whom Jack had a friendship.

Jack ran for twenty-two minutes before turning back into the McClain's driveway.

⌁∾⌁

"Would you like a cup of coffee, Jack?"

Mrs. McClain had been up early and was reading her Bible at the breakfast counter when she saw Jack walk in the kitchen.

Jack felt a little embarrassed that he had walked in on her reading, and was taken aback for a moment to see such a refined southern woman sitting in her nightgown and winter robe.

She almost looked to Jack like he imagined the normal middle-class mom, but her hair was pulled back and pristine, which Jack knew had taken significant primping. He stood in the entrance to the kitchen, not sure whether to come in.

"I'd love one," Jack said, "but don't let me take you away from your reading. If you'll just point me in the right direction, I'll be happy to get it."

"Don't be silly. I'm nearly finished, anyway."

She got up and walked around the counter and pulled a cup and saucer down from the cabinet. She placed them on the breakfast counter, and then carefully set out a small sugar bowl, spoon, and cream pitcher. Jack was amused at how careful she was to properly arrange each piece of the perfectly matching set.

"Most Virginia men that I know prefer a little cream and sugar with their coffee. Heaven knows, Teddy likes his to be sweet as syrup," she said.

"I'll take one small spoon of the sugar, but I don't care for any cream. It ruins the taste of the coffee. I like it bitter," Jack said.

"Tough guy?"

"Tough? Not really," Jack said.

"It's certainly not reading tea leaves or anything, but I've always thought you can tell a great deal about a person by the way they drink their coffee or their tea," Mrs. McClain answered with a smirk.

"Oh, I see. I'm not bitter about anything, though," Jack said.

"Well, I see my boy is still sleeping in this morning," she said as she poured the coffee.

"Exams and all, I suppose. He drove last night. And being that he's back home in his old bed, I guess we can cut him some slack."

"But not you, Jack? You don't get tired? You *don't* sleep in?"

She had already put two healthy spoonfuls of sugar in the cup.

"Guess not. Sometimes I wish I could. I suppose it'd be nice to be normal. I just can't do it."

"And you ran this morning?" She handed Jack his coffee and then pushed the cream pitcher toward him.

"Yes ma'am. Just three miles. Can't get outa shape, now. Be back in the Ratline pretty quick."

"You're eager to get back, aren't you, Jack?"

"I think just ready to get it over, the Ratline and all. I don't think getting back early will make that happen. Rumors are February or March, probably March. Guess you never really know until someone finally pulls the plug on this thing." Jack obligingly poured a splash of cream in his coffee.

"Well, it'll all be over with soon enough, and you and Teddy will have a thousand stories to tell, and you will tell them over and over for the next fifty years." Mrs. McClain laughed as she finished the sentence.

She walked over to the table and sat down again behind her Bible. She looked at it for a few seconds, but Jack could see she seemed to be struggling to get back into her reading. She closed the book and looked over at Jack.

"Jack, do you mind if I ask you a personal question?" she queried.

"No Ma'am." He answered.

"How serious is your interest in Anna?"

It was more than a motherly question. It was a shot across the bow, and Jack recognized it immediately for what it was.

White trash. Too poor. Too orphaned. Too something for their daughter. Shake it off. Not the first time I've been looked down on.

"I, uh, I like Anna."

Jack was stunned by the shot.

"I suppose I'm okay with 'like.' Maybe we can keep it there. We have plans for Anna."

"And I suppose those plans don't include a varmint from the wrong side of the tracks," Jack said, smiling.

"Touché. But that is not what I meant, Jack. It's just simply that this family is not for everyone."

"Who's it for, then? How does a guy get a ticket?" He kept a smile on his face to hide the rage swelling inside him, to let her believe he intended to be humorous.

"What is it that you are aiming for in life?" she asked him.

Jack cringed defensively. He frantically began trying to figure out how to answer politely.

"If you're asking me what my plans are after VMI," Jack started, pausing for a confirming nod of her head, "well, I plan on going into the army. You know, see where it takes me from there."

"No, I'm asking about something a bit deeper than that."

"Deeper?"

"Yes Jack, I want to know what is important to you. Why do you get up in the morning and put yourself through whatever you put yourself through? I'm sure I know why Teddy does it. He has a dream of being an officer in the army. But it's more than that, really. Teddy has decided that the military is his ministry. It's where he feels God is leading him. He's looking into being a chaplain, you know. So what is it for you, Jack?"

"Well, it's kind of hard to explain. I started working hard when I was fifteen, you know, when my dad died. I was just trying to make some money so I could go to school somewhere. At first I wasn't concerned about where, I just wanted to do something more with my life. I was like, 'Maybe I can go to a community college or something.' Everything else seemed out of reach, I guess."

"VMI was a leap?" she asked, genuinely intrigued.

"Oh, yes, ma'am. I didn't live far away, and had been there to check it out a couple of times. I don't know, the idea just grew on me. I guess really it all boils down to getting away from where I came from and wanting something better. The army made sense to me, so college and a commission made even more sense. I suppose that's why it's so tough to put a finger on it, on exactly what it is that I want. Sometimes I feel like I'm pushing toward a dream, but it's out of focus, or I don't know what it is, or something like that."

"And your past is what drives this," she paused briefly, "foggy dream?"

Jack could feel Anna, or at least the hope of a life with her, slipping away.

Losing ground, here.

"I don't know. Maybe it's what started it, and maybe it still keeps it going, but I've grown up a little in the last year or so, and I'm starting to look forward to finding something that pulls me instead of pushes me. Until then, I stay out of trouble and live a good life, and I'm going into the army, too. I may not have it all planned out yet, but I think I'm heading in the right direction. I suppose I'm kind of taking the same path as Ted."

"One more question, and then I'll leave you alone."

"Oh, it's okay, I enjoy the conversation."

Not too fond of inquisitions, though.

"Alright then, what do you think God wants you to do with your life?"

"Ooh, uh, that's a tough one."

Jack was still uncomfortable with the God stuff.

"You do believe in God, don't you?" she asked.

"Yes, of course."

Jack knew better than to answer any other way. He did not want to be offensive. He had lived in the South all his life, and knew that everyone was a member of one church or another, and most of those even believed in God.

"And so, what do you think He wants of you?" Mrs. McClain asked.

"I guess He wants me to live a good life, help other people, go to church. I think a person should do more good than bad."

"Hmmm," she said. "I said only one more and I've used that up. But that's enough for right now, we'll talk again later. I need to get ready for the day. Help yourself to anything else you need. Mr. McClain is taking all of us to breakfast at nine-thirty."

And with that, she stood up and walked down the hallway to her room.

※

"I hate Christmas," Jack said.

Ted had been driving Jack around Richmond all afternoon, trying to pick up a few Christmas gifts before things got too hectic to get anything done.

"What? How can anyone hate Christmas? It's when we celebrate Christ's birthday, not to mention the chow is usually pretty good, and we get to be on vacation. You're just stupid, dude," Ted replied.

"All that stuff is good. That's not what I hate about it. It's just that I'm always broke, and I can't afford to buy anything nice for people I know," Jack said.

Like Anna.

"Why do you even worry about it?" asked Ted.

"I dunno. I guess I shouldn't," Jack replied. "Y'know, your mom was talking to me about life this morning."

"Uh-oh. Did she give you the twenty questions bit?" Ted asked.

"Something like that. I don't think I'm well liked."

"What did you talk about?"

"Nothing of any real consequence. Just what I wanted to do with my life, that kind of stuff," answered Jack.

"You're such an idiot," Ted said with a big smile, "always thinking that everything in your life is worthless. Look, your life is important and God's got a plan for it whether you believe or not."

"Great plan, so far."

"Yeah, I know. Sometimes doesn't seem like it."

"I suppose somebody has to start from the bottom," said Jack.

They drove for another minute without talking.

"Don't mind Mom, she's just inquisitive. She always wants to know what people want to be when they grow up and what their dreams are. With you it's probably more than that. She's starting to worry about you and Anna."

Jack laughed, and said, "I suppose she is. I wish sometimes I came from better means. I'd probably fare better with your folks. And I don't blame God for all of it. I've just come to the conclusion I'm not on his radar."

Ted had stopped behind a couple of cars at a traffic light. He was pensive, and seemed to be thinking through an answer.

"I guess," Ted continued as the light turned green, "that it's kind of a random thing. Who knows? I just don't think that the garbage you go through here on earth is any indication of whether God loves you or not."

"I suppose, but if it was me up there," Jack pointed up as if he was pointing toward heaven, "I'd have given my garbage to someone like Phelps."

They both laughed.

"Maybe Phelps had worse. You don't know all the details of his life," Ted added, suddenly serious.

"I knew Phelps in high school. He was pretty well-off. He was a jerk then, too. He's been given a pretty good shake. He ain't hurtin' for anything," Jack said.

Ted pulled the car into a parking space, put it in park, and turned the key off. He cracked his door open, but Jack sat still, looking forward in a daze.

"You just gonna sit there?" Ted asked.

Jack sat silent for an awkward moment and then turned and looked at Ted.

"Ted?"

"Yeah, what?" Ted asked.

"The one thing I know for sure is I love Anna."

"Yeah," Ted said, stepping out onto the parking lot. "Does she know that?"

The McClain's loved their Christmas music. Andy Williams, Nat King Cole, The Johnny Mann Singers. Jack was being introduced to them all that evening at the dinner table. The smell of ham and fresh dinner rolls still hung in the air, though Anna had already cleared the table. Jack and Ted sat with Mr. McClain, talking and laughing while they finished their desert.

Mrs. McClain had complained she was a day late getting it finished before the boys arrived, but was determined not to let Anna see the house half-decorated. She had Mr. McClain pull down all the bags and boxes of decorations, and had quite a pile in both the study and the family room. But Anna arrived in time to help frock the stairway.

Jack had never even been in a home with the quality and array of décor as the McClain's. The garland was thick and had the look of authentic pine branches, and covered every surface which could reasonably be decorated. Mr. McClain had set up the trees several days earlier, and Mrs. McClain had spent her time dressing all three of them in their individual thematic garb.

Every table top was draped with red, green, and gold cloth, and finished with a holly and pine cone centerpiece. Then the candles—Annabelle loved them. She loved them year 'round, but during the Christmas season, especially.

"Mom, the house looks great," Anna said as she walked back into the dining room. "You really outdid yourself this year."

"It's the first year both of you have been away from home," Mrs. McClain answered. "I wanted it to be memorable."

"Oh c'mon, Mom, you'd have done it even if we weren't home for Christmas," Ted interjected from his seat at the table.

"Don't even say such a thing. I don't know what I'd do without both of you home for this, my favorite holiday," she replied from the kitchen.

Anna sat down at the table directly across from her father.

"Daddy," she whispered, "please tell me you were in charge of the gifts this year."

"Only yours," he answered.

"Good, because I would be so embarrassed if I opened up something meant for a twelve year old. You know how Mom is."

"I heard that," Mrs. McClain called out from the kitchen.

They all laughed.

"Anna, you are my princess," Mr. McClain said. "After we are finished here, let's talk in the study. I'd like to hear about the last semester. I'd also like to know what you're working on with your writing."

"Okay, Daddy, but you're not going to like it. My latest work is littered with all kinds of horrific foul language," she said, giggling.

"I doubt that. I raised you to be a straight arrow, and you've proven yourself to be just that, time and time again. Do you even know any foul language?" he asked.

"Of course, I'm in college, but don't worry. I haven't picked any of it up," she answered.

Jack sat quietly and listened to a family communicate in a way far different than he was used to hearing.

One day I'll have this. I'll have family and tradition and such.

"Jack, what about you? You don't cuss, do you?" he asked. He was very matter-of-fact, showing no signs of playfulness.

Mrs. McClain walked to the doorway of the kitchen. She had a dish in her hand and was drying it with a small red and green dish towel. She leaned against the door frame and looked directly at Jack. No one was talking, and the silence rattled Jack a bit.

"Dad, don't put him on the spot," Anna said.

"It's okay, I'm not on the spot. I suppose to answer your question, Mr. McClain, not really," Jack said.

That was weak. Sounds like I'm quibbling.

"I guess what I meant by that," Jack added, "is I don't normally cuss, but I've let a few slip. I swore it off when my Dad died. It's just something he did all the time and I didn't want to be that way."

"Good to know, Jack. I was kind of joking," Ted's dad said. "Didn't mean to sound so serious, but, good to know."

The trailer park trash might ruin their ears. Say something, Jack. Retaliate. Don't just let these people step on you.

"Thank you, Sir," replied Jack.

"Ted, the Institute hasn't colored up your language, has it?" Mrs. McClain asked from the doorway.

"I don't think so," Ted answered.

"Don't think so?" his dad asked.

"Well, if I say 'hell', let's just assume it is still a scriptural reference," he replied.

"Very funny," Mr. McClain said. "You know your mother and I fought about sending you to VMI. She was afraid that you'd come out of there with a real potty mouth."

"And I suppose it wasn't an unfounded fear," Mrs. McClain interjected, "as it certainly happened to Theodore."

"Oh, and your grandpa, my dad, was mad as a hornet when he heard me use a swear word. It took me a few years being out of the army before I got my language cleaned up. I was a captain in the Rangers where the language was pretty rough," Mr. McClain said.

"You were a Ranger, sir?" Jack asked.

"First Battalion in Ft. Stewart, then Regiment where I served with Fifth Ranger Training Battalion as a Ranger Instructor in the Mountain Phase. Six years in all."

"I think that's what I want to do," Jack said.

"What?" Ted asked. "Be a Ranger or cuss?"

They all laughed.

"Ranger, of course. Maybe a little cuss word every now and then for old times' sake," answered Jack.

Anna was in the middle of a drink of sweet tea when Jack answered. It caught her off guard and she spontaneously laughed, spewing tea all over Ted, who was sitting across from her.

"Anna, on that note," her dad said, "let's go sit and talk in the study. Don't dare bring your tea with you, I'd prefer not to be wearing it."

———

The next morning Jack got up early to run. He did not need an alarm clock. Every morning at five-thirty, he would jolt awake, sweating and heart racing. It was a response to morning that Jack had acquired as a Rat in anticipation of the door being kicked open for Rat PT. So every morning at five-thirty, Jack's brain ordered a shot of adrenaline.

He slipped downstairs and out of the front door quietly enough not to wake anyone. It was before Mrs. McClain was up for her morning routine, and it was still dark out.

The run was uneventful, painful as usual. The air was colder that morning, and Jack felt the sting on his face again, but worse. It had started to snow, though the flakes were tiny. Windswept almost sideways, they swirled around the black iron street lamps like swarms of crystalline gnats.

Jack felt his feet beginning to slip with each step, so he cut across a street to shorten his run. By the time he arrived at the front gate of the McClain home, the snow was thick with larger flakes and had already begun to coat everything. He opened the rod iron gate, being careful to close it behind himself, and then turned to walk up the long, straight cobblestone walkway.

When he made it to the front steps, Anna opened the front door and stepped out onto the porch. She had a thick knit ski cap pulled over her ears and grey sweats with the Hollins school name and logo across the chest. She did not have any gloves on, but almost immediately tucked her hands under each opposing armpit.

"I see you had the same idea I had," she said as she shivered briefly.

"I had no idea you were a runner," said Jack.

"*Were* is past tense. I *am* a runner," she answered.

"Oh, I'm sorry," Jack replied, "I had no idea you *am* a runner." He flashed a grin. She laughed.

"Truth be known, Jack Hartman, I run three or four times a week, but never this early. I don't see how you guys do it. You must hate sleep or something."

"Well, truth be known, Anna McClain, I don't hate sleep, but it sure doesn't care much for me."

"Mom said you liked getting up early to run," Anna said. "I figured I'd come out and give you some company."

"My guess is your Mom giving you a heads-up was more a warning than an invitation."

"Never mind them."

"I've already run, but I'll go with you if you'd like," Jack said.

"Looks like I timed that perfectly. Let's just walk," she said.

They walked down the steps and along the brick front walkway. Neither of them said a word. Jack opened the gate and ostentatiously gestured for Anna to pass through. He followed, and they began to walk along the sidewalk at the edge of the street.

Jack's heartbeat had slowed since finishing his run. He noticed his breathing wasn't as labored, but he had started sweating considerably and the wetness soaking his back and chest chilled against his skin. He could feel his heart beating stronger, different from exercise, more in the head than his chest. Anna always did that to him.

"So," Jack broke the silence, "are you going to graduate school after all of this?"

"I doubt it," Anna replied coyly. "I guess I'll see how it all pans out. I'm only a sophomore now, anyway, plenty of time."

"I'm going into the army when I graduate. I don't know what I want to do yet, probably an infantry officer."

"Do you have to?" she asked.

"I don't have to do anything, I suppose. Why?" he asked her.

"I'm so scared of a war breaking out and you and Teddy being right in the middle of it," she said.

"What? Don't tell me you think the Russians are going to cross the border in Europe and plunge us into World War Three."

"Yes. That's exactly what's going to happen, and you know it," Anna answered.

"I doubt it," Jack replied. "I think that the day of the big war is over. It's just so stupid when one sniper can tie a whole company up. Like Viet Nam."

"I don't care if you're both snipers in a little war or generals in a big one. I still like both of you better alive. Besides, the most horrible thing I can think of is being killed by a bullet. I'd rather have heart disease or cancer."

"I doubt any of those are any better that the others," Jack said. "If I died in a war, at least I think I'm doing something for some good. I don't want to live a mediocre life because I'm scared to put it all on the line."

Jack felt a passion stirring inside of him. It was starting as a feeling in his gut, and was working its way up. There was always something about talking manhood to Anna that stirred him.

I love this girl. I love this girl. I love this girl.

It flowed through his mind with every heartbeat. This cadence that had begun weeks before, echoed inside of him like a military snare in the barracks.

"Ah, such a southern gentleman – all full of courage and honor and male bravado," she said, looking straight ahead, but smirking.

"I *am* a Virginian," Jack said as he took off his gloves and handed them to her.

She took them, smiled at him, and began putting them on her hands.

"Yes, yes you *am*."

CHAPTER TEN

BREAKING OUT

"Guys, there's something going on out on the stoop," Ted whispered.

Jack pulled out his watch and pressed the backlight.

Zero four-thirty hours. Great. What can this be?

They listened for a few seconds.

"Drum out?" Darryl asked sleepily.

"Don't think so, no drums," said Jack. "I think we're about to get our doors kicked in."

"You've got to be kidding me," said Darryl.

Within a minute, they heard the telltale *clink* of the PA followed by the greeting, "Good morning, Rats!"

Surprisingly to Jack, a first classman walked in, flipped on the lights, and said firmly without yelling, "Get your PT gear on, and get out on the stoop. Winter PT gear."

Like clockwork, everyone in the room dressed in less than a minute and piled out of the room and onto the stoop. Even though they were in the PT sweats, Jack shivered in the brisk, moist March morning air as he strained facing the courtyard against the railing.

It was still dark out, with a hint of illumination spilling out of Jackson Arch. Other rooms were operating at similar efficiency, as the stoop railing filled up quickly and they were sent scurrying along the Ratline down to a likely workout somewhere. The first class seemed very subdued, and Jack noticed they were all dressed in grey blouse.

As they exited the arch they were turned left, but instead of the usual trip down the parapet steps they found themselves straining in the pews of J.M. Hall. The lights were very low making the mural of the New Market charge look very ominous. Phantasmal figures of cadets past moved along spirit ranks, shouting their rebel war cries.

Suddenly, the front doors swung open behind them, and once again, they heard the cadenced sound of unified heels on the hollow wooden floor. The echoes of the march sent chills down Jack's spine. As they approached the stage, he could see the group included all of the first class officers, the RDC and the regimental commander, executive officer and S3. They sat with solemn faces in a semicircle behind the podium, where the first class president had posted himself.

"Rats," he started, pausing as he looked around the sanctuary, "when you entered VMI seven months ago, I spoke to you on your first night, and I told you your Ratline would be hard, and I believe we have delivered on that promise."

Yeah, you delivered. I'm still here, though.

"Your RDC president, Mr. Thompson, told you one of the Rats to your right or left would most likely be gone before this Ratline was over. We matriculated four hundred and seventy-two of you and only three hundred and seven remain. More than a third are gone. Delivered. I told you this Ratline would last a long, long time, and the seasons would change again and again and you would still be Rats. Already the spring is on us, and look at you—still Rats. Signed, sealed, and delivered."

"What qualifies you to be a VMI class? Not time or effort, but unity."

Jack had already tired of back mouthing Mr. Warner. His mind was drifting. He sensed the unity and love for his Brother Rats long before Warner and his pompous speeches would ever confirm them.

"Now it's time to test you. Morning, noon, and night you will endure the toughest sweat parties we can give to you. Every moment of your existence here will intensify as never before. Some of you will quit this week because you will lose hope. It won't be because your Brother Rats are not supporting you and helping you. You have begun to feel a spirit of unity, and as a group you are evolving into something better than a self-serving mass of individuals."

There it is. Yes, yes.

Jack felt a warm rush of pride and satisfaction.

"On your feet!" He shouted.

The entire group of 306 Rats jumped to attention in a single thud.

The first classmen marched out the same way they came in. When the doors closed, the Rats stood awkwardly at attention for a moment. A first classman posted at the back of the sanctuary shouted for the Rats to fall out and return to their rooms.

Back in their room, Daryl was the first to talk.

"We could actually be real humans in a week or so. Well, as real of a human as a VMI cadet can actually be."

"Leave it to you," Ski said, "to always have the positive spin."

"Come to think of it, the way I see it, we just got ourselves a freebee," Darryl replied.

"Oh Lord," Ted said, "How's that, D?"

"Almost time for BRC. No workout this morning narrows it down to only fourteen more opportunities."

Darryl smiled big, raised his eyebrows, nodded his head and winked. The others laughed. Inside, though, Jack was nervous. They may have gotten the morning off, but dinner was coming quickly, and Phelps was still out there.

———

By Friday afternoon, Jack, Darryl, Ted, and Ski had reached a point of hopeless exhaustion. Mr. Warner had been on the money in his assessment of the intensity of everything Rat. It seemed there was no place to hide from the constant bombardment and harassment.

Every morning had started with the doors being kicked in just like they were the first week, and from that point it never let up. After DRC, the Rats were marched up to a sweat party in the courtyard. Monday and Tuesday, the sweat party was administered by the third class, while Wednesday's and Thursday's were hosted by the second class. Each night the first class threw a sweat party on the fourth stoop at 2230.

In between, the Rats were harassed AD nauseam. There was a feeling among all of the Rats this was it, and if they could just hang on, they would become a class, and be done with this misery.

Tuesday and Thursday afternoons were the usual days for Rat training, and of course, they were equally diabolical. Tuesday's started with a three-mile rifle run, and finished with something called a sandbag challenge that included a very long, steep hill and about a thousand thirty-pound sandbags. They had to move the huge pile of sandbags, one at a time per man, up the hill to a point on top as a group.

After a little organization, they set up a couple chains, with a few guys at the bottom feeding them both, and a few at top stacking. When they finished, First Classmen were screaming about something up top, so the entire Rat mass rushed up the hill to find the guys stacking at the top had arranged the sandbags into a giant "84."

They ended up doing push-ups and mountain climbers on the side of the hill for quite some time before being run back up to the barracks. The first classmen were trying to act mad but Jack and others could hear them joking about how "squared away" it was.

Thursday afternoon wasn't any better with each squad carrying a sixteen foot long, twelve inch diameter pole for a short mile and a half squad run, then completing the obstacle course as a unit.

So by Friday afternoon, Jack was content to curl up near the radiator in the back of the room on the floor. His arms were shaking as a result of the muscular exhaustion. His hands had the start of some pretty nasty and painful blisters. Ted was also in as bad of shape, and Darryl sat in his chair trying to wrap his twisted ankle. Ski hadn't made it back to the room as his boxing class was at 1400 on Fridays.

"Man, this is completely psycho," said Darryl, admiring the swelling on his ankle.

"If I could just get an hour of sleep, I think I could recoup—maybe get the pain back to a reasonable level," Jack said.

"That ankle looks bad, dude. You gonna be able to make it?" Ted asked Darryl.

"Do I look like some kind of gim rider?" asked Darryl, using the slang word for the injured or sick cadets that weren't required to stand formation or walk the Ratline. "The only way you'd catch me on the gim, is cold, stiff, and feet first."

Jack started singing a jodie to the tune of an old Doors song. The other two joined in.

> Riders on the gim,
> Riders on the gim,
> They are not friends of mine
> 'cause they never walk the line,
> Riders on the gim…

They laughed, making up other punch lines till it was time to get ready for SRC. Ski still hadn't made it back.

—◦◦◦—

"Where is your roommate, Rat Hartman?" Corporal Johnson yelled the question from his position at the end of the squad.

"I don't know, sir. He never came back from Rat boxing this afternoon."

"How about you, McClain, do you know?"

"No, sir," replied Ted.

"I suppose you don't have a clue either, Rat Burkes."

"No, sir," answered Darryl.

After the evening cannon and retreat, they marched down to the mess hall. Jack was considerably worried about Ski, but knew that they would try to track him down after SRC. A second class private gave thanks over the mess hall PA in the usual manner and they were seated.

"Brother Rats, I messed up! Brother Rats we might not break out because of me!" It was Ski, running in place near the RDC table, shouting at the top of his lungs.

"Look up there, Rats!" Corporal Johnson commanded.

They all snapped their heads around to see Ski getting worked out.

"I get all the good Rats! Seems like every time someone's up at the RDC table, it's one of mine," Corporal Johnson shouted proudly above the mess hall din.

Ski remained at the RDC table for the rest of the meal. When Echo Company marched back up to barracks, Ski joined them in formation.

"I guess you really screwed up, Kolwinski," Master Sergeant Hall yelled as they were still marching. "What exactly did you do, Rat?"

"I beat up a first classman!" Ski yelled loud enough that adjacent units could hear him.

"Geez, you *are* an idiot!" Corporal Johnson yelled.

They continued to march as one of the line sergeants called out cadence.

"The difference between you and Rat Hartman," Sergeant Hall said, "is Hartman was smart enough to smack a third around and you're such an idiot you took on the first class. You know, those guys in charge of letting you out of the *Ratline*."

"Yes, sir, I am fully aware of that. But this first classman deserved to get his butt kicked!"

Rats throughout the formation burst with laughter. This, of course, infuriated the corporals and sergeants who were marching them up.

"Guess what, idiot? When we get up top, we're gonna wear you out. You'll wish you had shut up when you were ahead," Sergeant Hall yelled.

As soon as Echo Company was back up on the bricks and halted, several corporals and sergeants converged on Ski and began screaming at him.

"Wooooh! Hoooooh!" Ski let out a primal scream that was part rebel yell and part lower primate.

"I think our roommate has finally lost it," Jack whispered over to Darryl and Ted as the staff was ripping into Ski and he dropped to do push-ups.

Jack thought about the times he had been singled out, and how his roommates and all of his Brother Rats had joined him. He was overwhelmed by a sense of brotherhood. Deep inside, he sensed Ski had not done anything wrong, because he knew him well.

"It doesn't matter how crazy he is, I'm with him all the way," Jack said.

Jack dropped down and started cranking out push-ups in unison with Ski, as did Ted and then Darryl. The whole company followed suit, and though the corporals had Ski off to the side, every time a command to do one exercise or another was given, they all executed it together. Other companies who were released from their formations ran over to Echo Company and joined in.

"They sure are gonna catch it at breakout tomorrow!" One RDC members said just loud enough for Jack to hear.

"Oh yeah," replied Gonzales, Ski's dyke. "Good job, Rats!"

———

"What was that all about?" Ted asked Ski as soon as they cleared the door of their room.

"I was finishing up Rat boxing this afternoon and, well, you know my dyke, John Gonzales, right?" Ski asked.

"Yeah," answered Jack.

"He comes down into the gym and says he's gonna try me out for the boxing team. Then he goes on to spar with me in the ring. I don't know if you guys know this or not, but John's on the boxing team and he went all the way to nationals this year. He lost to a guy from air force, but John's one heck of a boxer."

Ski got into a boxing stance and began to act out his narration.

"Anyway," said Ski, "we're movin' around and I'm scared 'cause I know John could really hurt me, and he tags me a few times with his jab. That stung a little but I didn't go crazy or anything. All of the sudden he came in square to me and I saw it and gave him a one-two. Caught him hard on the bottom of his chin. I caught him so hard with it I saw his head whip down, then he crumpled into a pile against the ropes. Coach Kennedy had to break out the smelling salts on him!"

"Okay, so that was the part about you whipping a first, but what about the craziness? You were scoring major points with the Echo Rat staff," said Jack, leaning back in his desk chair.

"John was so proud of me, he had me form up with the RDC staff for SRC and march with them to the mess hall. All that screaming and working out there was them having a little fun at my expense. They even told me what to do when we were marching back up. I was so glad that we have such a nosey staff, 'cause if they didn't ask, I was going to have to act all kinds of crazy and just start blurting it out. And, yes, they told me to yell *wooh hooh*."

"Suddenly, everything in the world makes perfect sense," said Darryl as he plopped down on his rack.

"Really? Everything?" Ski asked.

"No, not really," said Darryl.

"Hey, did you guys see the fire trucks hosing down the trench on the hill above the rifle range?" Ted asked.

"Yeah, that's where we'll be breaking out," said Jack.

"Are we sure this time?" asked Darryl.

"Oh yeah," Jack answered, "I got to overhear a conversation between Jim and some other regimental staff guys. Instead of the old way of breaking out through the classes on each stoop up the stairwell, We'll go through 'em back there. Thirds have the mud cliff to the trench and Seconds are in the trench."

"And John just flat out told me the whole schedule," Ski added. "Doors kicked in at 0530, rifle run, BRC, classes, and DRC. Then we'll get a briefing in J.M. Hall and it all starts–Big sweat party in the courtyard hosted by the Firsts. Then it's to the rifle range where we'll break out up the mud wall through the Thirds and into the trench through the Seconds."

"Hmmph," said Darryl, "our last night as Rats."

Exhaustion beyond comprehension, Jack had nothing left. His arms felt like bags of liquid hanging off his throbbing shoulders. He tried to summon one last squirt of adrenaline, with the hope that he could muster enough power to crawl, if movement was necessary. When the platoon halted, they were immediately given the left face command, which they executed sloppily.

A sudden roar of men's savage voices rose from the top of a thirty foot high clay wash out that stood about fifty feet in front of them across what was normally used for the rifle range. The adrenaline squirted into Jack's bloodstream. As the roar of war cries rose to a fevered pitch, so did the fear brewing in the guts of the small gaggle of Rats.

It looked like an army of nearly a thousand men, faces painted with war paint, some half black and half white, others striped in red and black, while still others angled with camouflage. They were screaming frantically, with crazed expressions and wild eyes.

The eyes made Jack's heart sink.

As they stood there, taunted by the screams of the upperclassmen, Jack was hit by the pungent odor of rotten food that had been stored up by upperclassmen for weeks prior. It was the hideous type that summoned gags from all of them, and Jack could only assume that the warriors above had worked themselves into such frenzy, they were immune to it.

"On my command," shouted the first classman in charge of the group, "you will assault the bluff!"

The first stood there for a moment, basking in the strong sense of fear and anxiety of the Rats around him, as if preparing to give the fateful command for the legendary charge of the Light Brigade.

Then, in a rather melodramatic, almost operatic voice, he belted out, "Ready...attack!"

And they did. The fifty of them ran to the bluff with reckless abandon, the care and fear left in a spiritual pile of ash behind them, running up the slippery red clay, digging their fingers into the wall in an effort to get as high as possible before grinding to a halt. They were impervious to the barrage of rotten garbage that rained down on them. Hands full of potato chunks in a slurry of milk and fish that had decayed for weeks in containers hidden behind the barracks were slung at the attacking pack of Rats at high velocity.

Jack and the rest of the platoon had begun using the backs of their Brother Rats to scale the last ten feet of the wall that had become completely vertical, but just as one would reach the top, a third would push him back, and he would tumble to the bottom, taking several of his comrades along for the ride. Occasionally, a third would sacrifice himself and roll down as a human bowling ball into the oncoming mass, completely destroying any gains they had made.

Finally, Jack had made it to the top and was only a couple feet from the lip of the wall, when he looked up to see Phelps, covered in war paint, squatting down looking over the edge.

"C'mon up Hartman. You won't make it through the third class. You're gonna die for sure."

He held out his hand to grab Jack.

Through eyes plastered with rotten food, Jack looked down to see who was supporting his right foot. It was Ski, who was also looking up, and judging from his expression had heard him through the din, too. He grimaced and looked directly at Jack.

"Get him," he said, and Jack could feel him push harder on his foot.

With every bit of energy he could summon from a place he did not know he had, Jack surged upward with a guttural scream, and launched himself to the ledge with the help of a powerful arm push from Ski. But instead of grabbing the ledge with both hands, he grabbed only with his right, allowing him to push himself even higher. Slinging his left arm from behind himself, he latched onto Phelps's collar, completely taking him by surprise.

Phelps grabbed Jack's arm.

"Oh no you don't, idiot!" Phelps yelled.

They grappled there on the edge, grunting, Jack burning with anger and vengeance.

"You won't stop me today!" Jack yelled.

"We'll see you…"

"Use your other hand. I've got your feet," Ski yelled up to Jack. Jack went all in.

He surged upward one more time and punched Phelps between the legs as hard as he could drive his fist. Jack was certain those in the packed rabble saw him strike Phelps. He didn't care.

For a split second, Jack felt the euphoria that a hitter feels when he hits the sweet spot of the ball, low and driving up, and on that perfect connection, feels the homer about to happen— and the homer was about to happen. With not much more than a quick yank, Phelps launched clear over the top of the pile and was airborne beyond the face of the bluff.

Phelps screamed an expletive when he realized he'd lost his balance and was headed for a long fall over the edge.

Jack did not look back; he was sure whatever happened was not good. He slid back down for a second, but still had his right hand over the top edge, and used it to get a grip and pull himself up. He quickly reached back and grabbed Ski's extended arm, and as he was being pulled into the fray, he pulled Ski with him.

The two of them jammed forward on all fours in the sloppy mud and mire until the press of the warriors around and above them became too much to bear, and they collapsed face down. They were pulled up over and over again while rotten muck was violently jammed into their faces and clothes. Each time they were raised they would struggle to move a few feet forward.

Can't see. Keep breathing. Keep pushing.

Finally, Ski moved alongside Jack, and barely being able to recognize each other, they linked arms and pushed through, digging their feet in behind them and pile driving toward the pit. They had made the twenty-five yard push through the throng of thirds and could see the entrance to the pit a few feet ahead.

Jack gasped for air as his nostrils were becoming packed with the rotten muck and his mouth was half full of mud. Neither could see much of anything anymore from the mud caked on their faces, and suddenly Jack felt himself being picked up by the back of his shirt and trousers. He was slung into the pit, which was packed shoulder to shoulder with seconds. He was spent, but hoping for some bit of energy to surface from somewhere.

Fighting was utterly futile, and he was finally numb to pain. Back and forth, he was slammed against each wall and twice trampled under the waist deep muddy soup that filled the entire pit. Scratched, bleeding, and still gasping for air he finally began to show some fight, as his fear instinct kicked in and squeezed out the last few drops of adrenaline that his body could manufacture.

Jack fought off two second classmen and pushed toward the berm along the back wall of the pit. He saw an unrecognizable Brother Rat struggling to get up the muddy wall out of the pit with a Second hanging onto him, pulling him back down, so he jumped on the second, prying his hand off. They both fell back down in the pit, neck deep, now, in the muddy water. The second laughed.

"Hey, it's my Ring Figure dyke!" It was the second Jack served as a Rat-dyke during Ring Figure week. "That's what I call

Brother Rat spirit. Now get your rear up over the top and be a free man!" he yelled as he pushed Jack with the help of another second onto the berm.

Jack low-crawled up and over the edge, and then rolled down the back side. He lay there, sprawled out facing upward. He could finally feel the sun on his face. He realized that he had lost complete control of his emotions as mucus and blood ran from his nose. He heaved a deep broken sigh.

"Do not open your eyes, Cadet Hartman. Gosh, I almost didn't recognize you."

It was Jim Donahue, his dyke.

Jim began squirting a water bottle over his face and wiping it off with a rag until Jack could see again.

"Now, blow some of that garbage out of your nose, spit that blood, out and go see the guys with the spray hose up there." He pointed Jack up the hill to a spot where a number of Brother Rats were being hosed off.

Jack limped up the hill at a slow jog and immediately got in line to be washed. One of his Brother Rats hugged him, unrecognizable, covered in muck.

Within a minute Jack had been blasted nearly clean and had drunk a half canteen of water. He was still digging garbage out of his ears, and blowing it out of his nose, and his lip was bleeding pretty badly. He just spit the blood out and got in the formation of Brother Rats getting ready to lead themselves back to the parade ground.

When Ski made it up, Jack hugged him tightly, like two fighters at the end of a long bout. They were beaten and bruised and bleeding. Strangely, they had never been happier.

They were finally free.

———

They stood, filthy and exhausted, arms around shoulders supporting each other as they filled the courtyard of Old Barracks to give the traditional "Old Yells," finishing with an Old Yell for the Class of '84. They were finally able to say the number 84 in the barracks.

"Rah Virginia Mil…Rah, rah, rah…Rah, rah, VMI, '84, '84, '84!"

It took two hours to get in and out of the showers. It was a normal shower with no one yelling at them, and their heads were still packed with mud and garbage. The foul smell was impossible to clean off, but no one seemed to mind as the elation overrode their senses.

SRC had been moved to nineteen-hundred hours, and the fourth class formed on the bricks one more time as a separate unit. They were treated, however, like upperclassmen and finally could walk into the mess hall to their tables.

With the lights down and candles at each table, brief congratulatory speeches were given by the First Class President, the Commandant and the Superintendant. They were victors in a struggle that had taxed them intensely for six months, and the whole group could sense the power of their brotherhood. Jack made eye contact with each of his roommates.

He relished the feeling of eating a meal slowly and in a relaxed atmosphere. Regardless of the smell of rot still imbedded in his nose, he enjoyed the flavor of Crozet Hall food as a free man. When they finished, Jack joined with his roommates, and together the four of them walked back to their room.

"This weekend is going to be the best," Darryl said.

"Sounds like trouble," Ted mumbled.

"I'm game for a little trouble," said Jack.

"Jack, hold up!" someone shouted from behind them.

It was Jim Donahue. They all stopped as he caught up with them.

"Jack, just to let you know, your buddy, Phelps was the only casualty of the whole breakout."

Oh no, someone saw what I did.

"Apparently, he fell off the bluff and busted his collar bone pretty bad," Jim said. "Stupid idiot got too close to the edge for his own good. Well, just thought that if breaking out of the Ratline was good, that would really make your day!"

"Good thing it didn't kill him," Jack said.

"Oh yeah, everyone says he did a swan dive like one of those cliff divers, only there was no water to land in, of course. Hit head first. Crack! What a moron."

"Thanks for letting us know. I suppose next he'll try to blame me."

"No doubt. Well, I'll see ya'll later. Congrats, fourth classmen."

Jim walked away, but they all stood there, smiling.

"Poor guy, footing must've been terrible up on the edge of that bluff," Ski said.

CHAPTER ELEVEN

Sandfiddler Road

Ted invited Jack to spend the summer working with him at a construction site in Virginia Beach, a job he had gotten through one of his dad's Brother Rats. Jack agreed–he needed work, and Ted was the closest thing to family he had. The morning they left the Institute, they stopped by Jack's farm so he could get the rest of his belongings.

They wandered down to the river. Jack was melancholy, thinking about his childhood—those good days when he camped along on the bank, fishing and doing whatever his mind could conjure up to do.

"This ain't too bad," Ted said sitting on a large rock at the edge of the James River.

"I used to love it here. As long as I could stay away from the old man, it wasn't too bad," Jack answered as he skipped a couple rocks across the familiar waters.

"You've told me about some of the situations, you know, when he beat you up pretty bad. Was it like that all the time?" Ted asked.

"Started as far back as I can remember. It got worse as time went on. I told you about some things, but I've never told anyone about the worst stuff."

"Is it hard to talk about?"

"Oh, I don't know," Jack answered. "I get sick sometimes when I think about it, so I try not to. I'd like to think I could tell you more than most people. You're the first good friend I've had since I was a kid, really the only good friend I've had since I was about eight or nine."

"I'd have never even thought that about you. You're a stand-up guy. Best I can tell, you make friends pretty easily," said Ted.

"VMI forced me—the friendship microwave, I guess. You put a bunch of guys inside, turn the timer and wham! You've got three hundred guys that think they're brothers."

"You're right about that," Ted said.

"I mean Darryl and Ski have been pretty good friends," Jack continued, "but you're different. Somehow, we think a lot alike. Plus you and Anna come as a package deal right now so I guess I'm stuck with you."

"I guess we share something in our upbringing," Ted said.

"Oh yeah? What's that?"

"Didn't really know our real parents."

"What do you mean by that. Your folks are awesome."

"I was adopted. Yeah, my folks are great, and I have no desire to track down my birth parents, but maybe we make a connection because of that."

"Maybe," Jack said.

Ted reclined on the rock facing the afternoon sun. Jack walked about fifteen feet along the river bank, wishing he had the old boat.

"That rock you're on, it's always been an important place to me. I used to hide below the overhang when I had to escape from my dad. It was my hiding place and my fortress, and the place I'd go to think," Jack said.

"How often did you have to hide out here?"

"Oh, I don't know. Spent a lot of time here, though. A lot of nights waiting for the old man to pass out," answered Jack.

"I can't imagine that," said Ted.

"It wasn't quite as bad at first, but the older I got; the worse he got with the drinking. He was unpredictable."

Jack slowly paced back and forth along the river bank. He was nervous. He had never told anyone what he was telling Ted. He was too ashamed of his past to let anyone in on it.

"When I was twelve," Jack continued, "I forgot to shut down the power take-off on the tractor. I drove the tractor across the field behind us into the barn. My old man came runnin' in behind me drunk and mad. He said I almost burned up the hydraulics. He called me a stupid SOB over and over till he worked himself into a rage. Then he cornered me and beat me senseless there in the barn with a hoe handle. He'd have killed me but he finally broke it in half across my back."

"You were only twelve."

"He didn't care about that. I kinda staggered down here to the rock. He came and found me about an hour later. Carried me back in his arms cryin' the whole way back to the house, tellin' me he was sorry. It's weird, but I felt bad for him. I laid up in the house for two weeks before I could even get out of bed. He cared for me like a mom nursin' a sick child, but that didn't last long."

Jack's voice was becoming weak and shaky.

"We don't have to talk about this anymore if you don't want to," Ted said.

"No, I've gotta get this out of me, I've gotta tell someone. I used to just be embarrassed by it. Guess I just wanted to be normal, to have a normal family. There were times when I was little that I can remember that I wasn't afraid of him. I remember him pickin' me up and carryin' me around. He would even give me hugs, and I can still smell his after shave and feel his whiskers on my face," Jack said, his voice breaking.

He turned away from Ted to hide tears that welled up suddenly. He sniffed once and wiped his nose on his sleeve.

"Let's go back up to the house and get your stuff packed up," Ted said.

Jack ignored Ted's request. He went on.

"That night, the night my dad died, it was raining hard. Some lightning and thunder, and real windy. It had been raining for a couple days. The ground was soaked, and everything was filling up the river. It had started flooding all of the farms along her banks, had made it right up to our barn, even into the barn a little.

I had done something' to set my dad off that night and he took a swing at me with his belt, but I wasn't havin' any of it, so I took off. I waded through waist-deep water out here to the rock, but he came lookin' for me. I hung under the rock a little in the current when he came out with a flashlight.

It was pitch black and the rain made it impossible to hear much. Somehow in all of that, he decided to move the tractor. Guess he was afraid that the barn might get flooded too deep."

Jack looked out over the river and threw a rock into the middle.

"They say he ran the tractor into the door frame, and it was enough to stop it, but bein' in first gear it had the power to keep the wheel drivin' in the mud. No one knows how it happened, but he must've got his leg caught and it pulled him right under the tractor tire. Ripped him apart."

"I'm sorry, Jack," said Ted.

"The worst thing is I could hear him through the rain screamin'. I'd climbed up on top of that rock to get out of the water. I didn't know. I thought he was screamin' at me 'cause he was still mad at me. He was callin' me to come help him, to come save him, I suppose."

Jack was stoic, but tears had crested over the bottoms of his eyelids as he struggled to get the last sentence out. He was not hiding it anymore.

They sat there for a few minutes, and then walked back up toward the house. Neither needed to say anything. Jack had spilled his guts down on the river bank, and it was time to move on.

As they walked back up past the dilapidated old barn across the field, kicking through the waist-high brush toward the house, Ted stopped. He turned and looked back at the barn.

"Would you have?" Ted asked.

"Would I have what?"

"Saved him," Ted replied.

Jack thought for a few seconds as a breeze stirred the seed heads in the overgrown fescue and brush around them.

"Yeah," he replied, "even if he killed me."

———

The boys left Jack's place the next morning and headed to Richmond, spent the night, and then left for Virginia Beach. The McClain's arranged for Anna to stay with some friends on Sandfiddler Road during her usual visits to the beach, so the boys had the place to themselves.

The house was an aged, low-key bungalow with white stucco walls that made it seem like something more west coast than Virginia Beach. Two beige brick columns marked the opening of the matching brick drive, lined with an abundance of Southern Virginia flora most notably accented with several twelve foot Norfolk Pines. A generous back deck pressed into the sea grass with a narrow, fifty-foot boardwalk that connected the deck to the sand and tide.

Even in its modesty, it overwhelmed Jack.

Two weeks had passed before Anna made her first visit of the summer. When she arrived that afternoon, both of the boys had just gotten in from the job site. Ted was taking a shower while Jack was standing on the back deck, drinking some water and watching the surf break.

There were still salt rings on his shirt where sweat saturation terminated and his arms had dirt streaks on them where his sweat had dripped down them as they worked in the dust. Jack did not hear Anna standing in the sliding glass back door until she spoke.

"Hey guy, looks like you had a fun day at work."

Jack's body surged with endorphins when he heard Anna's voice. He tried to be as cool as he could, so he calmly turned around and gave her a lopsided smile.

"It was good. We got a lot done."

Love her. Yes, I do. I do.

"Well that's wonderful. And what about your weeks without me?" she asked.

"Hmmm. It was horrific. I hope it never happens again," he replied, grinning widely this time.

"I guess that remains to be seen. I don't think they allow women at the 'I,' however. So it seems that you fellas will be on your own."

"Your dad knows the superintendent, maybe an exception?"

"Doubtful, but well worth the effort. I'll get right on it as soon as we have supper. I picked up a few things on the way in. Send Teddy in to help me. You go get a shower." She pinched her nose and giggled and then turned back in toward the kitchen.

Jack finished his water and then headed in to his room. On the way, he ran into Ted in his shorts and white t-shirt.

"Anna requests your assistance in the kitchen."

"She's here? How long has she been here?" Ted was walking backwards as Jack had just passed him.

"Just got in. Seems a little giddy," Jack said over his shoulder.

"Yeah, I'll bet she does. Y'know, *you're* here," Ted said grinning and shaking his head in mock disapproval. He turned around and walked toward the kitchen.

Jack went to his room and quickly showered. It was outside of his normal routine, but he shaved anyway. He wanted to impress Anna. He wanted Anna to look at him. Sometimes she would look straight into his eyes. He could see at those times that there was admiration, but he was not sure about desire. He wanted her desire.

His hair had grown out a little since the summer had begun, so he took the time to brush it, though it was still pretty short and wanted to stick up in the back.

Forget it.

He grabbed an old ball cap that he liked to wear and headed back to the kitchen where he saw Anna was cooking some spaghetti in a large pot on the stove. Ground beef sizzled in a pan next to it. Jack could smell onions and oregano. Ted had sliced some bread, and was buttering the individual slices and arranging them on a cookie sheet to put in the oven.

"There's some sweet tea on the counter if you're thirsty," Anna said.

"Yeah, and if I were you, I'd grab a glass and get out of the kitchen as quickly as possible or you will be put to work," said Ted.

"I don't mind," replied Jack.

"You are a guest, Mr. Hartman," Anna said, "and I will not have you working in this kitchen." She paused and then she said, "Except when it comes time to do the dishes."

Ted laughed.

"That's fine. I need to do my part," answered Jack.

Anna turned and smiled. She had her left hand cupped under the spoon she had been using to stir the sauce. She tasted the end of the spoon and then walked over to Jack.

"Try it," she commanded.

Jack leaned over and tasted the sauce on the spoon. He straightened up and pursed his lips, looking at the wall across the room like a critic formulating an opinion.

"It's not from a jar," was all he could come up with.

Ted slid the bread in the oven.

"No, no it's not," she said giggling.

She tapped him playfully on the nose with the spoon, leaving a good amount of sauce behind. Jack turned and grabbed a dry towel hanging on the edge of the sink behind him, and wiped the sauce off his nose.

"Hey, it smells great anyway," Jack said.

"Thanks for nothin'," she replied with a smirk. "Everything will be ready in about fifteen minutes. I'll call you guys."

The boys went out back and Ted cleaned off the table and chairs on the deck. It was dusk, and the cool evening air was tempting. Ted went in and found a blue table cloth and four thick candles. They set up the table and candles as Anna prepared their plates in the kitchen.

The three of them brought everything out and they sat at the table on the deck as they ate supper. The sun had long since retreated to the west, but no one considered turning on a deck light. As the sky grew darker, an occasional ship marked the horizon with her running lights, and the four candles lit the faces of the three in a soft orange glow. Further north, Virginia Beach blazed with all of her nightlife, pressing deep into the evening sky.

"There's a thing that Anna and I always do when we're here at the beach house," Ted said to Jack as they were finishing and sitting back in their chairs.

"Oh yeah? What might that be?" Jack asked.

"The beach?" Anna asked Ted.

She looked at him with a puzzled look, hushingly, as if he was about to reveal something deeply secret.

"Yeah," Ted answered, shrugging off her concern. "Every time we've come out here for about the last eight years, we go out to a place on the beach just over there, past where the grass breaks, about half way to the water." He gestured almost straight to the beach, but just slightly south.

"We'd just sit out there for hours when it got dark, and talk about everything," Anna said.

"Mostly dreams, you know, what we wanted to do with our lives," Ted added.

"I think those were the best times. I think they were what made us so close," said Anna.

"If you guys want to go sit on the beach, don't let me hold you back," Jack said.

"Oh no, since we're so liberally giving away our secrets tonight, you come with us," Anna replied. "It's nice out there this time of night."

"Yeah, Jack. You're not an outsider here. I think we can include you in our little sybling tradition," Ted said.

"But first, let's clean up," Anna said. "I'll take care of the dishes. I'm sure I'm faster than both of you put together."

They put away the dishes and Anna loaded the dishwasher. Ted snuffed the candles and put them away, while Jack cleaned the table cloth and folded it.

Before long, they were crossing the deck walk through the tall sea grass to the beach. Ted carried an old lantern he had lit, and the flicker of yellow flame sent shadows of their legs into the grass.

As they walked down the wooden stair steps to the sand, the lights of Sandfiddler Road faded. The noise from passing cars and a distant deck party were soon drowned out by the rhythm of the surf.

They walked only about thirty yards down the beach and Ted stopped and plopped himself down in a shallow hollow between the dunes.

"This is it," Anna said as she began to sit.

"Oh it's a good one tonight. The stars are perfect," Ted said as he lay back.

The sun's radiant heat that had penetrated the beach throughout the day was releasing from the sand, and as Jack sat down beside Anna, he could feel the stark difference in the temperature. It was cool out when they stepped onto the beach, but a couple feet from the surface the air was comfortably warm. He lay back, his hands behind his head, fingers interlocked.

Warmed by the sand, he nestled down into it. He did not care that it stuck to his legs, slightly perspiring, or that it found its way inside the back of the collar of his tee shirt. Jack was comfortable with the earth. The warm sand felt every bit as good to him as the cold, loamy soil along the banks of the James.

"How are you with your constellations, Jack?" Anna asked, breaking the silence.

"I'm pretty sure I know which one of those lights up there is the moon."

"Alright, it's time for a lesson," she said.

"No, please, I'm escaping anything that even slightly resembles school," Jack replied.

"But you need to know your stars, Jack. It's how you find your way home," Anna said, turning on her side to face him.

"I'm not sure I have one anymore. If I do still, I don't think I'll ever want to go back," Jack said still looking straight up at the stars.

It was, to him, simply a factual statement. He had said it, though, teasingly, as a way to fend off Anna's attempt to mother him.

"You always allude to that. It's time to quit alluding and be truthful. This is the holy place where there is no allusion or illusion, where we are honest, where we reveal our hearts and secrets," she said, then rolled on her back again.

"Jack," Ted said, "you don't have to tell Anna anything you don't want to. I know a lot of that is still hard for you. You don't need to get into it tonight."

They lay silent for a few minutes, all looking up into the dark night sky with its specs of light, too tiny to do anything about the powerful black that surrounded them.

"I'll tell you."

"Only if you want to, Jack," Anna replied.

"I doubt that he wants to," Ted said.

"I suppose it's about time to let Anna know," Jack said.

"Was it bad? Your home, I mean," she asked.

"You already know that my mom left us right after I was born, and you know my dad died when I was fifteen."

"And I know the little bit you've told me about him, your dad, how he was an alcoholic and was hard on you," she replied.

"Well, Dad always had it out for me. He always thought it was my fault, what happened with Mom and all. I don't know, but I guess it made him feel better to thrash me pretty good if he lost his temper, especially when he was drunk. There were a lot of times when I was little that I should've gone to the hospital. I was only seven when he beat me with his fists. Up till then, I kinda blamed it on his belt, or the stick, or even myself."

"Yourself? You were a little boy. It wasn't your fault, Jack. It was *his* f-fault, not *your* fault," Anna said.

Jack could tell that she almost swore, though he knew she wasn't one accustomed to using foul language.

"I know that now, and when he beat me with his fists and kicked me, that's when I couldn't blame belts and sticks anymore. I guess even back then, as much as I wanted to make him proud, I was too afraid of him. I still blamed myself a lot. You know 'I shouldn't have done this or that' or 'He got drunk because I messed up.' But when I got into my teens I got pretty angry. I started to blame him."

Jack sensed the deep grief stirring inside him. It was both the anger and the sadness blended to make an ugly knot in his gut. It would happen every time he thought about his childhood and his father. It always stirred the beast, repeating the labels his father had spewed at him even when he wasn't intoxicated.

You're an idiot. You're worthless. You can't do anything right.

Over and over again the mantra repeated itself, bubbling up from somewhere in Jack's cerebral cortex.

"Was it always that way? Were there any good times?" Anna asked.

"I remember Dad pickin' me up in his arms when I was little and carryin' me," Jack answered. "That's it. It's a good memory. I must've been two or three, but I can still feel his whiskers and smell his Old Spice. He didn't drink as much then. I've probably blocked stuff out, but I think it started getting' bad when I was around six, best I can remember."

A blanket of sadness lay over Jack heavily. His bottom eyelids filled with tears.

"The weird thing is, I still loved him and I just wanted him to love me. I wanted so bad to hear him say 'I love you.' I wanted him to say he was proud of me."

"Were you afraid?" she asked, wiping her nose on her sleeve.

Jack heard the grief in her shaky voice.

"Yeah, I practically lived on the river. I'd hide from him for days at a time. I suppose it wasn't that bad. I learned to fend for myself pretty well."

"He almost killed Jack," Ted interjected. "Beat him close to death with a hoe handle once. Show her your back."

"No," answered Jack.

"I told you that you didn't have to tell her all of this. Now you're all-in. Now she needs to see it. If you're going to tell her what happened, she needs to know all of it, Jack." Ted grabbed the flickering lantern from the sand beside him, and set it in the sand behind Jack.

I'm ashamed. It's ugly.

Jack sat up, pulled his tee-shirt off, and then leaned forward, resting his forearms on his knees. Anna leaned back and looked. She said nothing, but reached behind him, lightly running her fingertips down his back, feeling the rough skin along the raised scars.

"I was older then, twelve."

"You were twelve, and your dad almost beat you to death? He did this then?" Anna.

Anna brought her hand back, and looked out forward again. She had tears running down her cheeks as she sat with her arms wrapped around her knees, staring out at the ocean.

"It was madness like that as I got older. All the time running and hiding. I learned how to be invisible, to blend in. It helped keep me out of trouble. I had gotten to a point where I feared everything and everyone," Jack said.

"Where were your friends, or teachers, or someone who could've done something. How could anyone let him get away with it?" Anna asked.

"It was always hard for me to have any friends. I was kinda weird, I guess, quiet and all. I kept to myself, got in a few fights. Some kids made fun of me, I'd get mad pretty quick, like my dad. I figured out after he died that I didn't want to be that way. That's when I quit all the cussing and stopped getting in fights. Ted and you, Anna, and our roommates at VMI are the first real friends I've had in a long time."

"Did he die from his drinking?" Anna asked.

"I suppose in a way he did," Jack answered. "He was killed by his tractor one night when he was drunk. He had run me off to hide in the river. It was storming out and the river was up. He couldn't find me 'cause I hid on the backside of my favorite rock, a big one that's about the size of a truck. He finally lost interest and went to get the tractor out of the barn. I stayed in the river all night, shivering cold though the water had gone back down. I found him in the barn, his body ground up by the tractor tire. It was pretty awful seeing him like that."

Anna was weeping with her face tucked into her knees. "I – I," was all that she could muster. She stood and walked toward the beach.

"Anna wait!" Jack said, sitting up.

"She's okay," Ted said. "Give her a minute. She goes nuts when she hears about kids being abused. Then again, who in their right mind doesn't? She's real sensitive to it, though. Anna loves kids."

They watched her walk into the surf, still weeping. She stood there, looking out into the darkness of the ocean, with the foam of broken waves washing up around her ankles and calves, and the wind blowing her hair to one side. Jack studied her, too far from the lantern to see clearly, her figure illuminated only by the dim starlight.

"Maybe I shouldn't have told her."

"No, you needed to tell her. She needed to know," said Ted, propped up on one arm.

"I just don't like to see her hurt like that," replied Jack.

Ted lay back down, looking up at the stars again. "It's supposed to be this way," Ted said.

"What way?" asked Jack, still watching Anna.

"It's weird, but I think God lets me see little glimpses of what he's doing," Ted said. "I mean, what if all of those things you went through and Anna's sensitivity for kids who are abused were supposed to come together in our secret star-gazing spot tonight? What if he intended for this to make her love you like never before? I know that's a lot of 'what ifs,' but it just seems like God's got something going on here."

"You think all of this is part of some divine plan?" asked Jack.

"It could be," Ted replied. "I just find it hard to imagine that everything is random. Sometimes it seems obvious that God is weaving something together so much greater than we could've come up with on our own. Don't you think it's at least possible, Jack?"

Jack thought about it for a moment.

"What about your folks? Does God's plan include bucking them?" asked Jack.

"I don't know. That part is weird. Everything isn't always so obvious. His plans always seem to leave us with some questions. Yeah, you've got an uphill battle with Dad and Mom."

"I suppose I think that every time we have a conversation like this it gets harder and harder not to believe that there is a God, and that he's somehow got his hand in what we're doing," said Jack.

Ted did not press the subject any further. Jack was marinating in his thoughts, still mesmerized by Anna.

"She's praying, you know," said Ted.

"Her feet must be freezing," replied Jack.

They both stood up and brushed the sand off themselves. Anna turned and joined them, and they walked quietly back to the house. Anna hugged each of the boys and said goodnight. They saw her out to her car and watched as she drove south on Sandfiddler Road and pulled into the Morgan's driveway twelve houses down.

"I've never seen her so affected by someone as she is with you," Ted said as they walked back in the house.

"I love your sister, Ted," Jack replied.

"I suppose," Ted said. "Let's go in. I've got a splitting headache."

CHAPTER TWELVE

PROMISE

Anna drove back to Richmond the next morning. She had not told Ted or Jack she was leaving so abruptly, and it left Jack wondering if he had revealed too much about his past. She assured him on a phone call the following evening it was not because of him that she had left.

"It's me, Jack," she told him.

"Whadya mean?"

"I'm getting close to you so fast. I—I worry that things might get out of hand."

"Look," Jack said, "come back for a week. I promise things won't get physical, if that's what you're worried about. Well, at least not out of hand. Ted will chaperone."

"We'll see," she answered.

The conversation left Jack feeling better, but more in need of her than ever before. It was really the first time in Jack's life he felt he needed someone. Jack liked being independent and even alone.

"So is my sister gonna make it out before we run out of summer?" Ted asked the next morning at the job site.

"I don't know for sure," Jack replied. "I think so. I hope so."

"She'll be back. She can't stay away from the beach too long," Ted said.

"She's a bit worried that we're getting too close, too fast, that things might go too far."

"I'll be watching like a hawk. I'd beat you to a pulp if you took advantage of her, but I expect you won't dishonor my sister," Ted said.

"No way," replied Jack. "I mean, I'm a red-blooded guy, but I value her too much, and she ain't that kind of girl."

Jack said it, but deep in his mind he knew that he was quite capable of taking his relationship with Anna to a level Ted would deem inappropriate. It had been a battle raging inside him since he first met her.

—◦◦◦—

It seemed to Jack the looming return to VMI for their third class year was going to snub out a beautiful and worthy summer in its prime. The Atlantic had not begun to cool yet, and the August sun blistered hotter than it had since they arrived.

Anna showed up for a final few days of sun, and the three of them had eaten supper together twice, but little else had transpired. The boys were working their last couple of twelve hour days, and it left little time to do anything other than eat and sleep. With their summer employment wrapped up, and two weekend days left, Jack and Ted were both interested in enjoying the beach and some freedom before returning to school.

Late Saturday afternoon Jack and Anna sat on the beach together in the secret stargazing spot just beyond the grassy dunes, while Ted stayed at the house on the deck, sunning himself. Anna talked about music with Jack, and both of them made fun of each other's tastes.

"I want to see a Broadway play, *on Broadway*," she said.

"Oh, that should be exciting."

"It would be, Jack Hartman," Anna said, "and I've heard they're quite the production."

"It's not very realistic, people breaking into song and dance. People just don't do that," Jack said. "Even if they did, where would all that orchestra music come from? Are we supposed to believe that they're just following certain people around, waiting for them to start singing?"

"Quit being so ignorant, Jack. You know better."

"I prefer realistic things, not a musical. They don't make a lick of sense. That's all I'm saying."

"The singing isn't supposed to be a reflection of real life. It's just a way to tell the story, to tell the audience what someone is thinking or feeling in a creative and entertaining way."

Jack loved Anna's reaction to his teasing. He watched her hair tossed around behind her neck as the breeze came in off the ocean. She reached over and took his hand in hers, and they both watched the surf quietly for a few minutes.

"Growing up like you did, how did you make it?" she asked. "How did you manage to turn out to be such a good guy?"

The question was innocent, but it felt like a sharp stab in his gut. He knew he should be content with his decisions to do better than his father, but always felt shame and defensiveness when thinking about his past.

"I guess I could've gone the other direction," Jack said. "It would've been easier, I suppose. I could've been a real whacko. I guess I am sometimes. Come to think of it, I'm pretty much a disaster most of the time."

"Let's walk," she said.

They stood and brushed the sand off their legs, and then began walking together toward the edge of the surf where the firm sand still held the dampness of a higher tide. She held his hand again as they walked south in the cool late afternoon breeze, the sun sinking to their right somewhere beyond Sandfiddler Road.

"So you just decided to be different than your dad?" she asked.

"I did."

"Just like that, after your dad passed?"

"It took a couple years to come to figure it out. I got into some trouble in and out of school. Some very good people got a hold of me, took me under their wing. I made some promises."

"Promises?"

"Like how I would live my life and such. It was a first step in really deciding to do things right."

"And how *are* you going to live, Jack?"

"Well, one thing for sure, I'll never treat my kids bad."

"How many kids do you want to have?"

"Oh, a couple dozen would be good," said Jack.

"I don't think I could do *that*!" Anna said, laughing.

She looked down, blushing. Jack realized she had just tipped her hand, that she was asking these questions with their future in mind.

"I would like four, though," she finally said as her embarrassment wore down.

"Well, four was my minimum. I could live with four," Jack said, smiling.

"Okay, Jack Hartman, let's just say it was me and you and four kids. What would our life be like?"

"Let's see. I'd leave for work every morning, spend the day killing commies. You'd get the kids to school in the morning, go for a mile walk, eat a late, lazy breakfast, sneak in your one guilty pleasure of watching your favorite soap opera, clean the house, pick up the kids, and get yourself doozied up for me. I'd get home after a long day just in time for my slippers, the paper, and a great steak dinner," Jack said, hoping to raise her ire.

"I ignored your chauvinism enough to hear you say you intended pursuing a career in the military. Is that true?"

"It's part of my promise, serving my country."

"I guess Dad would like that about you," Anna said.

"You wouldn't?"

"I just don't want to be moving every three years. Neither do our four children," she answered.

"Oh yes, them."

"Jack, really, I'd go wherever you wanted me to. If you want to be career military, I'd support you. I could write along the way. It could work," she said.

"It should work, Anna, because I want you to be with me. I want to be the guy that wins your heart. I want to do everything I can to be everything you need."

She stopped walking and pulled Jack's hand till he stopped and turned around. She took his other hand so that she held them both as he faced her. They stood there looking at each other. Anna was smiling and blushing. She seemed to Jack to melt into an awkward shyness.

This is it.

It was the moment he had longed for and feared. He looked directly into her eyes.

"I love you, Anna Marie McClain," he said.

"I love you too, Jack Hartman."

They kissed.

They walked back along the beach, quietly at first, but resumed their talk about pasts and futures until they reached the boardwalk back to the house. Though the sun had been gone for almost a half-hour, it was still not dusky. Ted sat up when he heard them climb the steps.

"I was about to send out a search party!" he yelled.

"The only thing you were searching was the inside of your eyelids!" Anna yelled back. "You're a poor chaperone, Teddy."

"I can't help it," Ted said, "I've been having another headache. I think I'm getting those migraines."

"Excuses, excuses," she replied.

"Should we tell him?" Jack whispered.

"Yes, but let me," Anna answered.

As they approached the deck, Ted looked at them as if he was sure he had really failed in his chaperone duties. Jack could see he looked worried.

"We didn't do anything, if that's what that look is all about," Jack said.

"No, but we said some things," Anna added.

Ted looked confused.

"Just like our parents, we're officially in love," she said.

"Oh," Ted said with a sigh of relief, "you had me worried."

"I was more worried," Anna said.

"Huh?" asked Jack.

"I was worried that you were never going to love me, that there was something blocking you from that, or at least from saying it, maybe something from your past."

"See Jack, I told you," Ted said.

"You mean the thing about God's plans, or the thing about how I should tell her what I've been telling you since Christmas?" Jack asked.

"Yes," answered Ted, "exactly."

"You've been telling Ted since Christmas, what?" Anna asked.

"That I love you," answered Jack.

"I told him to let you know," Ted said.

"That's okay. I knew you were at least close to madly in love the night of our first hop," Anna said, "but I'm not so sure how strong my feelings were then. I don't know. I'm glad it worked out like this. Now walk me to my car. I need to go down the street and pack. I leave tomorrow, too."

Jack took Anna's hand and walked with her through the house to the driveway. They hugged tightly for a minute and she kissed Jack again. Jack opened her car door and she slid into the driver's seat and pulled the door shut behind her. She rolled down the window and started the car.

"Goodbye Jack Hartman, do well in school. You'll need the good education to pay for our four kids."

Jack smiled, and then laughed.

"I like my slippers warm and my steaks medium-rare."

—◦◦◦—

The hint of a new day's light crept across the ocean the next morning.

It was still early enough that the cool dampness of the dew on the sea grass wetted Jack's ankles as he walked the narrow boardwalk to the beach. A layer of grey stretched across the eastern horizon as morning rains fell on waters miles offshore.

The clouds muted what might have been a stunning sunrise, only allowing the increase in light that spoke the day into existence.

Jack found his way to the edge of the surf and began walking slowly south as the tide rhythmically drenched his feet and ankles. He breathed in the sea spray carried on morning gusts, and it laid heavy on the back of his tongue. It occurred to him how he would dearly miss this time of closeness with Anna, and the secret place in the sand.

I've never felt this before, this strange mixture of excitement and grief. I've liked other girls, but not like this.

It had been coming on for some time now, but this confirmation from Anna made it real and certain.

How do I start to love someone? I feel attraction and desire. But love? Isn't it something more than that?

The sense of something stronger, something deeper was taking hold in his mind. All the while, he feared becoming his father, an instrument of destruction and pain. He did not ever want to hurt her. He wanted to be better.

Anna is so beautiful. But can I get past that? What if it faded? Would my desire for her evaporate? She has been a friend. Is friendship enough?

And will it last? Is this as real for her as it is for me, or is this only for a summer?

Am I deeper than all of this? Are we?

There was, again, a pain inside of Jack.

He stopped and turned to face the ocean. He had a longing in his gut he couldn't shake, and it brought him close to the edge of his emotions. As he stood looking out over the surf tasting its saltiness in the spray as he breathed it in, he mourned the summer, now passing.

He couldn't stop seeing her face in his mind. He felt it welling up inside him, and it came to him with such force he couldn't subdue it. Her name repeated in his mind, echoing powerfully over and over, like a hammer driving a spike through his chest.

Anna, Anna, Anna.

CHAPTER THIRTEEN

OF DEEPEST PERIL

"Pop to, Rat!"

Jack felt the rush of adrenaline laced blood pumping through his body—the excitement of leading for the first time. A cadre corporal, he was assigned a squad of Rats for matriculation. What he thought sadistic just a year before, now made much more sense.

Certainly, Jack had reservations as to the intensity of his discipline, but he could understand the necessity to shock them into the seriousness of the VMI system. He knew not to be overbearing or harsh—he'd seen the failure of it—but firm and detailed.

And so he started with his first Rat, a slightly overweight, spectacled kid named Gifford. Jack thought Gifford was too short for Echo Company, but somehow he had fooled the tape enough to make the minimum height requirement.

"Name?" asked Jack.

"Gifford, B. A., sir!"

"Rat Gifford, where is home?"

"Onancock, Virginia, sir," Gifford answered.

"Eastern Shore, nice. Do any crabbin' up there?"

"No Sir, come from a family of cops, sir!"

"You gonna be a cop, Rat?"

"Not planning on it, sir."

"Why did you come to VMI, Rat Gifford?" asked Jack.

"Dad said I was too smart not to go to college, sir."

"And you decided to do that here?"

"Yes, Sir. Had a good friend talk me into it, sir."

"Your choice of friends is questionable at best. Who is this maggot? Is he in our Squad?" asked Jack.

"No, sir. He decided to go to Washington and Lee."

Several other corporals began laughing loudly.

"Let me get this straight. Your good friend, who talked you into going to VMI and suffering through the toughest military indoctrination an eighteen year old can legally be submitted to, only to be followed by three more years of Spartan life, accented by its military and academic cruelty, is now over there," Jack said, pointing across the parade ground to the W&L campus, "sucking down a beer at the frats with a blonde hanging off his right arm. Is that correct, Rat Gifford?"

"Uh, no, sir. They don't start classes for another two weeks."

Now, Jack laughed out loud.

"One more question," Jack said.

"Yes, sir?"

"How smart are you feeling right now, Rat?"

Jack let him chew on the question for a moment.

"Carry on, Rat Gifford. You may be smart to your old man, but you'll always be an idiot to me."

Jack went down the line harassing each of his Rats in like manner. Jamison was the last.

Rat Jamison was a momma's boy in every sense of the word. He came from Texas, but in no way exemplified the heartiness of his home state. He was pale and thin, barely over one hundred twenty-five pounds, and sensitive. Twice already, the harshness of the cadre had brought him to tears.

"Rat Jamison, are you gonna quit?"

"No, sir."

"Alright, Rat," Jack replied, "just what I want to hear."

Jack almost felt guilty for not coming down hard on him, not testing Jamison's mettle. He did not want his Rats to think he was a soft leader. But more insidiously, he did not want to look weak to the other cadre.

Something deep inside him, however, told him not to be hard on this one – at least not now. He felt a bit sorry for the kid. Jamison reminded Jack of himself – not because he was a twig of a kid that cried, but because he was somewhat of a reject like Jack had been.

"Tell you what, Rat Jamison," Jack said, "you make it through this first week, and I'll let you throw me into the Maury River. Deal?"

"Yes, sir," said Jamison.

"Company atten-shun," yelled the first sergeant. "Fall out!"

The Echo Company Rats double-timed out of the formation toward Jackson Arch. Jack headed in the opposite direction, toward Smith Hall. He had been given a detail to run for the Superintendant.

"Where you headed, Jack?" asked Ted.

"Detail at the Superintendent's office. Picking up something for the Regimental staff. Be back up on the stoop in twenty minutes."

A light breeze carried the scent of fresh-cut grass off the parade deck. Jack walked along the sidewalk that led directly to Moody Hall, enjoying the shade of the trees that dotted the edge of the parade ground.

"Good afternoon, Ma'am," he said, tipping his hat to a lady sitting on one of the park benches along the walkway.

She sat with her legs crossed, purse in her lap and a tissue in her hand. She looked to Jack to be in her early forties, dressed nicely in a floral summer blouse and tan slacks. She acknowledged Jack, but did not say anything, and as Jack passed, he noticed the tears.

Jack stopped and turned to her.

"Are you okay, Ma'am?"

She nodded and pursed her lips, as if she was trying to stem a wave of emotion.

"My boy," she said, pointing toward the barracks. "It's his first year."

"I don't know if it will help, but he'll be well taken care of, here," said Jack.

Like that's going to help.

"I'm sure he will be fine," she answered, then fanned back another wave of emotion. "I suppose it's more me. I've never been away from him for more than a couple days, and even that was hard."

Jack looked toward Smith Hall and then back to the woman.

A few minutes won't hurt anything.

"Mind if I sit?" asked Jack, pointing at the other end of the bench."

"Not at all Cadet, um." She tried to read his nametag.

"Hartman, Jack Hartman."

Jack sat on the bench, leaning forward, looking out over the parade field.

"What's your boy's name?"

"Mitch Jamison."

It can't be.

"From Texas?"

"Yes, do you know him?"

"I've run into him a few times."

"Now, don't go back and be mean to him because his mama was out here cryin' for him."

"Ma'am, there ain't nothin' wrong with you cryin' because you miss your boy. I'd have given my right arm to have a mama cryin' for me when I was a Rat."

She looked at Jack with tears still welling up in her eyes.

"Where was your mother? Did she not come with you when you started here?"

"I never knew my mom. They say she took off when I was a baby."

"I'm sorry to hear that, Jack."

"Well, it was probably for the best."

They sat there in awkward silence for a minute.

"I know I've done so much in my own life, so much wrong in the way I lived, the ways I messed up with my own boys. Mitch, well he's my one chance for redemption," she said.

"I'll tell you what, Mrs. Jamison; I'll talk to your boy. I'll make sure he writes you a letter every week. And the best thing you can do for him is to do the same. Just make sure that you keep him encouraged – he's gonna need it."

"Okay, Jack."

"And don't get to feelin' sorry for him if he gets sad, and sounds like he's gonna quit. You be strong and don't let him. Just keep tellin' him how you believe in him."

"I can do that."

Jack stood and tipped his hat to her.

"Well, Mrs. Jamison, I've gotta go. Supposed to be on a detail right now."

"It was nice meeting you, Jack Hartman. I feel better. I don't know how to thank you, but I'm sure I'll send you a letter someday," she said, sitting forward on the front edge of the bench.

"Have a nice day," Jack said.

He turned and began to walk away.

"Oh Jack," Mrs. Jamison said, standing up. "How will you know that he's writing me?"

Jack stopped and turned around.

"I'll have him bring them to formation before he mails them."

"Can you do that?"

"Sure, I'm his corporal."

—⌘—

Two days into Cadre, Ted left on a medical furlough. The headaches he had been experiencing throughout the summer had gotten more frequent and more intense. Jack waited till the end of the Cadre week to call him. He could not get anyone to answer at Ted's home, so Jack called the hospital in Richmond, where Ted had gone to get some tests done.

"A tumor," Mr. McClain told Jack, when he finally got him on the phone, "in the brain." He said it with a quiver, and Jack could sense his fear. Jack was stunned. He had never been close to anyone affected with cancer, or brain tumors, or anything like them.

"What are they saying? I mean, can they get it out?"

"Well, it's malignant and aggressive, Jack. They aren't making any promises right now." McClain had said it with a touch of irritability. It bothered Jack, but he couldn't react. He knew Ted's dad had to be hurting. Jack struggled to get his mind around the fact that Ted had cancer.

"Do they operate on something like this?" asked Jack, his face beading with sweat in the clammy heat of the VMI concourse phone booth.

"Yeah, they do, and they will. Then chemo and radiation after he recovers from the surgery."

It was as if darkness had fallen. Suddenly, nothing would be the same. The hope that had defined Jack's last two years shriveled and slithered away in the middle of a conversation on a pay phone in the concourse. Still, Jack found it hard to feel anything emotional. He did sense the return of a shadow, a warning of sorts. The stirring of blackness inside him.

"Jack, are you there?" Mr. McClain asked, breaking the silence.

"Yes, sir," Jack said, but as quickly as the words left his mouth, he knew he was lying. He felt apart from himself, somewhere other than on his side of the phone.

Ted of all people. He's one of the good guys.

"How are you and Mrs. McClain?"

"We're tired," McClain answered, "but Anna should be here soon. Ted will be up in awhile. We'd appreciate your prayers, son," said McClain.

"Most definitely, sir."

Jack said it, but didn't know the first thing about praying, and was certain that anything he prayed for would fall on deaf ears.

God doesn't care about anything I say.

"Thanks, Jack. I'll send you guys a status slip after we talk with the doctor tomorrow afternoon. Have a good evening. Tell the fellas Ted said hello."

He's asleep. Now we're both lying.

Jack hung up and picked up his books. He had a pile of reading to do and a paper to write. It seemed almost surreal to him everything would go on as normal, and he would be writing a paper, reading *Hamlet* and four chapters of Western Civilization, when just an hour and a half down the road, his roommate struggled for his life.

Just pray for him. Just pray for him.

Jack heard himself say it over and over, as concerned Brother Rats stopped by the room throughout the week to find out about Ted's status. It was an awkward position for Jack. He did not normally dispense prayer advice.

Do people really care?

They did. Everyone loved Ted.

———

Jack called cadence for the Rats on the march back up to the bricks from the mess hall. Already late October, it was a cold night, the clear sky speckled with the dots of a hundred constellations. When they halted, the corporals had a few minutes to give their Rat squads instructions.

"Rat Jamison, have you written your mama?" asked Jack.

"Yes, sir."

Jack detected a break in his voice.

A whimper.

As Jack approached, he could see Jamison had tears in his eyes.

"Why you cryin', Rat?"

"I'd rather not say, sir."

"Why would you rather not say, Rat?"

"Because I'm in a lot of trouble, Sir," Jamison answered quietly.

"That is a given. You're at VMI. You're a Rat. What could be worse?"

"A different kind of trouble, sir."

He had lowered his voice to a barely audible whisper.

"When the other Rats fall out, you stay on the bricks. Understand?" asked Jack.

"Yes, sir," Jamison answered.

When they fell out, the Echo Company Rats quickly moved to the entrance to Jackson Arch, while Jamison remained on the bricks, straining. Stephen Murphy, a line sergeant in Echo Company walked over to them.

"At ease, Rat Jamison," Sergeant Murphy said.

Jamison assumed the non-straining at ease position.

"So what are you all torqued up about, Jamison?" asked Jack.

"I, I'm, uh, having trouble with a Second, sir."

"What kind of trouble, Rat?" Sergeant Murphy asked.

"He's been harassing me pretty hard, Sir."

"Oh, don't give me that, Jamison," Jack said. "Every upperclassman worth his salt is harassing you pretty hard."

"This is different, sir."

"How so, Rat?" Murphy asked.

"Permission to speak to Corporal Hartman in private, sir?" Jamison asked.

"Permission granted. I don't even want to have anything to do with your bellyaching, Rat," answered Sergeant Murphy, then turned to Jack. "Don't keep him long. CQ is in fifteen."

Murphy turned and headed for the arch.

"Why in private, Rat?" asked Jack. "You know this is all a bit weird."

"Yes, sir. I'm just not sure I should say this in front of Sergeant Murphy."

"Is he involved? Is it some kind of hazing?"

"No, sir. Sergeant Murphy is mean and all, but he's just military. He is a second classman, though, and I'm not sure who to trust."

"So what's this second doing?"

"At first, sir, I thought he just had it in for me. Well, me and Brother Rat Gifford. He cornered us in the Ratline almost every day, screaming at us, saying all kinds of evil things. He'd get me alone and strain me real hard, and write me up to the RDC a lot. He said he was gonna run me outa here, that I didn't belong, that the corps had gone to pot 'cause of losers like me and Gifford."

"Sounds familiar," Jack said. "I had a corporal harass me like that when I was a Rat. Look, the system works. Report this moron to your dyke. He'll bring the heat down on him, and you won't have to listen to it anymore. Anything else, Rat Jamison?"

"Yes, sir, it's a lot more than that. And Gifford's situation is even worse, but he won't tell, he's scared to death."

"Well, it's about to be CQ, and I don't want to get you in trouble."

"But, sir…"

"Alright, meet me in Scott-Shipp Hall, room two hundred and thirty-two, in two hours. It's the small classroom at the end of the hall. No one ever uses it because it's too hot or too cold. Don't tell anyone. It would be considered fraternization and we'd both be in trouble. Understand?"

"Yes, sir. Scott-Shipp, Room two hundred and thirty-two at twenty-one hundred hours."

"Alright, you're dismissed. Go study till then."

Jamison snapped to attention, did an about face, and headed toward the arch. Jack realized he'd forgotten one thing.

"Rat Jamison!" he yelled.

"Yes, sir," Jamison answered, snapping back into a strain.

Jack walked over to him.

"Who's the second?"

Jamison suddenly looked nervous, standing in front of the arch. "His name is Mr. Phelps."

Jack sat tapping his pencil over and over on the blank page in front of him. His stomach churned, leaving a burning sensation creeping up his throat. Waves of fury left him cussing in his mind, and murdering Phelps in a hundred different ways.

He looked at his watch. Twenty fifty-five.

"Corporal Hartman?"

The door was only half closed, and Jack had not heard Jamison walking down the hallway over the clamoring going on in his thoughts.

"Come on in, Jamison."

"Yes, sir."

Rat Jamison walked in the door and stood straining at the opposite side of the table from Jack. He was shaking visibly. Jack could not tell if he was nervous or cold, though Jack could see his own breath.

"At ease, Jamison, and sit down," Jack said. "Now tell me everything that's been going on, including what you know about Gifford."

"Yes, sir," Jamison said as he took a seat across the table. "I guess it all started matriculation day. I know he singled me out then, maybe Gifford later. I guess it doesn't matter, but since then it's just gotten worse and worse. He traps me on the stoop and threatens me with the worst things, and he stops me in other buildings. It's like he's following me."

"So you've told your dyke?"

Jamison turned his head to look behind him. The hallway was sill empty. He turned back.

"He doesn't want to hear it—thinks I'm being a crybaby. I was waiting till it got real bad, till he did something that really crossed the line to talk to my dyke again."

"And he hasn't, yet?"

Jamison's face fell. He fidgeted in the chair.

"No, sir. Well, not till yesterday."

"What did he do?"

"He had me and BR Gifford meet him in the old gym. Said if we didn't, he'd turn us in to the honor court."

"For what?"

"I don't know, sir, he didn't say. We haven't done nothin' wrong, but I don't know who this guy is, or how much power he has. I assumed the worst, especially after my dyke's response when I talked to him about Phelps."

"Yeah, I get it, go on," said Jack.

"Anyway, we met him down there. He made us follow him to one of the locker rooms downstairs – over by the boxing room. He strained us for awhile, chewed us out pretty good, then put us both in the front leaning rest."

"He's lost his mind," said Jack.

"Well, then it got really weird, sir," Jamison said. "He said if we were tired of bein' harassed by him all we had to do was turn you in for hazing. But whatever happened, we both had to agree to do it."

"Did you agree?"

"I said we'd think about it, but I never had the slightest intention of doing it. He was talking some bad stuff. He wanted us to say you did stuff to us that would definitely have gotten you kicked outa here. He has it out for you somethin' fierce Corporal Hartman."

"Why didn't you go right to the Honor Court with this?"

"Gifford was scared awful bad. He's been too upset to do anything ever since. It's like he's gone completely paranoid."

"Why's he so whacked out about it?"

"Phelps said he'd kill him if he messed this up, except he said it with some pretty rough language. I think he meant it."

"You believed him?"

"I don't know if I did. I don't know if Gifford did. It was just weird, and we didn't know what was going on."

Jack felt rage well up inside him like water violently boiling over the edges of a soup pot onto a hot stovetop. He grabbed his books and slammed them on the table twice. It helped relieve the steam in him for the moment. He stood and walked to the door.

"Go get Gifford right now. Meet me in room one twenty-four in five minutes. Phelps messed up bad this time."

━☙☙☙━

Cadet Lieutenant Chris Carpenter sat on the edge of his bunk as Gifford and Jamison told their sides of the story. He was efficient, questioning the two in order to draw out the relevant aspects of the event. His dark brown eyes focused on each of the Rats as they spoke, only looking down to jot an occasional note on a yellow pad.

"You both need to realize how serious this is," Carpenter said, "and that you should have come to one of us prosecutors or the Honor Court President immediately. You should not have discussed this with your Cadre Corporal. When you witness an act that even might be a violation of the Honor Code, you are certified to speak to no one about it except myself or the other two I just mentioned."

"Yes, sir," they said.

"I just wasn't sure whether this was an honor violation, or what," said Jamison.

"Well, ask your dyke next time, not a Third," Carpenter said. "You Rats are certified not to talk to anyone about this. Do you understand?"

"Yes, sir," they both said in unison.

"Then you're dismissed," he said. "Corporal Hartman, stay here for a minute."

The Rats gathered their hats, placed them on their heads as they stepped out on the stoop into the Ratline. The gravity of their first real encounter with the Honor Court had them darting their eyes nervously, and Gifford's hands were visibly shaking. Lieutenant Carpenter waited till they cleared the door.

"Corporal Hartman, you should have stopped them when this even started to sound like something to do with an honor violation. You know that. You understand certification."

"If this had been something obvious, I would have," Jack said. "I mean, technically no one's even told a lie yet."

"It is a confusing situation, I'll give you that, but a violation none-the-less."

"How is it that cut and dried?" asked Jack.

"Coercing someone to lie is itself not a lie, but it is a form of toleration, and that is an honor code violation."

———

Jack walked along the sidewalk at the edge of the parade ground on his way to Preston Library. The moon gave off a bluish glow, enough to light the facades of the row of academic buildings along the other side of the street. The old gas lamps beamed yellow, but only in small circles around them and in the highlights cast on surrounding trees along the perimeter of the parade ground.

Jack switched the two books he carried from his right arm to the left, and the coffee from his left hand to his right.

The windows of each building glowed yellow and orange through ancient panes of glass, the light warming the hedges, and even creeping out to the street in a few spots. It was always an inviting sight when the autumn was giving in to winter. Steam curled from the Styrofoam coffee cup in his right hand, still nearly full from the PX. It did little to warm his fingers.

Shoulda worn gloves.

It was cold enough to make Jack shiver, and tree leaves crunched under almost every step. Six weeks had passed since Jack had brought the Rats to see Lieutenant Carpenter. Six weeks and no word. Now it was cold, and everything was dying.

Jack trotted up the steps of Preston, the building still aglow with every light blazing, even so close to taps. Inside he quickly followed the stairwell down to the lower stacks, where he planted himself at his reserved desk at the end of the row of books covering Ancient to Angst. He snickered to himself, thinking about the irony of it–his past and his anger.

Ah, late study. Taps in thirty minutes.

He set his books on the desk, switched on the desk lamp, and took a swig of coffee.

As he nestled into his chair, he could see he was the only one down in his part of the stacks. He loved the stacks; so barren of noise he could hear his heart beat. He began to read.

A voice startled him.

"Cadet Hartman."

He heard no one walking up. Lieutenant Carpenter stood at the end of the row in duty jacket, hat tucked under his left arm.

"Sorry I jumped. You scared me. Didn't hear you walk up," Jack said.

"Follow me to the Timmons Music Room," Carpenter said. "There are a few listening rooms up there that are about the only places we can discuss something certified."

They climbed the three flights of stairs, Carpenter leading and both not saying a word. Jack was certain this had to do with Phelps, but his heart still pounded hard inside of him.

When they reached the music listening library on the second floor, Carpenter looked around some of the rooms till he found one separate from the others and unoccupied.

"In here," he said, motioning Jack ahead into the room.

He pulled the door till it latched.

"Cadet Hartman," Carpenter said, "there will be an Honor Court hearing tomorrow. You have been selected to take the stand in the trial of Cadet Phelps. You are certified, and in this case understand that this means you cannot talk to anyone about even the fact that there is a trial going on. You will not be prepared in any way. You will be asked questions and expected to answer, regardless of what you believe the impact on the case will be."

"I understand," said Jack.

"Good. Report to Kilbourne Hall at fourteen hundred tomorrow," Carpenter said. "There will be an Honor Court member to meet you and escort you to the courtroom. Uniform is grey blouse. Any questions?"

"Yeah, why would you use me as a witness? I never saw a thing. Gifford and Jamison are your guys."

Carpenter turned to Jack as he took a step toward the door. "Who said you were a witness for the prosecution?"

―◆◆◆―

Jack tried to read. He sat at the desk in the basement of Preston Library, buried in the stacks, trying to study, but getting nowhere. The thought of being a witness for Phelps's defense burned deep in his gut.

Why would he want me to be a witness for him? Has he lost his mind? I'm the last guy he'd want up there, vouching for his character.

He closed his book, pulled on his duty jacket and tucked his work under his arm. Jack moved quickly up the stairwell and through the front door. The heavy ancient oak squeaked as he pushed through and then clanked with a thud as it closed behind him, sounding like a door on a medieval castle.

The cold night had turned heavy and wet with dew. Jack walked at a brisk pace back to Old Barracks, to the glow of Jackson Arch. He slipped quietly through the arch and up the sally port stairwell to the third stoop.

The rest of the room lay quietly asleep. Jack undressed quickly and nestled down in his hay. Lying there, hands crossed behind his head, he wrestled for a hint of reason. Nothing about the whole thing made any sense.

Is he calling me as a witness just to trip me up, to discredit what I say, and therefore discredit my report to the Honor Court? Is there something I know that would exonerate him? I would be truthful even if I thought it would. Maybe it would change his outlook. Maybe he would change.

He looked at his watch. It was just after midnight.

―◆◆◆―

"Cadet Hartman, you can come in now."

The runner, a first classman dressed in grey blouse held the door open with his left arm. Jack had been sitting for over an hour outside of the courtroom in the narrow hallway in the basement of Kilbourne Hall. He had begun to wonder if he would even be called to testify.

Jack followed the escort to the front of the courtroom. The room was set up like a standard courtroom with two tables facing the front of the room for the prosecutors and the defense. A dark red wood desk sat central, facing the back of the courtroom. The Honor Court president sat behind it.

Jack looked over to his right front to see a jury of first and second class Honor Court members, seated and also in grey blouse. There was only one pew-like bench behind the prosecution and defense tables. Two men sat in the bench. As he passed by the bench, Jack saw the commandant seated behind the prosecution, and the Honor Court faculty representative, Lieutenant Colonel Gore behind the defense.

The escort motioned for Jack to take the stand. Jack hesitated for a moment, then walked up and sat in a chair between the Judge's desk and the jury box.

Lieutenant Carpenter rose and approached him.

"Cadet Hartman, you have been called to the stand as a witness for the defense."

Jack looked over at Phelps, seated between two suits at the defense table. The lawyers, seated on both sides of Phelps leaned back, whispering over something on a yellow pad. Phelps looked at Jack, but instead of the intense face of hatred he had seen before, Jack saw a softness, the pitiful face of one in deep need.

Life or death. He needs me to say something. He must have no defense.

"Cadet Hartman, you know that we do not swear in a cadet who takes the stand. You were sworn in the day you matriculated. A cadet is always under oath, so to say," Carpenter said, standing at the front corner of the Honor Court president's desk.

"I understand."

"Defense, the witness is yours," Carpenter said, and then walked back to his seat at the prosecution table.

A short, thin and slightly balding man who had been sitting on the end of the defense table stood up. He spoke from his position behind the table.

"Cadet Hartman, what is your relationship with Cadet Phelps right now?"

"Um," Jack said. "What do you mean by relationship, sir?"

"Just simply describe the current relationship you have with Cadet Phelps."

"Okay, we don't talk. I don't care for him, and last I knew, he felt likewise. Other than the fact we are both cadets at VMI, there is no relationship."

"How do you know Cadet Phelps doesn't care for you?"

"He told me last year in no uncertain terms that he hated my guts, and would do everything possible to make me leave VMI."

"You had a problem with Cadet Phelps last year?"

"No sir. I did not have a problem with Cadet Phelps. He had a problem with me. I never did anything to him."

"Say it however you want, but the fact is you didn't, and still don't, get along with Cadet Phelps, correct?"

"I've got to object to that," said Carpenter, as he stood quickly. "No such thing has been established as fact."

Cadet Captain McGuire, the Honor Court president, held up his right hand, palm toward Carpenter.

"I think everyone in this courtroom is aware of the incident last year," McGuire said. "I think we all know of the friction between these two, and we are all aware it continues to this day. I'll allow the counselor to continue for the moment. Go on, sir."

"Thank you, Cadet McGuire. Semantics aside, are you and Cadet Phelps at odds right now?"

"Yes, sir."

"Could you describe your dislike for Cadet Phelps on a scale of one to ten, one being only slight dislike, like you would feel for someone who bugs you or has bad breath, and ten being hatred so deep you would consider murder, if the situation was right."

"I guess a five or six, sir."

"Well, is it five or six, Cadet Hartman?"

"Six, sir. I'll go with six."

Jack felt a sudden flush of adrenaline. His face flushed, and he could hear his heartbeat in his head.

"So you would say you are closer to murder than to just being irritated."

"I don't know if I would put it like that, sir."

"You just did, Cadet Hartman."

The counselor walked from behind his table and stood at the very front corner, supporting himself with his left hand. Jack felt his heart pounding.

Thud, thud, thud.

"Cadet Hartman, please describe for us your relationship with Cadets Gifford and Jamison."

"I'm their Cadre corporal."

"You are responsible for their well-being. Correct?"

"Yes, sir."

"If the well-being of one of your Rats is being threatened, would you say it is your responsibility to correct the problem creating the immediate threat?"

"Yes, sir, as much as I can."

The counselor turned and walked back to his original position behind the table. Jack felt his right hand shaking. His heart continued going at it, but even harder.

Thud, thud, thud, thud.

"Now are you aware, Cadet Hartman, that on numerous occasions Cadet Phelps passionately addressed your two Rats, Gifford and Jamison?"

"That's a very kind way of putting it, sir."

That's it, stay calm. Give it back to him the same way.

"Okay, you got me on that one, Cadet Hartman. Guess I shouldn't quibble here. Let me rephrase the question. Are you aware that on numerous occasions Cadet Phelps viciously harassed your two Rats, Gifford and Jamison?"

"Yes, sir, I am."

"And are you aware that Cadet Phelps coerced the same two Rats to report to the basement locker room in the old gym?"

"Yes, sir."

"And are you aware he worked them out in an unauthorized fashion?"

"Yes, sir."

He stepped back to the front of the table. Sweat beaded on Jack's face.

Thud, thud, thud.

"Tell me, Cadet Hartman, how are you aware of these things?"

"Jamison and Gifford told me."

"So you didn't witness any of the incidents we just talked about?"

"No, sir."

"But you believe Cadet Phelps did them, anyway?"

"It sounded like something he would do, sir."

"The truth is Cadet Phelps has been harassing these two for quite some time, but he never took them down to Cocke Hall and never coerced them to do…"

"Objection. He can't just say that unless he has a witness to refute the charges," Carpenter said, standing.

"That is sustained, Lieutenant Carpenter," said McGuire. "Counselor you know you can't do that here."

"Then I move to strike Cadet Hartman's testimony as hearsay."

"But he's your witness, counselor," McGuire said. "However, the Honor Court will disregard that particular part of Cadet Hartman's testimony, as it is hearsay. Any further questions for him?"

Phelps's lawyer smiled and nodded.

"Cadet Hartman," the counselor said, "is it possible your Rats have concocted this story because they hate Phelps more than a five or six?"

"Objection."

"Overruled. Cadet Hartman is their corporal. He should know if they're capable of it."

"I suppose it's possible, sir," Jack said.

"Well, I suppose it opens up a number of possibilities. Do you think it would be more likely for someone who knows the system better than a Rat to come up with the same kind of set-up?"

"Objection. That's complete conjecture," said Carpenter.

"Sustained. I thought you actually had a point, which is the only reason I let you go on with this."

"I have a point, Cadet McGuire."

"Go on, then, counselor, but you'll need to quit fishing."

"Do you believe Cadets Gifford and Jamison look up to you, Cadet Hartman?"

"I think so, sir."

"Do you also think they fear you?"

"I am their cadre corporal," said Jack, "they better."

Jack heard whispering among some of the Honor Court members in the jury box.

"Then was it out of respect or fear that they agreed to meet you in the basement of Cocke Hall, where you gave them a private sweat party?"

"I didn't meet them anywhere."

"Oh really? I have a witness that can place you in Scott-Shipp Hall with Jamison shortly before you brought Jamison and Gifford to turn in my client."

The questions were coming fast. Sweat dripped from the end of Jack's nose.

"I didn't mean I never met with either of them afterward. I meant I didn't meet with either of them to coerce them to do anything."

"Isn't it true that you worked them out in the basement of Cocke Hall?"

"No, sir."

"Isn't it true you convinced them to make this story up about Cadet Phelps?"

"No, sir."

"Isn't it true you met with Jamison and then Gifford before you went to the prosecutor in order to get their stories straight?"

"Yes, sir. I mean no, sir. I mean I met with them before we went to the prosecutor so I could find out what happened."

Thud, thud, thud, thud.

"Isn't it true you set this up because you hate Cadet Phelps so much you are only four numbers away from wanting him dead?"

"No, sir!" Jack yelled, standing up. "I hate him bad enough I'm zero numbers away from wanting him dead!"

"I object to this whole line of questioning. Counselor is badgering Corporal Hartman," Carpenter yelled.

"Sustained. Anything else, counselor?" McGuire asked.

"No, I'm done with him."

※

Jack hung up his grey blouse, damp with his perspiration, in its spot between two others. His arms felt limp as he struggled to hook the dowel. The sweat had dried on his skin, but the film of salt felt dirty and chalky.

It was a bad testimony. Too nervous. Almost sounded like I did it.

Jack had been replaying the whole thing over and over in his mind, then beating himself up mentally for every flub, every confusing, disorienting moment. He felt foolish and indecisive in front of some of the most respected members of the Corps of Cadets. Worse, he knew his loss of composure may have been what Phelps needed.

If he's exonerated, he'll come after my Rats. He'll still try to get to me through them.

"Get your chin in, Rat."

Jack turned to the doorway and saw Ted standing just inside. Ted wore his civies, consisting of blue jeans and a light jacket with a white tee shirt underneath. He looked better than he did last time Jack saw him at the hospital in Richmond. He had some color in his face.

"Hey, Ted," Jack said as he moved quickly toward him.

They hugged briefly.

"I thought you weren't back till the end of the semester," said Jack.

"I'm not. Just came by to pick up my stuff and say hi to you guys. I won't get back till next semester."

"What about your classes. I mean, you're gonna get a semester behind."

"Guess I'll be a five-year man. But don't worry about me, I'll be around."

"Are you going to need surgery?"

"Remarkably, no. It's shrinking so quickly, they think the treatments are going to knock this out."

"Well, that's some good news."

"You getting dressed up for something?"

Jack realized he was still wearing his suspenders and tee shirt with his white ducks.

"No, I'm getting changed back into class dyke," answered Jack.

Mr. McClain stepped in the door behind Ted.

"Hey, Jack. How's it going?" he asked reaching out to shake Jack's hand. Jack obliged.

"We need to collect Ted's gear and get back up to Richmond before he starts wearing down," Mr. McClain said. "Doin' alright, son?" he asked Ted.

"Dad, I'm fine," Ted answered then turned back to Jack. "He spends more time worrying about me than he does anything else."

"I certainly understand that. Let's get your stuff packed," said Jack.

He was glad they had showed up.

———— ❧ ————

That night Jack returned from late study around one-thirty in the morning. He had struggled all night to finish his work, his mind frequently drifting back to the Honor Court and thoughts of Ted.

I messed it up. Phelps will get out of this somehow, just like he did with his constant abuse of Rats he perceived not worthy of the Institute. Mr. McClain was cordial. Could things be changing?

As he gently laid his books on his desk, he noticed the silhouette of Ski against the dim light of the back window. He leaned against the edge of the window, looking out, not even turning to acknowledge Jack's entrance.

"You're up late, Ski."

"Wow. I was so deep in thought, I didn't even hear you come in. You scared the daylights out of me."

"Sorry, BR. What's on your mind?"

"Oh, just thinkin' about Ted, and how crazy everything has been this year. First Sergeant asked if I wanted to be a Rat corporal."

"Makeovers aren't till January."

"Yeah, one of the fellas is stepping down. Demerits, I think."

"You gonna do it? I mean, it would be awesome to have one of the roomies out there with me."

"I guess so. I guess there's a part of me that wants to be a private and not deal with all the extra garbage. Then there's this other part that wants to rain a little scunion down on some Rats."

"I say, do it."

And then they heard it. It was the faintest hiss coming from somewhere in the echoing hollows of the Old Barracks. At first, it was as if a rattlesnake had interrupted the silence with a long shake of its tail, but it never trailed off. It grew and grew. They both looked at each other knowing what it was. It had been three months since they heard it last and it always took them by surprise. It was the roll of drums.

They woke Darryl before the coateed Honor Court member made it to their door, and they took their place along the rail of the third stoop, looking down into the courtyard, well lit by the bright March moon. The snares rolled over and over. The bass drum sounded its solo stinger announcing that another had fallen. The corps sleepily assembled one room at a time in the ghostly four story huddle. Cigarette meteors fell. Drums ceased. Court marched. On their halt, the Honor Court President began his ceremonial announcement.

"Tonight, your Honor Court has met, and after a trial hearing has found cadet Phelps, J. A. guilty of toleration of a breach of honor! He has placed personal gain above honor, and has left the Institute never to return! His name will never be mentioned within the walls of these barracks again!"

No one said a word. They didn't have to. The nemesis of the room, the one who had tormented them all the previous year, was gone, and in a way that none of them would have ever believed, not even Jack after *his* testimony.

Jack knew Phelps loved the Institute. But Jack knew he was a bad seed. Whatever the guys felt about Phelps, the silence in room three hundred and thirty-two was indicative of their shock.

They each quietly returned to their respective racks, slid under their respective comforters, and stared at their respective parts of the ceiling.

"Who's calling Ted?" asked Ski.

"He'll probably just want to pray for Phelps," said Darryl.

Jack said nothing. His hatred suddenly waned. All he could see was the desperation in Phelps's eyes.

There was a long silence in the room.

"Couldn't have happened to a nicer guy," Ski said.

CHAPTER FOURTEEN

GOSHEN PASS

Ted came back. Though he was drained of it months before, he was filled with more life and energy every day. By the middle of March Ted was feeling pretty normal, and he looked, to Jack, as if he had never even been sick, other than his head being more bald than buzzed.

The winter faded, too.

Spring danced into the Shenandoah Valley as a southern debutante with all of her charm and regalia. Drizzling showers twisted and turned in alternating steps with warm, sunny days. As they swirled through the valley, they left behind the thick greens and yellows of ferns and goldenrod, bright violet azaleas, and dogwoods in full bloom.

A perfect shifting of the jet streams brought pleasant weather with only moderate rainfall. The cold of what had been a relatively harsh winter had now been set aside, while another Virginia summer hung in limbo, waiting for her card to be called.

The warmth beckoned hand-holding couples, and soon the streets of Lexington were filled with the co-educated of Washington and Lee University in their pastel pullovers, khaki shorts, and docksiders. And after all the required trumpets, cannon and barracks turn-outs, the men in pressed military white.

Jack walked in the room on a Thursday evening about a half-hour before SRC, and noticed Ted donning his white blouse.

"You going to town?" he asked Ted.

"My folks are waiting for me. They want to take me to dinner. I'm sure they're going to grill me about how I'm feeling and make sure I'm taking my medication."

"I'll save you some slop from Crozet," said Jack.

"I can't wait. And Jack, I'd invite you, but, um, Anna may be coming up, and I think Dad is wanting time alone with family. You don't mind, do you?"

"No, not at all, I'm fine with all that. I realize I'm not a McClain. I hope to be there, someday. I know I'm gonna have to grow on your folks first."

"I don't know, Jack. Y'know Dad's still a little iffy about you and Anna."

"Sorry, Ted, but I just can't turn it off. I'm not going to quit on her."

"I'll see ya when I get back."

Ted checked his gig line in the mirror, then squared his hat on his head and walked out onto the stoop. Ski lay in his bed, his eyes closed.

"That was cold," Ski said, eyes still shut.

"I guess I understand it. They have their minds set on a specific kind of guy they want their daughter to marry," said Jack.

"Oh yeah?" asked Ski. "Just what kind of guy is that? Is it some Mink from next door, or some mama's boy from Richmond? I mean, just what kind of pedigree will make the cut with Ted's folks? You've gotta quit believing this garbage that there's something wrong with you."

"I can think I'm good enough for Anna all I want. It still doesn't change the way her folks see me."

Jack turned in time to see a runner clipping a status slip to the door. He walked over to the door, opened it and pulled the slip off. As he read it, he smiled.

> Name: Cadet Teddy McClain
> Room: 332
> Message: I'm in the arch.
>
> Anna

Jack grabbed his white blouse and quickly put it on.

"What's up?" asked Ski.

"I think Anna's in the arch."

"Nice timing."

Jack bolted out of the door and jogged down the stoop to Ghetto corner. Before he even made it to the first stoop he saw Anna standing in the arch, looking out toward the parade ground. His heart began racing as he got closer to her.

"You looking for someone, Miss?" asked Jack.

Anna turned, startled.

"Jack, you scared me," Anna said.

"Sorry, but I couldn't resist."

"Where's Teddy?"

"I'm surprised you didn't run into them. Ted just left with your folks, they're going to dinner somewhere."

"I guess that means you don't know where," said Anna.

"He didn't say, but I'm sure you could track them down."

"I'm not going to drive all over Lexington looking for them. They weren't really expecting me. I told Teddy on the phone yesterday that I might drop by. I guess Mom and Dad needed to check on him."

"You hungry?" asked Jack.

"Are you offering?"

"Why not? I still have time to sign out. Dine-with date, you know."

—◦◦◦—

They had a small table in the back of The Palms. Anna was radiant and Jack was completely consumed. Jack chose The Palms, as he knew Mr. McClain would not typically want to eat there.

Walking back from the restaurant, Jack and Anna turned down Washington Street onto the Washington and Lee campus, past the rows of quaint red brick shops, and the Old Episcopal Church with its grey stone and high steeple. Just past the church's rod iron fence, they turned right and walked along the sidewalk that ran straight across the lawn in front of the plantation style white-columned buildings that made up the façade of the University.

It had started getting dark, and the black silhouettes of the trees splashed against a purple sky. Anna laughed shyly. They held hands as they walked, saying little. The old black gas-lit street lamps that lined the sidewalk shed orange-yellow light at intervals, and just before they crossed in front of Lee Chapel, Jack stopped in the darkness between.

Anna turned and grabbed Jack's other hand, giving a tug as if to say "Let's go." Jack didn't budge, but looked at Anna intently.

"And what are we doing, Cadet Hartman? A little late for a tour of the Old Chapel, huh?" she asked with one eyebrow raised.

Jack smiled, but remained silent. His heart was pounding, and his mind feverishly searching for something. He wanted more than just holding hands. He wanted to be closer to her, to hold her, and feel her need for him. It was that perfect moment that he had longed for since they had first noticed each other on Parents' Weekend over a year before. More so than the day on the beach.

Private, dark.

He pulled her up close to himself, still holding both of her hands, but bringing them in to his chest. She obliged, still smirking and with one eyebrow up. He let her hands go, and in a fluid movement she slid her forearms to the top of his shoulders and overlapped her hands behind the back of his neck so that her fingers extended to the bristly hair on the back of his head. He leaned his forehead against hers, and wrapped his arms around her waist.

They stood there for a moment; both feeling the pounding of the other's heart, almost equally fast but slightly out of unison. Jack wanted to kiss Anna, but was not sure if she would go along. Before he could think of a way to ask, he felt her move her face close, pressing her lips against his.

He felt a flush from head to toe, and the kiss quickly became passionate. He pulled her closer and held her tightly. Somehow in his mind, he wanted to blend with her. They went on for almost a minute, Jack getting more feverish as they progressed. Suddenly, she pulled away.

"Jack, we can't," she said, breathing hard.

"What?"

Jack looked shocked, disbelieving.

No, no, no we can't stop this now!

Anna seemed suddenly confused, as if she was grasping for a sliver of a reason.

"Out here, in public—the EC, or whatever you call them. You know, the public display of affection thing."

"I don't care about that. I care about you. Nobody is going to see us doing anything."

They were both whispering, but with passion. Jack was still trying to pull her up close.

"Okay," she interrupted, "it's not so much that."

She pushed to get a little separation.

"It's just, we can't keep going, Jack. It's going too far."

"But *you're* the one who, who kissed *me.*"

"You're right, and I'm sorry. It's my fault. I care for you. I love you, but I don't want to throw all of that away for a few minutes of misspent passion."

Jack felt infuriated. He knew that she was right, but she had crushed his ego. He felt cut-off, rejected, dismissed. Inside of him, he could feel the beast stirring. He could hear the ringing in his ears.

Strike back, strike back! She started it. She owes it to you!

His only recourse was what he knew instinctively. He had to lash back. He looked at her so that she could see how wounded he was.

"Misspent?"

He shook his head and then turned to walk toward Letcher Avenue. Anna stood for a moment, and then turned to follow him.

"I didn't mean it like that, Jack," she said as she chased him across the cobblestones in front of Lee Chapel.

He would not stop walking.

"C'mon, we've gotta get back before CQ," he said coldly, still moving at a brisk pace.

She reached out to grab his hand, but as she held it, his was limp.

"Please hold my hand, Jack."

He did not say a word, and would not oblige. They walked for a minute without saying anything.

"Jack, I'm sorry."

"Whatever."

Jack knew that he sounded heartless, but his pride would not let him stop. The beast was dancing.

Jack could sense every rejection was like a knife slashing her soul. She started to cry quietly. They walked quickly through Limits Gates, Anna hanging on to Jack's limp hand, as Jack was slipping away.

"I'm…so…sorry," she said quietly in between sobs.

Jack's anger had subsided somewhat, but now his pride began to make excuses for his behavior. When they reached the edge of Moody Hall, Jack could see the McClain's with Ted standing by her car where she had parked earlier about a hundred feet away along the parade ground. He stopped.

"Well, I'm going to head back to barracks. Looks like your folks are waiting on you. They certainly don't want to see me," He said, emotionless.

"It's not like that, Jack."

"Oh yeah? Well what is it like? They don't want us together, and I guess that's what it's coming down to between us, too. I've gotta go."

"Goodnight, Jack," she said quietly.

She finished drying her eyes and then turned to walk to her car. Jack walked along the parade ground sidewalk, still mad, but now also at himself for making Anna cry.

But it's her fault. More so, it's her parents' fault. They're the ones who have judged me out of her life. The only reason they don't want me is because of my dad, and because of the life I've had till now, and because of how it's made me mad and all. Maybe I'm not a good guy, and they know it. They're really right. I'm not good enough for Anna.

The longer he walked, the more his conscience seemed to hold him in contempt. He knew he had been ridiculous, and foolish, and selfish. He wanted to turn around and go back and start all over.

His pride taunted him. His insides were twisting as the beast clawed its way back in. He thought that maybe he should run back across the parade deck and tell her he was sorry for treating her badly when all along she was right. But his pride said he had gone too far, so he waited. Finally, he decided to stop, to go back and make amends.

He looked back, but her car was gone.

So was the beast.

—◦◦◦—

It had been a restless and frustrating attempt to finish his English Literature theme paper and Jack closed up his books. He had accomplished little, and everything he had on paper seemed to be irrelevant drivel. Though it had been almost a week since their argument, he could not clear his mind of the overwhelming guilt he felt for the way he had treated Anna.

The lonely, cold late-night walk back to barracks seemed a reminder to Jack of earlier days when he felt so alone on the river. Sometimes the nights were cold and windy and miserable, but they were far better than the alternative of a raging father. So he slept on the banks of the James in a threadbare sleeping bag, keeping his mind off the cold by staring at the moon and listening to the sound of the waves of wind as they stirred the willows.

But Jack was tired of loneliness. This whole struggle with Anna had brought him to realize how much he really longed to be close to someone, and how much he stood to lose. He wanted to somehow fix this, but he wasn't sure if he would get the chance. His selfishness and callousness had finally cost him dearly.

He fought back wave after wave of pride telling him that he didn't need her. It was a futile battle the beast waged. Jack had tasted her love—a wonderful, beautiful, good love—and there was no convincing him that he didn't need her.

The moonlit courtyard of Old Barracks was eerily silent as Jack made his way up Sally Port to the third stoop. Every step echoed almost obnoxiously as he walked from Ghetto Corner to his room. He quickly wiped away the grease pencil mark for authorized late study on the door status card, and then stepped inside. Jack's eyes adjusted quickly to the dark room, and he could make out the silhouette of Ted sitting on the edge of his bed by the window looking out.

"You just get back, Ted?" Jack asked.

"About fifteen minutes ago. Thought I'd wait up to talk to you."

Here it comes.

"What's up?"

"I don't know, Jack, you tell me. What's going on with Anna? I've kept my mouth shut 'cause I thought you guys would work this out. I'm just being straight up with you, but it bothered the heck out of me the other night when she hardly said a word when she came over to see Dad and Mom off. I didn't notice till she kissed my cheek, but her eyes were wet. She seemed really upset. I couldn't get her to tell me. She just took off."

"We just had a little argument. No big deal."

"When it comes to my sister crying, it is a big deal, Jack."

"I didn't mean it like that."

"She's obviously pretty broken up about something. You just gonna shrug it off?"

"I'm not shrugging it off."

"I guess you seem a little cavalier. That's all."

"Look, we had an argument. I was way out of line, but…" He paused as if he couldn't figure out what to say next.

"But what?"

"Well, she was, too."

"And?"

"I don't know, I guess we both got our feelings hurt."

"So what? Did you break up with her?"

"No," Jack answered quickly, but then rethought. "I don't know. Maybe I've messed it up forever."

"Why do you think that?"

"The way I acted. How I treated her. I wouldn't forgive me."

"First of all she's not you. She's not the vengeful, unforgiving maggot that you are. What in the heck did you say to her, anyway?" Ted asked.

"I was just being ugly, and selfish—really selfish."

There was a moment of silence between them.

"Look, Jack, I know how she feels about you. I mean, she's head over heels and all. I know how Dad's not real comfortable with the idea of you two, but I don't know if it would matter if it was you or someone else. I just don't want her to get her heart broken, if she hasn't already."

"I don't either, Ted."

—◦◦◦—

Sunday, Jack lay on his cot near the window, reading the weekend edition of *The Lexington News Gazette* that he picked up after breakfast. Ted popped into the room singing, just back from Chapel. He was making all kinds of noise, much to Darryl's dismay, who was just getting up from trying to sleep off a hangover.

"Ted, have some consideration for those of us that still drink the demon rum." Darryl said rubbing his eyes.

"It's a nice day out, Sunday and all," Ted said.

Darryl got up and half-walked, half-staggered over to the sink and began washing his face.

"As soon as Ski gets back from church, let's all head out to Goshen Pass. Some of our BR's are goin' out there to catch a few rays," Ted said.

"I'm game. Lord knows I could use some fresh air and sunshine. You game, Jack?" Darryl asked.

"You guys go, I've got a paper for English Lit due Friday."

"Friday! Friday?" Ted said, and then laughed. "Look, you never know when you are going to have another Sunday like this. C'mon."

"I just don't feel like it."

"Dude," Darryl said, "I'm gonna go out on a limb, here. If this is all because your girlfriend, who happens to be Ted's sister, is having a little spat with you, maybe you've gotta think about moving on."

Ted looked at Darryl with a puzzled expression.

"All I'm saying is that you gotta make a decision," Darryl continued. "Either your gonna sit around here on your dead butt, wallowing around in self-pity, or you're gonna get up and start living like you're some kind of a normal human being, not some self-absorbed whiney pants."

"Whiney pants?" Jack and Ted asked in unison.

"Yeah, and I'm not finished."

Darryl walked back over to the mirror and started to lather up his face to shave.

"Your roommates need you to participate. I always stand a better chance with the ladies when I'm around you and Ted. So you can't say no. It's the unwritten rule. Right, Brother Rat?"

"C'mon Jack," Ted chided in, "we'll be back well before SRC, and after supper you can work on your paper."

"Alright, I'll go," Jack said, defeated.

They waited a half hour for Ski. His new girl came by with her roommate to pick him up, so Darryl decided he should go with them.

Ted and Jack put on their PT gear, with their unauthorized trunks and civilian tee shirts in a back pack, and headed out on the two mile trek to Ted's car, parked in an old guys garage half-way across town.

On the way to the Pass, Ted and Jack didn't talk much, opting to crank the stereo and sing with the beach music. It was the first time Jack had been to Goshen Pass, and he stayed transfixed on the river as they began to wind up into the canyon. By the time they arrived, Ski and Darryl were already there.

They *stopped* at a riverside picnic area that was about two hundred yards long, and had a pavilion and some picnic tables. Ted pulled the car into the parking area that was little more than an exaggerated shoulder retained from the picnic area below by an eight foot high rock wall that ran the length of the park. He shut the car off, took out his keys, and began to get out.

"C'mon, let's go down to the river," he said.

"Saw Anna's car. You didn't tell me she would be here."

"What? Am I supposed to clear everywhere I go with my sister to make sure we don't cross paths?"

"Ted, she goes to Hollins. It's not like this is her back yard."

Ted let out a breath of exasperation.

"Alright, alright. I told her to come. No time like the present to make amends. Chop-chop!"

"I don't know what to say. It's gone on too long, now."

"Well, I guess you'll never know what to say if you don't get off your dead butt and at least try something out on her."

Jack opened the car door and got out. He followed Ted down a set of stone steps, across the picnic area and along a path through some tall grass that opened up to the river's edge. Ted went to a big rock and began taking off his shirt and shoes.

Jack stood in the area along the bank that was covered in large smooth rocks that had washed down through the canyon for eons. Some of the boulders were only big enough to step on, while others were big enough to scale and have a picnic. Jack spied a rather large one that jutted out well above the rest about fifty yards upstream. He began to make his way toward it.

Out in the river, a handful of cadets and girls sat around sunning themselves on beach towels or in the water on inner tubes. Jack climbed the rock and looked over at Anna.

I'm scared. Will she ever talk to me again? I've ruined it. I've ruined everything. She's so beautiful. She seems happy. Just a sign things are over, I suppose. She's over me.

Jack lay back on the rock and closed his eyes. He was tired of fighting himself.

I'm tired. I can sleep, here.

He was there for quite awhile. The sound of the water running through the rocks, making small waterfalls and rapids that gurgled and splashed, calmed him and had him on the edge of a sound sleep, when he heard someone climbing up beside him.

He thought it might be Ted, but as he carefully peered through slightly cracked open eyelids, through his eyelashes, so that whoever it was would think that he was asleep, he saw that it was Anna and his heart immediately began to race. She climbed up and sat beside him, holding her tan knees in her arms, as she looked out at the rest of the group, downstream goofing around in inner-tubes.

They sat there like that for quite awhile; Jack playing possum and Anna too scared to talk. She finally let go of her knees, took one of Jack's tennis shoes for a pillow, and lay back on the rock beside him.

Oh, how Jack ached to apologize, to end this ridiculous charade, to shower her with affections and affections and affections. He wanted to go back to the beginning and feel the tingle and thrill of their mutual flirtations. He wanted to sit up and shout out loud how much he loved her and how he would be willing to wait for whatever she needed to wait for.

The clock was ticking, but his fear of her rejection was like a wall of Goshen boulders.

As he lay there with sweat pooling up in the corners of his eyes, he felt the most subtle touch on his right hand's little finger. A wave of tingle ran down his body. It was the slightest unintentional brush; as if her hand had just relaxed and accidentally touched his.

Jack decided at that moment, that he would take a chance.

He slowly lifted his little finger and laid it over the top of hers. She breathed in softly and obliged by interlocking her little finger with his. Jack flushed warmly with relief, turned his head to look at Anna, and Anna's eyes filled with tears, as the apparent pent up anxiety of weeks came flooding out.

Her tears ran rapidly down her cheekbones and off the back of her neck. They clasped their whole hands together, intertwining their fingers and squeezing tightly. Then, Anna moved her left foot until it touched Jack's right. Jack acknowledged by rubbing the top of his foot against the sole of hers, as if to say everything was going to be alright. They lay there for a moment, silent under the sun.

"I'm sorry. I'm so sorry for everything, Anna," Jack said just above a whisper.

"I love you, Jack Hartman."

"I love you, too, Anna McClain."

PART 3

THE
BROTHERHOOD

CHAPTER FIFTEEN

THE RING

Summer faded. Blood red sunsets brought them closer to another winter with all of its gray sky wind that blew steadily down the valley. Leaves turned a thousand shades of autumn as they drained of green and the life of trees receded somewhere deep inside, sleeping.

The corps would lose the white ducks by late October and begin wearing "woolies"—the all-wool uniform pants—though the ducks would remain a uniform option. White blouse gave way to grey wool blouse, the more recognizable blue-gray cadet uniform with the black collar that resembled that of a priest, minus the white vestigial tab. A hush of drab settled over the Corps as it began its descent into winter.

The Dark Ages. That was what they called it.

Jack returned for his second class year with rank again. He had earned the Echo Company master sergeant position, a job that had him hopping long before Cadre week kicked off for the new Rats. Ted, having missed a semester, was overlooked for rank; a fact that clearly bothered him. Ski had outdone them all, being made over to Regimental S-1 sergeant.

Most importantly for all of them was the fact that this was the blessed year, the year of Ring Figure.

Ring Figure was more than an occasion. It was a zenith, an event that peaked for a moment, certainly, but the whole crescendo leading up to it was every bit as exhilarating. It was a special time particularly marked by southern genteel tradition.

It was the official welcoming into the circle of VMI men.

Every event culminated in another. Second class week when the seconds took charge of the corps, the somber Ring Ceremony, Ring Figure Hop—more the traditional pre-Civil War southern ball, passing through the ring with the ladies in their white southern belle gowns, brandy and cigars at a swanky hotel in Richmond or Roanoke. It was certainly the largest and most memorable event in the life of any cadet, rivaling even graduation—their Independence Day.

"Hey Jack," Ted began one afternoon, breaking the silence as they lay in their respective bunks, "you've seemed a bit distant, lately. What's up?"

Jack sat up and dropped his feet off the edge of his bunk.

"I promised myself I wasn't going to make a big deal out of this; that I wasn't going to share it ahead of time unless someone asked me," said Jack.

"Okay, so what exactly have I asked?"

"Well, I know I've gotta ask your dad first, but," Jack paused, "I'm gonna ask Anna to, y'know, marry me."

Ted looked stunned. He sat up and shook his head, got up from his bunk and then walked to the back window. Several leaves flitted by, carried on a random gust.

"You're not thinking about any time soon, right?" He sounded flustered, awkward.

"No, obviously," Jack replied, plopping back flat into his mattress. "We both have school. Anna graduates in the spring and, of course, I have first class year. So, probably right after graduation. I haven't formally asked her yet, and won't until I talk to your dad."

"She's not pregnant, right?" Ted asked.

"No. We've somehow managed to stay out of that kind of trouble."

"Her idea?"

"Well, I guess, but I agree with it. I love her, and I sure don't want to mess things up."

Ted turned and looked out the window.

"I don't think you understand how tough it's going to be to get Dad to go for *this*. He thinks you're a decent guy, but he has plans for her."

"She's never discussed any plans with me. What plans?" asked Jack.

Ted turned back and looked directly at Jack.

"He will not agree with Anna marrying a man that is not a professing Christian."

Jack felt as if Ted had just struck him. He'd been hinting around it for over a year.

"You could've told me this a while back," Jack said.

"I know. I just didn't know how to approach it. Anyway, I've been talking about faith to you, and what that means. You're just hard-headed."

"Doesn't matter, I'm ready to make that happen."

"It doesn't work like that. You can't just become a Christian because you want to marry a certain girl. And Dad isn't going to buy it. There'll need to be some track record."

"C'mon, man, we've been seeing each other for two years. Your dad should know by now I'm a pretty good guy."

"He ain't interested in a good guy. He wants to know his daughter is marrying someone who follows Christ," Ted said.

"After two years being around you and Anna, I think I'm ready. I think I can handle your old man."

"Well, bottom line is Anna can do whatever she wants, but she's always been a daddy's girl. She'll want his blessing, bad. Dad just isn't going to give it to her without assurances. He'll have to be pretty sure of you."

"Fine, I'm okay with that."

"Great, let's sit down as soon as possible, and talk about how a person becomes a Christian."

"Fine, but right now, we need to go lead Rat PT."

Jack wore his long johns under his grey wool uniform to go downtown. It was the Saturday before Ring Figure week, and it was another biting and windy November day, with temperatures in the low thirties. Remnant leaves, last left hanging by fading autumn winds, were finally giving way to winter. They twirled in eddies along Letcher Avenue as Jack crossed Limits Gates.

Most of the Corps was headed to Richmond for the football game that would start at nineteen hundred hours. Jack was planning on catching a last minute ride with Mark Johnson, their old cadre corporal, who was now a much laid-back first class private and fellow English major.

But it was more than a routine Saturday in the fall with all of its details and arrangements and football games and goofing off somewhere other than the Institute, somewhere cadets could enjoy a fleeting moment of normalcy. This was a big Saturday. There were waves of adrenaline and nervousness and excitement that Jack could feel as he walked down Letcher Avenue towards downtown Lexington.

The ring.

It was, of course, one of the most important purchases Jack would make in his life. Anna would wake up every morning and look at it and be reminded of how much Jack loved her.

A ring. Jack was on his way to buy it. It was going to cost him every penny he had and would have for quite some time. It had, however, created a bit of a dilemma, the whole reason he would not have the money for his VMI ring.

Ring Figure had come too quickly. Jack burned inside for his VMI ring. He had seen all of the upperclassmen's rings, his dyke's and others, but they were not quite as impressive as the old one he saw in the VMI Museum.

It caught his eye because it had no antique shading in the finish and the stone was the light green Peridot that was also his birth stone. Jack wanted one just like it on his finger. He couldn't wait to wear it, and be reminded of the sweat parties and Phelps and all the stress of the system, every painful and agonizing thing he and every one of his Brother Rats had suffered.

As disappointed as he felt, he would not have enough money to buy one in time for Ring Figure. So he buried his disappointment in thoughts of Anna.

—◦◦◦—

"Ted! Ted!" Jack yelled across the parking lot as he made the long trek from the odd and impermissible parking spot that Mark Johnson had found between some frat row dumpsters. They had walked quite a while to get near the stadium parking, and Jack saw Ted a hundred yards or so away.

"Getting worried you weren't gonna take advantage of this permit." Ted laughed.

"I got it." Jack grinned.

"Got what?" Darryl said as he walked up behind them, tipping Jack's hat down over his eyes.

"It," Jack replied, holding up a small black box. "Look."

They stopped and huddled under a bright street lamp. Jack opened the box to reveal a rather underwhelming solitaire.

"Nice, Jack, but what's your plan for Dad?" Ted asked.

"I guess I'll ask him tonight."

"Geez, dude, you're really gonna tie the knot?" Ski asked.

"That stinks," said Darryl. "The townies are going to be in mourning for months, at least the two ugly ones that know *you*, Jack."

"Very funny," Jack replied.

"So how much did that thing cost?" asked Ski.

"Hey, hey, hey!" Ted interrupted. "It's not polite to ask someone how much they spent on anything like that. Besides, I'm her brother, and I for sure shouldn't know!"

Jack closed the box and put it back in his pocket. They began walking toward the gate.

"You're just afraid that you might find out that your future brother-in-law is cheap," said Darryl.

"Me, cheap?"

"He ain't cheap," Ted said.

They were becoming part of the crowd, only about twenty feet from the gate.

"How do *you* know I'm not cheap, Ted?"

"Because I know how much you spent on that thing!"

"Oh, really? How much?" Jack was genuinely curious.

Ted looked at him and grinned.

"Educated guess says everything you had."

"Theodore, the boys are here!" Annabelle shouted upstairs to Mr. McClain.

Ted, Jack, Darryl, and Ski were filing into the living room at the McClain's home, each dropping his bag at his feet, and then plopping down on the sectional sofa that wrapped around three sides of the sunken center of the floor. "Nice place ya got here, Mrs. McClain," said Darryl.

"Why, thank you, Darryl. I am pleased that you were able to visit," she replied in her best Southern Belle accent.

"Sorry we got in so late, Mom."

"Don't be silly, Teddy, I didn't expect you in any earlier than this."

"It didn't help that we almost got in a brawl over by the frats," said Ted.

"What happened? Or, do I want to know?"

"Some frat boys tried to pick a fight with Mark Johnson because he parked his car between their dumpsters," said Jack, "and it turned into a bit of a stand-off. People yellin' and all. Kinda like bein' in high school again."

"Ah, the Richmond juvenile elite. They live here for three or four years, spending their time in their squalor of a frat house, protecting Richmond from undesirable out-of-towners, such as yourselves, and especially yourselves. They listen to their professors only enough to garner the dross from their liberal teaching until they have nothing left to say but socialist anti-military drivel they don't even comprehend. But, it makes them feel intelligent," Annabelle said.

"Geez, Mom, that was really different."

"I guess I can see where Anna gets her passion," said Jack.

"Ted's mom, thrashing some Richmond Spider Greeks, very nice," added Darryl.

"Jack, I see you made it up alright. What kept you in Lexington till the last second?" she asked.

"Uh, well." Jack was taken off guard. "I just had some stuff to do in town to get ready for Ring Figure. That's all."

"Oh yes, Anna is so excited about Ring Figure. You know, it was the weekend that Theodore and I officially fell in love."

"This is creepy," said Ted. "Anna is excited now about something that has to do with VMI, and Mom thinks that falling in love can have an 'official' date!"

"So I've heard," said Jack.

"Teddy, you know your father and I are both very organized and efficient. We have an official date for just about everything."

"Well, we officially lost tonight, but it was quite a game. We were down by a touchdown and had gotten the ball to about the twenty-five yard line when we coughed it up on a fumble. Anyway, they ended up scoring again and we couldn't answer in the last minute and a half."

"So we heard. Tragic, I suppose. Football is everything to everybody around here. Let's go to the kitchen," Mrs. McClain said. "I've prepared a sandwich tray and some soup. You boys must have frozen half to death at that game tonight. It was thirty-five degrees."

"Yes Ma'am," they all said in near unison.

They made sandwiches and Mrs. McClain entertained for a half hour. She was a master at asking questions and pulling out every detail of a person's life and then committing them to memory. They ate and talked and laughed. Eventually, Theodore McClain II came down to the kitchen. He had on a fresh jogging suit and his hair was wet, but combed neatly.

"Gentlemen, gentlemen, gentlemen…and lady," he said boisterously as he walked in and shook hands with each of them, ending at Mrs. McClain. He took up her hand and kissed the back of it gently as he bowed to her.

"I understand we didn't do so hot tonight," he said, still looking at his wife.

"The score looks a lot worse than the game. We hung with 'em till the very end," Ted answered.

"Well, that's something, I suppose. I see you fellas have had a chance to eat. We've got two beds set up in the guest room and Ted's room, of course, has two beds."

"We haven't gotten to that part, dear. You come rolling in like a hurricane, always in a hurry. Give the boys a chance to wind down."

"Which reminds me, Dad, when did you and Mom officially fall in love?" Ted asked, winking at his mother.

"Easy one. My Ring Figure."

"Weird," said Ski.

"Uncanny," said Darryl.

"I tell ya, they're real fans of their calendar," said Ted.

They laughed, though Jack seemed in another world. Ted looked at him with a raised eyebrow. That's when Jack committed in his mind to go through with it. It was one of those all of the sudden things when he saw a gap in the conversation barely big enough to drive a bike through. It just seemed like it might be the best time.

"Mr. McClain," Jack said, turning to face Ted's dad, "can we talk?"

"Of course, Jack, what's up?"

"Well, I was hoping that we could talk alone."

"Sounds serious," said Ted. "I'm sure we won't be any imposition. Go ahead, Jack."

"I don't think so," Mrs. McClain said. She shot a nervous glance at her husband. "Why don't you show the other guys upstairs, Teddy?"

"Alright, to the room," answered Ted. "Might as well grab your gear, guys."

Ted headed upstairs with Darryl and Ski. They joked on the way up the stairs, Ted pausing to look at his mother, nervously.

"I suppose this is man-talk. Why don't you two talk in the study so that I can get this kitchen back in order?" she said.

Jack followed Mr. McClain through the living room and across the two-story foyer to the rather large ornate mahogany doors that opened to his study. He felt nauseous. Though Jack had been in the study before, for some reason it took on a completely different appearance. It seemed bigger and more imposing than the last time he had been there.

Jack felt the nervousness he used to get when he started a new school as a small child. He was here in this sacred place, surrounded by the ghosts of a multitude of forefathers whose eyes bore down on him, about to make the most sacred request that a man can make to the father of a daughter. He was not prepared. His confidence fleeting, he could not speak.

"Have a seat, Jack, while I light this fire. A good fire brings out the best of our thoughts." He pointed Jack to one of two chairs that sat in front of his desk and pulled the other one close to the shallow hearth.

Once the pilot was lit, Mr. McClain had Jack pull his chair up close to the hearth as he closed the screen and locked the glass doors back.

"Alrighty, Mr. Hartman, what's up your sleeve?"

"Well Sir, I...um...wanted to talk to you about Anna. Well, and me, Anna and me."

"I understand you two are still dating, right?" he asked.

Jack could already feel the resistance.

Still? Still?

"Yes, sir. But it's more than that."

"I'm guessing you are going to tell me you two are getting serious."

"Oh, yes sir, very much so. I…uh…I love Anna."

"Well, isn't that just something?"

Mr. McClain stood up and walked over to the window behind his desk. He did not say anything else, just stood there with his hands on his hips, looking out.

Then it came.

"There was a time during your Rat year Annabelle was talking seriously about adopting you. She was crazy about bringing you into the family, and helping you get through college. I didn't oppose it in principle, but when I saw the way you looked at Anna, I wouldn't have it. I knew it would be nothing but trouble," he said, still facing the window.

"You were thinking about adopting me?"

McClain turned and stood, crossing his forearms, resting them on the back of his office chair.

"For a brief time. I don't know, we may have even talked about it for a year."

"But you thought I would move in and take your daughter?"

"I suppose, and that just wasn't in the plans. Look, Annabelle is oblivious to what goes on in a young man's head when it comes to girls, but I'm not. I wanted Anna to have a chance to mature a bit after college, and then there would be plenty of decent guys she could consider."

"I guess I'm not one of the decent ones, then."

"It's not that you're not decent, it's just that I don't want to have to worry about her."

"Because my dad was an alcoholic, and he had a temper?"

"It's certainly in the back of my mind. But to start with, you're not even a Christian. I will not allow Anna to be in a serious romantic relationship with someone who doesn't share our beliefs."

Too late for that, sir.

Jack thought better than to say it, though. He sunk with a wave of depression.

Guess I won't be asking the question tonight.

He felt the urge to say something, to not be put off summarily. He felt a tinge of anger swell up.

"I'm guessing that if I became a Christian right here and now, and Jesus appeared and personally confirmed it, you still would object to me marrying Anna."

McClain looked stunned.

"Marry? We weren't talking about marriage."

"That's what I came in your study, to ask you for Anna's hand."

Mr. McClain looked flabbergasted.

"Whoa. When did all this happen? Last I heard, you two were only dating occasionally."

"The summer was short for me. I worked a lot of hours to get some money for the year saved up. We went out a few times. Then I had to be back to VMI early for Cadre. We've been out almost every weekend since."

"Look, before you ask, the answer is no."

"Why does it seem I'm not good enough for your family?" Jack was angry, the beast rising in him. He fought it back.

"It's not a matter of good enough or not good enough. It's a matter of right and wrong."

"I'm wrong for her?"

"Right now, yes."

Mr. McClain sounded emphatic, like there was no turning back, but he had left the door to Anna slightly ajar.

Right now?

It emboldened Jack.

Is he bending?

"By that, do you mean there might be a chance, in time?"

"I suppose, but you will really have to show me you can walk the walk. Do you even know what it means to believe in Christ?"

"Ted's talked with me. I think I get it."

"I don't want you becoming a Christian just because you want to win my daughter. You need to be genuine about it, and I need to see a lifestyle change that lasts for some time before I can even think about the two of you getting married."

"Alright Mr. McClain, I can live with that."

"So does she know about this?" Mr. McClain asked.

"No, but she recently asked me if I was thinking about asking you. She said it probably would not go so well. I guess she was right."

"She usually is."

CHAPTER SIXTEEN

Brotherhood

"Sound Adjutant's Call!"

The Regimental Band played the fanfare from their position in Jackson Arch, followed by a loud rebel yell from the entire Corps, the traditional kick-off to every parade, reminiscent of a Confederate unit about to assault.

The drums began their cadence and the Regiment began maneuvering onto the parade ground. Platoon by platoon they marched out of the arch in perfect rows and columns. The band marched into position at the far side of the field playing a medley of marches, drums echoing off the surrounding buildings and even, at times, off of House Mountain that loomed in the distance.

They had planned this parade and walked through it and practiced it until they were nearly sick of it. With simultaneous crisp saber salutes, the three battalion commanders snapped their sabers back to the carry position and executed an about face.

One, two, three.

Snap.

Now facing the first battalion, his battalion, Jack prepared to give the command that sent chills up his spine when he saw the parade as an eight year old boy. For a brief moment he relished the bite of the light breeze against his face and the sound of the feathers in his officer's plume above his shako, rustling. He took a deep breath.

It was almost a song, stretching the end of 'battalion' and the middle of 'attention' as his head swiveled from left to right across the three companies. Jack ordered the battalion to attention and present arms.

The loud and succinct rattle of four hundred twenty-three M-14 rifles through the three count movement stunned Jack from this new perspective. The delayed echo off of the academic buildings behind, gave Jack a chill.

The battalion at present arms, he executed an about face and gave the low voice command to his staff to present arms. The seven sabers moved in crisp unison through the two count saber manual to the present arms position. Second battalion and Rat battalion commanders followed suit, calling their battalions to attention and present arms, and then their staffs likewise.

"Bring your battalions to order arms and parade rest!"

Ted had not been qualified to be given rank because of his semester off, but would qualify at the end of the semester. Jack knew it would mean Ted would probably only get a line position, but if he did well, he might make battalion staff. He hoped could both serve on battalion staff together.

All up to the powers that be, I suppose.

The rest of parade seemed routine. Jack was in his element. Manual of arms. Ceremonial presentations. Jack's mind wandered.

The ring. Tonight the ring. Giving her the ring.

His heart beat harder for a moment, and then settled, distracted by a gust of wind that challenged the feathery plume above his shako. His concentration on the order of commands slipped in and out, wistfully dancing with the anticipation of Anna.

"Pass in review!" the Adjutant commanded.

Jack called out the appropriate commands to the companies, and they began to march. Sharp, crisp. Rows of rifles in exquisite symmetry. Rows, columns and angles. Glistening brass breastplates clasped on white crossdyke, and rows of cupped left hands with crisp white gloves, swinging in synchronized rhythm.

Jack had never been more satisfied, and as he passed in review with his staff, he sensed the honor of it. Only the best of the best could earn a battalion command, as there were only two. He wanted it, though, and knew his current ring figure position might be a hint he would get it.

It meant everything to him. The prestige and honor of it, especially for the one who believed he came from the lowest existence. It would mean the verification of his victory over his past.

And he wanted his best friend with him.

———

Jack sat between Troy Henson and Jeff Harrington, shoulder to shoulder, in J.M. Hall. His golden master sergeant stripes rubbed against Hinton's line sergeant chevrons on Jack's left, and Harrington's color sergeant chevrons and star against his right. The class squeezed in tightly in each row of pews, in alphabetical order, coatee and white gloves.

Jack's mind raced in a different direction. He would walk the stage and receive his empty box in a few minutes. While others around him tried on their rings he would sit and admire them. But he wasn't thinking about that.

Anna McClain, will you marry me? That's too old fashioned. Anna, I have something for you. That doesn't even ask about the marriage. Anna, your dad would kill me if he found out, but… Yeah, more like it.

The chapel was filled with the parents and girlfriends from the balcony that wrapped the entire sanctuary to the last fifteen rows of pews on the floor level. Jack and three hundred and seven Brother Rats sat in the first twenty-five rows, somewhat nervous, smiling, looking forward to holding their rings for the first time.

After the chaplain's convocation and brief speeches by the superintendant and the second class president, the wait was over. Row by row, they stood, walked across the stage and received their boxes. In those boxes, nestled in red velvet, a ring perched perfectly with a glistening stone of green, red, blue, or even black onyx.

As each of them sat back in his assigned spot on the pew, he nervously opened the box as he carefully cradled it, stared at the beauty of it, and then offered a proud glimpse to others like the father of a newborn might do.

Jack knew his box was empty, so he admired Troy Henson's ring first, then Harrington's. He then held his box clasped in both hands to hide its barrenness, remembering how he covered torn old shoes on his feet in grade school.

"Jack, let's see your ring," Troy said.

"I didn't get one. They gave me the box so I would still be a part of the ceremony. Pictures and all," Jack said, shrugging.

"No way, dude. Your roommates couldn't help you out?"

"I refused to let them. Well, I mean by that I didn't tell them I wasn't getting one right now. But I'll get one down the road. Just gotta put together some more funds."

As Jack was whispering to Troy Henson, he felt someone open the box in his hand. Instinctively, Jack yanked it away.

"Sorry, Jack. I just wanted to get a look at your stone. Didn't mean to startle you," said Jeff.

"Jack, what's with the note?" asked Troy.

The box had clamped shut again, but a folded piece of paper hung a couple inches out of it. Jack pulled the paper so that it slid out of the closed box. It was stationary, folded over three times and then obviously rolled up and stuck in the box. Jack unfolded it and began to read carefully penned words.

Dear Jack,

When I heard what had happened—what you had done for Anna—I could not allow you to miss this moment. You have proven to me you are an honorable man, willing to sacrifice greatly for the one he loves. We may have some work to do to convince Theodore, but you have won my heart and my approval. I cannot know what your future will hold, but if you do marry Anna, then she could not have done better, and you will be a part of a loving family.

If you don't, then know that you will always be a son to me, and you have a place in our home, if you desire.

Love,
Annabelle

Jack sat, stunned, tears filling his eyes. He could not discern whether it was the sensation of a mother's love torquing his heart, or the joy at being half-way home to marrying Anna. Jack burned for family as much as he had burned for Anna. For the first time, he truly sensed the love of a mother, unconditional and unwarranted.

Jack slowly pried open the wooden clamshell. There perched in red velvet, the ring, lightly antiqued with the light green Peridot sparkling in the bezel.

Just like the one in the museum downstairs. How could she know?

His heart raced with excitement he hadn't felt since Breakout. His hands were shaking, and Jack stared at the ring, breathing slowly trying to control them.

"I thought you weren't getting a ring, Jack," Troy whispered.

Only then did Jack look up just as tears spilled over the bottoms of his eyelids.

He handed Troy the letter.

"I didn't know," was all he could say and still maintain control.

Troy read the letter, then looked at the ring.

"That's really cool. That's Ted's mom, right?"

"Yeah."

"You must've made a good impression. I guess Anna's the one I've seen you out with around town?"

"Yeah, that's her," Jack whispered.

"I met Ted's dad last year. They seem to be some fine people."

"The best."

—⁓⁓⁓—

"Cadet Jack Hartman, escorted by Miss Anna McClain."

They stood in the walk-through ring long enough for Anna to slide Jack's VMI ring on his finger, and to look in each other's eyes. Anna smiled shyly and her face flushed. It felt to Jack like something permanent, something marital.

Jack felt the flash of several cameras, and knew it was time to turn and take their place on the gym floor.

"Tell me we'll be doing this again, soon," said Jack as he held out his arm.

Anna wove her hand under and through his arm in genteel escort fashion, and they began the walk down the ramp from the ring and over to their place on the floor.

"I hope," Anna said.

Jack smiled. His heart pounded. He had anticipated every moment of this night, every soft touch, every look filled with an eager love. But it hadn't worked out exactly as he had envisioned.

Anna had been sick off and on for the last couple of weeks, and tonight had been rough for her. To make matters worse, she had seemed depressed lately and unsure of the plans they had toyed with in conversations throughout the summer. She was a trooper, though, and was doing everything possible to make the evening enjoyable, regardless of how badly she felt.

I love her. I love her.

They took their place in the formation of coateed cadets and white-gowned debutantes on the ballroom floor watching the other Brother Rats and their dates presented.

I love her. I love her.

Over and over, Jack hung on the refrain. Anna squeezed his arm tightly when Ted McClain and Jenny Lipscomb were presented.

"Our dear Teddy," she said, then looked at Jack and smiled.

Yes, he will be ours. He will soon be my brother-in-law.

"What was that?" Anna asked quietly.

"Nothing. I didn't say anything," replied Jack.

"I'm sorry, I thought I heard you say something."

She can almost hear my thoughts. Am I thinking that loud?

Following the presentation and the first formal dance, Jack and Anna found Ted and Jenny. They made their way off the dance floor and through the throng of parents, cadets and other onlookers till they found the McClain's.

"Where are Ski and Darryl?" Mr. McClain asked Ted.

"I'm sure they're making their way over. I told them you and Mom wanted a picture of all of us."

"Yes, I do. And I snapped some great shots of all you boys and your lovely dates," said Mrs. McClain.

"You got all the roommates, Mom?" asked Ted.

"No, son. She means she got the whole class. All three hundred and whatever. Ten rolls of film," Mr. McClain said, holding up the camera bag.

"Well, I just started with the first one and I couldn't stop."

"Hey, guys!" Ski and Darryl walked up to them, leading their dates through the crowd. Darryl introduced both the girls to the McClain's. They all walked outside to the parapet and gathered for a few pictures.

"That's it," Mrs. McClain said.

"What?" asked Ted.

"Well," she said, then paused to grin sheepishly, "it seems I've run out of film. I sure hope these come out."

Darryl and Ski exchanged courtesies and returned to Cocke Hall with their dates. Jack, Anna, and Jenny waited for Ted, who had been pulled aside by Mr. McClain, up to the top of the parapet beside one of the French cannons, where they were engaged in a stern, but whispered, conversation.

"Mrs. McClain," said Jack, "I haven't had the chance to…"

"To finish our small talk about your goals in life, I know," she interrupted. "I'm certain we will resume our conversation exactly where we left off. What was it, almost two years ago?"

Her interruption was distinctive and swift. It took Jack off guard. His mind raced.

No one knows what she did. She doesn't want anyone to know.

"You read my mind," he replied.

Mrs. McClain looked at Jack, smiled and winked. He knew, then, they had an understanding, that she had accepted the expression of gratitude she had severed so abruptly, and he was not to tell anyone about it. He bowed his head back to her.

"Daddy, let Teddy go, please," Anna called out.

"We're on the way," Mr. McClain replied. "Remember what I said, Ted, and don't let me down on this."

Though he apparently didn't mean for anyone but Ted to hear it, they were far enough apart he had to speak over a whisper. It was barely audible, but Jack could hear what Mr. McClain said in the echoes of the courtyard.

He can't tell her to say no. I won't let it happen. I love her and I've done nothing wrong. I will ask her as quickly as I can find some privacy.

Ted and Anna kissed their parents before they left. Then Jack, Anna, Ted, and Jenny walked back into Cocke Hall.

"It's amazing what you can do with a few thousand rolls of streamers and a ton of linens," said Ted.

"The hop and floor guys are pros, look at this place," Jack said.

"You'd never know this is an old gym if it wasn't for the smell of sweaty socks," said Jenny.

They all laughed.

"Jack, come over here. Ladies, we'll be back in a second," said Ted.

They walked about fifteen feet away from the girls, and then Ted turned to Jack.

"Look, man, I'm supposed to tell you not to ask Anna to marry you. They're assuming you were going to, and though Mom isn't bothered by it, Dad doesn't want it to happen."

"Well, here's a news flash, Ted. Your mom is for it. She wants me to marry Anna, and I'm leaving it up to her to square it with your dad."

"You know I'm okay with it. I mean, I think it would be great. But Dad, Jack, It's gonna be a problem."

"What do you want me to do? I've got this ring, and my hearts been set on this for a long time. And Anna, well, I'm pretty sure she's expecting it. I can't just shut all that down."

"It's a ring and some emotions, and you're a man. Get a grip."

"This is the best grip I've ever had, and I'm not going to let go," said Jack, and he turned to walk back to where the girls were waiting.

Ted stood there for a minute, hands on his hips and head down. Jack looked back when he made it to Anna. He felt bad for Ted, knowing he'd been stuck in the middle of this against his desire. Ted finally joined them.

"Alright, you win," Ted said as he walked up, "but promise me you won't make a big deal of it, that we can hold off on telling Dad and Mom."

"Promise."

They shook hands, then switched to a thumb-wrap grip and pulled each other close to the chest.

"What are we not telling Mom and Dad about?" asked Anna.

"Well, uh," said Jack.

He looked at Ted, who looked back at him and shrugged.

In the awkwardness of the moment, Jack heard it.

> I love east coast beaches,
> We'll have some fun in the sun,
> Build a castle in the sand,
> 'Cause I love east coast beaches,
> Music and fun on the boardwalk
> With the girl I love…

"Follow me," said Jack.

He held out his hand to Anna. She looked at him with a half-smile and raised her right eyebrow.

"And what, may I ask, is this all about?" she asked.

"Just follow him, Anna," Jenny said. "You've always said you like adventure."

"I suppose."

Anna reached up and grabbed Jack's waiting hand.

Jack did not skirt around the edge of the dance floor, he walked straight through the middle of it, sometimes cutting between dancing couples. Ted and Jenny hurried behind them.

When they made it to the far corner of the gym, Anna remembered where they were.

"The stairwell," she said. "We danced in the stairwell."

"Yes, we did," replied Jack, as he opened the door.

Anna walked through.

The safety lamp above the doors was out, and the only light was that which filtered in from the stairwell doors above and below. An emergency exit sign painted the walls a dim red-orange, the warmth of which seemed in opposition to the coolness of the stairwell.

"This isn't so bad. I thought it would be much colder in here," said Jack.

"It's certainly a nice spot to escape a hot dance floor. So tell me, Jack, why are we here?"

"Remember when we sat in the window that night?"

"The night I tried to teach you to dance, you were so pitiful," Anna answered, then laughed.

"Hey, I was catching on."

"You were. And the window," she said, walking over to it, "yes I remember it. You were so sweet. Your hands were shaking, you know."

"Yeah, I know. I was nervous. I was falling in love."

She put her hands on the window sill, and looked back at Jack. There was no moon out like the first night they sat there, but her face glowed again in the red-orange radiance of the emergency exit sign.

"And did you keep falling, Cadet Hartman?"

I can't do it. I'm not sure she'll agree. What if she's worried about her dad? But I have to do it. I need to ask. I need to know.

He walked to her and she turned to face him, leaning against the bottom of the window sill. Jack wrapped his arms around her shoulders, and Anna slid her arms around the middle of his back.

"Yes, hopelessly," Jack said. "And I don't know if I'll ever stop falling in love with you. Every time I think I've reached the deepest part, it just gets deeper."

"Me too, but I need to say something."

Oh no, here it comes. Please don't say no.

"Say it."

She laid her head against his chest, as if she could not look him in the eye. Jack's heart was pounding like the heart of a petrified witness in a courtroom. He was suddenly overcome with nausea and fear.

"I'm worried, Jack."

Anna turned and looked out the window into the blackness of the night. Jack wrapped his arms around her from behind, his hands clasped at her midriff.

"About what?" he asked.

"Jack I…I…"

Jack sensed a quivering in her voice. He leaned forward over her right shoulder and glanced at her face from the side. He could see her tears.

"What's wrong?"

She said nothing. No response. Just staring into the blackness and tears.

Nothing is going right. I need to ask her. God, if you can hear me, help me ask her.

Anna wiped her tears quickly and turned in Jack's arms to look at him again.

"I just can't talk about it now."

"But you'll tell me soon, right?"

"Yes, I promise," said Anna.

Thank you, God.

"Well, as I was saying, the night we sat in this window, and I fell in love with you, I want to do that again."

"You want to fall in love again?"

"No, sit in the window, silly."

Anna laughed hard with her head thrown back. Her eyes were still wet and her nose reddened. The odd combinations of her emotions penetrated Jack's thoughts, and he sensed her fragility.

I love this girl. I love her.

"I don't think I can get up there in this gown."

"Hmmm. Let me help you."

Jack swept her up in his arms, and set her in the box window.

"This must be important for you to pick me up in my white gown, and set me in this dusty window sill."

"Trust me, it's clean. And yes, it is important."

Here goes.

Jack unbuttoned a button on his coatee and reached inside around his chest. He fumbled for a moment, and finally pulled out a small envelope, of which he opened the top, and let the ring slide out into his right hand. Jack pulled up Anna's left hand, then looked up into her eyes.

"I know I need to get things straight with God and all, and that will happen. I know your dad needs to approve, and though I can't control what your dad decides, I know we have your mom's blessing. It may sound kind of conditional, but Anna, will you, um, would you be my wife? Will you marry me?"

Tears streamed down her face, and the flood of emotion restrained her speech. She sat in the window, Jack holding the ring and her left hand, as she wept softly for about a minute. Finally, she did not try to dry her face, but took in a deep breath.

She pulled her left hand away.

Wha...what?

"Jack, it's too soon," she said, turning her face toward the window.

Jack stood for a moment, waiting for something more, some deeper explanation.

Too soon. Too soon for what? We're in love. She knew I was going to ask this. What's going on?

"I don't understand. I mean, I thought we were ready for this," Jack said.

"I know, Jack, I know," she said turning back to face him. "I knew we were ready, and I knew you were going to ask me, and I knew Dad would probably interfere, but you would do it anyway. I knew what you were doing when you set me in this window sill. I knew all of this, but I couldn't stop any of it. Like everything, it just came at me and I couldn't stop it."

She crumpled over almost fetal and leaned into Jack's chest. From a place deep inside her, that abyss where the deepest hurts lie in wait, a place from where most never dare draw emotion, Anna began to overflow. Her sobs turned to wailing—broken, twisted, and painful wailing like Jack had never heard before.

Jack stood, holding her and comforting her, but saying nothing. He was broken and confused, and his heart was pounding. Whatever heart-wrenching hurt he was feeling, he knew it was nothing like what Anna was experiencing. All of it was only more difficult, because he didn't know why she was hurting.

The door to the stairwell opened quietly behind Jack.

"Is everything okay?" Jenny asked.

Jack turned to Jenny and shook his head. She slowly walked over, her face covered with shock and sadness, one hand over her mouth.

"Anna, are you okay?" she asked.

Ted stood just inside the door, holding it shut. Jack shot him a nervous glance. Anna began to soften her cries till she was no more than whimpering quietly.

"Anna, let's go outside, away from all this," Jenny said.

Anna nodded her head, and then brought her legs over the side. Jack picked her up and set her on her feet on the landing.

"Jack, I'm sorry. I just feel sick and I think I have some hormones working me over. It's not you, I promise," Anna said.

She kissed Jack on the cheek, and then walked toward the door. Ted opened it.

"I think we'll just get some air," Jenny said. "We'll be back."

The door swung closed with no regard to noise as it slammed like a clap of thunder.

Ted stood looking puzzled.

"Guess that just shot our Ring Figure," he said.

"Yeah," Jack replied, "a real disaster."

"What happened?"

"I don't know. I thought my proposal was good enough. I didn't expect a reaction like that."

"No kidding, genius. Have you guys been having problems or something?"

Ted walked over and sat on the steps leading to the running track upstairs. Jack pushed himself up in the window sill and sat facing into the stairwell.

"Not that I'm aware of," answered Jack. "I mean, we haven't seen each other as much as we wanted to since school started. Last month we went out twice. The second time she was sick, and didn't want to talk much. That was two weeks ago. Then we had Richmond last week and Anna couldn't make it out Sunday. I mean, we've been on the phone every couple of days."

"Do you think she's starting to cool on your relationship?"

"I don't think so. Not with the things she's told me. She was acting fine when she came out today. It's weird; she was perfect right up until I asked her to marry me."

"I've never known her to blow up like that. It is weird." Ted stood up. "I'm gonna go get something to drink. You want anything?"

"Naw, I'm fine," Jack said. "I'm just gonna sit here and wait, in case the girls come back."

Jack pulled his legs up and sat completely in the window sill, looking out into the blackness of the night, broken up by an occasional street light along North Main and the neighborhoods in the hills beyond.

I know Anna's been a little distant lately; maybe even more than I let Ted in on. Surely she hasn't found someone else that has caused her to doubt. It seems like she's been depressed. I know she was sick for awhile, and with what Ted has been through, it may have scared her. Maybe that's what's on her mind, holding her back.

"Jack?"

"Yes Anna."

"I'm sorry, I was wrong. I've just been emotional lately. Ask me again."

"Ask you what?"

"The marriage question, ask again."

"Okay. Will you marry me?"

"Yes, yes, yes, yes a thousand times, yes… Kiss me, now."

It would be nice, I suppose.

Jack wallowed in his fantasy for quite some time, imagining the sound of her yes and the feel of her lips. He knew it was a long shot at this point, and that he may never hear her say it, but it gave him some satisfaction as he ran through the scene over and over in his mind.

"Jack?"

He turned, shaken out of his daydream.

"Jack, I'm so sorry," said Anna as she stood just inside the door of the stairwell, under the glow of the exit sign.

This time she was real.

"Anna." It was all Jack could muster.

"Do you still have that ring?"

"Yeah, I do."

"Is the offer still good?"

"Of course it is, Anna."

Anna walked toward him. When she stood a few feet from him, she held out her left hand.

"Does that mean you will?"

Anna laughed. "Maybe," she said. "Of course I will, Jack."

Jack carefully slid the ring on her finger.

The doors opened behind them, with one swinging all the way and slamming into the doorstop, making quite a loud bang. Jenny ran straight to Anna, pushing Jack aside. Jenny and Anna hugged.

Ted held out his hand and Jack shook it.

"Guess we're both in trouble, now," Ted said.

"I suppose."

"I hope this stairwell isn't off-limits," Ted said.

"Wouldn't matter. We're officially on Ring Figure permit. Nothing's off-limits," said Jack.

"I wouldn't go that far."

CHAPTER SEVENTEEN

BLOOD

Rain followed on the heels of Ring Figure. The week after saw cold front after cold front push across the valley, and each carried a wave of rain that soaked the earth and filled the small creeks and rivers beyond their banks. Then it stopped.

As if God himself turned off a switch for a couple of days the sun was out and temperatures warmed to the upper seventies.

Anna had asked Jack if she could drive up and meet him in order to talk. She seemed better, still apologetic, but her voice and her words more upbeat, more positive. It gave Jack the hope he needed, but did not relieve the nagging doubt in the back of his mind.

With the unseasonably warm weather, the commandant had authorized the use of summer uniform off post, which allowed them to wear the white short-sleeve blouse and white trousers, a more warm-weather friendly attire.

"Where are you going in white blouse?" Ted asked Jack.

"Uptown to grab a bite with your sister. I think she wants to talk. You don't think she's having second thoughts, do you?"

"Doubt it, but maybe you can get to the bottom of the whole deal the other night. I haven't had much success on the phone this week. She seems down about something, though."

"Same here, though she seemed upbeat when I talked to her earlier."

"Hey, you mind if I just go down to see her before you guys take off?" asked Ted.

"Of course not."

Ted changed into white blouse and they met Anna in the parking area in front of Nichols Engineering Building at four o'clock. After talking with Ted, she asked Jack if he would mind if Ted came along.

"I don't mind," said Jack.

"No way. You guys are engaged. I'd be a fifth wheel."

"Please Ted, come," Anna said. "I have something to talk to both of you about, and this is the first day in a while I've felt up to it."

"Yeah, Ted. Let's just go," said Jack.

Maybe Ted can pull it out of her. Maybe both of us together.

She suggested that they use her car, but both guys wanted to walk. The day had turned out to be too nice, the sun too warm in an almost cloudless sky. So they walked and talked past Limits Gates and down Letcher Avenue. Jack held Anna's hand.

Ted walked beside Anna on the left. They took Henry up to Main and then made the mild ascent up Main to the Southern Inn. They made plans for Thanksgiving, and then Christmas along the way, and laughed about Ted's latest failed relationship with another of Anna's friends.

"Ted," Anna said, "I'll be completely out of friends if you keep this up."

"I just appreciate the fact that you always seem to have a decent supply of good-looking friends to pick from. It would be great, however, if you could find one that wasn't so stuck-up."

"You do understand, Ted, that there will come a time when it will no longer be appropriate or necessary for you to chaperone us, and your excuse for using Anna's deep well of friendship from which to draw a mate will completely dry up," Jack said as he winked at Anna.

She smiled and sighed, but did not laugh as she usually did at Jack's dry wit.

"So what's wrong?" asked Jack.

Anna looked away for a few seconds. Jack could see she was stemming something emotional.

"Soon," she said quietly.

Ted held the door for both of them and Jack talked to the hostess. She secured menus and led them to a table. Jack was overcome by that feeling again, the one induced by endorphins that flowed into the bloodstream when everything in the world seemed wonderful and good and right.

Finally, Jack knew family. It was a comfort that he had only glimpses of during his whole childhood, especially around his father. Jack secretly wished there was a way to flush out everything in his mind that had to do with growing up, and start fresh with all of this.

When the meal was served, the two boys ate heartily, but Anna picked at her food.

"Not hungry, sis?" Ted asked.

"Not really. I haven't felt great today. I'm thinking…"

"About May twenty-fifth, nineteen eighty-four?" It was a question, but Jack did not inflect much, almost as if he was sure he was correctly finishing her thought.

"That is a year and a half in the future. Besides, even if you were right, I would be thinking about two o'clock in the afternoon, and you would be thinking about midnight," she said.

They laughed, again.

They ate silently for a moment, and then Ted looked up at Jack with a rather serious expression.

"Anna," said Jack, "whenever you're ready to talk about whatever is on your mind, feel free to go ahead."

"Jack, to change the subject, or maybe not, this might be what's bothering Anna, if you and Anna are really gonna get married, I'm wondering how you are spiritually. I mean, you seem like you're getting it, like you understand things."

"Ted, you can ask me anything when it comes to this stuff, and I'll listen to you. I trust you on this."

Anna remained silent, but watched the two intently.

"Okay, Jack, if you died today do you know where you would go? I mean do you think you'd go to heaven or hell?"

Jack thought for a moment. "I don't guess I know for sure. I mean, I hope that the way I've been living lately I'd go to heaven. But, how could you know for sure?"

"If you could know for sure, would you want to?"

"Of course."

"The Bible says you can know. In the book of First John it says these things have been written to you, so that you may know you have eternal life. Basically, he says the evidence of the Gospel at work in your life allow you to know, not guess, but know you have eternal life."

"You had just talked to me before Ring Figure about this," Jack said turning to Anna.

She nodded and looked over to Ted.

"That's because she loves you and wants you to know the same kind of love," Ted replied.

"I know, I know." Jack looked into Anna's eyes for a moment, then turned back to Ted.

"Okay, so how do I know for sure?" asked Jack.

"Can I ask you another question, first?"

"Shoot."

"If you died today, and stood before God, and He asked you why He should let you into His heaven, what would you say?"

"Geez, can you make it any harder? I guess I would say I've been pretty good. I don't really cuss. I don't drink. You know I've started going to church, that kinda stuff."

"How about the Ten Commandments, you follow all of those, right?"

"Hard to say. I don't even know them."

"Let's just take a few. No lying, no adultery, and no stealing. Have you ever told a lie?"

"Yeah."

"Then what does that make you?"

"A liar."

"The Word of God says that if you look at a woman lustfully, you have already committed adultery. Have you ever looked at a woman lustfully?"

"Uh, yeah."

"So if, by your own admission, you have looked on a woman lustfully and God's Word says that it's adultery, then what does that make you?"

"An adulterer."

"Ever taken anything that didn't belong to you, without permission, even something small?"

"Yeah. I guess that means I'm a thief," Jack said.

"By your own admission, you are a lying, thieving, adulterer. God's word says that people that do those things have no place in Heaven."

"So what's the point? I mean, why try to be good, then?"

"The point is that you are not good enough to work your way into heaven, and have eternal life." He paused for a few seconds. "Look, here's another example," Ted said. "The Bible says that all have sinned and fallen short of the glory of God. So we really need to think about what sin is to get the big picture of just how sinful we all are. Name some sins, Jack."

"Okay, how about murder? Oh, yeah, and stealing, we just talked about that, and adultery, of course."

"There's a vast number of things you can do on the outside that are sins. What about things we say?"

"You mean like foul language?"

"Yeah, and using God's name in vain, gossip, telling dirty jokes, and on and on."

"And lying, a lot of stuff."

"How about our thoughts, lust, greed, hatred?"

"Agreed. Especially hatred."

"Those are all sins of commission. How about sins of omission, stuff we don't do, and because we don't do it, it's a sin?"

"Like what?"

"Like not worshiping God, or not praying, or not studying our Bible, or not sharing our faith with others?"

"I don't think they can get you for that one!"

"Well, I confess that I'm guilty of that even with you, Jack. We should've had this conversation a long time ago." He paused to take a drink of his tea. "So with all the sins we can commit by our actions and words and thoughts and even things we don't do, would you agree that the average person sins at least thirty or forty times a day?" asked Ted.

"More than that, maybe hundreds."

"Let's imagine that we know the best guy in the world, and he's got it narrowed down to just three sins a day. He'd be a pretty good guy, right?"

"Real good."

"Do the math. That's over a thousand sins a year, or over seventy-thousand sins in an average lifetime."

"Wow, never thought of it like that."

"So do you see how we stand before a holy God? Can you say guilty? Isn't that what a judge would say if you presented yourself in court with a rap sheet of seventy-thousand crimes?"

"Probably give me the chair."

"That's exactly right, and it's what our sins have earned us. The Bible says that the only thing we earn with our sin is death, that's the penalty that we face and deserve."

"But..." Jack said, "There is a 'but' here, right?"

"Well, there's some good news. Heaven is a free gift. That's the beauty of it. You can't earn it or deserve it. Remember our 'good guy,' he's still a heinous criminal, and that was better than we could imagine a person could be. That's why it has to be free, because if we try to earn it we will most certainly fail. You see, God can't have sin before Himself. That means that even one sin in an otherwise perfect life would be enough to separate us from Him."

"Which brings us back to how do I know for sure?"

Jack was very interested, now sensing the truth of what Ted was saying.

"God loves us. The Bible says that God *is* love. God also must punish sin. And that means death and eternal separation from him in hell," Ted said.

"Not a great outcome."

"No, it's not. But I want you to imagine you were in that courtroom with your dictionary-size rap sheet, and the judge imposes the death sentence on you. Just before they take you off in your handcuffs, the judge steps down from the bench, takes off his robe, puts on the same jail clothes you're wearing, holds out his hands to be cuffed, and says he'll be taking your place, and you are free to go. They release you, and cuff him, and he goes to the chair, instead."

"Not a great outcome for him."

"Essentially, that's what God has done for each of us. He had to judge our sin, but then he stepped down from His rightful throne, put on the body of man, and paid the price for our sin. The Bible says that all of us just like sheep have strayed away, everyone in his own direction, and God has laid on Him, Jesus, all of our sins."

"I guess that makes sense."

"That's why Jesus went to the cross, for you and me. Jesus is God's son, but He is God. The Bible says in the Gospel of John that in the beginning was the Word, or Jesus in other words. It goes on to say that the Word was with God and the Word was God. Then after that it says that the Word was made flesh and lived among us."

"Alright, so it says that Jesus is this Word?"

"Yeah, only John, of course, was writing in Greek and he used a word that translates to 'the Word.' But when he says the Word became flesh, we can know he is talking about Jesus."

"Okay, so is it automatic? Does everybody get to go to heaven because of that?"

"They have the opportunity, but here's the deal. If someone gives you a present for, say, Christmas, do you get your money out and try to pay for it?"

"No."

"You just accept it, with gratitude. It's the same thing with this gift, you don't pay for it with your good works, but you have to accept it."

"Okay, how do I do that?"

"By faith. Now, the Bible says that it's by grace we are saved through faith, and not by our own power or works, but it is a gift of God, so no one can boast and say they did it themselves. So you have to get rid of the whole concept that doing good works will earn you eternal life with God in heaven, and you have to put all of your trust in what He did on the cross. Remember, we don't deserve it and we can't earn it. Jesus even said anyone who believes in him has eternal life. That word for believe is a very strong one that indicates total trust and commitment."

Ted paused to drink some more of his tea.

"It makes sense, but give me time for it to sink in. I'm still trying to get a grip on it."

"That's fine, I'm not trying to sell you something. This is your decision. But it is a decision none the less. You need to understand that now that you've recognized your sin, you need to repent, or turn away from it. You remember that old movie about the Alamo?"

"Yeah."

"When Colonel Travis dramatically draws that line in the sand, and asks for anybody that will stay and fight to cross it. One by one they began stepping across it, even though it meant certain death. That's a good illustration of what must take place in our hearts. We can never go back across the line to our old self because we die to the old self. That's how strong the decision must be."

Jack sat quietly for a minute, looking across the room at an old painting.

"I've gotta soak this in. Let's talk more tonight."

"Jack, I believe God's calling you, but you need to think about it and make a quality decision for life, not a hasty one."

"Rooming with you, and getting close to Anna, has really changed my life. I wish God would let me know in a more physical way that this is what I'm supposed to do."

"He has already, in a way he is accustomed to doing. Maybe he's been revealing himself through us, Jack."

Jack thought again. He was certain that Ted was right in all of this, but something inexplicable was holding him back. He had sensed that a decision of sorts about his faith was on the horizon, but it seemed to have overtaken him all too quickly.

"I know the chaplain said we're not all going to have a 'burning bush' experience, but sometimes it seems to be what I need."

"If it's a 'burning bush' experience you need, then I pray God will give it to you," Anna said, taking Jack's right hand in both of hers.

They finished their meal.

It was a bit cooler outside when they left the restaurant, as the next cold front had begun its push across Virginia. The wind had picked up, and what was a warm, sunny afternoon had turned into a cool, breezy late dusk.

"Such are Indian summers in Virginia," Anna said, "born in unpredictability, so they die."

"So Anna," Jack said, "about…"

But she held up her hand in front of his mouth to stop him.

"When we get back. Let's not mess this up."

What could possibly mess this up? She has to tell me, eventually.

They walked up Main to Preston and then down to Jefferson to head back to the Institute. Jack still held Anna's hand and Ted walked again on her left. The sun was setting quickly. A wall of clouds covered the sunset.

"That's coming in fast. Hope we can get back to barracks before we get soaked," Ted said.

"Ah, another wonderful date with Jack, and Teddy has consumed his every attention," Anna said, staring at Jack walking beside her.

"C'mon, you both know good and well that neither of you has anything to say to the other. I've heard you on the phone. I don't think you've missed out on any earth shattering conversation tonight," Ted replied.

"When we get back to the parade ground, Jack and I are going to get some one-on-one time, without you, so we can talk privately. As privately as can possibly be, anyway."

She had become serious, almost stern, but with an urgency Jack had not heard from her before.

"I guess as long as you're at the Institute, I can forgo the babysitting duties," Ted agreed.

Jack remained silent as the two of them flitted back and forth with their sibling banter. He was twisting and torqing in his gut over what Anna was holding back, what she would soon reveal.

He tried to think about everything Ted had talked about in the restaurant, still contemplating eternity. But it was all becoming convoluted as all of the other thoughts about the secret of Anna's sadness and shattered weddings and fading futures intermingled.

Stop it! Probably nothing. Torturing myself. Everything is crashing down, crushing hope.

As he listened to Anna talking, he burned with desire for her. He wanted to be alone with her, to kiss her passionately, and surrender to whatever would come next. He was aware it would not happen until the honeymoon, but it seemed eons away.

His heart raced as he began to think about ways they could move the wedding date up. He could not imagine that he would be able to stand this. If there was an eternity, these eighteen months seemed to be it.

They were walking slowly along the sidewalk that made its way down Jefferson to the Palms. Ted was unconsciously grabbing the top of every other black ornamental rod that made up the short rod iron fence surrounding Hopkins Green, as if he was using them for support. They walked lazily in the cool dusk air and soft breeze that warned of the coming storm.

"I can smell it. Rain is coming," whispered Anna.

"Wonder how Juice and Mackie and the rest of the fellas are doing at…" Jack stopped short of finishing his sentence as a car angled in toward a vacant parking spot a few yards behind them hit the curb and came to a screeching stop with one tire up on the sidewalk.

The three turned to look, but when the driver opened the door and appeared from the far side, Jack got a sick feeling in his stomach. He never anticipated seeing him again, and had not prepared in his mind how to handle such an encounter. It was late dusk on the fringes of night, but it was clearly Phelps who had stepped out of the driver's door of the Cutlass that had found its way onto the sidewalk, up the hill behind them.

He walked around the front of his car, crossing the headlight beams, stumbling slightly on the curb. Jack noticed that there was something weird about the way Phelps walked, and after a few steps toward them, Jack realized that Phelps was drunk. Phelps let out a couple choice expletives directed at the three of them.

Jack saw the fight in his eyes from the moment he cleared the front of his car and it made the hair on the back of his neck stand up. Ted let go of the fence he was still gripping and began to move to get in front of Phelps.

"Ted, I'll get this!" Jack said.

"I'll be more than happy to kill both of you," Phelps slurred, "but I'm here for this one!"

He walked straight to Jack and slid a large pistol from under his jacket, pointing it directly at Jack's face.

"You've ruined everything. Now it's your turn. Now I'm gonna hurt you!" Phelps was concentrating to keep from slurring his words.

Jack's heart pounded. He felt as if his chest might explode.

Thud, thud, thud!

"Hey, man. This is insane. I mean, you don't need to do *this*," Ted said, keeping his hands in front of himself, about four steps to the side of Phelps. He kept his voice low, though he was obviously shaken.

"It was you, you did this. You took my life away," Phelps replied in a hiss.

He waved the pistol around again, his hands quivering. Jack could see the sweat beaded on Phelps's forehead and nose.

Jack thought desperately about how he could tackle him and get control of the weapon, but he was afraid that Phelps was about to begin shooting, and he feared for Ted and Anna.

"How does it feel? Do you like this?" Phelps shouted.

Thud, thud, thud, thud!

"Phelps, we've had our issues, but how did *I* ruin your life?"

Jack could feel Anna hiding behind him. He could hear her breathing and feel her hand touching the small of his back. She was shaking hard with fear. Jack motioned to her behind his back to move away, as he feared that Phelps could shoot anybody at this point. Anna began slowly backing up toward the black rod iron fence.

"How did you ruin my life? You got me drummed out, idiot!" Phelps shook the pistol toward Jack.

"I was just a witness. I had to tell the truth…"

"The *truth*? There was nothing about the whole trial that was true," Phelps interrupted, "and now look at what's happened. I've been disowned by my family, screwed up the family tradition. Honor was everything. VMI was my life."

"Phelps, it was never my intention to do anything except tell the truth at that trial," said Jack, slowly taking a step toward him.

Thud, thud, thud!

"Your truth…*your* version of it!"

"It's what my Rats told me. I had no choice but to report it," said Jack.

Thud, thud, thud, thud, thud!

"I didn't do it. I was…" He paused, losing track of what he was saying.

"Look, what's done, is done. There's no need to screw everything in your life up for some misplaced revenge. C'mon, man, put that thing down," Ted said, almost pleading.

"Shut up!" Phelps said. "You were, and still are a piece of…" He easily rolled the foul insult off of his tongue. He waved the pistol at Ted, but quickly returned it to Jack.

"You can't believe that killing *me* is somehow gonna fix all this," Jack said.

"Why? My life is trashed. So what's it to me if you die?"

Jack glanced back and saw Anna now a good twenty feet away, behind him, and standing near the rod iron fence of Hopkins Green. Ted held his ground near the sidewalk curb, three or four steps to Phelps's right.

Jack looked Phelps in the eye, and in that moment made the decision to call his bluff.

"Go ahead, then… Shoot me."

Thud, thud, thud, thud, thud, thud!

Jack held his badly shaking hands out slowly, till they were stretched straight out to each side.

Phelps gripped the pistol with both hands and aimed it right at Jack's face. Jack stared intently over the top of the barrel into Phelps's eyes. Ted prayed in a whisper off to his left.

Phelps's hands began shaking more and more until he could almost no longer hold onto the pistol. The stalemate went on for less than a minute, though it seemed to Jack like ten. He lowered his weapon, still breathing hard, still staring at Jack. It appeared that he had come to his senses to some degree.

His arms went limp and he looked around nervously, still holding the pistol slightly in front of him. It was as if the adrenaline of his fury had suddenly overcome his drunkenness, leaving him startled and confused. Jack and Ted looked at each other, neither moving.

In a moment his face changed from the confused expression to one of total calmness and control. He raised the pistol in a swift and decisive moment pointing it at Jack's head.

Bang!

Jack cringed, jerking his head toward his right shoulder. He was blinded by the flash momentarily, and his ears were ringing. In his mind he analyzed what had happened. He knew the pistol was pointed at him, so he assumed he had to be hit.

His left hand found his own face and he felt for a hole, or broken skull, or worse, brain. But there was no real pain other that a slight burning sensation on his left cheek and ear. Jack looked at his hand.

No blood. He missed. He had to have shot to my left on purpose, to scare me.

Still he would take no chances. In a split second after the shot was fired, Jack took two running steps and leapt at the stunned Phelps. When he tackled him, the pistol dropped to the ground, and both of them crashed into the side of a car that was parked in the space below Phelps's Cutlass, and then fell in a heap on a curb near the back tire.

Ted was frozen in place for a second longer, then stepped over and scooted the pistol away from Phelps and Jack. This time, Jack did not wrestle with Phelps, but rolled on top of him and struck him several times with his right fist.

"I said I would kill you!" Jack shouted.

He had no control of himself, his mouth and body operating on some instinctive level. He could not even feel the blows he landed on Phelps's face.

Stop! Stop! Stop!

Another voice screamed inside his head trying to call Jack back to his own senses. Jack stopped with his fist in the air, breathing hard still straddling Phelps, who lay on his side, covering his head with his arms.

In that moment of silence, Jack heard a cough. It wasn't a simple, throat-clearing cough, but a long, loud cough that gurgled at the end. His head snapped around to see Anna holding onto the fence as she slowly sunk to her knees. Her left hand was shaking violently and she was trying to hold the front of her throat. Jack thought she was having some kind of panic attack.

"Ted, Anna!"

Ted had already spun around and was running to her. Jack jumped up off of Phelps and followed. When he got to her, Ted was holding her up slightly, but he slid down against the iron fence and laid her back in his lap. Jack's heart sunk as he saw the blood that soaked the whole front of Anna and already covered Ted's arms.

"I've gotta move your hand, Anna!" Ted yelled, his voice quivering and loud.

Two cadets ran through the front door of the Palms and into the street toward them.

"Call 911! Call an ambulance!" Jack screamed.

They both turned and ran back in to call. Jack knelt down beside Anna just as Ted was pulling back her hand. A stream of blood the diameter of his little finger squirted out across the front of Jack's blouse, spattering on his face. Ted gasped as he shoved her hand back over it.

"Oh God, oh God, no…no!" Ted yelled.

It was surreal. Ted and Jack were covered with Anna's blood. It seemed to Jack that he was moving in slow motion, that he could not react fast enough. He pressed his hand against Anna's trying to stop the bleeding, but it seemed to almost make it worse as blood kept flowing in surges between their fingers.

"Ted, press down on the wound. I've gotta use this blouse!"

He leaned back and ripped his white blouse off, wadded it up and then peeled Anna's hand back again. It was more of a v-shaped tear than a hole, with a large flap of the flesh inside the "V" shredded, exposing a deep wound that flooded and gushed with each heartbeat. Anna's eyes were frantic as she saw all of the blood covering her brother and Jack.

"I don't want to...die now," she said in a frightened whimper between coughs. Tears pooled in her eyes.

"You're not gonna die, Anna. Just gotta get the bleeding stopped. It's not that bad," Jack lied trying to reassure her, but his trembling voice gave away his fear.

His blouse was already half-saturated, and he noticed that her skin color was pale and bluish. He looked up at Ted, who was stroking the top of Anna's hair with short, gentle strokes, looking down at her face. Tears were streaming down his face, mixing with the blood and his sweat as they ran down his cheeks.

"I don't know what to do," Jack whispered.

Ted looked up at him with a blank stare. He was in shock. Jack slid his fingers under the wadded blouse to see if he could press directly down on whatever was bleeding.

"No! No! No!" he shouted in frustration.

It seemed that blood was coming from everywhere at once. He realized that it was futile, that he just did not have what it would take to repair the damage, if it could be repaired. He pressed the blouse against the wound again and grabbed Anna's right hand. He hoped beyond hope that the ambulance would show up in time. Anna was struggling to breath and kept coughing, she had been shaking all over but Jack noticed her legs were limp.

"Anna, you've gotta stay awake. The ambulance will be here in a minute," Ted reassured her.

The two cadets from the Palms came running up. Several others were behind them.

"They should be here in a minute!" It was Ted and Jack's classmate Mackie, and another classmate they called Juice was following.

"Give me your blouse, Mackie!" Jack said hastily.

Mackie yanked his blouse off and handed it to Jack, who replaced his blood soaked one with it.

"Oh no...Oh my God!" Juice exclaimed as soon as he walked up and saw the three of them covered in blood, sitting in a pool of it.

"How did it happen?" asked Juice.

"Him," Jack said, motioning frantically at the sidewalk behind them.

"There's no one there," said Mackie.

Jack glanced back over his shoulder. Phelps was gone.

"Stay with us, Anna!" Jack yelled, turning back toward her.

The wail and warble of the ambulance and police sirens winding through Lexington sounded so distant.

"Don't go to sleep on us, Anna!" Jack was pressing the blouse against her neck with his left hand, while holding her arm against his chest with his right, squeezing her hand over and over, trying to keep her awake. Her breathing was faint and gurgled. She had stopped shivering.

"I love you, Anna Marie," said Jack, through flooding eyes as he pulled her hand up to his lips and kissed it.

She looked at him and smiled. Suddenly calm seemed to come over her whole body. Her face flushed for a moment, and her eyes looked beyond everyone toward the sky. She opened her mouth and reached her left hand upward.

"What is it, Anna?" Ted asked in a breaking voice.

"It's...it's okay...Teddy... I can see him, now," she said in a soft, raspy voice.

She laid her hand back down on her stomach, and her body began to go completely limp. Jack looked at her for a moment, knowing that she was slipping. The hair on one side of her head was matted with thick, coagulated blood, and his fingerprints were smeared in blood across her right cheek.

Her skin now appeared a bluish tint in the beam of the street lamp that arched off a wooden telephone pole planted a few yards away near the fence along Hopkins Green. She lay quiet and limp across Ted's legs, grotesque, almost inhuman. Her eyes were still half open, and there was a slight smile in her thinning lips. Jack put his ear to her face.

"She stopped breathing!"

No God, please don't. Don't let her die.

He leaned over her and pinched her nose while cupping his mouth over hers. He had let go of the blouse he had used as a compress and it fell to the side. He breathed once into her and her chest rose slightly. But on the second breath, her lacerated trachea gave way and the air blew through the wound hole, expelling the blood that had pooled in the wound in a single blast all over Jack and Ted.

"Stop!" Ted yelled.

"The ambulance is almost here! We've gotta keep her alive!" Jack was frantic, helpless.

Mackie restrained Jack, pulling him back, but Jack shook him off and grabbed Anna's lifeless right hand in both of his. He lay down on the concrete next to her, half in the puddling blood along her side, and held her hand on his lips as he began to weep.

"No, no, no, no, no!"

Ted sat with Anna still lying across his lap, his hands grabbing the hair on both sides of his head, shaking as he sobbed uncontrollably.

It had been less than five minutes since the shot was fired.

Ted and Jack were in hell.

Anna was not.

CHAPTER EIGHTEEN

VINDICATE HER HONOR

Rainwater gushed through downspouts pouring into the parking lot below, turning the asphalt into a shallow, swift river. At ten o'clock, it had begun again. The autumn rains flooded the valley and chilled the air unbearably. Another cold front ushered out the brief Indian summer.

The four Lexington police officers, a Lexington police detective, and one state trooper that came to the scene of Anna's murder had held Ted and Jack as the ambulance took Anna to Stonewall Jackson Hospital.

The detective, an older clean-cut man in jeans and a solid light blue long sleeve dress shirt named Watts, questioned the two boys for a few minutes, enough time to walk through everything, then drove them to the hospital. Jack saw him once more after Mr. and Mrs. McClain arrived. He assured Jack they were looking for Phelps, confident that they would find him soon.

The McClain's arrived just a little before midnight, but Jack only saw them from a distance. Ted went back to meet them with Chaplain Campbell and Colonel Jackson.

Jack looked up. He had been sitting in a chair, one of several along the hallway wall between the ER and ICU, for a couple hours. He was drained, numb inside. His right hand throbbed with a dull, pulsating pain that would come and go at unpredictable intervals. The outer edge of his left ear stung from powder burns. No one had attended to them yet. He didn't care.

Ted walked down the hall toward Jack.

"Dad and Mom, well, they're pretty messed up," Ted said, stopping in front of him a few feet away. "They're going in to say bye to Anna. I'm going in with them."

"Tell your folks I'm sorry," Jack said as he stood up.

"It wasn't your fault, Jack."

"We both know he meant it for me," Jack said. "If I just hadn't dodged to the side…"

"You'd be dead, and maybe Anna, and maybe me," Ted interrupted. "You did what you could to stop him. For some reason, this is how it ended up. I just wanted to let you know what was going on. I gotta go."

Ted turned to walk back down the hall, but stopped after a few steps and turned back to face Jack.

"Oh, I didn't want to make it worse."

He held his clenched hand out toward Jack.

Oh no, not that.

Jack stepped toward him and held his right hand out open, still shaking. Ted placed the ring, still smeared with dried blood in Jack's palm. Jack flushed with anger and sorrow.

"It's better this way," said Ted.

"I don't want this, Ted. I want it to be on Anna's finger."

"I'm sorry, Jack, but Dad, it would make it harder on him, right now."

Jack closed his hand around the ring, as Ted headed back down the hallway and through the double doors at the end of it.

Standing there, he felt overcome with guilt and fear. Thoughts of the recent years and his conflict with Phelps tormented him. His actions hours earlier were a blur, but he was becoming convinced it shouldn't have gotten so far out of hand, that he had somehow pushed the wrong buttons, sending everything spiraling out of control.

Rain hammered the world outside. Jack could hear a downspout shudder with the volume of water pouring through it. Lightning flashed again and again. It was distant. Thunder rumbled in waves.

Jack began to wonder if he would be allowed to see the McClain's. He looked at himself, for the first time realizing that he was still covered in Anna's blood. He had washed it from his hands and arms earlier, but there was dried blood still matted in his hair, and the front and left side of his shirt was still stained heavily with blood. His white uniform pants were blood soaked on the left thigh.

The knuckles on his right hand were swollen and skinned. A flap of skin hung open on his middle knuckle where he had caught Phelps squarely in the open mouth and a tooth had sliced through his hide.

Why would they let me back there? I'm covered in her blood.

He felt betrayed and alone again, haunted by the solitude of the isolated sterile hallway, the stillness broken only by the occasional shuffle of surgical shoe covers, or muffled conversations from the nurses' desk around the corner. With each nurse or patient passing by, Jack looked up with hope that it would be someone sent to retrieve him and bring him into the fold of those grieving, that he might have someone with whom he could grieve.

But they never were. They never came for him or sent for him. It became clear he did not belong with the family. He would have to grieve on his own. So Jack ran.

Jack pulled up in front of his old farmhouse, the beams of his headlights barely trickling through the weeds and tall grass. He got out and stood beside his truck, the rain beating fiercely on his head and his shoulders.

In his mind, he could see his dad standing on the front porch in every flash of lightning, sneering with his belt hanging from his right hand.

It was you.

He reached down and picked up a rock and hurled it at the front porch as his mind boiled over with rage.

"You did this to me! You did this to me! You cursed me!" Jack screamed, rushing toward the old house, now fully overcome with anger.

You did this to me. You cursed me.

Jack tripped and fell into the mud and water, puddled in front of the rotten porch steps. He sobbed bitterly.

Why, God? Why did you let him do this to me? Why am I cursed?

Soaking wet and covered in mud, Jack slowly stood and began to walk, stumbling over fallen limbs and large tufts of neglected, overgrown grass. He walked around the old house into the field behind it.

A flash of distant lightning revealed the river creeping up the light slope to the barn, about where it had been the night Jack's dad went in to move the tractor. So much death swirled around in Jack's mind that it made him nauseous. He waded into the water in the blackness of the rain, first his ankles, then his knees.

By the time he made it to the rock, Jack was waist-deep, and the cold water was pushing hard. His legs ached from the cold, wet bite of the river, and he had to fight to get to the downstream side of the rock, and then pull hard to extricate himself from the current.

Jack sat for a couple hours, hoping to become hypothermic in the cold rain, hoping that the river would creep up the rock and overtake him, hoping for something to eclipse his guilt and anger and pain. An occasional flash of lightning would startle him enough to shake him from his despair for a moment, but his mind would quickly spiral back down into it, deeper. He was alone.

Lightning flashed. Then a bright beam of light bounced along the river to the shore on the far side, moving back and forth till it landed on Jack.

"I knew you'd be here!"

Jack spun around. He could barely make out the image of someone wading deeper into the water, approaching the rock, holding a bright flashlight.

Ted?

"Jack, we need to talk!"

Jack could hear the voice cut through the downpour and the roar of water against tree trunks and brush along the banks. It was Ted.

"Stay back, Ted! I don't feel like talking right now. I'm fine. I just want to be alone," he yelled over the rain.

"I'm coming over there," Ted yelled back.

Jack turned around and faced the river.

What if I just rolled off this rock. There'd be no findin' me for a couple days.

He imagined in a flash the movements it would take to roll over the edge into the swift, blackness. Jack trembled as he thought of the icy cold water sucking him under and consuming him. It caused him to push back from the edge, quivering.

He was content to wait on the James.

Then he heard a splashing behind him.

"Jack, I need your help!"

Ted was clawing into the rock. He had made it to the back side, but stepped too far and lost his footing. Jack got on his knees and scooted down toward Ted.

"Hang on! I'll grab your shirt," said Jack. "I told you not to come out here."

"Just give me a hand!" Ted said desperately.

Jack slid down to Ted and grabbed Ted's shirt sleeve just over the shoulder. One good tug had Ted clawing his way up out of the murky, cold water.

As soon as he got his footing, Ted leapt at Jack, grabbing his shirt collars and slamming him back against the rock. Jack was caught off guard, and could only hold his arms in front of his face defensively.

"You knew, you knew all this time!" Ted yelled, shaking Jack by the collar.

Jack swept his right forearm across Ted's wrists, ripping Ted's grip away, but busting his own lip with one of Ted's hands. He backhanded Ted hard enough to knock him over backwards, sprawling headfirst on his back, sliding down toward the water. Ted rolled on his stomach in time to catch himself, then immediately got his footing and crouched several feet away from Jack, lower on the rock.

Jack pushed himself up almost immediately. He stood at the top of the rock looking down at Ted.

"Get back, Ted! Leave me alone! What are you talking about?" he yelled out viciously.

Jack stood like a frenzied animal as he spat blood from his mouth.

"Anna, Jack. You knew about her…"

Lightning struck.

"That's right, God!" Jack yelled, shaking a fist skyward. "This is your fault!"

"Quit blaming God," Ted yelled. "God didn't do this!"

"Well where is he? Where is God, and where was he tonight? Huh?" asked Jack.

"I'm pretty sure he wasn't the one pulling the trigger," Ted replied.

"Oh yeah, he never is," yelled Jack. "Why couldn't *he* save her, Ted? I mean, what kind of God would let Anna die? Why does everything in my life have to be like this?"

"You're so selfish that you still think it's all about you? 'Cause you had it bad growing up. C'mon man!"

"What the…" asked Jack.

"You think you're the only one hurting? Who do you think Anna was? She was *my* sister, and my parents only blood child. You were her boyfriend who knew her for a couple years."

"I'm sick of God sitting around, not doing anything. I'm sick of him taking days off, like with Anna, and yeah, with me growing up," Jack said.

"It's just how things are, Jack. God didn't do any of that. We did."

"Oh, we did?" Jack continued. "What? I thought he was supposed to take care of his people. Where was he when Anna was getting shot? Where was he when we were covered in her blood, when we watched the life drain out of her?"

Jack's backhand had less effect on Ted than that statement. Jack could sense Ted choking up. Ted looked defeated as he sat down near the edge of the water still creeping up the rock. He hung his head as the rain poured around the edges of his face.

"I suppose," he began, looking back up at Jack, "I suppose he was in the same place he was the night his son was hanging on the cross."

Jack had no argument. He had no more questions. Ted had struck deep into Jack's heart with his answer. He sat back down on the rock and began to quietly weep, his tears blending in with the rain, but his anguish leaking out in soft sobs. Ted crawled up the rock and sat beside him.

"She was going to be my wife," Jack said.

"I suppose sooner than we all thought. It's why you left tonight. Isn't it?" Ted asked.

"I left because I didn't belong," Jack answered.

"Jack, my dad wasn't too keen on the idea of you and Anna being together. It's no mystery, I guess. So tonight was sort of a confirmation of his fears. You've gotta understand. You've gotta let them grieve."

"I understand. They just lost their daughter."

"But the way you…" Ted paused, "well, why didn't you just tell us?"

"Tell you *what*?" asked Jack.

"You had to know that when they examined her, they would find out. That's why I figured you left," said Ted.

"I don't know what you're talking about."

"C'mon, Jack. You didn't know?"

"What?"

"You didn't know that Anna was pregnant?"

—⟋⟋⟍—

The rain had diminished to a light drizzle by the time that Jack walked into the room. Ski and Darryl were both sitting on the side of their beds, talking.

"Where have you been?" Ski asked, as he stood. "We've been drivin' around like crazy the last couple hours, looking for you and Ted. Man I'm sorry, Jack."

"You heard?" asked Jack.

"We heard at about oh-three-thirty," Darryl said.

"We cleared it with the OC, and headed to the hospital. They said you'd taken off and Ted went to find you," said Ski.

"We waited for a while," Darryl said, "and then figured we should go find you. Never did. Ended up back here. You gonna be okay, Jack? I'm sorry about Anna."

"Thanks, guys. I, uh, yeah it was bad," was all Jack could muster.

Jack sat down on his bed and took off his wet shoes. One by one he slowly removed each piece of wet, muddy, blood-stained uniform and stuffed them in his laundry bag. It was painful and methodical and neither Ski nor Darryl knew what to say. Jack put on his robe and sat on the side of his bunk.

"I'm still trying to figure out how it all happened," Jack said, breaking the silence.

"We didn't get the whole story," Darryl said, "but you guys ran into Phelps and he shot Anna 'cause he was drunk and all. Someone said it was an accident."

"It was an accident that Anna got shot. It was intended for me. Anna was standing behind me. I tried to stop the bleeding, but I couldn't… I miss her," Jack said, tears in his eyes and his voice cracking.

"Sorry, Jack," Ski said.

"If you don't want to talk…" Darryl said.

"It's just hard," Jack said, cutting Darryl short.

They sat for about fifteen minutes, no one talking. Darryl busied himself with folding some laundry, while Ski stared out the back window. Jack sat in his chair at his desk and pulled out an old letter that Anna had sent him Rat Year. He held it to his nose.

"Jack, was Anna pregnant?" asked Ski.

"So I've heard," Jack replied, curtly.

"I guess that means you didn't know," Ski said.

"No, she never said anything to me about it."

"She never told you that you were going to be a dad?" Darryl asked.

"No, she didn't, but I guess I can understand why," Jack answered.

"Why's that?" asked Ski.

"Because I wasn't going to be a dad," Jack said. "I never slept with Anna."

No one said a word for a moment. Jack sensed their uncertainty.

"Everyone thinks you were the father," Ski finally said.

"Everyone's wrong!" Jack snapped back.

"Well, what are you gonna do? I mean, you can't just leave it like that. You can't leave everyone thinking you got her pregnant, if you didn't," said Darryl.

"Anna's gone. Does it even matter? I don't really want to drag her name through the mud," said Jack.

"I don't know. Maybe not. Maybe it's not the right time to talk about this. You need to take it easy, Jack. Get some rest. We also need to find out what we can do for Ted and his folks," said Ski.

"Yeah, Ski's right," Darryl added. "Sorry we even brought it up. I'm just sorry about everything."

"I need to think about it, about what I'm supposed to do," said Jack. "The funeral service will be in a few days."

Jack paused standing by the front door, looking out its window into the courtyard.

"It was the most horrible thing. She shouldn't have died like that," Jack said.

"Get some sleep, Jack," Ski said.

"I'm going to take a shower. I still have her blood on me."

———

"Jimbo?"

"Yes, this is Jimbo. How can I help ya?"

Jack was calling from one of the courtesy phones in Lejuene Hall. It was early Sunday afternoon. He was quiet, almost whispering.

"I, uh, I've gotten into a situation, and I thought you might be able to help me. I hate asking for help, but you're the only guy I really know that might be able to give me a hand."

"I'm sorry, I didn't catch your name," Jimbo said. "Who is this?"

"Oh yeah, It's Jack. Jack Hartman, Mr. King."

"Jack, good to hear from you. I think," said Jimbo.

"It's good to talk to you too, Mr. King, uh, I mean Jimbo," answered Jack.

"What's this about, son?"

"Well," Jack started, then took a deep breath, "did you hear about the girl that died in Lexington last night?"

"Yes, I heard," replied Jimbo. "She was shot. Wasn't she?"

"Yes," Jack said. He fought off an urge to choke up. "She was Anna McClain, my fiancée."

"Oh, Jack, I'm so sorry."

"I was there. I tried to stop the guy. It was actually meant for me…"

"Who did this, Jack?" Jimbo interrupted. "I mean, did you know him?"

"You remember Phelps? He was the guy that hated me Rat year. He was drummed out last year, and he's a real mess. He saw us in town last night and chased us down. He had a pistol.

I thought he was just trying to scare us, but I ended up looking straight down the barrel. He was out of his mind. I tried to stop him, but he fired right by my head. It hit Anna. She died before the ambulance could even get there."

"My heart goes out to ya, son. Did they get the guy?" Jimbo asked.

"He left when Ted and I were trying to keep Anna alive."

"That's really sad. She was a beautiful girl, Jack. Are you going to be okay?"

"Mr. King," Jack said, his voice breaking with emotion, "she was pregnant."

There was an awkward silence.

"Sorry, Jack, I'm just not sure what to say. How far along?"

"I don't know for sure," answered Jack. "I didn't know she was pregnant. I think Ted said around a couple months. It was a shock to everyone. I suppose it really hurt her family. They won't talk to me."

"Well, I'm sure there are a lot of emotions driving things right now. You may have to give things a little time. You must still be in shock, yourself. I'm coming over there to talk to you. I'm sorry about Anna and your baby."

"It wasn't my baby. Anna and I never did anything to get her pregnant. We never did anything more than an occasional kiss. Sure, I wanted to. She just had this whole thing about staying pure till marriage. Ted was with us most of the time. There were all kinds of rules to keep us out of trouble. That's what I don't understand."

"Where are you right now?" asked Jimbo.

"Lejuene," answered Jack.

"I'll be there in fifteen minutes. Can you sit tight?"

"I'll wait out front."

⸺⟨ʘ⟩⸺

"Cadet Hartman, I'm sorry you've been through what you've been through, but I wonder if it wouldn't be prudent of me to put you on barracks confinement until this is over," Colonel Jackson said in his drawl that was more a product of his Texas upbringing than anything he might have picked up in Virginia.

Jack stood at parade rest in front of the commandant's desk.

It was Monday.

After talking with Jimbo Sunday afternoon, Jack had gone back to his room and lay in bed, wrestling with his overwhelming loss and hopelessness that hung over him like a thick shadow. He could not fathom going to formations or classes, or doing anything that he had done before Saturday night. So he lay there, fetal, tormenting himself with a thousand "what ifs" until he slept.

Jimbo was afraid Jack was still in shock. He insisted that he would look into this while Jack rested, but Jack would not agree to sit and wait. He had to do something. He had to be moving.

They did agree it would be a good idea for Jack to gain an emergency furlough before they tried to figure out this mystery of Anna's pregnancy, and Jimbo secured the appointment with Colonel Jackson. Jack met him there after morning formation.

"I would prefer otherwise, sir," Jack replied, from his spot in front of the desk.

"I'm considering doing it for your own safety. The police have yet to find Phelps, and I'd hate to think what might happen if you run into him, to him or you. You're safe, here," the commandant said.

"How long is my confinement, sir?" asked Jack.

"Two weeks."

"What about Anna's funeral?"

Jack had tears welling up in his eyes.

"I am not liberal with confinement, as you well know, Cadet Hartman. I do not hand out confinement, and then let you run off post, especially in this..."

"That's ridiculous, Bill," said Jimbo, stepping forward, almost in front of Jack. "We're not talkin' about some bystander here. She was his fiancée. You can't keep him from her funeral. Is there somethin' more to this?"

Colonel Jackson stood up from his chair and walked to the window behind his desk. He stood there with his back slightly to Jimbo and Jack, looking out at the drizzling rain on the parade ground.

"Truth is, son, they don't want you at the funeral," he said without turning around.

Jack was stunned. He felt as if he had been gutted right there on the commandant's floor. He was suddenly weak and washed out. He breathed a deep labored breath, but could not force any words. The smell of cherry pipe tobacco hung loosely in the air.

"What is wrong with those people?" Jimbo asked. "From what I've gathered talking to Jack, he did everything he could to save their daughter's life. He'd have gladly takin' the bullet if it would've saved her. They were going to get married. Help me out, here, 'cause I'm not getting whatever's going on in McClain's head."

"Theodore McClain is a good man and my Brother Rat, and I need to do what I can to abide by his wishes. You should know that as well as anyone, Jimbo. You taught it to me," replied the Colonel.

"I taught you about loyalty and watchin' your Brother Rat's back, but not like this, not to the detriment of others."

"Cadet Hartman," Colonel Jackson said as he walked back to his desk, "please excuse us so we may talk privately. You may have a seat in Mrs. Henning's office."

"Yes, sir."

Jack snapped to attention, offering a salute to the commandant. Colonel Jackson returned the salute. Jack did an about face and walked out of the office into the Colonel's secretary's office.

Though he was mentally exhausted, he could not sit in any of the chairs that were normally reserved for cadets answering some significant violation, fearfully awaiting an appointment with the commandant. Jack knew he had done nothing wrong, but he certainly felt the sting of it all. He determined not to rest until he cleared this up, until he faced the one who had stolen Anna from him.

He was tired, but at least Jack did not feel alone anymore. Whatever was going on behind the thick, ornate door was muffled, and though he couldn't hear just what was being said, Jack could tell the argument was heated.

If I'd only known.

CHAPTER NINETEEN

DEFEND HER RIGHTS

Jimbo pulled the taxi into the student center parking lot and parked along the sidewalk. He had secured a forty-eight hour emergency furlough for Jack, but Colonel Jackson would not bend and allow Jack to leave the barracks during Anna's funeral.

Jimbo had called ahead to a friend that worked in the administration at Hollins. The best he could manage was a note left for Anna's roommate, asking her to meet them at the student center.

As they walked up the steps to the front tinted glass doors, Jack stopped.

"That's her," he said, gesturing toward a girl with short brown hair, smoking a cigarette nervously, sitting on the other side of the steps.

"Lisa!" Jack shouted.

"Jack?"

"Yes," answered Jack, walking to her.

They embraced briefly.

"I'm sorry, Jack, sorry about Anna," she said.

She looked at Jimbo.

"You must be Mr. King. I'm Lisa, Lisa Nichols."

She shook Jimbo's hand.

"Nice to meet you, Lisa," Jimbo said.

"What happened, Jack? I heard it was some crazy guy."

Jack looked down. Suddenly, all of his courage faded. He could not find words. He did not want to relive it.

"Would you mind if we go inside? It's very important," Jimbo said.

"Oh, of course."

They began walking toward the glass doors.

Jack saw tears building up in the bottoms of Lisa's eyes, and heard her sniffle twice. They walked quietly through the double door to a common area with a group of round tables.

"Is this okay?" she asked.

"Yes," said Jimbo.

They sat around one of the tables.

"What happened?" she asked.

"She was shot by a former cadet. It was an accident. The bullet was meant for someone else," Jimbo answered.

"This is horrible. Rooming with her, it was so easy to get close. It was our first semester rooming together. I met her this summer. She was such an awesome person," Lisa said, beginning to cry.

"She was, and it is horrible," said Jack.

"Jack, this has got to be hard on you. And what about Anna's parents? How are they doing?" she asked.

"Not so good," answered Jack.

"Lisa, this may seem like a weird question," said Jimbo, "but do you know if Anna was ever seeing anyone else?"

"No, I don't think so. She never really talked about any other guys that much. She talked in terms of Jack and her brother, Teddy. Why?"

"Something happened. I can't talk about it right now, but it brought up questions I couldn't answer. I have to find out," said Jack.

"Did she ever talk about anything out of the ordinary with Jack, or any guy for that matter?" Jimbo asked.

"Not really. Other than how she was head over heels. Oh, and the time you guys had that fight."

"That was over a year ago," said Jack.

"No, I'm talking about right after the semester started. She came in one night a real mess, sobbing and angry. Messed up. I asked her what happened, and all she would tell me was she had a fight with her boyfriend. I can only assume it was with you."

Jack looked over to Jimbo.

"We never had a fight."

"Is that all?" Jimbo asked. "Did anything else come of it?"

"Not really. Her friend from Richmond came and picked her up later that night. It was a Friday. I didn't see her again till that Sunday night. She seemed fine then. I didn't pursue it 'cause I figured she would bring it up if she felt like it."

"Who picked her up?" asked Jack.

"I didn't know her, and Anna never said. I'd guess they were pretty close."

Jack looked over at Jimbo, his mind racing.

"What are you thinking, Jack?"

Jenny, Jenny, Lip...

"Jenny Lipscomb."

———

"You gonna be okay?"

Jimbo sat forward, his forearms on his knees and his hands folded together. He was sitting on the edge of an overstuffed couch that faced the row of windows overlooking Westhampton Lake. The University Commons Building was nestled on the end of the lake near the middle of the University of Richmond campus.

Jack stood at the windows looking out over the water, exhausted and broken.

"Yeah, don't have much choice."

"Jenny is on her way. Don't worry, Jack. And don't be afraid of what she might tell us. You need to know."

"I'm not afraid, I just miss Anna."

"I know, son."

"Jack!"

The shrill shout broke across the hollow room, and Jack turned to see Jenny running toward him. When she got to him, she gave him a tight hug with both arms around his neck. Jack was overcome by a flush of his shyness which echoed sensations of his first dance with Anna.

"I heard about everything on Sunday," she whispered, still hugging him tightly.

He could feel her tears against his cheek. He didn't want to let her go, but instead wished he could unashamedly explode, pouring out his emotions on her shoulder. He wanted to bury his face in her hair and be lost in weeping. Her hug was the first he'd had since Anna died.

"Why, Jack, why?"

"I don't know. I can't make sense of it."

Jenny let go, and noticed Jimbo who stood up from his seat on the couch.

"Mr. King?"

"I am."

"I'm Jenny Lipscomb."

"Yeah. Sorry it has to be like this, though," Jimbo said.

"Let's sit down," said Jack.

Jenny sat on the couch beside Jack. Her knees tilted toward him so she almost faced him. She took his left hand in hers.

Jimbo pulled a leather footstool over from an adjacent couch, and sat in front of them.

"I'm still in shock, Jack. And I'm angry and sad. I really don't know what I'm feeling."

"I guess I'm struggling with things right now," said Jack. "I mean there are things that came to light through all of this, things that have me pretty mixed up."

"Came to light?"

"Yeah. Maybe you can help me."

"Help you?"

"Jenny," Jack said, "was there ever anyone else? I mean another guy that Anna was close to or hung out with?"

"No, no, no, Jack. She loved you. She was mad about you. Why would you think that?"

"I just had some questions I had to settle so I could go on and deal with this. Something happened."

"Jack, I'm a flirt. I can't keep a boyfriend for a minute. Anna was devoted. Loyal to a fault. Once she got teamed up with you, I could never get her to do anything that might have even been remotely around any guys. She was a lost cause for fun. The perfect girlfriend, I suppose."

"Fiancée," Jack said.

"Yes, fiancée."

"At the beginning of the semester, you picked her up from Hollins. She was emotional. What was that all about?"

Jenny flushed for a moment. Her hand went limp in Jack's, then she pulled it away. She stood and walked over to the windows and stared out at Westhampton Lake.

"Girl stuff. She'd had a horrible day. One of those when a girl's time of the month lines up with every other catastrophe. She just needed time off, away from that place."

"And that's it? Anna was just having a bad day?"

"That's it."

Jack looked to Jimbo for help, but Jimbo remained silent.

"And you don't know anything about any other guy close to Anna?"

"She loved you, Jack. *Only* you."

Thursday. A cool morning with an occasional flash of sunlight through another band of thick, flowing grey. As long as Jack was in barracks he was required to attend all his military and academic duties. He stood on the stoop at the railing, waiting for each brief appearance of sunlight between his first and third block classes.

Colonel Jackson had only granted Jack emergency furlough through Wednesday taps, and only under the odd agreement to be under close supervision of Jimbo King. Jimbo proved to have a great deal of influence over Colonel Jackson, apparently stemming from their days as cadets. Jack never even considered his cab driver friend was not only a former cadet, but one with considerable pull with the administration of the Institute.

Jack had reluctantly reported back to barracks Tuesday afternoon. The officer of the guard informed him that the commandant had instructed the guard team to remind Jack of his barracks confinement. As much as the colonel thought it was the best thing for the Institute, it only served to send Jack spiraling into a deeper depression and had him thinking about leaving VMI altogether.

"Jack, I just got word on the funeral arrangements." Ski walked down the stoop toward Jack. He had just come from his second block class, and had a satchel of books slung over his shoulder. He dropped the satchel at his feet and stood beside Jack at the rail looking out into the courtyard.

"I've decided to leave," said Jack.

"You've gotta do what you've gotta do, but I don't know where you're more likely to find support than here with your BR's."

"I know. I just can't deal with it all anymore. I don't see the point."

"You came here looking for a better way. Better than the way you grew up. You've got a chance at doing something great here, and beyond here. That's the point."

"I've messed everything up. I've lost my fiancée, and in a way, my best friend. I thought I was doing everything right, and this is what I have to show for it."

"It isn't what you have to show for it. Everything you've done here, geez, don't you remember where you came from?"

"I understand. But if my life is in a shambles anyway, does it really matter?"

"It will someday, Jack."

Jack turned and looked at Ski.

"They won't even let me attend her funeral."

"I know. It doesn't make sense for the commandant to get involved in all this."

Jack turned and looked back out over the courtyard.

"I'm going, regardless."

"What about the McClain's?"

"I don't know. I just need to say goodbye."

"Hmmm," Ski said, turning to look at Jack.

"What?"

"If you do it right, and maybe with a little interference from the right guys, I mean, you might miss a stick, but what's a few more weeks of confinement?"

"What are you suggesting?"

"Well, Eric's the OG Friday. The service is at fourteen hundred in Richmond. You don't have any afternoon classes on Friday, typical English major. You can make DRC formation. We pre-stage the car down by Cameron Hall. We'll be late for the service, but somehow we can figure out how to get you in without causing a stir. Still not sure how that would shake out, though."

"Okay, I'm listening."

"Anyway, we'll need to leave the service at fifteen-thirty and be back in time to make SRC."

"It might've worked, but I'm on confinement. Barracks status checks."

"That's why I mentioned Eric. He has two status checks to make during that time. It's his discretion when he makes them. One a minute after DRC, one a minute before SRC."

"What about the TAC? Can't he tell Eric when to make them?"

"I think it's 'No Bones McGee.' He has afternoon ROTC classes and never comes on till after SRC."

Jack turned to Ski, and for the first time in several days, smiled.

"You had this figured out before you even walked up here."

"I wasn't going to let you miss Anna's funeral."

Had everything gone as planned Friday afternoon, Jack and Ski would have made the funeral about twenty minutes after it started. But the commandant ordered the OG to post a sentry at room 232 to ensure that Jack stayed put. Lucky for Jack, he did it right after BRC, so Jack and Ski could make an alternate plan.

They brought several of their Brother Rats back to the room directly following DRC formation, harassed the Rat sentry enough that he would be afraid to look into the room, and Jack climbed down from the second story window on some rope that one of the other guys had brought from his room.

The whole event cost them some time, and it began raining hard on the way to Richmond, slowing them considerably. By the time they made it to the cemetery, the graveside service was well underway with everyone pressed tightly under a large canopy tent.

Jack looked up the hill from inside Ski's car.

"I need to go up there," he said.

"No, Jack, it'll cause a stir, and it won't be pleasant. Who knows what the McClain's might say? You've gotta respect them. It's their daughter."

Jack popped the door handle, but Ski grabbed his shirt behind his shoulder.

"If you take off up there, you'll do it without a shirt."

"I have a right to say goodbye."

"Not like this, you don't."

Jack closed the door. Tears of grief and frustration were building up in the bottoms of his eyes.

"Look, let's drive around this place. I see some woods about sixty yards up the hill. Maybe you can go up from the back side and observe from there," Ski said.

"Fine, just get me out of here."

They drove out the front entrance and made a series of turns that took them to a road that bordered the back of the cemetery. As Ski suspected, there were woods that would allow Jack to get close enough to observe the funeral without being too obvious.

"Want me to go with you?"

"No, I need to be alone."

Jack got out of the car and climbed over the short wall. Before he made it to the wood line, he was already soaked from the steady rain. It was a steep hill, and the ground gave way several times under his feet, once causing him to fall and be saturated with mud and water. It was as if nature took offense to him attending Anna's funeral, as if every force possible had lined up to stop him from being present there.

He found a spot by a cluster of trees near the edge of the woods from where he could watch and not be easily seen. He watched as the rain began to come down in sheets, and a steady line of umbrellas began to make their way back to the long row of vehicles that lined the small road through the cemetery and filled the parking lot below.

Finally, the McClain's left, and no one remained but a single member of the funeral home and cemetery, an older gentleman with thin white hair and a black overcoat. Jack could see his gold nametag pinned neatly to his lapel. He waited till most of the cars had made their way out, and then waved to a crew in an older truck parked on the service road nearby.

Jack watched as they adjusted the casket, and then began to lower it slowly. When the casket was half-way into the grave, Jack was overcome with a sudden flush of realization that he would never see Anna again. She was gone.

He held out his hand as if to reach for her, as if maybe this gesture could somehow bring her back. But the louder he wept and the harder he reached, the louder and more determined the rain came down, taunting him. Finally, he slid down against a tree onto his knees, sobbing.

"I, I didn't mean to let you go like this. I didn't mean to bring you into my hell of a life. Why did it have to be you? I, I'm so sorry, Anna...Anna."

...*Anna.*

"Those who wish to do so may fall out at this time."

It was a welcome command, business as usual following the SRC formation. Upper classmen had the privilege of choosing not to attend mess at any meal formation. Jack was not hungry.

Ski and Darryl also fell out with Jack. Both were concerned. On the way back from Richmond, Jack was despondent. They broke through the trailing edge of the rain shortly after leaving. Jack rolled the window half-way down because he said he was sick, but he did it to cover up bouts of weeping that seemed to overtake him in waves.

"Hey, Jack. Wait up," yelled Darryl.

Jack stopped and let the two catch up with him. The trio walked through Washington Arch and made the quick right to the corner stairwell.

"Have you ever noticed that this corner is the only one in Old Barracks without a name?" Darryl asked. "I mean, you've got Sally Port, Ghetto Corner, and Gold Coast."

"Wait up Jack, who's that?" asked Ski.

He pointed to Jackson Arch.

"Yeah, isn't she one of Anna's old friends?" asked Darryl.

"Yeah, Jenny Lipscomb."

Jack did not hesitate, but jogged quickly to ghetto corner, down the stairs and across the courtyard.

"Jack!"

"Hey, Jenny. What are you doing here?"

"I came to see you. We need to talk. Ignore the slip I just sent to your room, you're here already."

"Let's go to Lejeune."

"That's fine," she said.

As they left the arch and turned along the walkway to Lejeune Hall, Jenny grabbed Jack's arm and hung her arm through it. She was solemn and quiet.

"I don't even know how to start," she said.

"What is this about?"

"Well, you remember when we talked about the night I picked Anna up from Hollins?"

"Yes."

"I lied to you and Mr. King. I didn't mean to. I was, I was just so afraid. I didn't know what to do."

"What do you mean? It wasn't just because of a bad day the night you picked her up?"

"Yes Jack, it was an awful day. It was a nightmare of a day. I wish that day had never happened. I wish I could erase it from history. I wish I could rip it out of my mind."

Tears welled up in Jenny's eyes.

"What happened?" asked Jack.

"Anna was…she was raped."

Jenny began to cry. They stood in front of Lejeune Hall and Jack held her up. She buried her face in the shoulder of his grey blouse. They stood there while she cried, and then collected herself.

"Why didn't she tell someone? You mean she didn't even go to the police?"

"No, I couldn't get her to talk to anyone. I tried, Jack. I told her to tell her dad or tell you. She just wanted it to go away. She knew that if you or Ted found out, you'd kill him, and then you'd go to jail. She didn't want to destroy everyone's lives. Then, as if she hadn't had enough, she found out she was pregnant."

"Why did you lie about it?"

"I lied because I had promised her I wouldn't tell anyone. I guess I was also afraid everyone, even you, would think badly of her, think that she was somehow to blame. I was afraid that you would hate her for being pregnant by some other guy, even if it wasn't her fault."

"No, Jenny. I would have loved her more. I would have been the father to that baby. But she was right, if I'd have found out who did it, yeah, I'd have killed him."

"I know. I was so scared at Ring Figure. She was going to tell you. Then you proposed. She promised me she would tell you the next weekend as soon as you two were alone. I guess that never happened."

"No, Ted was with us the whole time."

"That's the other thing. I didn't know who shot Anna till this morning. No one ever mentioned it. I just assumed it was someone I didn't know, and it didn't matter. The guy would get caught and go to jail. But this morning I read it in the *Times*, and everything made more sense."

"What?"

"She was afraid to tell you, Jack, because of the way it happened. She blamed herself."

"I don't get it. How could she even think something like that could be her fault?"

"From what I understood, she got a call the first week in the semester at Hollins. The guy told her he needed to meet her, that he had to tell her something about you, something extremely important, something life-changing."

"So she met with him?"

"Yes, at a party. She tried to set it up to be as public as possible. She felt she needed to know what he was going to tell her."

"And?"

"Somehow he got to her. We never could get into the details, she would get emotional. I think she drank some, which is totally out of character for her. I don't know why. He did tell her something, Jack. She never would tell me that either. Whatever it was, it shook her up almost as much as the rape."

"Did you ever find out who did it?"

"Yeah, it was him, Jack, the same guy. John Phelps."

Jack saw Jenny off and rushed back to the room. He was overcome with a rage that was building to a point he couldn't control. The mercy he'd shown Phelps by not killing him when he fired the shot that killed Anna was gone. Jack was determined in his heart to find Phelps and kill him regardless of the consequences.

"I've gotta get my civies and get out of here!" Jack said as he burst through the door.

"Whoa, Jack," Ski said. "What's gotten into you? Did Jenny say something?"

"Yeah, she said something," Jack answered, climbing on his chair to pull down his misc box.

He pulled down the top box and set it on the chair seat.

"Anna was raped," he said without looking up.

Ski and Darryl didn't say anything for a moment. They both seemed stunned.

"That's how she got pregnant?" Darryl asked.

"Yeah."

"Hey man, I'm sorry," Ski said. "Did anyone other than Jenny know?"

"No. Anna was trying to figure out how to tell me and Ted and her folks, I guess. I don't know if she'd have ever told me who did it."

"Someone she knew?" asked Darryl.

"Yeah, someone we all knew, Phelps."

"Corporal Phelps?" asked Ski.

"Yeah, him. And now I'm gonna find him and kill him."

Ski got up from the edge of his bed and picked up a green message slip from the guardroom.

"Sorry, man, I almost forgot this, but it may change your mind about killing someone."

He handed it to Jack.

> Date: 11-21-82
> Room: 232
> Time: 1745
> Message: Jack, I'm waiting at Lejuene Hall.
> Please come quickly. Important development.
>
> Det. D. Watts

Jack folded the message slip in half and put it in his pocket.

"Maybe you ought to tell him what you told us before you do something crazy," said Ski.

"Yeah, I suppose."

Jack took off his grey blouse and laid it on the desk. He grabbed his duty jacket and put it on over his tee-shirt and walked to the door.

"See ya in a few, guys."

———⟶———

"One of these days, this college will enter the same century the rest of us live in, and the coffee won't taste like something from a wagon train."

Detective Watts was standing in the lobby of Lejeune Hall, nursing a styrofoam cup of coffee he had bought in the cadet canteen. He was easy to recognize in his black jacket and a badge clipped onto the front of his belt.

Watts held out his hand.

"Cadet Hartman, you doin' alright, son?"

"Yes, sir," Jack said as he shook the detective's hand.

"The colonel let me borrow a small room upstairs so we could talk privately." Watts motioned to the stairs and they both began walking up them.

"Have you been getting any sleep since Saturday night?" Watts asked.

"Well, not the first night, but okay since then, I guess."

"Do you prefer I call you Jack or Cadet Hartman?"

"Jack is fine, sir."

Detective Watts pointed to the door of the small upstairs conference room. Jack could see another officer standing beside the table surrounded by a half dozen chairs. A warm wash of adrenaline caused Jack's heart to beat faster and harder.

Why the room? And why two of them?

"This is Officer Wharton, Jack. He is here to assist in our conversation. You know how it is with a government job. Always gotta have two to do one guy's work. He will be recording our interview to help us piece all of this together."

Jack shook Officer Wharton's hand. Watts closed the door behind them.

"Have a seat, Jack."

They all sat down, Watts to Jack's right and Officer Wharton directly across the table. Officer Wharton pushed the record button on the cassette recorder, and it began to rotate, giving off a strange oscillating hum.

"First, I have a couple questions I need to ask you, Jack," said Detective Watts. "I know this can be hard right now. If you need to take your time, then take it. I just want to get a few things straight."

"Okay."

"Jack, where were you Saturday night?"

The question struck Jack as odd, and boosted his adrenaline again.

"You know where I was, sir. I was with Ted and Anna."

"I understand you left the hospital later that night. That's more of what I'm getting at. Where did you go."

"Oh, yeah. I was feeling kind of like an outcast at that point. Thought it would be best to leave. I ended up picking up my truck where I hide it behind the SPCA, and headed down to my dad's old farm."

"What time was that?"

"When I left?"

"Yes, and when you made it to the farm."

"It was a little before oh-three hundred when I left. Probably took me a half hour to get to my truck. I ran, but it was raining hard. It's about thirty minutes to the farm. Had to be before four, 'cause I was there for a good hour before Ted showed up."

"Ted showed up at five?"

"About that time. We got into it when he got there before he dropped the bomb. Then we cooled down and talked. He talked me into going back."

"Here, I assume."

"Yeah, I was ready to quit VMI. Heck, I was ready to quit life till Ted talked me down off the rock."

"The rock? What's that?"

"That was where we were sitting. Middle of the river bank. Only, that morning it was surrounded by water. We had a tough time getting back on land. Fought a pretty good current. It took us fifty yards downstream from where we jumped in."

"What happened then?"

"Oh, I just drove my truck back to the SPCA. Walked back to barracks."

"You mentioned Ted dropped a bomb. What was that?"

"Anna was pregnant. He thought I did it."

"And you're saying you didn't get Anna pregnant."

"That's correct. Anna and I never slept together," Jack said.

"What have you done since then?" The question this time came from Officer Wharton.

"I talked with the guys back at the room, and then took a shower."

"And then?" asked Watts.

"I called Jimbo from right here in Lejuene, and he came and talked to me."

"Jimbo King, right?"

"Yeah, you know him?"

"Who doesn't?"

Both officers smiled and nodded.

"He made me go back to the room and get some sleep."

"Colonel Jackson said that Jimbo took you away on furlough. What was that all about?"

"Just trying to find out how Anna got pregnant. I thought maybe one of her friends would know."

"Well, did you find out anything enlightening?"

"Not when we went to Hollins or Richmond."

"And where have you been since then?" Wharton asked.

"Here. Well, and the funeral. Ski took me to Richmond."

"Alright, that's enough for now, Jack," said Detective Watts. "Do you have anything you want to add?"

Jack thought for a moment.

"You don't have a clue, do you?" asked Jack.

"About what?"

"Anna."

"I thought you said you didn't find out anything enlightening about Anna," Watts said.

"Not at Hollins or Richmond. I found out the truth tonight."

"And what would that be?"

"Anna was pregnant because she was raped."

"How do you know that?" asked Wharton.

"Her friend from Richmond, Jenny Lipscomb, told me. You want to know the kicker?"

"Go ahead," answered Detective Watts.

"The guy that raped her was Phelps."

Watts gave a single nod to Officer Wharton.

"Cadet Hartman," Wharton said, "we found Phelps's car today."

"Well, was he in it?"

"No," Wharton answered, "but before we go any further, we need to take you to the station, where we can hash this out. Understand you're not under arrest, and this is strictly voluntary. We'd like to ask you a few more questions. We have others we're talking to. It's not about you being a suspect, it's all about getting this cleared up."

"I suppose," Jack said.

They think I did something to Phelps!

"Officer Wharton?"

"Yeah?"

"I need to make one call before we leave. Is that okay?"

"You can, but if you call a lawyer, it'll sure make you look like you've got something to hide."

"Well, if this is not about me being a suspect, then I suppose it shouldn't make a difference," Jack replied.

He turned and walked to a phone on a table just outside of the room.

CHAPTER TWENTY

NOT MY WILL

Jack sat at the police station in a small room that closely resembled his barracks room—drab off-white walls of painted cinder block, cracked plaster ceiling with one fluorescent light fixture in the middle. Spartan and cold.

Jimbo will be here soon.

Jack couldn't understand how they could suspect him of doing anything to Phelps. He had given them a reasonable accounting for his time. There were witnesses to every move he had made since Anna was killed Saturday night.

Except for one.

When I left the hospital. No one saw me for a couple hours.

He began to mull over the timeline again and again. He thought hard about what he did from the moment he left the hospital to the moment he pulled Ted onto the rock. He was unclear about every detail of it. Jack had operated in somewhat of an emotional haze that night, making it hard to remember, as if he was trying to recall the details of something that had happened years ago.

I should've never left the hospital. Why did I leave the hospital?

He tormented himself, replaying the events of that night, finding it difficult to produce the same results twice. Jack hoped there would be something he would remember that would give him a reasonable alibi, but no matter how many times he covered it, there was still a two hour gap he could never get back.

Someone opened the door.

"I thought I told you to stay out of trouble."

Jimbo walked through the doorway smiling, taking off an old World War II bombardier jacket. Another man followed Jimbo into the room and closed the door. He was tall and broad shouldered, appeared to be in his mid-fifties, well-dressed in a dark brown leather dress jacket, impeccably pressed jeans and tan ostrich cowboy boots.

He had dark brown, almost black hair, parted on the right and combed back with a few loose locks hanging on his forehead. Handsome, confident.

"Jack, meet J.D. Harvey."

Jack stood and shook hands.

"Jack Hartman."

"J.D. Harvey," the man said, smiling, "the third."

"I asked Mr. Harvey to come over and help you out. Told him what all was going on. He called over here from his office and had a conversation with Watts," Jimbo said.

"Are you a lawyer?"

"Yes, I'm a lawyer."

"Good, I need one right now."

"Jack, I spoke with Detective Watts," Harvey said. "He seems to think you may have been involved in the suspected death of former VMI cadet, John Phelps. Here is what I know, and feel free to set me straight or fill in the blanks: John Phelps shot Anna McClain Saturday night. You and Ted McClain were with her when it happened. Phelps fled the scene."

"Yes, sir," said Jack, "just like you said."

"Alright, fast forward to now. They found Phelps's car this morning partially submerged under water. But, *viola*, no body."

"Could it have been an accident? Do they think he's dead?" Jimbo asked.

"Let's say they suspect foul play, and want to get a jump on this thing before they drag the river. Couple problems that make you a person of interest right now. One is obvious: Phelps shot Anna, Anna was your fiancé. Phelps's car is found banged up in the river, and no body."

"I confess to doing only one thing to Phelps," Jack said. "I punched him three or four times as hard as I could in his face after I tackled him. My knuckles are proof. I had to have come close to knocking one of his front teeth out. That's what happened to my middle knuckle."

He held up his hand and made a fist, revealing the gash across his knuckle.

"And that happened when Phelps fired the shot?"

"Right after. I jumped him and pinned him between the curb and a parked car. Like I said, I hit him several times until Ted yelled at me. Then I ran over to Anna. I didn't even hear him leave."

"Did you see Phelps after that?"

"No sir, haven't seen him since."

"Well, I personally don't think they're going to hold you here. They may have a few questions, but unless there's something you're not telling me, they don't have any reason. If they did, they'd have arrested you."

"When can we get this over with?"

"They'll be in soon. They've got Ted McClain across the hall. When they're done, they'll talk with you."

"Ted's here?" asked Jack.

"Yeah, I'm sure they're checking your story against Ted's," Harvey said.

They sat for a minute, waiting quietly.

"Mr. Harvey?"

"Yeah, Jack."

"What was the other?"

"The other what?"

"The other problem," said Jack. "You said there were two problems with it being an accident, but you only mentioned one."

"Right. Well, it seems they're a bit hung up on some rather convenient geography and timing."

"I don't understand," said Jack.

"Right now they seem to have some reason to believe the car's been in the water for a couple days. They say since early Sunday morning."

"I was at the farm then."

"Yeah, so I've been told. And that's the rest of the problem. They found it in the James, mostly under water, near the railroad bridge about two miles downstream from your farm."

—◦◦◦—

There was a time when Jack longed to be someone great, as a cadet, the Honor Court president or prosecutor, regimental staff or even the regimental commander. He longed to go on from VMI and work his way up through the army's officer ranks, and just maybe to leave his mark on his country as a great soldier or politician.

Now, he just wanted to breathe.

He just wanted to survive long enough to get out, to be gone, off into the sunset, rejected and spit out again by the rest of the world. Just to breathe a breath of escape, of freedom.

The walls were getting closer as Jack felt freedom slipping away. The reality of everything—Anna gone, the McClain's rejection which felt to Jack like the worst kind of betrayal, and now the tenor of all these questions being hurled at him—sunk deep into his heart. Tired and afraid.

I didn't do anything wrong. Why can't I escape this curse?

"That'll be enough, fellas!" Harvey yelled.

"Mr. Harvey, we have a possible dead boy who murdered a girl connected closely to your client. If we need to make an arrest, we will," Watts answered.

"I seriously doubt it. With your ridiculous lack of anything with substance, you wouldn't dare introduce Miranda into the conversation and turn a fully cooperating Jack Hartman into a sphinx."

They'd been going at it for a couple hours. A half-hour of brow-beating questions for Jack, then back over to Ted. Then they came back, and then returned to Ted. Now they were back and J.D. Harvey was fed up.

"Look, Jack, I can't seem to make sense of the coincidence here," said Watts. "Give me something to work with. Like a good reason Phelps was on your road right after he killed your fiancée during the same small window of time you were there."

"Phelps went to school at James River High."

"Yeah, but he didn't live on that road."

"He had friends that did."

"Zero four-hundred, Jack. No one goes for a friendly visit then."

"No one rapes a girl then shoots her two months later, either," said Jack.

"Yeah, good point. There isn't much about this situation that has any precedence, is there?" Harvey asked.

There was a knock on the door. Wharton entered with Ted.

Jack suddenly felt good, his fear flushing away. His friend was back. Ted would not look at Jack, though.

"Alright," Wharton said, "I think we've figured something out here. Go ahead, son, tell 'em what you told me."

"Jack didn't do anything," Ted said, looking down.

He looked back up quickly and directly at Jack.

"I'm sorry, Jack. I should've told them everything I know, and this would've been over. I was mad, mad and scared, I guess. Anna was everything to me. Then Officer Wharton told me the truth."

"So what's the big revelation?" Watts asked.

Jack felt the adrenaline shoot into his body. His heart began pounding fast and hard and he could feel the sudden thuds of pressure in his temples. His neck began to feel constricted, and he fought to keep from gasping for air. He knew that what was about to be said would change someone's life forever.

Ted looked around the room. He was visibly shaking. He took a deep breath. His face became expressionless.

"It was me. I did it."

Watts read Ted his rights as Harvey whisked Jack out of the room and had him processed out of the station. Jack agonized about Ted and his family as he rode back to the Institute with Jimbo.

"Ever since I showed up here, there's been a curse that seems to have no end. It's like a dark cloud I can't get out from under, and everyone who gets close to me gets sucked into it."

"You're not the one to blame for all of this, Jack. It's certainly tragic for them, and you've had to endure a good part of it, but you can't blame yourself."

"I suppose," said Jack, taking up refuge from the conversation in polite, southern agreement.

He stared out the window the rest of the way, and neither of them said a word until Jimbo let Jack out at Jackson Arch. Jack thanked Jimbo for his help and the ride and headed up to the second stoop.

"What happened now?" asked Darryl when Jack walked in.

"Ted's in a lot of trouble, guys," answered Jack.

"What's going on?" asked Ski.

"I don't even know where to start with this one," Jack said.

Ski was sitting at his desk shining his shoes, while Darryl reclined on his cot with a book.

"They found Phelps, well his car, at least, in the James," said Jack.

Darryl sat up and threw his legs over the side of his cot and tossed the book onto his desk. "Was he hiding?"

"No, they haven't found his body, yet. They figure he's dead."

"Phelps is dead? How?" asked Ski.

"Most likely drowned in the James. They found his car in the river this morning. They've got some evidence it's been there since early Sunday."

"Geez," said Darryl, "what else could possibly happen?"

"Well, for starters they thought I did it."

"C'mon, you've been a bit busy lately. I doubt you'd have found much time for that," replied Darryl.

"Well, they don't think I did it anymore. Ted told them *he* killed Phelps."

"What? Ted? No stinkin' way!" said Ski.

"That just doesn't make sense," said Darryl. "I mean, I know he might have been pretty messed up right after Anna was killed, but I just don't see him killing someone."

"Yeah, I don't either, but there's not much I can do about it at this point," replied Jack.

"What's his story? I mean, how did *he* kill him?" asked Ski.

"I don't know. The lawyer Jimbo brought with him was pretty eager to get me out of the room. They were arresting Ted when I left."

"Something's wrong," said Darryl.

"Yeah," Ski said. "Didn't you say they found Phelps's car in the James?"

"I did, and I know it looks like this is a cut and dried accident, but these cops have it in their minds that someone had something to do with it."

"So *what*? Are they questioning him?" asked Ski.

"His dad just got there. I'm sure they'll lawyer up just fine. I don't know any details, so I guess we just wait till tomorrow and see what happens."

"You know what the good thing about all this is?" asked Darryl.

"No, what?" asked Jack.

"It can't get any worse."

Jack heard the door opening behind him, and turned quickly to see a silhouette standing in the middle of the doorway.

It was Ted.

Jack froze, shocked for a moment. He could feel himself wanting to move, but not really knowing what he should do.

How did he get here? He was being arrested just an hour ago.
Jack felt awkward and couldn't speak for a minute.
He's still your friend.

But it felt to Jack as if they had lost their friendship. The admission Ted made at the police station, however, was as much of a sacrificial act as Jack had ever witnessed. Though it may have been true, Jack knew Ted didn't have to do it.

Ted began to speak, almost as if in the middle of a conversation. "I said it for you, Jack, to get the heat off you. I guess I realized when I saw you in the woods up on the hill at the cemetery how hard we'd been on you. We pushed you away, and you had nothing to do with it," Ted said.

"So, how did it happen? Phelps, I mean," asked Jack.

"I said I did it, but I didn't do anything really wrong," Ted said. "When I took off to go find you, I knew you would head for your farm. I headed straight out there, hoping to catch up with you. I really thought you'd lost it. I didn't know what you might do."

"Like kill myself? I don't know. It was bad. I was in a bad mental state, I guess. Anyway, I could never have done anything like that."

"I'm sorry we treated you like that," said Ted.

"It's okay. I understand how painful it would be, especially for your mom and dad."

"But you, Jack. You loved Anna deeply. I shouldn't discount that, and neither should my folks."

Jack felt the warmth of peace flush through him. It was the mention of Anna.

Anna.

"Brothers, again?"

"Yeah, brothers," Ted said. "Jack, speaking of which, I've got something very important I need to tell you."

"Wait," Jack said, as if stuck by an epiphany, "you saw me at the cemetery?"

"Yeah, Mom saw you, too, as we were leaving. It broke her heart."

———⟨✦⟩———

Ted had killed no one. He had given chase to Phelps in his car after seeing him on the interstate on his way to find Jack. As if fate had stepped in, Phelps took the exit into Buchanan, then raced up Narrow Passage Road toward James River High.

They ended up barreling down muddy roads, through a farmer's field and over a set of railroad tracks. Ted lost him, but the wild flash of headlights, and immediate disappearance of his car made Ted believe he had probably wrecked. Filled with anger, he turned around and headed back to the highway toward Jack's farm, never knowing Phelps rolled his car a number of times and ended up submerged in the James where he most likely had drowned, and would probably show up somewhere miles downriver in a few more days.

Police closed the investigation, deeming it a missing person case, until they could confirm an accidental death. Though it seemed a relief to be through with it, the most difficult winter was on them. Jack and Ted struggled with despair and grief. Ted buried himself in helping Jack with his master sergeant duties, while Jack lost all motivation for the military aspect of his life at VMI.

A solemnity fell over the room like a thick shadow that hushes the sun and cools the air, and by the end of March, Ted broke the news his cancer had returned, and he would need treatments to start immediately.

"Well, Jack, as much as I dreamed of being a first battalion commander, it's probably not going to happen," Ted said one evening before he left.

Darryl and Jack sat on their respective bunks in the room.

"Good, we'll be privates together," said Jack.

"You know Colonel Jackson is going to forgive you for all of your insubordinate behavior, and make sure you get some serious rank next makeover. Not just as a staffer, but probably a command position. The guy loves you, Jack."

"I doubt it. Besides, I'm looking forward to the stress-free life."

"You're a natural leader," Ted said, "and the strackest cadet in the corps. Your grades are top-notch, and you never get a demerit. You'd make a rather poor first class private."

"I don't know. I used to love chasing rank. I thought it was the only thing that could break me away from my past. Now, I don't have the desire. I don't know, maybe it will come back."

"I think the only thing that has kept me here this long is you, Ted," Darryl said.

"And now you need to stay and finish for me," Ted replied.

"I'm not going anywhere," said Darryl. "The whole medieval thing we have here has kinda grown on me."

Only a few months later, Darryl announced his intention not to return for first class year. His girlfriend was pregnant, and the reality of life and death with Anna and Ted had convinced him there were things in life more important than graduating from VMI. It was difficult for all of them to watch the room fall apart, but Jack and Ski promised to be back and keep half of the room together through graduation.

Though Jack was no longer motivated by the military aspect of cadetship, he was healing, finding respite in his studies and his writing. Secretly, Jack desired the life of a first class private. The last three years had drained much of his desire to do anything he did not see as having a definitive purpose. All of the responsibility for the corps could fall on another's shoulders, and the thought of it satisfied him.

But Colonel Jackson wouldn't allow Jack to fold. After a session with him, Chaplain Campbell, and Colonel Gavin, Jack had accepted command of first battalion. He assured the triumvirate he would execute his duties professionally.

Ted wanted this, not me. Ted loves this stuff. I used to love it, but not as much, anymore. So this is for you Ted.

—◦◦◦—

As soon as the corps was released from military duty for summer furlough, Jack headed north to Richmond. Ted had been receiving treatment at St. Mary's, and Jack hoped to be able to see him. He planned on finding a cheap place and getting back on a construction crew, where he could earn some decent money before reporting to Ft. Bragg for the army ROTC leadership course, affectionately known as "Summer Camp."

Ted had written him, sending him a couple good contacts for work, but insisted Jack stay with Ted's folks. Jack knew he couldn't do it, that he would need to take care of room and board on his own. He still felt on the outside. The idyllic thought he would be accepted into the McClain family had slipped too far away for any real hope.

The same day he left the Institute, he stood outside a thick wooden door on the fourth floor of St. Mary's. Ted lay inside, a nurse waking him up following a treatment. The door slowly opened in front of him.

"You can go in, now," said the nurse, "but don't expect too much. These treatments take a lot out of him."

Jack nodded and walked in. Ted lay on his left side facing a window with the shade pulled down. The light of the bedside lamp was dim, but Jack could see Ted was gaunt and yellowish. His hair was patchy, almost gone in the back and the front thin in sparse tufts. Jack moved around to the far side of the bed, to see if Ted was awake.

Ted opened his eyes only slightly.

"Hey, man. I knew you'd make it up here," Ted said, then smiled in a way that looked more like an expression of pain.

"I came straight here. Is it a good time, now?"

"It's fine. I always feel like this after a treatment, like I've been hit by a truck."

"Where are your folks?"

"They were here before I went in. They probably left to give me time to sleep this off."

"Or they knew I was coming."

"I doubt it. I think they're getting over all of the blame. I think they know it really wasn't your fault."

"Yeah, but there'll always be that nagging voice in the back of their minds."

"It doesn't matter. They're capable of forgiveness, Jack."

"I suppose."

"I hope you are, as well."

"No problem, here. I'm a forgiving machine."

"Really? How's that working out with your dad?"

I can't forgive him. He cursed me. It's his fault Anna died.

"That's different," said Jack.

"How so?"

"Well, he's dead."

"So why is that stopping you from forgiving? You don't have to be face to face. It's something you do in your heart. You just let it go."

Jack turned toward the window, and pulled the side of the shade slightly open to look out. Steam sputtered from exhaust vents on an adjacent lower rooftop. The sunlight warmed his face.

"I wake up every morning in fear, Ted. I cower like a beaten dog when I hear a door open behind me. I can constantly I feel bones in my body that were once broken. I'm reminded of him every day."

"Forgiveness doesn't mean you'll forget it. It doesn't mean you approve of it. It means you release it. You erase your responsibility to own it."

"I still don't know how to do that." Jack sat down in a chair by the window. "So, when do you get out of here?" Jack asked.

"I think in a week or so, depending on how I do with this round of treatments. I get to be home for a month, then back here for another week."

"You gonna make it back for Cadre?"

"I doubt I'll make it back for the semester," Ted said, then paused for a few seconds. "You know, I'm glad you made first battalion commander. It was the job I really wanted. At least we kept it in the room."

"Had you been there, it would have been yours. I was definitely second-string on this one."

Ted rolled onto his back and stared at the ceiling. His eyes were now wide open.

"Jack, I've been working on something, something important. I don't want to tell you just yet. I'm not sure if I'll ever need to, but I sense that I will. Right now, I'm still working on it. Just promise me, if anything happens to me, you'll find my back pack. It'll be in there."

"Nothing's gonna happen to you. You'll outlive most of us, I'd guess."

"Maybe not, but you never know," Ted answered and took in a labored breath. "I sure don't feel very invincible right…and… you…" Ted trailed off in the middle of his sentence. Jack waited for a few minutes, listening to Ted's breathing rise and fall slowly. Finally, Jack got up and left the room, and headed out to his truck.

Time to leave. He needs sleep.

Jack had never spent the summer in Richmond.

CHAPTER TWENTY-ONE

Morning

Summer flashed by quickly and furiously. Jack found work in Richmond till mid-July, then spent five weeks at Ft. Bragg attending the mandatory army leadership course. He wasn't sure if he would go on active duty after graduation. He wasn't too sure about anything.

Jack longed to write. He wanted to concentrate on the one thing he felt he could do well. It might, he reasoned, be his one shot at doing something really significant in this world.

He sat in class one morning, the second week of his first class year, mulling over these thoughts, dreaming of what he would be doing his first year in the real world, only about nine months away.

He was suddenly overwhelmed.

Anna, Anna, Anna.

He could feel her hair blowing across his face, and smell the salt water. She was laughing on the beach, propped up on her elbows watching the tide. He could feel the sand on his back as he listened to her laughter, and the dampness of perspiration where his shoulder touched her forearm.

It was real. For a moment he lay beside her on the beach again, in the secret place among the dunes. But as quickly as the vision came, it went, and he was left sitting in a cold classroom, listening to his Language, Myth, and Meaning professor, Dr. Junger, ramble on about all things Aboriginal.

He stopped suddenly when his eyes fell on Jack.

"Jack, are you okay?"

Jack realized there were tears rolling down his cheeks. He flushed with embarrassment.

"I'm, uh, I'm fine, sir," he answered. Jack wiped his face with the palm of his right hand.

"Well, that's it for today, anyway," Dr. Junger continued. "Let's finish with chapter five of the textbook on Thursday and finish your reading of the Stanley book, also."

He looked at Jack as the nine cadets around the table assembled their notes and books.

"Jack, do you have a moment?"

"Yes, sir," Jack answered.

Junger was an eccentric man in his late sixties. His hands trembled, but he was never nervous. He smoked considerably, and frequently did so in class. No one cared. He was one of the few civilian professors. His teaching style was loose and engaging. Cadets loved his classes.

When the last cadet left the room, Dr. Junger spoke.

"Jack, you do realize there are things in life more important than VMI. Or do you not?"

"I realize that, Dr. Junger."

"If you require time to grieve, then take it. I'm sure the military system will not collapse in your absence."

"I'm fine, sir," said Jack. "I just get these waves of emotion that hit me from time to time. I'm not going anywhere."

"So be it. I wonder how it all ended up. The papers dropped the story almost as quickly as it sprung up. Did you ever hear anything else?"

"They were never able to find Phelps's body, but I think they have it pretty well wrapped up. They've determined it was an accident. It's closed now."

"Hmmm."

"What?"

"Someone told me there are people still asking questions, that's all."

"I don't know. Maybe the cops are still looking for answers."

Dr. Junger paused and walked over to look out of his office window. He pulled a curtain from the outside edge to look behind to the street below.

"Do you have any siblings, Jack?"

"No, why?"

"Just something else I heard. I may have been mistaken, though."

"What did you think you heard, Dr. Junger?" Jack flushed with feverish curiosity.

"I thought someone said you and Cadet McClain were brothers, maybe half-brothers or something like that, but I probably misunderstood."

"We're close, but we're only Brother Rats. Maybe that's what whoever said it meant."

"Maybe so, then."

Jack heard an uncertainty in his voice. It seemed he was dropping the subject too easily. Jack felt he had to be bold before Dr. Junger closed down.

"Who did you overhear talking?"

"Well, it was strange, but early this morning I was walking up the hill to Scott-Ship when I heard two men talking about you and Cadet McClain. It was foggy and I didn't realize who it was till I got fairly close. It was Colonel Jackson and some other guy who got in a cab and drove away after I passed by," Junger said.

"So what exactly were they talking about?"

"They clammed up when I passed them, but they sounded urgent before they saw me. Anyway, I heard what I heard before I passed them."

"The part that made you think I have a brother?"

"All I know is I heard your name mentioned as well as another whom I'm sure was Cadet McClain. I guess I keyed in on your name because you're one of my best students and a battalion commander. The cabbie said something about being brothers. He did not say *Brother Rat.*"

"And you think he was saying Ted and I are brothers?"

"I don't know. I suppose the curiosity it aroused in me had me asking you all of this. It's probably a misunderstanding."

Jack thought about it for a moment. Suddenly everything took on a new strange tint. But Jack knew he was an only child. Ted had been adopted in Richmond. It would be ridiculous. Then, something suddenly stood out in his mind.

"Dr. Junger, did you happen to see the name of the cab company?"

"It's got that symbol, you know, like a crest."

"King Cab?"

"That's it."

———

"Jack, you have a status slip on your desk," Ski said as Jack walked in the room. "What did you do, now?"

"What do you mean?"

"Says something about you seeing the commandant at fourteen-hundred."

"Nothing like having your life planned out for you by Big Brother," Jack said.

"You gave up privacy and freedom three years ago, signed your life away to the man, Brother Rat. Not to mention how little regard you must have had for personal freedom when you agreed to wear those stripes."

"I suppose," answered Jack.

Jack set his books down and read the status slip. The message, scrawled in black ink, in handwriting nearly illegible, was distinctive. He recognized it immediately. It appeared on every letter Ted ever received from home.

Meet me in the commandant's office at 1400.

That was all. Nothing more, and no signature. It didn't need one.

"It's Mr. Mack," Jack said.

"He's here?"

"He's at least been here, and according to this, he'll be here at fourteen-hundred."

"News about Ted?"

"Yeah, could be. If it is..."

Jack stopped.

He wondered how he would even finish his sentence. He wondered if Ted had died. He had been expecting a call such as this. Expecting, but hoping somehow it would turn out differently.

It shook him.

He sat down at the desk, pulled out an old letter from Anna, and waited for two o'clock.

It had been several months since Jack last stepped foot in the commandant's office. Nothing had changed. Still the same dark paneling and cherry pipe tobacco. Colonel Jackson was a creature of habit.

"Cadet Hartman, be at ease," the colonel said as Jack finished his salute.

Jack stayed planted in front of Colonel Jackson's desk, assuming the more relaxed position with his hands behind the small of his back and his eyes on the colonel.

"Jack, you know I don't often give cadets this privilege, but special circumstances call for, well, you know," Colonel Jackson said. "Please, have a seat." He motioned to a chair to the left front of the desk.

When Jack turned, he noticed for the first time Mr. McClain sitting in another chair several feet from the left side. He reached out and shook his hand, but before he would let go, Mr. McClain stood.

"I'm sorry, Jack, for everything. I've been a mess and it caused me to make some rather poor decisions. My judgment has been way off, I haven't been thinking clearly, even before Anna's murder. Please," he paused, and then finished, "forgive me."

There was something stirring inside Jack, something unforgiving, something raging.

Am I capable? Is there anything left?

He forced his emotion back down his throat.

"Yes, sir. It's in the past. Good to see you again."

Jack was not sincere. He wanted to be forgiving, to let things go no matter how personal and hurtful they were, but he couldn't yet.

Immediately, Mr. McClain let go of Jack's hand, sat down, and began to wipe tears that were filling the bottoms of his eyes. Jack looked nervously at Colonel Jackson, who nodded and eyed Jack approvingly.

It lasted for less than a minute.

"I'm sorry, Bill," Mr. McClain finally said, looking at the commandant. "Seeing Jack, again, well, it all comes back. But I feel like a weight has been lifted off me. Jack, your forgiveness means everything. I was wrong, and you've taken the brunt of it."

Mr. McClain's reaction and comment struck Jack deeply. He now began to feel as if he could move closer to authentic forgiveness. He could sense that Mr. McClain's outburst held more pent up emotion than could be accounted for by Jack's mercy.

"There's more to it than my forgiveness," Jack replied. "You're not here just to be forgiven."

"Ted."

"How is he?"

"Fading fast. Radiation was horrible, and not that promising. He's not taking the chemo well, since. The center doesn't give him much time. We've believed all along God could heal him. It hasn't happened, yet anyway. We started making hospice arrangements."

"I'm sorry. Can I see him?"

"Well, that's another problem. He's gone."

"Gone?"

"Yeah, gone. He was in pretty good shape, seemed to be resting fine. We were only away for a half-day. When we returned to the center, he wasn't in his room. No one knew where he went."

"When did this happen?" asked Jack.

"Yesterday."

"And no one's seen him since?" the colonel asked.

"No one. We have people looking for him. Haven't been able to file a missing person report. It hasn't been twenty-four hours, yet. I hired a P.I."

"Any ideas?" asked Jack.

"I thought you might have heard something, or remembered something he said these last few years. I didn't want someone else asking you. I wanted to see you."

"I can't think of anything off the top of my head. I mean, nothing obvious."

"Nothing about where he'd like to go, some place he'd like to see? Dream stuff?"

"No." Jack thought for a few seconds. "Well, except Rat year he talked about the time he spent with his Grandfather fishing on the Yukon River in Alaska. But surely he wouldn't…"

"I don't know why I hadn't considered it, but hearing you say it now, it makes sense," Mr. McClain interrupted.

"Why would Alaska make any sense?" asked Colonel Jackson.

"It's not just the location, it was his grandfather, my dad. It was also a difficult time for Teddy. He was struggling with some things. Dad had asked if he could take him to his cabin up there. Said the man time would do him some good. It did."

"It was his turning point," Jack said. "He really found God there."

"Yes it was. Yes he did," Mr. McClain said.

"So Theodore, do you think he really may have taken off to Alaska?" Colonel Jackson asked.

"It would be a good place to look," Mr. McClain answered. "Any other thoughts, Jack?"

"Do you know where on the Yukon?"

"Somewhere near Circle or Fort Yukon. A cabin, right on the river."

"You been there, Mr. Mack?"

"No, I never made the trip. It was kind of an escape for Dad in his later years."

Jack was silent, waiting for Mr. McClain or Colonel Jackson to speak. But no one said anything for what seemed to Jack an awkwardly long time. It seemed that all were in deep thought.

"Jack, can you help me? Can you come with me? Just a few days," Mr. McClain said.

"What about Mrs. McClain?"

"I'll speak with her, but she's in a rough state. No doubt, she'll want to come and find her son. It would be best if she stays. We don't know for sure Teddy's even gone this route."

"Jack, you have the emergency furlough you need," Colonel Jackson said. "Let's find your son, Theodore. You know you have any resources the Institute can offer, any help you need."

Jack stood up.

"I don't know if Ted left to go to Alaska, and if he did, why he would have. It doesn't make sense. But if Ted's in trouble, we need to do something."

"Thanks, Jack," Mr. McClain said. "Oh, and Ted left you a note. I was wondering if it would mean anything to you. I mean, what he wrote is pretty straight forward."

He reached into his coat pocket, and pulled out a note, folded in quarters.

"Here."

Jack took the note and unfolded it quickly. He read it through twice.

"He says that I'll see it soon, this whole thing about God weaving everything together. He wants me to be there."

"Yeah, it seems so," Mr. McClain said. "I think it would help him. I don't know what kind of shape he'll be in."

Jack stepped in front of Colonel Jackson's desk. "Permission to be dismissed, pir."

"Permission granted Cadet Hartman."

Jack executed an about face and walked to the office door.

"When can I contact you, Jack?"

"I'm gonna tell Ski what's going on, and grab a few things from the trunk room. I also need to make a call. I'll meet you in the arch in thirty minutes."

CHAPTER TWENTY-TWO

ON DARK WATERS

The Yukon was beautiful and mesmerizing. At times it spread out like a lake, laced with large islands, weaving among them with undetectable movement. Otherwise, it moved with a deep current, powerful and consuming. The boat was finally back on a stretch of river that actually resembled a river. They had spent several hours moving purposefully back and forth in and around islands, making sure they missed nothing.

They had investigated several cabins and about a half dozen different smaller boats that had been banked. So far, they had no luck in locating Ted, his boat, a cabin that fit the description Mr. McClain's father had given years ago, or even an eyewitness that had seen Ted on the river.

"Johnboat, up on the right!" Mr. McClain shouted back to Jack, who began to work the boat out of the current and toward the right bank.

"Yeah, it looks like it came from Caraway's. Got the same kind of numbering," Mr. McClain said as they approached the boat that had been tied to a tree that hung out over the edge of the river.

Jack nosed the boat up hard onto the bank, while Mr. McClain jumped off and secured it to the same tree.

"Looks like there's a pretty good trail up here," he said, pointing up the hill as Jack stepped over the bow. "Think I saw a cabin as we were closing in."

They headed up the trail, and about seventy yards up the hill found a small cabin. Mr. McClain took a look inside.

"Two campers. You don't think Ted would've come with anybody else, do you?"

"No way," Jack replied. "I don't see that happening."

"I doubt this is him, then. It doesn't look like any of his stuff." Mr. McClain paused for a moment, thinking. "Okay, Jack, go down to the river. Make sure nothin' passes and he doesn't float right by us. I'm gonna take a quick trip up to the top of this hill and see if I can run into someone."

Jack walked downhill to the boat. When he got to the river, he climbed back in and took a seat on the bow. The Yukon moved quietly by, powerful and slow. He saw something in the other boat that caught his eye. He had missed it completely when they had first pulled up. A tackle box was neatly stowed under one of the seats, and there was a name written on it.

He got up, reached out to the limb and pulled the line with which the other boat was tied to the tree. When he pulled the boat alongside, he stepped over the gear in their boat, careful not to step on the rifle, and into the other boat. He sat down and pulled out the tackle box and read: "Don Jenkins," and then underneath, an address in Orofino, Idaho.

Definitely not Ted. Could've saved us some trouble if we'd seen this first.

Jack stepped out of the boat. He determined to find Mr. McClain before they wasted any more time. A fear swept through him, and he did not know why. He reached back into the boat and grabbed the rifle and a box of rounds.

Just in case. May need this. Big country.

When he made it to the cabin, he saw Mr. McClain another fifty yards further up and off the side of the trail in a cluster of scrubby trees waving frantically at Jack. He continued his sprint as he yelled to Mr. McClain.

"What is it?"

"Bear," he answered, out of breath, "and he's hurt someone bad, up there!" He pointed directly up the trail.

Jack could see a man curled up in the fetal position lying right in the middle of the trail, not moving. He could not see the bear. Jack pulled the bolt back to check and make sure there was a round in the chamber. He nervously fumbled with the box till he had it opened and the rounds half spilled on the ground. He gathered a few in his hand and pocketed them.

Almost as quickly as Jack began moving up the trail toward the injured man, the bear stepped out of the thicket beside him. It was a monster brown, thick and powerful, with light brown greasy looking fur that grew darker around the eyes and the paws.

It grunted twice, but did not look up, and seemed totally preoccupied with the man, still holding a tight fetal position. The bear gave him a couple of scooping swats, the second sliding him around so that his face was looking down the trail. Jack saw his eyes blink, and knew he was alive.

He was, however, a bloody mess, and his left leg was badly mangled half-way down the calf and around the foot. A large flap of his scalp on the left side had been peeled back over his head and hung flopping over toward the ground. His jacket was intact, but his jeans were soaked with blood around the waist, leading Jack to believe that there were injuries they couldn't see.

Jack froze for a moment in the middle of the trail, realizing that he was only a few seconds from being the next play toy for this bear if it decided to attack. He slowly eased the rifle up, gripped the hand guard and firmly planted the stock in the front of his shoulder.

The bear presented a flank, but Jack felt unsure where the best kill shot was on a bear. He aimed mid chest just behind the front shoulder and squeezed off his round. For a second, Jack was stunned by the recoil. He saw the bear shudder, and knew he had at least hurt it.

The bear swung its head violently in a circle a couple of times, a string of saliva trailing. It drew a bead on Jack and took two steps in his direction. Jack knew he had to act quickly. Shaking, he cranked the bolt back dropping the expended shell casing, allowing the next round to slide into the chamber, and the slammed the bolt closed forward. He quickly took aim again.

The bear had stopped, and then started again favoring its left front leg. But the wound caused it to move slowly, shoulder first at an awkward gait. He quickly squeezed the trigger and the second round hit just in front of the same shoulder down toward the center of the chest. Both front legs collapsed, and the bear went chin first into the dirt.

"Jack, be sure you killed it!" Mr. McClain yelled.

Jack was already racing up to the man on the ground, with Mr. McClain only a few feet behind. He nervously jacked the bolt back and forth, reloading it with a fresh shell. Without stopping, Jack slowed and trained the barrel on the bear as he passed it.

The bear was definitely dead, and Jack did not even bother wasting time to check it. When he got to the man, he could see that the bear had bit his lower left leg and left him with an obvious compound fracture, as the lower leg just above the ankle had been snapped like a small twig. The muscle was exposed and torn badly.

Jack grabbed the scalp that was flopped over exposing the skull, and carefully laid it back in place. Before turning him from his side to his back, Jack had Mr. McClain peel his jacket off of his side. The bear had pawed his back under the rib cage on the right side, and had ripped out a good size chunk of flesh.

"You must've pissed that bear off pretty bad," Jack said.

"Yeah. You've gotta get me outa here. Blasted thing just ambushed me, didn't even see it till it was on top of me," the man replied in a weak, shaky voice.

Jack could tell he was in immense pain, but he was more worried about the blood loss that he had suffered and the state of shock that he was in.

"Mr. McClain, run down to that cabin and kick the door in. See if you can find some things we can use for first aid."

"On it!" he answered and was immediately running back down the trail.

Jack put as much pressure on the wound as he could. Before Mr. McClain ran back up the trail, he had the bleeding down to a seep, and was collecting some sapling trunks to make a splint for the leg. He had laid the man on his back and covered the top of his torso and arms with his own jacket, trying to keep him as warm as possible.

"I've got it," panted Mr. McClain. "Found a first aid kit and some things we can use for bandages, and a blanket."

"Good. Alright, sir, we're gonna have to put you back together. Then we'll haul ya down to the boat. Now tell us while we're workin' here where we need to go to get you to a hospital."

It took both ace bandages in the kit and both rolls of tape to finally get him wrapped enough. He was in no condition to get on his feet, so Jack prepped a couple of thick saplings and rolled them up in two opposite sides of the blanket to build a stretcher. Jack slung the rifle across his back and they both lifted the man onto the makeshift stretcher and trudged down the trail, past the bear carcass and the cabin, to the boat.

They wrestled the stretcher onto the boat and set him down near the cargo in the center. He was still a little dazed when they got him positioned on some padding, with his splinted leg propped up. He didn't want to lay completely flat because he was feeling nauseous, and was afraid that it would just get worse lying on his back, looking at the arctic sky.

"Are you Don?" Jack asked.

"Yeah, Jenkins," he answered, cringing with pain.

Jack stuffed a pack behind his shoulders and head, allowing him to see where they were going. Though it seemed the worst of the bleeding had stopped, Don was a bloody mess.

Mr. McClain was back on the motor and had gotten it started, so Jack jumped over the bow and pushed them off. They were quickly heading downriver, while Don told them how to get to Circle, a small community on the Yukon a good number of miles further downstream. They ran steadily with the current as fast as they could push the boat for well over an hour. Jack was not sure that they would make it in time. Don was in extreme pain, had lost a great deal of blood, and was slipping in and out of consciousness.

As they approached a bend in the river where they could see an obvious boat landing, Jack shook Don awake.

"What is this landing?" asked Jack.

"It's Circle," he said gasping. "Follow the road."

Mr. McClain nosed the boat hard into the sandy landing, where it resembled a small beach at the edge of the bend. Both immediately jumped from the boat and began wrestling Don onto the stretcher and over the side. After quickly adjusting the poles to hold the blanket tight, they headed over the bank, and immediately could see a small store about a hundred yards up the sandy road.

It seemed to take forever to trudge uphill through the deep sand, but somehow they got a call for help out, and the store tenders, a couple of middle-aged men, ran down to help them.

They swore a great deal, redressed Don's wounds and got him coherently talking. They had an I.V. they used and it was effective. Some of his color began to return, and he began responding verbally.

The helicopter was a military dispatch from Ft. Wainwright. It arrived surprisingly quickly, the huey kicking up half of the landscape around the old country store. The army medics were extremely fast treating Don, securing him and getting him on the bird, and like that, he was gone, on his way to Fairbanks.

Jack and Mr. McClain sat on the edge of the porch in the ensuing silence, exhausted. They both realized how far off their own mission that this event had taken them. The two men from the store, who had identified themselves simply as Butch and Andy walked up to the porch after seeing the helicopter off.

"So you fellas are lookin' for your son?" Butch asked, pointing at Mr. McClain.

"Yeah, though we've gotten a bit off track with the bear and all," Mr. McClain answered, "but, yes, it is my boy we're looking for. You wouldn't have happened to have seen a young man traveling alone pass through here?"

He went on to describe Ted to them.

"Your boy's down river about twelve miles," said Andy, after listening to Mr. McClain's description.

"How can you be so sure of that?" Mr. McClain asked.

"He came through about three days ago. Picked up a couple things. Nice kid, looked pretty sick, though. Kinda felt bad for him. He hardly had any hair left on his head, just like you said. He was goin' to that old cabin just downriver on the north bank. Only one on that side for about twenty-five miles. Belongs to an old guy about my age, maybe a bit older. Ain't seen him in a few years, though. Cabins near fallin' apart."

"Does it have a road?" Jack asked.

"Naw. It was a trapper's cabin the old fella fixed up. Take forever to try to find it by land, so I think you need to stay on the river," he replied.

"Now the river opens up 'bout ten miles down. Keep your nose pointed west. Dodge them islands and it'll skinny back to normal after five or six miles," said Butch.

"Will we be able to see this cabin from the river?"

"Oh heck yeah, it sticks out through the trees. They're pretty scrubby on that hill. It's got a pretty good rock trail goin' down to the river. Just stay right on the river, but don't bottom out on the shallows. There's a couple low spots in between here and there," said Andy.

"What was the guy's name that owned that cabin?" Mr. McClain asked.

"Theodore, uh… hah," Andy laughed, "Mack something. Oh, what was that? Not Macdonald, but uh…"

"McClain?" asked Jack.

Andy pointed at Jack and smiled.

"Bang, that's it!" He said.

"Let's go," Mr. McClain said.

"Thanks guys, we'll be back this way today or tomorrow," Jack said.

"Now it's already three-thirty," Butch yelled as Jack and Mr. McClain were jogging toward the river. "Sun's gonna drop like a rock around four. Don't try to come back in the dark, or we'll have to come downstream and pull ya out of a sandbar."

Jack and Mr. McClain headed quickly for the boat. Within a few minutes they were moving down river again. The river began to widen as they trekked west. Dusk was falling, and it looked more like a lake again. As they rounded a wide bend they saw the islands.

They slipped passed the first several on the narrower side, but when they neared the last of the group, Jack's heart surged.

Tied up at the island's leading edge, a small outboard bobbed in the lazy current.

Ted was sitting in it.

CHAPTER TWENTY-THREE

ON THE FIELD OF HONOR

"**W**here's the cabin?" Mr. McClain asked.

Jack maneuvered the boat alongside Ted's.

"We're not even close. We've only gone ten miles, maybe."

Ted looked bad. His skin was a pale yellow, and he was shivering uncontrollably.

"This life we have, our time here on earth is the one chance we have to make an impact on the universe," Ted said in between bursts of shivering.

"Yeah, Ted," said Jack as they pulled Ted's boat tight against theirs, "let's get you back to Circle before it's too late."

McClain stepped over into Ted's boat. It was sitting on a shallow silt bar, making it fairly solid to stand on. Jack felt a twinge of nervousness, unsure how to handle Ted. Jack carefully stepped into Ted's boat behind his seat.

"It's a moment in eternity that God allows us to move in our own free will, and we…and we…"

"C'mon, son."

Mr. McClain grabbed his son by the collar and stood him up while Jack grabbed him from behind and under his armpits. Once he was standing, Mr. McClain squatted and pulled Ted up over his shoulder.

"Let's go," he said, grunting under the weight.

Suddenly, Ted exploded with energy. He wrestled himself off of his dad's shoulder, and then stumbled backward in the boat to the back seat. His eyes were vicious and fiery. Almost comatose a moment before, Ted was now alert and very alive.

"I'm not going anywhere! I've made it this far, and I finally have him where I want him," said Ted.

Jack looked at Mr. McClain. Mr. McClain shrugged, his expression somewhere between bewilderment and fear.

"Who are you talking about, son?" he asked Ted.

"Phelps. I got him here, and now I have him trapped."

"What?" asked Jack.

He's hallucinating.

Mr. McClain looked at his son with a look of pity.

"Son, Phelps is dead. You're not thinking clearly right now."

"Ted, Phelps died in the James a year ago," said Jack.

Ted laughed and shook his head.

"No one ever found a body, did they?"

"No, but it's reasonable to assume…"

"Reasonable! *Reasonable?* Has anything been reasonable in the last two years? Reasonable would be both of us marching in a parade on Friday, and you and Anna going out on a date afterwards. But that really wouldn't be reasonable, would it, Dad?"

Mr. McClain looked shocked and his face flushed with embarrassment.

"Son, I haven't told him, not because I didn't want to, but because I didn't know how."

"No time like the present, Dad. Jack needs to know."

Ted coughed hard twice; painful looking coughs that made him wince, and drew blood from his nose. He pulled his shivering hand away from his face and looked at the blood drizzled over the back of it.

"This is new," he said.

"We've gotta get back to Circle," Mr. McClain said.

He stepped out of the boat to try to free it from the silt bar, but slipped almost immediately into a hole just off the back corner. He sloshed around, fighting his way back up to the edge of the boat. Jack reached over and gave him a hand up. McClain was soaked from the chest down.

"We ain't going nowhere, Mr. Mack. It'll be pitch black out here in another ten minutes, and neither of us knows this river well enough to get back to Circle safely. Let's get Ted on the shore and I'll build both of you a fire. I don't need you hypothermic," said Jack.

Ted stood on his own, and Jack and Mr. McClain helped him over the bow. They moved about twenty feet off the river's edge, cleared an area of rocks, and Jack set out to gather some deadwood. Mr. McClain busied himself back at the boat bringing up some supplies.

It took Jack about twenty minutes to gather a good pile of wood, and get a fire started. Mr. McClain made sure Ted was warm, and then stripped off his wet jacket, boots and socks, and laid them out next to the fire. Jack walked to the boat and secured his pack and the rifle.

Just in case.

The sun had already dipped below the horizon, and the last moments of twilight faded into something purple, something dark.

"He's watching us," said Ted. "I can feel him."

"You don't still believe Phelps is here, do you?" asked Jack.

Ted seemed lively and normal again after warming up. Jack knew it wouldn't last long.

"Tell him, Dad," Ted said.

McClain stood and walked slowly to the edge of the fire light in his bare feet, about half way down to the river.

"You know the commandant, Jack, and you know Jimbo King, right?"

"Yes, sir."

"The three of us are VMI grads, the commandant and I graduated in 'fifty-eight. We ended up in the army together—Fort Bragg—in the same battalion. Jimbo and Bill were in the same company. They were both in Alpha and I was in Charlie.

I had a sergeant in my platoon that caused a lot of trouble, a drinker. Everyone knew this guy, all the way up to Division, but especially Jimbo, who had to subdue him one night at a bar until the MP's could pick him up. Anyway he ended up getting an Article Fifteen around the summer of 'sixty, and getting a less than honorable discharge. I finished my four years and moved on. Bill and Jimbo stayed in and put in a couple tours each in Viet Nam."

"What about the sergeant? Why did you mention him?" asked Jack.

"His name was Hartman. He was your dad, Jack."

"You knew my dad? Why didn't you tell me this before?"

"It's not that easy."

Jack felt his hands tremble, and a wave of nausea. Still, he needed to hear more.

"So if you knew him, did you know my mother?"

"Yeah, but not very well until years later. The first time I met her, she had called the company barracks to ask for help getting back into her house, and the PFC on orderly duty sent the call to me. I drove over to their apartment on post and she was sitting on the steps outside, pregnant and bloody, badly beaten. I flew into a rage and drug him out onto the parking lot and beat him to a pulp; not much of a fight, because he was so drunk. MP's arrived a bit later. He got an Article Fifteen, but that was before he caused the trouble in the bar. It certainly contributed to him getting booted."

"Was I born yet?"

"I never got a chance to follow up before he was discharged," Mr. McClain said. "Then in February of nineteen sixty-three, I had just gotten out of the service, and was living in Richmond when we got a knock on the door late one night. It was her, your mother, Jenny. At first I didn't recognize her, once again beat up real bad and said she was pregnant. She was scared, and got our address from someone back at Bragg, thinking maybe we could help her get a bus ticket to the west coast."

He didn't finish the story, but Jack could feel it coming. Ted looked up and finished it for him.

"She was carrying me."

Jack sat down and leaned back against a boulder. He wasn't sure what he was feeling. Emptiness and anger. But more so, sadness, like a deep black well filled with liquid grief. He stirred his grief for a moment.

How could God arrange all of this, and wait till now to show me?

"All these years, I had a brother. Did you know?"

"Not till after Anna's funeral. Dad sat me down one night and told me. He insisted he be the one to tell you, to explain how it all happened. It was hard to keep that secret. Then the cancer and all. But I wasn't going to let it go another minute. That's why we're here. I knew you would come. Go ahead, Dad, finish it."

"Well, Jenny begged us to adopt the baby she was carrying. We agreed to do so. We always wanted another. Annabelle had just found out she couldn't have any more children. It was as if God had worked it all out. One of those amazing things you can't explain, and can't chalk up to coincidence."

"What happened to her?" asked Jack.

"That's the part I've struggled so hard to tell you, because I'm so deeply ashamed. Shortly after Teddy was born, she packed and left. California, I think. But it's what she said when I dropped her off at the bus station that stuck in my mind and has haunted me all these years."

He paused for a moment as if to push back an emotional surge.

"She said to tell Jack it was for the better he didn't know her, and that he would always have a special place in her heart, but she wasn't fit to raise him. It was just like her to say something wrong, to get a name wrong. So at first, I figured she meant Ted. The more I thought about it, the more I got curious. I had some law enforcement friends look into it and found out about you,

Jack. Not much, just you were there in Glasgow with your dad, still. I had assumed she'd lost that baby."

"But wasn't she pregnant the first time in 'sixty?"

"Well, I'd seen her in the spring of 'sixty. I figured she was about four or five months. I never knew she had you, till after we got Ted."

"I was born in December of nineteen sixty-one."

Mr. McClain thought for a moment.

"It doesn't add up, does it? Could you be older than you think you are?" Mr. McClain asked.

"No way. I stole my birth certificate from Dad's room when I was ten. I used to dream about her, about Mom, that she would come one day and rescue me."

"I tried to figure out the best time to tell you. It's one of the reasons I was so concerned about you and Anna."

Like puppets on a string.

"I imagine it wasn't by freak chance I ended up rooming with Ted."

"About a week before matriculation, I got a call from Jimbo King out of the blue. He called to tell me that Sergeant Hartman had died years before, but his boy was going to VMI. Of course, I called Bill Jackson to confirm, and pulled some strings to get you and Ted in the same Company, and even the same room. I thought it might be a chance to redeem myself for not pursuing you earlier."

Jack sat forward and stirred the fire with a stick. Inside he was settling in on a kind of melancholy, softer and kinder than the grief. No one spoke for several minutes. Mr. McClain walked back up at sat near the fire, across from Jack, sat and set his feet close to the fire. It was turning cold, fast.

"Now, it's my turn," Ted said.

What else could there possibly be?

"I told you that Phelps is here, and he is," Ted said, "but I didn't follow him up here, he followed me."

"What are you talking about, son?" Mr. McClain asked.

"He visited me in the hospital the day you and Mom were gone. I wasn't hallucinating, and I believe he'd been waiting for some time to get to me alone. When he got to me, he was irrational, like a rabid dog, crazy and vicious. He told me he found out at eleven he had been adopted, that his parents might as well have thrown him in the trash when he was a baby, but they just gave him up."

"He's alive? You're sure it was him?" asked Jack.

Ted looked at Jack for a few seconds, and then went on.

"He knew our birth parents names, where they lived, and enough of Jack's story to confirm that he had to be our mother's first child. He found out the details of it all when he was in high school and began to hate Jack with a passion. Don't you see, Jack, it makes sense – the whole reason he came after you, the reason he raped Anna and tried to kill you."

"John Phelps is our brother?"

"Born in August of nineteen sixty. Then you came along in December of 'sixty-one. They kept you, probably felt guilty for what they'd done to their firstborn. When she got pregnant with me, she'd apparently had enough of the abuse and left to drop me off and head out to the west coast to start over."

"He can't be my brother, I *hate* him," said Jack.

"He is, and he's out there," Ted said, motioning with his head at the tree line.

"How did you get him here?"

"Nurse kicked him out of the room right after I told him I was also your brother. He said he would finish the job he had started, so I told him he'd have to find me to do it. I let him chase me all the way up here. He even rented a boat about five minutes behind me. I checked back when I got to Circle, so I knew I had him. When he went looking for me on this island I sunk his boat out in the middle of the river. Been patrolling around the island for the last thirty hours or so, waiting for you guys."

Jack reached down and stroked the rifle lying beside him.

Just in case.

"What do you think, Mr. Mack?" asked Jack.

"Teddy's convinced he has him here. I think we need to round him up, and turn him over to the state police. They'll get him back to Virginia to be dealt with for what he did to Anna. Is he armed?" Mr. McClain asked, turning to Ted.

"He was," answered Ted. "I've got it now. Pumped a few rounds through the hull of his boat to sink it. Think I've got a couple left."

"You boys stay here," Mr. McClain said. "I'll go find him and bring him back."

"No disrespect, Mr. Mack, but you ain't dressed, and besides, he's my problem, and apparently my brother," replied Jack. "I'll go look for him. You stay here and be ready if I flush him out in this open area."

Jack picked up the rifle before Mr. McClain could object, and dug in his pocket for a round. He pulled all he had out and counted four. When he slid the bolt back, no rounds fell out. The chamber and magazine were empty. Jack shuddered.

Good thing the bear died when he did. I'd have been in trouble. Four should be enough.

The island wasn't large, about a hundred yards across at its widest, and three hundred yards long. It rose about fifty feet out of the river at its highest point toward the back side, and was covered in scrub shore pine and tangle thickets. Between the clusters of trees and brush, the muskeg muffled each step Jack took.

He moved as quickly as he could in the blackness of the new moon night, slowing from time to time to adjust his eyes, making the best of the limited illumination. Jack stayed close to the bank on the right side of the island until he reached the back. He heard nothing.

C'mon Phelps, move – if you're really here.

Jack decided to snake his way back and forth through the thickets, moving from back to front, hoping to move anything into the open area where Mr. McClain and Ted would be. He had made several trips from one side to the other before he finally made the apex of the hill and could see the glow of the campfire below about two hundred yards upstream.

Then he heard it. It sounded like someone whispering. His muscles immediately clenched, and he swung the rifle in the direction he thought he heard it come from.

Calm down. That was too noisy. What was that? Whispering?

Jack crouched slowly, and took several steps downhill to his right. He stopped again and listened. His finger on the trigger was already clammy, even though the air was cold enough to have a bite to it. He could feel his heart beating rapidly against the stock, pressed firmly into his shoulder.

"Jack...Jack Hartman."

What was that? Did he say my name?

This time, Jack could not tell where it came from, but it did not seem to be coming from where he thought he heard it before. He turned back upstream, toward the campfire. There was a thicket directly in front of him.

Jack took in a long slow breath and held it in for a few seconds. He squeezed the hand grip under the barrel, then let his breath out. With a burst from his right calf, he surged forward, leaning into his run. He ran past the left side of the thicket, turned sharply right, and spun around facing the back side of it.

Stay low, slow down. Head low, eyes up.

Crouching, Jack moved into the edge of the thicket. He took several slow, methodical steps, almost stopping completely each time he set a foot down.

Nothing. I'd swear it came from here.

Down the hill, halfway to the campfire, Jack heard a stirring in the brush.

He's getting away!

Jack spun around and ran down the hill toward the campfire, hoping to trap Phelps in between. Almost at the bottom, he fought through the thick tangle brush, and earth, marshy enough to be summer tundra. He saw movement in the darkness to his front, fifteen feet away. Jack stopped.

"Jack, you did this to me. You stole my father and you killed him. Now it's your turn."

The whisper was so faint, Jack could not be sure he heard it right. He wondered if he had imagined it.

His rapid breath fogged around him, and drifted back across his face now beading with sweat. Throat clenched tight, and heart pounding, Jack could feel adrenaline surging into his body. His hands trembled slightly as he raised the barrel of the rifle till he had it pointing directly at the blackest clot of darkness just in front of him.

Don't make me shoot him. God don't make me shoot him. Please don't make me shoot him, God.

Jack knew he wouldn't have a choice if Phelps came at him. He would have to pull that trigger.

"Jack Hartman, let's finish this."

Crash!

At first, everything moved in slow motion as the adrenaline gave Jack a hyper-sensitivity to movement and time. The explosion of the thicket in front of him revealed the dark figure was only about ten feet away and closing quickly, not like a train coming at him in a tunnel, but like a tunnel coming at him in a black hole.

Jack squeezed the trigger.

Crack, flash, recoil.

He could see only blue as he stumbled backward, his only thought being a flash of realization his barrel was too high to have done any good. As he hit the marshy turf on his back, the blue blindness dissipated enough to see the wings of an owl beating the air, about the height his head would have been had he not fallen.

It wasn't Phelps. And now Jack was convinced that Phelps was dead, not because of the round he had just fired, but because of a swollen river in Virginia the year before. He stood and brushed himself off, giving time for the flash blindness and ringing in his ears to fade.

All in my head. All in Ted's head, too.

Jack bee-lined for the campfire. When he broke through the wood line, Mr. McClain approached him.

"Jack, are you okay?"

"Yeah," answered Jack, "scratched up a bit, but I'm fine."

"What about the shot? Was it him?"

They had reached the fire and Jack stood near it, where he laid the rifle down and began warming his hands. Mr. McClain sat down and began pulling his boots back on. Jack looked across the fire at Ted, who lay back against and old scrub stump. He shivered uncontrollably on the ground, looking delirious again.

"He's going downhill fast," Mr. McClain said quietly to Jack. "We need to get him to Circle, even if we have to leave Phelps."

"There is no Phelps, Mr. Mack," Jack said. "He's been buried in the James for almost a year."

"So you think Ted imagined the whole thing?"

"I'm sure of it. He ain't here. Look around us. It's a cold, loud swim to the shore. Ted would've heard it."

"You're...right...I would've," Ted said, trying to sit back up. "He's here, Jack Hartman. I'm not losing it, and I swear he's still here." Ted hissed his words, vengeful and vitriolic.

"He's not here, and we are going to put you in our boat and try to find our way back to Circle, tonight!" Jack said.

Ted let out a painful laugh, then reached quickly into his coat and pulled out the pistol.

"You're so eaten up with it," Ted said, "you couldn't figure out you were walking into your own doom."

He held up the pistol with both hands and suddenly stopped shaking. Jack's heart jumped and his head filled with blood. He tried to form a question, but words would not come out. As he stared into the barrel, he could only shake his head.

No Ted. Why?

"Ted, what are you doing?" Mr. McClain screamed, holding his arms out, palms toward Ted. "Put that down. What are you doing?"

"This ends tonight," said Ted.

Blam!

Jack's vision went blue with flash blindness, again. His ears rang. He couldn't feel the shock of the round, but in a split second, it registered to him he had felt it clip the outside of his left hand, like a zipper catching some hide on the way by.

Blam!

Again the flash blinded even more, and now Jack could hear nothing. This time the round had zipped by about knee level, no grazing.

Not like Anna! Quickly.

But it wouldn't be. Jack felt his knees wobble and he used all of his strength to keep them from buckling. His ears were still ringing, but he began to hear around him within seconds. As the flash blindness faded, Jack saw Ted lay back down against the stump, his pistol slide forward and smoke rolling out of the open chamber.

He's spent his last round.

Still, no pain, except for a stinging on his left hand.

"Jack, behind you," Mr. McClain said.

Jack turned to see a body writhing on the ground behind him. He heard a noise – a man screaming. Jack knelt down quickly and pushed the shoulder of the man to reveal his face.

John Phelps.

———◄०/०/०►———

A hefty hunting knife lay on the ground beside Phelps. He was doubled over, fetal like, with his arms wrapped tight around his legs. Jack peeled his arms back to see what kind of wounds he had sustained. When he tried to pry Phelps's left arm off of his knees, the arm hyper-extended a full ninety degrees at the elbow, as if it was a piece of soft rubber. The elbow was blown apart.

Jack could see a considerable amount of blood around Phelps's waist in the flickering light of the fire. Mr. McClain grabbed him by the armpits and straightened him out. The bullet had entered about mid hip, but also on the left side. Phelps let out a scream when Jack and Mr. McClain straightened his left leg, and Jack thought he heard a crunching sound, like he was manipulating a bag of rocks. He figured the pelvis was in pieces.

"He's bleeding pretty badly," said Jack, "but we might be able to stop it. Or, we could let him bleed out, y'know, self-defense. But if we get busy, and try to help him, he might make it to Circle."

"You'll be a medic before this trip is over. Let's do the right thing, at least the legal thing. I'll get something from the boat we can use to treat him."

McClain fetched some materials for Jack to use to bandage Phelps's arm and waist. Jack didn't say a word to Phelps, who spent most of his time moaning deliriously, but busied himself getting his elbow splinted and bandaged while Mr. McClain poured coagulating powder on the wound just inside Phelps's hip.

Eventually, with pressure, gauze, and some strips of cotton shirts Jack had cut up, Phelps stopped bleeding profusely. He was nearly unconscious having lost even more blood than Don Jenkins had with the bear.

Still, they had to wait several hours for even a hint of daybreak to load Phelps on the boat. As the morning horizon began to glow orange, they were ready to be on their way, upriver.

They left Ted's boat on the shore, and once they were situated, Jack shoved them off the sand bar, climbed in and cranked the outboard up. He made a wide turn and headed up river.

"Look, Dad, the three brothers alive together. Probably be the last time," said Ted.

His voice was weak, almost inaudible over the noise of the outboard, his breathing slow and raspy.

"Don't think like that, son. We're gonna make it."

"I'm not, and I'm not real sure about him," Ted said nodding slowly toward Phelps.

Phelps moaned again.

"Don't give up on me, Ted. Hang on. We'll get you home," Jack said.

He won't make it to Circle. He's coughing blood, now.

Mr. McClain lay back against the bow with his arm around Ted, trying to keep him warm. Phelps lay fetal in the middle on the rack.

"Funny thing is," Ted said slowly and painfully, "it took all this…to finally get you two together, you and Jack…and brother Phelps…just a bonus, I suppose."

Mr. McClain looked at Jack with sorrow in his eyes. He shook his head. Jack saw Ted's lips move, saying something to his dad, but could not hear him over the whine of the outboard.

"What is he saying?"

Mr. McClain got up and scooted across the seats and gear to get back to Jack.

"I'll take over, here. You go up and talk to Teddy. He wants to tell you something."

Jack handed the throttle to McClain and worked his way forward. He sat down on the bow seat facing Ted.

"Don't you see it, now?" Ted asked in a whisper.

"See what?"

"The note I wrote you."

"Oh, the whole God weaving thing?"

"Yeah, that."

"I see your point. God put all this together."

"We get one chance."

"One chance for what?" asked Jack.

"This life…we have. It's like a battlefield…and we have one chance to get it right…and accomplish something…close to the mission God had in mind…when he dreamed each of us up."

Ted paused to wince at a wave of pain in his head.

"Yeah, brother. Just like that."

"If it takes me dying...for you to know Christ...then I will have gotten it right."

Jack sat back up straight and nodded his head.

"Field of honor," Jack said.

"What?"

"You know, Ted, *the field of honor*, when we do the New Market ceremony."

"Yes, I suppose...my field of honor," Ted said, almost squeezing out each word. He coughed twice, and winced with pain. Dark blood dripped twice from his nose. "Lose your pride, Jack. Make room."

"Get some sleep, brother."

They were the last words Ted would ever say. His breathing became suddenly shallow, and he slipped out of consciousness. Jack moved back and took over the outboard. Mr. McClain worked his way to the front and lay beside Ted, cradling him under one arm. He couldn't find Ted's pulse. He tried desperately to revive him, but to no avail.

Ted died in his dad's arms somewhere west of Circle on the Yukon River.

Hours later, they turned John Phelps over to the state police, who had him airlifted to a hospital in Fairbanks. It would be several weeks before he would be cleared for extradition to Virginia.

They flew on the Huey alongside both of Jack's brothers to Fairbanks, and from there, took Ted home to Virginia.

Four days later, the McClain's buried Ted next to Anna. Jack was there. He gave the eulogy at their church in Richmond.

The following Saturday, the corps marched in memoriam. The McClain's stood with the superintendant and Colonel Jackson as the corps passed in review. Following the parade, the first class and guests assembled in J.M. Hall for Ted's memorial service.

Chaplain Campbell opened the service with prayer and a message to the first class about the character and faith of their Brother Rat. Jack walked up to give the eulogy.

As he looked over the corps, he noticed that the sanctuary was filled, not just with cadets, but other friends from Richmond and Lexington and Roanoke and Virginia Beach. He suddenly was overcome by the impact of his younger brother's life on so many. He did not open the pages he had written. Words of truth flowed from him like fresh water.

"I had things to say. They were good words about the Ted I knew, about the Ted you knew, but I am overcome with grief, and overpowered by love. Ted's last words to me were, 'Lose your pride. Make room.' That was it. Now, I'm looking at a room full of hundreds and hundreds of people Ted impacted in his short life. He kept telling me what it was all about. But I guess he had to die to prove it to me.

I thought I knew what I wanted when I came here. I wanted to escape some dark things from my past. I wanted a name and recognition. I wanted this rank."

Jack looked at the five chevrons on each coatee shoulder. Then, He looked upward as tears filled his eyes.

"But now I don't care about any of that. I want to be like you, Ted. I want to be like you with God living in *me*, just as you proved to everyone who knew you that God lived in you."

Jack stepped out from behind the podium and walked quietly down the steps. He stood directly in front of Ted's coatee that lay on the memorial table in front of the stage, along with a framed photograph and flower arrangements. Jack reached into the small pocket on the waistband of his white ducks and found the pocket knife he had carried for fifteen years.

He opened the blade, reached to his shoulder, and began slicing through the threads that held the chevrons of his rank to his coatee. When he had removed his rank from both sleeves, he laid them on Ted's coatee, folded the pocket knife, and slid it back into his waistband pocket.

For you Ted. I wore them for you. But they have become the symbol of my pride. I don't need it anymore. Today, I choose to follow the Christ that lived in you. Forgive me, God, for doubting you. My faith in you is complete.

Jack turned to take a seat beside the McClain's. When he approached them, Theodore stood and embraced Jack with masculine passion, and both wept.

"I know what it means. I know what you did," he whispered. Jack took his seat next to Mrs. McClain. She held his hand for the remainder of the service.

In November, Jack drove to Richmond, where he spent some time with the McClain's, then went to the cemetery and laid some flowers on Anna's grave.

CHAPTER TWENTY-FOUR

LEAVING

"Jack, wake up."

Jack slowly opened his eyes, and in a blur he could see Ski standing over him, gently shaking his shoulder.

"Did I miss formation?"

"No, it's only fifteen hundred," Ski answered.

Jack plopped back down, rubbed his eyes and began vigorously scratching his scalp with both hands. He had fallen asleep in his bunk after DRC as he didn't have any finals left, and was exhausted from late night study. Ski walked over and sat at his desk.

"Let me guess, they need some filler for *The Cadet*."

Ski shook his head, looking a little more serious.

"Alright, I give up. Just don't say it has anything to do with going to see the commandant," Jack said yawning.

He turned to allow his legs to slide off the side of the mattress, and in a fluid motion, slipped his feet into his shoes.

"Just this note from the guard room." Ski tossed the message slip across to Jack's desktop.

Jack picked it up and read it. His eyes began to water, but just enough to fill along the bottom of his eyelids. He continued looking at the note as he fought it back. He was glad that he did not allow the tear to crest over and run down his face.

Time: 1330 hrs.
Message: Jack, we're here. Your graduation is the most important thing in our life right now. We've missed you. We're waiting in Moody Hall. Hope to see you, son.

T.McClain II

Since the Yukon and the last hours with Ted, it was as if Jack suddenly saw people with a completely different set of eyes that were not his own. Now with this note, a storm of thoughts rained inside him. Jack controlled his desire to let them spill out openly.

Does he? Does he think of me that way?

"What about it, Jack?" Ski asked.

Jack lingered for a moment on the picture in his mind of Annabelle McClain calling him in off the river for supper.

"Did you read the note?" he asked.

"Yeah, I read it."

"Did you notice he called me 'son'?"

"I saw it. So you're going to go over there, right?"

"Of course I am, but I'm not good at this sort of thing. I haven't seen them since November."

"You mean you're not good at being nice to people, or being someone's son?"

Jack thought for a moment. "Probably both, but I need to be there for them, to be a son for them, if it will help."

Ski smiled and nodded. "Stand in the gap," Ski said. "You may be surprised at who it will help."

"Yeah," said Jack.

"Well, go on, man. Go see them. Tell Mr. Mack I said 'hi,' and I'll link up with you guys later."

Jack threw on his white blouse and buttoned it quickly. He straightened the epaulets, grabbed his hat, and headed out the door. As he walked across the courtyard and through the arch, he could feel the light warm late spring breeze that hinted of an oncoming hot summer.

The cleansing, cool wind on his face, and light scent of honeysuckle reminded him how everything was new, and how all of the old ghosts of his childhood had been flushed out and washed away. There was still, however, a burning somewhere deep inside of him.

Anna, Anna, Anna.

Waves of her memory pounded against his heart. Jack knew that some day he would deal with that ocean, but it wasn't one he was giving up easily. He was afraid that if he lost it, he would lose the only connection he still had to her.

Jack stopped at the base of the steps leading to Moody Hall.

Anna, Anna, Anna.

It all began to pour back into his mind—how four years ago, he had walked up these same steps and met the two most important women in his life. The thrust of the emotional wave was so strong that Jack had to lean against the wall for a few minutes. He was fighting it again, beating it back.

"You know you shouldn't keep Annabelle waiting like this." Mr. McClain's voice echoed between the stairwell walls. He was standing at the top of the steps, smiling.

Jack jogged up the steps and shook his hand, but Mr. McClain pulled him close and embraced him.

"How are you holding up, son?" Mr. McClain asked as they hugged.

It was a good word.

Son.

"Fine. It comes and goes in waves, but I'm sure you know that better than anybody. How about you and Mrs. McClain?" asked Jack.

"It's been a bit of a struggle," Mr. McClain said and then paused. "Jack, I'm sorry we've waited till now to see you."

"But you didn't. You invited me over for Christmas furlough. I'd made plans with Ski. I should have stopped by to see you. I wanted to, but I was afraid. I wasn't sure if you were ready to see me again."

They turned to walk along the front patio outer wall that overlooked the parade ground as Jack listened to Mr. McClain.

"So many good memories out there, sweating in parade dyke waiting to pass in review. Now painful ones. At first it was all me. She was the strong one. My depression has been a battle since Anna passed. I try to think of her, radiant, full of joy incomparable to anything we can understand, but I lose that battle over and over."

I lose it too. It's crushing me.

"I mean, my reason says it's so," he continued, "that she's in a better place, but I miss her. I can still smell her, and hear her voice and her laugh, like a ringing in my ears."

They had stopped and leaned against the wall. Jack listened.

"After Ted died, I had to find myself all over again, you know, who I was, deep in my soul. I was mad. Mad at cancer and mad at the world. Mad at John Phelps. I guess I was mad at God, too."

"It's alright Mr. McClain. I've been mad, myself."

"I finally realized it was getting me nowhere other than a deep hole. So I started forgiving. You know, letting things go. Phelps, cancer, the world. Then God. It seems strange, I know, forgiving God. He didn't need my forgiveness. I just had to release the blame and anger that I was holding inside. That's what forgiveness is, I suppose," Mr. McClain said.

A group of next year's cadre ran by in a tight formation, singing a jodie. Mr. McClain waited till they passed.

"Finally, me," he continued. "I was so embittered at myself for all the things I forgot to tell them, and for not holding them enough. Y'know, before Anna went back to school that last semester, we were walking somewhere and she reached out and held my hand. I pulled it away after a minute because we were walking by other people and it felt weird, like I was treating her like a little girl or something." His voice broke, and tears welled up in his eyes. "I'd hold that hand a thousand times, if I was ever given the chance again."

"I suppose if everything we believe in is right, you will."

"True, but it's still hard, now. That thought haunted me for months. It made me hate myself for all of my stupidity and awkwardness. After holding onto Ted as he was dying there in the boat, I realized that God had given me the chance to make up for it, and I could finally start forgiving myself then. That's when things turned around for me. Well, kind of, on the road to turning around. Still in waves, like you, Jack."

He stopped and they looked over the wall at the parade grounds and the barracks beyond. They said nothing for a few minutes, but nothing needed to be said. Jack felt the coolness of the spring breeze slipping gently across his face. He wanted to say something nice, but there were no words.

Mr. McClain seemed deep in thought.

"Annabelle, well, she hasn't fared so well. I mean, she can put on a good game face when she needs to, but she's been getting worse. She'll hardly leave the house. Doesn't want to talk about it, but you can see it all over her, this torment," he said.

"I can't imagine how tough it must be," Jack said.

He knew he could imagine it. He struggled every day with his grief.

"Funny thing is we've always thought we were strong Christians," Mr. McClain said. "I mean, we always thought we'd be the ones that if somebody we were close to died, and we knew that they were in Christ, we would be able to handle it so well. You know, celebrate their life and so on."

"It would be nice, I suppose, but I can't do it," said Jack.

"I guess we never even considered that it would be our own kids. It took us by surprise. Anyway, she brought up adoption the other day. I laughed inside. Could you imagine, at our age?"

He smiled and looked at Jack.

"Mr. McClain, this world needs more good people. I wish you would raise more kids."

"No, Jack. Those days are over. We're probably a bit past the patience required to raise little ones," McClain said, almost laughing.

He looked at Jack and grinned for a moment. Jack tried to read his face. They both looked back out toward the barracks.

"I'm talking about you."

Jack was somehow expecting this. Still, he did not know what to say.

Can you imagine, at my age?

"Let's go in now, Annabelle is wondering where we are, I'm sure," Mr. McClain said.

They turned and walked across the patio to the large doors that led into the main gathering room on the first floor. Annabelle was sitting in a tall wingback chair with her purse on her lap, looking off to her left out the windows that wrapped around two sides of the room.

"Mrs. McClain," Jack said, walking quickly to her.

She stood and set her purse in her chair and wrapped her arms around Jack's neck.

"I can't tell you how badly I've missed you," she said into his ear.

"I've missed you, too."

She held onto him for what seemed to Jack more than a minute. He wasn't sure what to do.

I need to stand in the gap.

Jack pulled away and held out his arm.

"May I?" he asked her, in a way he knew Ted would have.

"Sure, Jack," she said, and wrapped her hand under his forearm. She was smiling, glowing.

"Would it be alright if we took a short walk?"

"It would be wonderful."

Mr. McClain looked at Jack and nodded.

Jack walked quietly with Annabelle down the front steps of Moody Hall, across the street and to the sidewalk that wrapped around the parade ground.

"This will always be my favorite place to walk. It's always beautiful, but especially in the spring and early summer," Annabelle said as she walked with Jack, still holding his arm.

"I've loved it since the first day I came here. The smell of fresh-cut grass, the thickness of the trees along the walkway. I especially like it at dusk, when the gas lamps first light up," said Jack.

"Teddy loved it, too. I'm glad you guys got to become best friends."

"I figure we made up for a lot of missed time as brothers."

"Oh, Jack, had things been different, had we only known about you and your situation when we adopted Teddy."

"You've done so much for me. I don't know, but sometimes I think I'm glad I went through all I did growing up. Ted helped me, Mrs. McClain. He was a good friend. He was a good brother."

"He was a good son."

Jack could feel a sudden coolness come over Annabelle.

"I'm just so sad, so broken inside."

She stopped walking, let go of Jack's arm and crossed behind him to sit on one of the park benches along the walk.

"I need to sit. This is too much, too fast," she said. Tears welled up in her eyes quickly, and she retrieved a tissue from her purse. Jack sat down beside her. Annabelle stared blankly across the parade field.

Then it hit him.

"Mrs. McClain, this may sound strange, but two years ago I sat on this same bench with a woman holding a tissue, crying for her son."

"Why was she crying for him?"

"It was late in the afternoon on matriculation day. She was heartbroken because she'd never been apart from him."

It came together in Jack's mind in a single wave of comprehension. God had done that, and he had arranged it just for this moment.

"What did you say to her?"

"I just told her that her boy would be well taken care of here, and I would see to it."

"And did you see to it, Jack?"

"Yes, Ma'am. He was one of my Rats. I had him write her a letter every week."

"I wish you could do the same for Anna and Teddy," she said.

She stared, almost catatonically, across the parade ground in the direction of Lejeune Hall, but Jack knew she was looking at nothing in particular. He could see by her tears and clenched jaw, she was fighting back what should have been sobs. She seemed so deep in her grief, buried in a flood of helplessness and anguish.

Jack wanted to give her hope.

I have something to give her.

"Mrs. McClain, Ted wrote this letter to me before he took off to Alaska. I want you to have it."

Jack took off his hat and retrieved the letter Ted had written him. He handed it to her, and she leaned forward, elbows on her knees, pulling a loose lock of hair aside and holding it pinned back with her hand holding the tissue.

As she read the letter, she began to weep more and more profoundly. She finished and held the letter against her chest, let the lock of hair fall loose, and covered her eyes.

Jack waited till she had wiped her eyes and nose. She put the tissue in her purse, retrieved another, and handed the letter to Jack.

"No Ma'am. You keep it. I have it memorized."

"Thank you, Jack. These are precious words." Annabelle folded the letter carefully, and placed it in her purse.

"Do you think God could be trying to tell us something?" asked Jack.

"I'm not sure what you mean, Jack."

"I mean, like Ted said in the letter, God's plans and all. It just seems to me to be more than coincidence we would find ourselves here on this particular bench, just like it happened two years ago."

"Well, I suppose it could be. But what do you think it is he's trying to tell us?"

"The first part makes sense. I think he's saying Ted and Anna are being well cared for, and he's making sure of it."

"I guess I can see that. What's the second part?"

"Well, I don't know how they can write letters from heaven every week, but somehow, I think God has figured it out."

Annabelle looked at Jack through reddish eyes and puffy eyelids. At first, she was almost expressionless and seemed to stare through him. Suddenly, she began to smile, mouth slightly open. It seemed to Jack her face began to glow.

She reached back into her purse and pulled out the letter.

"A letter from heaven," she said, holding it up in front of Jack.

"Yes, yes it is."

She leaned back, held the letter to her chest again, closed her eyes and smiled.

Jack woke to the sunrise warming his bed. Two weeks had passed since graduation, and he had made it. Finished. He lay there for several minutes basking in the warmth of a sun splashed comforter.

Ted's bed. I wonder how many times he woke up like this. The sun. The smell of breakfast. I suppose he does every day, now. We might have shared this room growing up. Wish we could have grown up together in this place.

The McClain's would not hear of Jack going out on his own. They said they needed him there. They convinced him of it, though it was not hard work. Jack wanted to spend time with them. He wanted to feel as if he'd been their son all along. He wanted a home.

For two weeks he had been sorting through Ted's room, boxing up things, helping the McClain's sort through his belongings. Both of them had tried to do it on their own the previous months, both unsuccessfully. Jack promised he would help.

Piece by piece, he took the trophies of Ted's life to Annabelle and Theodore, and listened to them tell the story of each, then decide which items they would keep. At first Annabelle resisted even letting go of a pair of socks, but as the weeks wore on, she loosened up a little at a time. She was getting better, and Jack could see the glow coming back to her face.

The room was finally clean.

He sat up on the edge of the bed and rubbed his face. It would be a good day.

After breakfast, pack. Run those boxes of Ted's clothes down to Goodwill in Charlottesville. Mrs. McClain won't ever see anyone wearing them there. It would hurt her to see that. Come back home for early supper. I called it home. It is home. Get on the road by six.

Jack was excited. He had found home and family. His orders for active duty gave him a month and a half of freedom, and he planned on making the most of it. With money left from the sale of the farm, he wanted to take the time to see some of the country.

Jack walked over to the closet to grab a pair of jeans and a pullover shirt. As he pulled out his duffel bag, Jack noticed Ted's knapsack.

Jack remembered he had dropped his duffel bag in the corner of the closet when he first arrived after graduation. Ted's knapsack ended up behind it, out of sight. He hadn't paid much attention to it, thinking at the time it probably contained little more than a change of clothes. Now, trying to help the McClain's get everything sorted out, he thought it best to empty it.

He released the keepers, dumping the small bag on the foot of his bed.

Wrapped up in a pair of jeans, Jack could see something white, paper-like. He carefully unrolled the jeans and grabbed a stack of several envelopes, flipped them to the addressed side, and began to read.

It can't be. Letters from Ted. They're to his parents. Post dated. Thanksgiving. Christmas. He never told us. I should've looked in this bag.

It was at that moment Jack remembered Ted talking about something he was working on the summer before he died, when Jack visited him in the hospital. There were seven letters. Ted had post dated each with a holiday, his birthday, and his graduation. Jack knew he needed to get the graduation letter to the McClain's right away.

And the rest. All of them. I will give them all of the letters at breakfast. It's up to them when they read them.

Jack grabbed some clothes, shaved and showered. When he was ready, he carried the boxes in a couple of trips, and loaded them in his car. He greeted Mrs. McClain as he walked by the kitchen. She was preparing breakfast.

Jack went to the room, put the letters in a small box, and walked back downstairs.

They sat around the breakfast table in the kitchen and ate blueberry pancakes and bacon. Jack loved the smell of bacon. It was always his favorite at Crozet.

Mr. McClain leaned back and sipped his coffee.

"So what's in the box, Jack?" he asked.

"I found something this morning," Jack said. "I forgot to go through Ted's pack, so I dumped it out on the bed when I saw it. These fell out."

Jack held the small stack of envelopes up, then laid them on the table.

"They're from Ted," Jack said.

Annabelle picked up the stack. Her hands trembled slightly. Mr. McClain stood, walked to her side and knelt on one knee. He pushed his reading glasses from the top of his head down to rest on the bridge of his nose.

"He wrote them for special occasions," she said as she thumbed though them.

"When? When did he find time to write them?" Mr. McClain asked.

"I suppose while he was in the hospital, when he knew," Annabelle answered.

"I want to open them, now," Mr. McClain said.

"I do, too," Annabelle said, "but I don't think Ted would want that. He took the time to spell out when he wanted us to read them. There's six of them here, a year's worth."

"Seven," said Jack.

He held up another letter. It was marked "VMI Graduation."

Tears filled Annabelle's eyes as Jack handed it to her. Mr. McClain grabbed a box of tissues from the counter, scooted his chair beside her and sat down.

"I'm going to take a walk, and let you guys be alone," said Jack.

"You don't need to leave, Jack," Mr. McClain said.

"I know," said Jack, "but I think it would be best."

He stood and walked to the front door as Annabelle began to carefully open the envelope with her shaking hands. Jack pushed open the heavy door and stepped out into the warmth of morning sun.

He knew where he wanted to go, his favorite spot he had found through the woods in the back yard along a trail that led to the south bank of the James. He could see part of the city jutting up beyond the trees lining the opposite bank. He had been spending time there since Mr. McClain showed him the trail his first day there after graduation.

Jack found a spot, close to the water's edge and lay back on a large, flat rock. The cool air that moved in brief gusts along the James reminded him of the farm, and even the Yukon, but the rock warmed his back. Jack lay there, almost dozing, for what seemed a half-hour, though probably even less.

"Jack."

It was Annabelle's voice, and it startled him. He sat up on the rock and focused his eyes.

"Yes, Ma'am?"

Annabelle walked out of the wood line, and carefully stepped along the rocks until she made it to the rock Jack lay on. She sat down beside him, facing the river.

"This letter, well, it's amazing. I would have never imagined Ted would be writing us letters from heaven, but somehow, like you told me two weeks ago, God worked it out."

"He did, Mrs. McClain, and it is amazing."

"Jack," she said, then paused as if thinking through something, "do you want to be our son?"

"I would be honored to call you and Mr. McClain my parents."

"Okay. Good. Then it's settled." She stood and took a couple careful steps heading back to the house. "Oh, one more thing," she said, turning back.

Annabelle held the letter out to Jack.

"I think you need to read this," she said.

He reached up and took it.

"Yes Ma'am."

She did not wait for Jack to begin reading. Jack watched as she tip-toed across the rocks to the wood line. Her dress flitted in the breeze from the river, and her hair blew across her face. She glanced back at Jack and smiled as she disappeared into the woods. He looked down and unfolded the paper.

Dear Dad and Mom,

I am gone. I know, because you wouldn't be reading this otherwise. Though I write this while I am still here, still coherent, I want you to know now, I am not in pain, but at perfect peace. I am in the presence of God.

And, of course, I'll see you here soon.

God has given Jack to you, to be your son. He needs you, and you will need him. I do not doubt you will love him as if he was me.

I wish I could have made it to graduation, Dad. I know how much it meant to you, but I believe it meant even more to me. Thanks for always being there when I needed you, and for being the man of God I could always look to. You are my champion, my hero.

Mom, you have always been a shining light. You have
taught me about the beauty of grace, the love of family,
and the joy that comes from being in the presence of God.
I am experiencing it now, eternally. You are a gift from the
Father, both beautiful and elegant.

As I write this, I am truly still in Richmond, still seeing
things imperfectly as through a glass, darkly. I only know
in part, but what I see and know makes sense. This plan
God has had for us leads to Jack.

What I can't see in Richmond is what happens next. I
sense it is for you to love and encourage Jack. God will, as
usual, do the rest. It must be big.

Happy graduation and see you in the fullness of time.

Love, Teddy

———

After returning from Charlotte, Jack finished packing, and
carried his gear down to the car. He loaded his duffel in the trunk
and stopped for a moment to notice the name "Hartman, J. M."
on the side in two inch block letters. A flood of memories of that
first Cadre Week swirled around inside of him. There was that
old familiar nervousness and flush of adrenaline, followed by a
new strange warmth.

Still, it took such a small movement of anything in his mind
to pull him back down into the grief that had consumed him for
so many months. Sadness haunted him.

As he made his way downstairs with the last of his bags,
Annabelle answered the phone on the third ring.

"Yes, it is," she said.

Jack stopped at the bottom of the stairs and set down his bags.
He was suddenly curious about the call. He did not know why.

"Yes, he is. Who, may I ask, is calling?"

Annabelle paused for the answer.

"Well, that's fine, I'm sure he will appreciate your call. I'll
get him."

Annabelle walked out of the kitchen and looked at Jack. Jack could see that she was either shocked or scared. Something was wrong with this call.

"It's Mrs. Jamison. She said you were her son's corporal."

"She's the one I told you about, the one on the same bench we sat on at graduation."

"She sounds familiar."

"I doubt you know her."

Jack went in the kitchen and picked up the telephone receiver. Annabelle did not follow.

"This is Jack."

She said nothing for a moment. It seemed longer to Jack.

"Jack, it's me, Mrs. Jamison."

"Yes, Ma'am. How are you doing? And your son, how is he?"

"Fine, Jack. We're both fine."

She paused again, as if waiting for Jack to say something, but he knew he didn't have anything to offer, other than trivial questions.

"Are you there, Mrs. Jamison?"

"Yes, Jack, I'm sorry. I just, um, wanted to talk to you, to tell you that Mitch is doing fine, and to thank you for taking care of him while he was there."

"Well, I'm glad to hear you're both doing well," Jack said. "How did you find me?"

"Oh, that. Well I, um, I called VMI, the guard room of all places, and I guess I got lucky. The man I talked to there said you'd left with the McClain's after graduation."

How would anyone other than Ski and a few others know that?

"Then I just had to find them in the Richmond phone book. Do you know there are eighteen McClain's in the Richmond phone book? You were the fifth," she said, then laughed nervously.

Jack knew something wasn't right. Mrs. Jamison knew way too much about how to find him, and about the McClain's.

Richmond. How would she know the McClain's lived in Richmond?

"Well, I just wanted to say thanks for talking to me that day, and of course, for all you did for Mitch."

"It was my pleasure. Nice talking to you again."

"Take care of yourself, Jack. Maybe we can talk again, sometime?"

"Yes, that would be good."

Jack placed the receiver back in the cradle, and stood for a minute with his hand on it, staring blankly through a window near the breakfast table. He walked over to the shelf in the kitchen where Mrs. McClain kept a Richmond phone book.

Jack leafed quickly through it till he found the first McClain listing, and then counted down the column.

Thirty-one. They're twenty-fourth. Mrs. McClain. That look.

Jack rounded the corner of the kitchen and through the living room. He did not see Annabelle, so he walked over to the door of Mr. McClain's study, which was slightly ajar. He could see Annabelle sitting in one of the wingback chairs in front of the desk, holding a picture in her lap. Her eyes were filled with tears. Jack knocked gently.

"Mrs. McClain?"

"Yes, Jack, come in."

Jack walked into the study and sat in the wingback next to Annabelle's.

"What's wrong?"

"I don't know. I guess I had this idea in my head that you would be around from now on, that we would talk from time to time about Teddy and Anna while you ate every bad dinner I made, that you and Theodore would become close and play golf and talk sports and work on cars. And even though Anna and Teddy aren't here, we'd still feel like we had a family."

"It sounds great. It's what I want," said Jack.

"I just feel like it's slipping away," Annabelle said.

"But, why?"

She turned the picture around so Jack could see it. It was a picture she had taken of him and Ted at VMI after a parade.

"You both look so much alike, almost twins. I guess it's why it was so easy to take you in as a son."

"Look, Mrs. McClain, I know I'll never replace Teddy in your heart, and I don't want to. But I'll be a good son for you and Mr. Mack."

"Oh, don't get me wrong. I'm happy you're becoming part of our family, Jack. But I'm worried about what you will do, now."

"Now?"

"Now that you've gotten that call."

She pointed toward the kitchen.

"Mrs. Jamison?"

"Jack, I don't know anything about a Mrs. Jamison, but I know the voice of Jenny Hartman when I hear it."

Jack stood in the McClain's driveway. He had finished loading his bags.

"You gonna be okay?" Mr. McClain asked.

"I'm good. How about you?"

"Day at a time, Jack, but we do have a new mission. Y'know, like Ted wrote about in the letter," he said as he smiled.

They said nothing for several seconds. It was a moment when truth and love and justice all collided, when God tipped his hand and tore the veil, and all he had done lay open and naked for Jack to see. The question begged to be asked.

"Should I call you 'Dad'?"

Mr. McClain smiled, then grabbed Jack by both shoulders and looked into his eyes.

"You're the only son I have now, Jack, and you will always be my son."

Jack noticed he was trembling and his eyes filled with tears. Mr. McClain held out his hand to Jack. Jack grabbed his hand and held it tightly in his as he hugged him. Quickly, as if relieved, he clenched Jack and began to weep.

Jack felt the tears from Mr. McClain's cheeks roll down onto his own neck. He felt his razor stubble touching the side of his face and remembered that feeling from his own father's face when he was a little boy, before he ever knew grief and pain and sorrow. He was, for a moment, in his father's arms again. They separated and collected themselves.

"I'll be back in a couple months," said Jack.

"Where are you going?" asked Annabelle, now holding her arms out to hug Jack.

"Texas. I need to forgive someone."

Jack kissed Annabelle's cheek and whispered to her.

"No matter what happens, I will always be *your* son." He paused for a moment, and then asked, "Can I call you 'Mom'?"

She leaned back slightly and cupped his face in her hands looking directly into his eyes. She smiled and nodded.

"Be careful on the road, and write us. Keep us in the loop," Mr. McClain said.

Jack pulled away and opened the driver's door. He paused and looked around, tentative for a moment, and then turned to face them both.

"I love you," he said.

They both replied likewise.

Jack slipped down into the driver's seat, closed the door and started the engine, and then headed down the drive thinking of all that had transpired between them. For the first time since he was little, Jack felt the joy of belonging to people who loved him.

He worked his way down Cherokee Lane and turned onto the highway heading north toward Interstate Sixty-four. When he crossed over the James, that beautiful river, he was suddenly overtaken by the thought that all this time it was the James that connected them, and it was the James that separated them.

From a small farm near Buchanan to the wealthy banks overlooking Richmond, the James wove its way through the heart of Virginia and beyond, where it joined the waters of other rivers until they came to the ocean and mixed with all of the waters of the earth.

He thought about how it was always a river that tied the events of his life together. He thought about the mother that neither he nor Ted ever knew, that someday he hoped to know, and to forgive, and to love, and to honor. It was not just for him, but for Ted, as well. Like the James that connected him with Ted, so did the blood of their mother.

And Jack thought about the plans Ted had always talked about. Those plans for his life God wove together through all of this. He settled on the thought that when this plan for his life had run its course, he would join Ted and Anna, flowing together like the rivers do.

At that moment, Jack knew it would be alright; that the pain would fade with time, but the gift Ted and Anna had poured out with their very lives to give to Jack, would last through all time, and even beyond time.

That's it, I will find a way to live this life as if it was theirs, and carry on everything they left in me. Our brotherhood, our love.

It was brotherhood, born of blood and forged in adversity. And it was the love he had for the woman who would have been his wife, for whom he still ached, day and night.

He decided he had no choice but to live differently than he might have had he not known Ted and Anna and their parents and even the Institute. He searched for something valuable he could grasp in the raging confluence of all these waters. And it occurred to him, not too suddenly, but little by little as he drove, that if the cutting short of Anna's, and then Ted's life could lead to the redemption of his lost soul, then living that redeemed life in a way that would honor them could bring maybe a flicker of hope to all of it.

So as he contemplated those thoughts, Jack drove toward the Shenandoah, evening falling hard on a reddened sky, and he committed in his heart from that day forward to be a man who would live for the truth, and for love, and for honor…

and honor…

and honor.